ALSO BY JONATHON BURGESS

CHASING THE LANTERN, *Book One of the Dawnhawk Trilogy*

ON DISCORD ISLE, *Book Two of the Dawnhawk Trilogy*

BENEATH A BURNING SKY

BOOK THREE OF THE DAWNHAWK TRILOGY

BY

JONATHON BURGESS

Cover Painting © 2015 Ksenia Mamaeva

Map illustration & Chapter Glyph © 2015 Vladimir Verano

Book & Cover Design by Vladimir Verano, Third Place Press

Edited by Susan Defreitas, Indigo Editing & Publications

ISBN: 978-0-9909604-2-3

FIRST EDITION

BRASS HORSE BOOKS

JBURGESS@BRASSHORSEBOOKS.COM
WWW.BRASSHORSEBOOKS.COM

For Willy

"What do you here?"

To Edrus
To Yulan and Breachtown
Stormhammer Isle
Graveway Lagoon
Haventown Lagoon
N
The Copper Isles

PROLOGUE

It was murky at the bottom of the sea.

Soft shafts of sunlight shone down from the surface above. They danced together, a shifting curtain only hinting at the twilight world of the ocean floor. Through this gloom swam lazy schools of fish, startled now into frantic activity by an armored mass that tore up the seabed and churned the water with its passing.

The Dray Engine was irritated. It wasn't built for such an environment— in these depths it was awkward and ponderous. Worse, every piston-driven step it took lifted more sediment into the water, blinding it. The Dray Engine did not like being underwater.

Something swam past, all grey fins and silver skin. The Dray Engine darted forward, catching the shark between its burnished, reptilian jaws. Water churned all about them as the fish struggled, fighting in vain against the relentless mechanical pressure that trapped it. The Dray Engine savored the moment, then bit down and severed its prey. Two still-twitching pieces of shark fell through a hazy cloud of its own fresh gore. For a brief moment, the Dray Engine felt marginally less annoyed.

That brief satisfaction faded all too quickly. Something like despair replaced it, ticking its way through the clockwork mind of the ancient machine. What was it doing? Where was it going?

Its primary commandment burned clearly: to protect the designated sanctuaries of Voorn foundlings from enemy action. Failing that, a second objective was inscribed: to eliminate any non-Voornish threats to the Dominion. Dimly, it could recall performing such tasks. The memories were cloudy, though, almost as if they belonged to some other automaton, one from a different place and time.

More recent events, it remembered clearly. It had awoken in the great Foundry of Garaam, roused by an irritating, golden-eyed slave-human prancing across its back. To the Dray Engine's disgust, the obnoxious creatures were everywhere, so numerous and appalling that creative interpretation of its second commandment had been immediately called for. Crushing them into paste had proven surprisingly amusing.

Afterward it left. But to the ancient machine's dismay, it found itself not in a great and glorious city but a rural tropical isle, the aether-bands almost completely silent. As if that weren't enough, *more* slave-humans appeared, and some even had the audacity to attack it. The resilient golden-eyed female, in particular, had proven so foolhardy.

One thing had led to another. When it was all said and done, the Dray Engine found itself far from the island, frustrated, lonely, and trapped on the silty bottom of the ocean. Even down here, though, the aether-bands should have been full of chatter. It should have been able to hear the voices of its masters. Were there even any Voorn still living left to command it?

The Dray Engine wanted guidance. Yet with none at hand, there were only two options: It could sit on the sea floor, waiting for authorized instruction. Or it could seek them out on its own.

A piece of it *wanted* to sit there. Some niggling built-in instinct said that this was exactly what it was supposed to do. Nevertheless, it gave a watery snort, chose the strongest still-existent signal on the aether-bands, and stomped off to find the source.

But it couldn't shake the feeling that the journey would be pointless.

An upward slope gradually appeared on the seabed floor. The water around it lightened, revealing great forests of kelp growing straight up out of the sand. Overhead swam shining schools of fish, chased by sharks and squid in a maddened and chaotic free-for-all unfortunately too far away to reach.

The Dray Engine shook off its reoccurring malaise. The aether-signal was growing stronger with every step it took—it was going the right way. Even better, there was enough strength and complexity in the signal to mark it as more than background noise; it was unused, but it was definitely being broadcast by a Voorn installation. The Dray Engine found itself so excited that it only took the slightest detour to crush a large armored sea crab.

Fronds of kelp gave way to rocky piles of shimmering coral. Anemones grew here from the living stones, a decorative forest of fringed and floating polyps. The Dray Engine did not care. It stepped on as many as it could, ponderously crushing them, sending clown fish and eels racing off in a panic.

Then it surfaced. Water streamed off of its head, gushing out from between the chinks in its armored carapace to pour back into the sea. The Dray Engine found itself standing in the surf before a sandy beach that sloped up sharply to a bare and rocky hill. Other islands stood in the distance, their jungle-covered cliffs shot through with shining veins of copper, all set against the backdrop of a midday sky.

The details were unimportant. The Dray Engine could feel the pulsing of the aether-band. Whatever the originating source, it was located just ahead beyond the hill.

The Dray Engine strode up onto the shore, clambering straight up the rocky slope towards what seemed a flattened cliff top. The rock was brittle, giving easily, and the Dray Engine slid backward more than once. It roared out in vexation, redoubling its efforts until, with one last great heave of the pistons in its legs, it surmounted the slope.

And found nothing. The island was round and not overly large. Its center wasn't simply flat but an empty crater with perfectly smooth rock walls dropping three hundred feet down to a forest of palm trees and wild vines.

Its masters had been here, once. In the center of the crater, rising from a grassy plain, shone the tip of a golden pyramid. Here, then, was the originating source of the aether-band signal that it had followed.

But the installation was broken, long abandoned. No watchful guardians patrolled the perimeter. No short-range communications were being sent. There was nothing for the Dray Engine here.

It bellowed in frustration. The roar echoed out across the crater, lonely and mocking. The Dray Engine roared again, then lowered its great reptilian head, sighing out a great gush of steam. It blinked its armored lenses and turned to leave.

The stony lip of the crater crumbled beneath the claws of its left foot. The Dray Engine shifted its weight in alarm, and the stone beneath its other foot gave way as well. It scrabbled desperately for purchase with taloned forelimbs, to no avail.

The Dray Engine slipped backward and fell into the crater.

CHAPTER ONE

Lina Stone peered out from the stairwell at the walking dead.

The Revenants milled about the cargo hold of the airship *Dawnhawk*. A single dying lantern provided illumination, revealing rotting jaws, cloudy eyes, and suppurating wounds. Tightly packed crates filled with plundered goods hemmed the monsters in. They would bump up against the waist-high barrier only to back away, staring down and groaning in confusion. A few would claw at the air reflexively.

One of them seemed to look at her. Lina swallowed, a thrill of fear climbing down her spine to mix with the disgust roiling in her belly. It probably couldn't see her there, in the dark of the stairwell. Probably. Still, Lina shifted in her crouch upon the steps, inching backward.

"Well?" hissed Captain Fengel in a stage whisper. "Do you see it?"

Her captain crouched on the steps above her—notably, out of view of the Revenants. Thin slivers of light escaped the hooded lantern he held, illuminating his features artfully—something he'd probably done on purpose. Handsome enough, with a neat beard that he didn't trim himself, the effect was somewhat ruined by the weirdly shaped monocle he had crammed into one eye. A tricorn hat and a blue Perinese officer's coat completed his ensemble, along with the saber hanging awkwardly at his hip.

"No, I can't," Lina stage whispered back. "There're crates and Revenants and the whole rest of the Goddess-damned hold in there. How did you lose your only other monocle?"

"It fell out of my pocket while we were bringing that last load aboard," said Fengel. "I'm sure it fell down here."

Lina glared at him. "If you hate the one you're wearing, and you found this other one, why weren't you *wearing* it?"

Fengel raised an eyebrow at her. "Because then I wouldn't have a spare," he replied. "Look, just get in there and find it. It's probably on the floor."

"I don't want to go in there!"

"What? Why ever not?" Fengel peered carefully around the corner. "I'm going to have the Mechanists replace that oil lamp when we get back into port. But it's not *that* dark. Besides, I brought this lantern."

He tried to pass it to her. Lina fought him off forcefully. "That's not—stop! If I go in there, especially with a lantern, the Revenants will see me."

"What? Rubbish. Some of them don't even have eyes anymore. At any rate, Omari says they're harmless. Mostly."

"You weren't in Breachtown!" she hissed. "And I trust that woman about as much as I do your grasp of finance!"

Her captain looked hurt. "That is uncalled for. I almost always pay off my debts. Anyway, look at them. Those things are hardly violent."

Lina glanced back at the herd of corpses. She had to admit they seemed fairly docile at the moment. Not at all like the ones she'd fled in Breachtown. Though these were all former crewmen who'd died in that affair three months ago. They'd been friends, for the most part. No one wanted them around. Yet they couldn't just throw them overboard into the sea either. Did that make the difference? Not for the first time, Lina reflected how awful it would be to be trapped, mindless, halfway between life and death.

A shuffling Revenant caught her eye. "Look," she said. "It's Jonas Wiley. He was an idiot, but not that bad, for a thug. He didn't deserve to end up like this. No wonder his brother Nate's been taking it hard." Lina paused. "Though Jonas *was* always trying to look down my shirt."

"I can't imagine why," mused Fengel, peering out into the cargo hold in repulsed fascination. "Not much there to see."

Lina glared at him.

"Oh, dash it all," said Fengel. "You've been too loud, Stone. They've heard us."

Lina glanced back into the hold. It was true; the Revenants no longer milled about. Now they faced the stairwell as one, eerily still, arms upraised towards them. The lantern on its chain above them flickered, flared, and went out.

Lina wouldn't have gone into the dark for all the tea in Perinault, and she held a moment's hope Fengel wouldn't ask her to.

"Well," said Fengel. "You're definitely going to need this then." He opened the shutter on his lantern, illuminating the darkened stairwell around them.

"No!" hissed Lina. "I'm not going digging for your spare eyepiece among a bunch of walking corpses!"

"Come now," Fengel said, before being cut off by the tromp of boots on the steps above.

A massive figure was coming down the stairwell. It was Sarah Lome, one of Fengel's officers and the gunnery mistress of his nonexistent gunnery crew.

"Captain," said Sarah, "we're almost back to port. You're wanted on deck."

"Oh?" replied Fengel. He stood, looking disappointed. "Well. I suppose we can come back down here later, Miss Stone."

Lina glowered. *Not if I can help it.* She rose to her feet as well, mentally reviewing all the bolt-holes and hiding places she knew aboard the *Dawnhawk*. At least for the moment, she had a reprieve. Lina brightened as she realized she was free to go hunt down Michael Hockton. Just the thought put butterflies in her stomach. She just *had* to see how things with him were progressing.

Captain Fengel led the way up through the bowels of the airship, reaching the mess deck and climbing higher, stopping only briefly outside the captain's cabin where two pirates were working. They were Andrea Holt and Ryan Gae, both repairing a damaged step under the watchful eye of the dour ship's Mechanist. Lina waved to her friends; Ryan gave a weak smile before bending again to his task.

It cheered Lina to see him up and about; the older pirate had been gravely injured three months ago. He was quieter now, with thin streaks of grey coloring his hair. Andrea, usually cheerfully remote, had grown quietly protective of the man. She nodded to Lina and took up a hammer.

Fengel tried to hurry past, but the Mechanist looked up sharply. "Captain," he said in a flat monotone. "We must speak. The *Dawnhawk* has sustained significant wear these last few months. And the Revenant presence in the hold is utterly—"

"Sorry!" said Fengel as he fled up the stair. "About to dock. Find me later, Mechanist!"

Then he was gone. Lina knew the last statement was a challenge, not an offer. By the sour grunt the Mechanist gave, he knew it too. Slipping by, she ascended the stair to the aft hatchway, with Sarah Lome trailing behind.

The midafternoon sun was bright enough to all but banish the shade on the *Dawnhawk*'s deck. Out past the curve of the gas-bag envelope stretched pale blue sky, only lightly touched by white, puffy clouds. Lina felt a warm breeze, scented with the salt spray of the Atalian Sea.

The Mechanist was right; her airship had seen better days. A pumpkin-seed-shaped hull attached to a spindle, the *Dawnhawk* was downright battered. The deck planking was furrowed, gouged by cargo and equipment. Heavy hawsers connecting the gas bag to the deck were frayed and had been poorly reinforced by additional cordage. Steam hissed from a crack in the port-side exhaust pipe where a great dent deformed it, accompanied by a constant teakettle whistle. Half of the linkages connecting the network of skysail armatures together were completely disassembled. Above, the envelope itself was a mess of roughly patched canvas held together by makeshift stitching that bulged oddly in places. Flopping in the breeze along the starboard hull dangled rope cordage running from bow to stern like the patchy locks of an animal's mane. A toll had been taken on the *Dawnhawk* after her recent adventures. She needed repairs—and a good long rest back in port.

"Captain!" cried a voice. "There you are!"

First Mate Lucian Thorne waved from the helm back near the stern. Beside him stood Henry Smalls, Fengel's short steward, covered in damp paint and looking particularly aggrieved. At the wheel stood the ship's magicians, Maxim and Konrad. Each aetherite gripped the *Dawnhawk's* wheel, fighting for control and glaring at the other.

"What in the Realms Below is going on?" asked Captain Fengel.

"It's these two idiots!" Lucian growled. He gestured at the two aetherites. "Each one keeps trying to slip away from the helm to woo that damned Yulani necromancer. And they keep setting *traps* to make each other look bad. Poor Henry here walked into a bucket of whitewash set above the door to the privy. I didn't even know we had whitewash aboard!"

A loud grinding came from the propeller assemblies in the stern, cutting across Lucian's complaint. Everyone stared up at the mechanisms in alarm. Then the moment passed and the linkages ran smoothly again. Lina winced. *We really need a good, long refit once we're back in port.*

Maxim pushed the wheel of the helm at Konrad. "If this buffoon would just stay at his post like he is supposed to," he said, his voice thick with the accent of his native Greisheim, "then it would not be so dangerous aboard."

"I was off shift!" chimed in Konrad, pushing back.

"You traded that shift yesterday!"

Lina backed away. *Time to make myself scarce.* A few months ago the two aetherites had been like peas in a pod. That all ended when the Yulani native, Omari, came aboard. Since then, both men had reverted back into rivals.

Captain Fengel held his hands up and moved in to mediate. Sarah Lome cracked her knuckles ominously. Lina slipped past the big woman and snuck off for the starboard exhaust pipe running up the ship. Just the thought of seeing Michael made her giddy.

A host of obstacles presented themselves as she made her way up the deck. Lina dodged a draping section of half-sewn canvas only to hop across a broken equipment locker, then a tangle of rope, loosely piled. The crew assigned to these tasks tended to them only lackadaisically. Everyone knew that once this trip back to Haventown was over, they would have a lengthy stay. All the real work could be done then.

An ear-shattering screech pierced her buoyant mood. Lina staggered, then whirled around with fists raised. *That damned bird …*

Butterbeak flew past. A rotund, singularly ugly parrot with a butter-yellow beak and brilliant rainbow plumage, Natasha's new pet was universally hated among the crew. Usually it avoided her on account of Runt, her own pet, a scryn. Still, no one was really safe from the parrot's malevolence, and there was active competition among the crew to make the bird suffer an inconspicuous yet permanent "accident."

Before she could take a swipe at the parrot, it landed on the upraised arm of its owner. Captain Natasha Blackheart was striding down the deck, straight for Lina. All thoughts of aviacide evaporated, and suddenly Lina wanted nothing more than to hide.

"There you are!" snarled the *Dawnhawk's* other captain. She stormed over, stopping just a little too close, within Lina's personal space.

Natasha Blackheart was the daughter of Euron Blackheart, the notorious pirate king of Haventown. She was tough, ruthless, and more than a little crazed, as likely to gut you as she was to hang you up by your toes. Rumor had been spreading among the crew that she was somehow worse of late … there were whispers that Natasha was trying to be *nice*.

"Where have you been?" demanded Natasha. "I've been looking all over for you." Butterbeak peered mockingly down at Lina, somehow looking smug.

Lina glared back at it. "What about, Captain?" she asked. "Only Captain Fengel had me looking for his other spare monocle—"

They both ducked as the port-side exhaust squealed sharply, belching a great gout of steam. When the sound died down, Natasha glared at it. "I've been looking for you because this airship is a damned wreck and I need to consult with the Mechanist. You always seem to be running about. Seen him? Also, I wanted to ask how you've been."

Lina blinked, certain she'd misheard. Once, Natasha had strangled a man for mentioning, in passing, that he was cold.

"Just…fine?"

The pirate captain relaxed. "Good." She shifted Butterbeak to her shoulder before retrieving a small leather folio out from her puffy-sleeved blouse and opening it to a dog-eared page. "Can't imagine what I'd do if you'd actually said anything of import. Now, I'm not going to smile, because to the Realms Below with that, but it says here that I'm supposed to act like I care to remember your name."

"I'm Lina, Captain."

"I'm sure you are."

"Lina Stone. I've been on this ship for almost a year now."

"Oh, I don't doubt it."

"I came up with the idea to mutiny against you and Fengel a short while ago."

"Really?" Natasha narrowed her eyes, and all the awkward friendliness evaporated. "Well, that's worth remembering." She shook her head. "Fortunately for you, you little mutineer, the book makes specific mention that I'm not to decapitate anyone without current reason. So be thankful for that."

Lina stared at the pirate princess. Then, curious, she craned her head to get a better look at the spine of the book. Natasha snapped it shut, shoving it back down her shirt.

"Enough. Where's the damned Mechanist?"

"Aft-hatch stairway," replied Lina, feeling very uncertain.

"Good. Be about your business, Stone." Then the pirate princess pushed past; Butterbeak glared at Lina until they were out of range.

Lina made a mental effort to put the strange exchange behind her. *Every day on this boat is an adventure.* She shook her head, glancing about the deck. Her mood lightened as she caught sight of Michael Hockton, standing along the port-side exhaust pipes, along with Allen, the apprentice Mechanist. Runt was there as well, lying in a coil atop the steam-heated pipe and chirping sourly in his sleep, ignoring them both.

Butterflies fluttered through her stomach. She ignored the feeling, trying for focus instead. Now it was time to *test* him. Again.

Michael wasn't tall or muscular, though compared to Allen he seemed a hero straight from some theater stage. Both young men leaned against the pipe, greasing the chain assembly that controlled the skysail armatures running alongside the ship. They shared the pot of grease sullenly, yanking it away from the other as each reached for another fistful.

Lina forced herself to calm. She put on a practiced scowl of disapproval and placed her hands on her hips. "You two need to work faster," she said as she approached, "if you're going to be done by the time we dock."

Both men whirled in surprise. Michael recovered first. "Lina!" he exclaimed. "You're looking radiant, as always."

She fought to keep the scowl in place, which she'd copied almost exactly from Captain Blackheart. He was just so Goddess-blamed *cute*. "You're sweet. But I know I stink of old corpse. The captain had me in the hold for a good half hour."

"Even were you entirely malodorous," said Allen, "you could not be more lovely."

Lina blinked. "Well, thank you, Allen. I think."

She stepped past them both to where Runt lay coiled. He slept soundly, tormenting something in his dreams. Lina grabbed him up, staggering under his weight, and wrapped him around her shoulders like a great wormy shawl. He stirred awake, chirping questioningly. Lately he'd been especially irascible. It seemed Runt was only happy after eating, which he had been doing way too much, competing with the White Ape atop the gasbag for seagulls.

She brought her mind back to the matter at hand. "As I was saying, though, you two had best finish up if you want to go out. Myself, I'm looking forward to having a drink or ten down at Garvey's Hole."

The ex-soldier and the apprentice Mechanist started, then glared at each other. Both leaped for the pot of grease at the same time.

It was clear Michael felt something for her, which made her want to squeal in delight. Allen was merely nursing a longtime crush, both painful and obvious. The two men feuded constantly whenever she was around. Which was a good thing, to her mind. For all that she was taken with Michael Hockton, she didn't really *know* him, just that he'd been a Bluecoat soldier—that is, before she'd thrown Runt in his face. So she'd come up with a kind of game; she kept both men in competition with each other for her favor, spreading her praise equally. The more Michael warred with Allen, the more she'd learn about him, and the more she could be certain he was worth her time. It wasn't that long ago that she'd sworn off romance entirely, after all.

"Land ho!" came a cry.

Lina glanced over to the starboard rigging, where Reaver Jane hung on the ratlines leading atop the gas-bag envelope. "Lookout spies the Copper Isles, off the starboard bow!" She gestured, and Lina followed her outstretched arm to spy a dim speck on the horizon to the north.

Everyone aboard the deck let out a cheer. She joined in and ran up to the bow, pressing through the crowd collecting there to watch the final approach. After a few minutes, the dark speck grew into a chain of islands.

The waves crashed high against beachless cliffs of dun-colored rock shot through with veins of coppery ore. Green jungle foliage grew atop each isle, thick and verdant.

Seen from above, the Copper Isles appeared shattered, broken and flooded by some great tectonic upheaval now eons gone. The only entrances into the interior of the island chain were the waterways threading it, a confusing and treacherous labyrinth whose single real approach lay along the western edge of the isles.

Unless you could fly, of course. Which made any such impediments moot. Still, Lina knew there was a loose agreement among the pirate crews of Haventown; in order to keep the pirate port hidden, all were required to approach properly, even in an airship.

The *Dawnhawk* lost altitude as Sarah forced the feuding aetherites to make the proper changes to their approach. Lina groaned at the thought of the route ahead, and judging by the muttered whispers of the crew beside her, she wasn't the only one unhappy at the delay. Swinging westward just so they could turn around and head east again … it would take another hour or more. And her poor airship was *so* battered. What was the point? It wasn't like there was anything out there they needed to see.

She glanced back at the helm where the captains stood. Fengel was arguing with Natasha now. He shook his head as she jabbed him in the chest and then pointed at the battered deck and the forest of draping ropes and canvas. Finally, he threw his hands up, turned on his heel, and stormed off. Natasha smiled, obviously having won.

"Continue course dead ahead!" she called out, for the benefit of the crew. "We're taking a shortcut and going home!"

The crew gave a cheer. Lina went back to watching as the *Dawnhawk* approached the Copper Isles, her bow aimed for the ore-threaded cliff tops. They grew and grew, then disappeared, replaced by a canopy of vine-shrouded palms fifty feet beneath the hull.

Then the jungle gave way to thin and twisty ravines, each fed by ocean-borne current. Jungle appeared again, only to disappear moments later. The airship flew across a thousand little islets of irregular shape until finally, after a quarter span of the glass, the waterways met to form a great lagoon.

This was the Graveway, and it was large enough for a frigate to maneuver freely within. A dozen small waterways fed it from the west, along with a single greater channel. The path to Haventown continued to the east through a long ravine. An old stone fort perched watchfully above, carved into the coppery walls of the cliff itself. Built in the Salomcani fashion, it was a relic from the early years of the original colonists. A handful of lazy sentinels paced along its crenellations, waving at the *Dawnhawk* as they flew by.

Vines atop the jungle cliffs shrouded the walls of the final approach, crawling down the sides of the ravine like a sleeping giant's hair. Small, brightly colored birds took flight as the shadow of the airship fell over them, and gibbons climbed up into the upper branches of palm trees to hoot their indignation. Then the waterway widened into one last lagoon, and Lina found herself back in port.

The Haventown lagoon was even wider than that of the Graveway. Several smaller channels fed into the water here, though only one was wide enough for the egress of a sailing vessel. The same thick jungle foliage topped the cliffs, unbroken but for an enclave built atop the far eastern end of the cove. There a town descended a series of natural terraces to the water of the lagoon, a ramshackle settlement of precariously hanging structures interspersed by rope bridges, boardwalks, and great brass pipes.

The *Dawnhawk* made directly for the highest point of the town, where it perched atop the cliff. This was Nob Terrace, home to the rich and powerful: Sindicato fences, important pirates, and even the Mechanists, huddling within the walls of the Brotherhood Yards. Most importantly, though, this is where the Skydocks were. Built at one end of the terrace upon the slope of a low hill, the Skydocks were a stair-step series of wooden piers jutting directly out from the cliff. Almost all of which were full, its berths occupied by airship dirigibles floating serenely in an ascending line. The *Dawnhawk* made to join them, aiming for an empty space near the bottom.

Lina glanced down, taking in the rest of the pirate township. Directly below the cliff top shone the Yellow Lantern Terrace. Easily the most popular district in the town, the Yellow Lantern was where people went to have fun. Bordellos, taverns, gambling halls, smoking parlors and even a small library resided here. And unlike the rest of the town, which was really only appealing after nightfall, Yellow Lantern businesses took pride in their appearance.

Farther down lay the Flophouse Terrace, with all of the hostels and homes that it contained. If Yellow Lantern was where everyone went for fun, Flophouse was where people went to sleep. Lina knew several decent taverns there but avoided it otherwise; most of the buildings were rife with fleas.

Beneath Flophouse lay the Craftwright's Terrace, the domain of the sailmakers, black apothecaries, and all the other independent professionals who serviced the town. The Gasworks of the Mechanists rose here as well, a mysterious facility of metal boilers and the source of the network of brass pipes that threaded through every other part of town. A towering collection of chimneys and struts rose from the center of the structure, supporting a wide platform that almost reached the terrace above.

At the very bottom lay the lowest and oldest portion of the town, the Waterdocks. Built directly atop the lagoon on a series of old-fashioned piers, the Waterdocks held warehouses and dockworkers' taverns in a mazelike warren. A few traditional sailing ships were moored at the moment, manned by those few pirate captains without an airship. Though poor and unimpressive, the buildings were paradoxically new; rebuilding had been necessary after the disastrous wedding of Fengel and Natasha burned the whole thing down.

"Make ready to dock!" cried Lucian from back near the helm.

Lina snapped from her reverie and ran to her post along the gunwales. The *Dawnhawk* slipped neatly into a berth between the staggered masses of two other airships: the *Windhaunter* below them, and *Solrun's Hammer*, above on the left. Lina leaped neatly off the gunwales with a heavy rope in hand and landed upon the planks. Two crewmates joined her in mooring the great airship: the reptilian Rastalak and dour Nate Wiley, whose undead brother still tottered about the hold. Lina made her rope fast to a cleat, then stood aside as Lucian ran out the gangplank.

The plank fell to the pier with a thump, and she went back aboard with the others. Everyone else was finishing their tasks, making things tight before assembling near the helm where the captains stood. Lina saw that even the outcasts from Almhazlik were here now, finally up from their rooms below. She was acquainted with Etarin and his big friend Farouk. The others—like the boy Paine and ex-soldiers Cumbers and Simon—she knew not at all. Omari was there, of course, looking peevish and uncertain at the small circle of space in the crowd around her. The necromancer was infamous aboard the *Dawnhawk*—Lina moved a bit herself to be farther away.

"Listen up!" cried Natasha, glaring back and forth among the crew. On her shoulder Butterbeak mimicked the motion. "We're finally home. Means we've got a lot to do, but first things first." She nodded to Fengel, who wheeled about to face Omari and the outcasts.

"To those who've found themselves unintentionally aboard the *Dawnhawk*," he said magnanimously, "you are now free to go. Haventown is full of opportunity, so if you really want a trip back to the continent, you'll be sure to find it here. However, Natasha and I have consulted; you've all proven yourselves, in some fashion, so if you seek a home and gainful employment, there is a berth here aboard the *Dawnhawk*."

Cumbers and his younger friend looked at each other, then at Etarin, who nodded. The young boy, Paine, sulked and kicked at the deck. "Don't *wanna* be a pirate," Lina thought she heard him mutter.

The ex-sergeant put a hand on the youth's shoulder. "We've talked it out," said Cumbers. "There's no place for us back on Edrus anymore. We'd all be hung as deserters. So we'll stay."

Omari folded her arms tightly. "Not I!" she said. "I have had enough of this ridiculous ship and your piratical endeavors. I've made my way in strange places before; I will do so again."

Fengel nodded sagely. "Good. I was hoping you would say that, Omari. I wish you the best of luck." He glanced at the boy in the crowd. "Young Paine? Don't sulk—it's unbecoming of both an officer *and* a pirate. See Henry Smalls in a moment. He'll take you into town shortly." Then Fengel clapped his hands together and smiled. "Ship's officers! Attend us here. The rest of you are at liberty until tomorrow morning."

A great cheer erupted across the deck. The assembled pirates moved to flee en masse. Henry Smalls peeled away from Fengel's side to gather up the newly inducted crewmen.

"Ship's officers stay put!" hollered Natasha above the din. "Lina Stone, Michael Hockton, and that Mechanist's apprentice, you get over here too. And the rest of you, don't go where we can't round you up tomorrow! We're off-loading the cargo then, and there's going to be a whole host of things needed to put this ship back together. Stick to Garvey's Hole if you're going to carouse, which I am fairly damned certain you're all going to."

Lina watched her crewmates flee the airship. *What in the Realms Above do they want me for?* It wasn't like she didn't have things to do in town either, aside from getting falling-down drunk. Lina adjusted Runt sourly, eliciting a grumpy chirp. She moved closer to the captains. At least Michael was still here. She sidled up beside him, bumping him with her hip and then looked dismissive as he glanced at her.

"What's going on, captains?" asked Lucian Thorne when the deck was otherwise empty. The first mate appeared mildly irritated. "I'm going to need a whole host of hands to get everything off-loaded and our stores restocked. Not to mention the rotting problem in the holds. We've got huge damned messes on all decks—there's cabling and loose canvas everywhere and a ton of things to fix. Now I'm going to have to spend half of tomorrow rounding everyone back up."

Fengel gave an understanding nod. "I know, Lucian. There's a task we need to accomplish quietly, beforehand. Those ... things down in the hold need taking care of. They need to go before we do anything else, even off-loading our booty." He turned to Sarah Lome, face grim and unpleasant. "Gunney Lome? Go into town and find a warehouse. Somewhere out of the way down in the Waterdocks. Get those walking corpses off our ship and into … storage. Revenant-Herder Hockton? Mechanist Allen? Go with her. Quick and quietlike. No witnesses. I'll figure out a better long-term solution later, but for now I don't want to hear that you've slipped up."

Michael started in dismay beside Lina. "But … sir. The Waterdocks are those piers on the bottom terrace, right? How are we to get fifty walking corpses—"

The captain raised an eyebrow at him. "Mr. Hockton. I thought you'd told me three months ago that you wished to be a pirate?"

"Well, yes." He glanced at Lina. "Sort of …"

"Then on this ship, at least, you'll follow the *captain's* orders. Which goes for both my lovely wife and myself. Am I clear?"

Michael hung his head. "Aye, sir."

Lina winced. For some reason, Fengel had taken an instant dislike to Michael. She couldn't fathom why, really. But he wasn't the only one upset at the news. Allen frowned in dismay, though he was too much the coward to protest. Even Sarah Lome grimaced.

Natasha caught the first mate's eye. "Lucian," she said flatly. "You're a slippery bastard when you wish to be, so you're busy tonight too. Get along after that Yulani witch, Omari. I'd have just dumped her overboard, but my little book says that's impolite." She paused to reach up and thump Butterbeak, who was chewing on her hair. "Walking around on her own, there's bound to be more Revenants. Especially once the locals begins drinking and gutting each other in earnest. Get them down to whatever lockup Gunney Lome here discovers. If it gets bad enough … take steps. Reaver Jane? You're in charge of getting the hold reasonably clean. Use plenty of bleach and soapy water."

The first mate gave a weary nod while Reaver Jane stared in despair.

Fengel clapped. "So! That's that, then. Off you go."

Lina frowned as the others went to their tasks. "Wait, captains? What did you call me up for?" Runt wriggled along her shoulders, and she put a hand up to quiet him.

Natasha looked at her. "We've got to give our obeisance to Father," she said. "Fengel insists you come along."

"Indeed," continued her husband. "I've come to see you as a bit of good fortune, Miss Stone. Also, like me, you're clever in a pinch."

"Even if you're a mutinous little traitor," said Natasha flatly.

They separated just after that, with Lina trailing sullenly along after Fengel and Natasha. The pirate king, Euron Blackheart, held court at the Bleeding Teeth, a Nob Terrace tavern just a short distance away from the

Skydocks. The trip proved quick enough, and before long she followed the captains into a wide taproom.

Lina *hated* the Bleeding Teeth. It was always sweltering, the heat coming from a plethora of lit lanterns and sconces that covered every available space. Souvenirs, it was said, from every place that Euron Blackheart had ever raided. Combined, they bathed the room in daylight brilliance.

It was also surprisingly busy. Lina stared at the collection of pirates milling around the room, like so many brilliantly colored birds.

Wait. There are captains here. Is something going on? She spied Khalid Al-Murdawzi and Brunehilde of the *Solrun's Hammer*. There was James Glastos of the *Powderheart* as well.

Euron Blackheart himself, the pirate king, sat in a great high-backed chair before the crackling fireplace. Beneath his outdated and faded finery, he was bent and gnarled, like an old tree grown in on itself. Eyes like hard glass peered out from above a hawk-like nose and a bushy grey beard shot through with black. A full tankard of foamy ale sat on an armrest beside him, but the pirate king was intently studying an older wooden mug, cracked and punctured as if someone had shot it with a pistol.

Beside Lina, Fengel stiffened. Natasha changed as well, her carefree nonchalance turning into something tight and brittle. They looked to one another, then strode forth as one across the taproom to stand in front of the pirate king. Lina followed, but she tried to do so inconspicuously.

Old Euron looked up from the wooden mug, his eyes widening at the sight of Natasha. "Avast!" he called out. "Why, it be my darling girl, returned home!" He glared at Fengel. "And her primping popinjay of a husband."

Natasha actually blushed, looking embarrassedly around at the assembled captains. Fengel, on the other hand, set his jaw. He bent in a low bow. "The crew of the *Dawnhawk* has returned to port," he said loudly, "and thus, I have come to give our obeisance to the rule of Blackheart."

"And it be my damned poor fortune that I have to take it," replied Euron sourly. He leaned back, still clutching the broken mug in his hoary old hands. "Ye know, back in my day a proper pirate captain wouldn't have been bowin' and scrapin' like so before me. He would have damned well stood straight and told me to go off to the Realms Below!"

"Yes," said Fengel tightly. "And you killed them all because of it." Lina actually heard his teeth grinding.

"So I did," said Euron. The pirate king sounded tired. "So I did. Reddon was the last of them. Glorious bastard he was. Arr! Remember when we came to it, down on th' Waterdocks? Said he didn't know what I be talkin' about, said he be perfectly loyal. But I saw the gleam in his eye, oh aye. I'd just caught him off guard, was all. What a fight we had!" He shook his head. "Glorious, glorious. Those days be gone, though. An' with 'em, all the *real* pirates." He glared at Fengel. "The only thing that be left is fools like ye."

Fengel returned the glare so hard that his monocle popped free to dangle on its chain.

Euron sighed, turning to face Natasha. "But arr, me daughter! Ye give me hope. How goes the pillagin'? Brought back a fat hold full o' bloody loot? I know ye haven't had a decent man to run things since Mordecai died, but even this overdressed popinjay should know how to keep order aboard a ship. And look, ye've even found a parrot, like I used to have!" The old pirate eyed it critically. "It do be a bit funny lookin', though."

Natasha flushed crimson. "I've been doing fine," she said, voice flat. On her shoulder, Butterbeak hunched down and puffed out his feathers, seemingly embarrassed.

Her father laughed aloud, slapping his thigh. "Of course ye have, of course."

"She has," said Fengel, voice flat and cutting, stepping forward to squarely meet the pirate king. "Natasha's brought the *Dawnhawk* back to port with a full hold. She's been in command just as much as I. She's the one who took our prizes. There have been a few … disruptions of late, but she doesn't *need* anyone to run a tight ship. Both our names are feared by those crossing the Atalian Sea—far more than *Euron Blackheart*."

Euron dropped his mug in surprise. "Ye pup! How dare ye? Why, back in my day—"

"Yes," said Fengel, "back in your day. But your day is *over*, you old fart. This is our era"—he gestured at the pirates around the room—"and while we offer you the respect due, it's we who make Haventown great."

Captain Fengel turned on his heel and strode away for the door. Natasha, looking torn, glanced back once at the old pirate on his throne. Then she followed Fengel.

Lina took one look at Euron's face and slunk away after them.

CHAPTER TWO

Admiral Wintermourn considered disowning his son.

It wasn't really a question of if he would. More a question of how. Official notice of the cessation of hostilities had been delivered this morning by courier ship, ending the long struggle between the Kingdom of Perinault and the Sheikdom of Salomca. The final conflict had occurred in Arquam Bay, ending any chance of enemy naval dominance and birthing a glorious new era for the Kingdom. A grand victory, to be certain, yet his worthless offspring had somehow managed to lose both his command *and* his life in the process. While he had taken two enemy vessels with him, that was no less than expected of a Wintermourn scion.

The admiral stood upon the quarterdeck of the *Colossus,* arms folded behind him as he inspected his vessel for any imperfection. The dreadnought flagship of His Majesty's Royal Navy, the *Colossus* had been built for the war and was still almost fresh from the yards at Darrenway. She carried a modern steam engine, paddlewheels, and a full complement of the most advanced guns available. The crew worked under the fading glow of twilight, checking rigging, lighting lanterns, and tying up the sails. His officers moved about calling orders, immaculate in their dress blues and whites. Along the deck rails stood the ship's company of Bluecoat marines, ranked at attention in their cerulean jackets and round black caps, waiting for any sign of trouble.

Beyond the *Colossus* stretched the Atalian Sea, calm, her horizon broken only by the cliffs of the Copper Isles directly to the east, which shone in the light of the setting sun. Dozens of other warships floated nearby, similarly at anchor. A more poetic man might make allusion to the formation of some aquatic city, moving with the ebb and flow of the waves.

Admiral Wintermourn was not a poetic man. He did appreciate the sight, though; the numbers meant strength. Almost the entirety of the Perinese Royal Navy had been directed to this action, save those ships necessary at Arquam. Victory against the Salomcani had been a foregone conclusion for over a year now, so much so that the fleet could be sent to pacify a lackluster rebellion in the Breachtown colony. That done, the only question had been what to target next. When Wintermourn received his new orders, he approved the choice. Now the strongest naval force in the world was in position just outside of the Copper Isles. The setting sun seemed particularly appropriate when he considered their foe.

"Almost ready now, sir."

Wintermourn glanced at Sergeant Adjutant Lanters, standing deferentially aside. The man was a side of beef in uniform, with little intellect, and worse, no patronage. But it wouldn't be said that Admiral Wintermourn didn't reward dedication; when trapped in a burning building three months ago, with unholy undead abominations clawing at their feet, the man had stood fast where all Wintermourn's other subordinates had fled. For that, he made Lanters his adjutant for this fleet action, commanding all the *Colossus's* Bluecoats. The man also made a good valet, he'd found. While giving a mere marine the same authority as a navy field officer had generated resentment among his own lieutenants, they were all canny enough to keep their complaints to themselves.

"I should hope so, Sergeant," replied the admiral, glancing past the man. "Any more time spent on this task is unacceptable. Subterfuge of this sort is quite unbecoming."

A dozen men worked at the port-side gunwales. They loaded weapons into a longboat launch along with casks of whale oil. Disgraced volunteers one and all, the men followed the direction of Able Seaman Hayes, who directed the preparations stiffly, his back only barely recovered from the bite of the nine-tailed-cat. The ex-pirate Oscar Pleasant sulked within the launch itself. Before long they would venture alone into the island chain to the east, hunting for the pirate port called Haventown and the airship Skydocks there.

"Aye, sir," replied Lanters. "No one's going to miss these sacks o' skin, though. And if they do succeed, the Goddess-damned sky pirates will be crippled. Assumin' that Pleasant fellow proves trustworthy."

Admiral Wintermourn sighed. "They won't succeed, Sergeant. The only thing they'll do is prod the bear awake. Which is the *only* reason I am allowing this dishonorable course of action. We've been at anchor all day, yet these damnable sky pirates haven't even noticed us!" He shook his head.

Cutthroats and rogues they may have been, but he couldn't imagine that the pirates were so miserably oblivious to the threat waiting on their doorstep.

"I would love to hang Mr. Pleasant," Wintermourn continued, "but it seems he can be useful in this instance. So yes, let him lead the way into that warrens. He will be trustworthy enough for that. The fellow has no home now but ours."

Still, this preemptive skulking rankled him. Things were done a certain way in the navy. Great battles full of sound and fury, the spent lives of common men wicking out like burned-down candles—that was the way to victory. If he had to goad the enemy to play their part, so be it.

Wintermourn watched as Able Seaman Hayes loaded a cask of oil into the longboat. *So be it.* He could almost see it now: wooden buildings afire, pirates and saboteurs both burning. Tottering blindly about, reaching up with fingers like claws as they died and rose again …

The false sun of a galvanic lantern bloomed above the crow's nest of the *Colossus*, cutting through the memory.

Ah. There he is. One last presence was required before the invasion could truly begin. Though it … complicated matters. The newcomer had taken a different route than that of the fleet. However, now here he was, right on schedule. The admiral cast one last look about the deck, then straightened his wig, adjusted his hat, and gestured to Sergeant Adjutant Lanters. Everything had to be perfect now.

The sergeant gave a nod. "Atten-shun!" he bellowed, both hands cupped about his mouth. Every man on the deck froze in his task, from able seamen all the way to First Lieutenant Lebam, and turned to face the admiral.

"Present arms!" continued Lanters. The marines along the rails stepped forward and raised their muskets to the sky. "Fire!"

The rippling thunder of a hundred shots echoed out across the deck and over the water. There were enough ships clustered nearby that the salute might prove dangerous. It didn't matter. Some things were just done, especially for a member of the royal family. And maybe the pirates would notice *that*.

The lantern above winked out, replaced by the silent, oblong hulk of an airship. Smaller than the ridiculous contraptions built by the Haventown Mechanists, this vessel was made for war. Its gas bag and gondola both were armored, and smaller propeller assemblies along either side of the hull helped the two in the rear to provide speed. Golden lettering up near the bow declared its name, and the sunburst sigil emblazed across the gas bag declared its allegiance. Still, to Admiral Wintermourn's eye, the *Glory of Perinault* was an ungainly vessel. It lacked the imposing grandeur of a proper oceangoing warship.

He could hear the whir of propellers as the *Glory* shifted in its position above their topsails. The airship floated to starboard, then lowered, coming down until its gondola deck sat just above the *Colossus's* own. Bluecoats ran out a boarding ramp, then lowered it down with a mechanical winch. One of Wintermourn's lieutenants barked an order, sending deckhands to secure it.

The time has come, then. Admiral Wintermourn jerked his head, then descended to the deck and the base of the boarding ramp. Sergeant Adjutant Lanters followed, and First Lieutenant Lebam gathered with the other officers. For all of his confidence and rank, a sense of trepidation lingered in Admiral Wintermourn's heart. He had never met the crown prince before, and what he had heard from correspondence back home did not reassure him.

The deckhands scurried away as he moved amidships to face the ramp, sufficiently far away to allow an honor guard to appear. He was not disappointed, as four men descended to the deck, ornate in uniforms of red, blue, and gold. They held long-bladed halberds etched with the sunburst sigil of Perinault and carried at their hips a far more practical saber, as well as a brace of flintlock pistols. The royal guard descended, splitting off to stand at either side of the ramp, glaring about the *Colossus* before turning worried gazes back up to the airship.

No one appeared. For a moment stillness reigned, disrupted only by a loose bit of sail flapping above in the tropical breeze.

Then Wintermourn heard it. A heavy tromp, as of many booted feet all taking a step at once. The clank of metal followed, both sounds repeating, quickly building into a monotonous rhythm that grew louder with every passing moment. The ramp to the *Glory* began shaking with some unseen force.

A figure in a brazen suit of heavy platemail armor appeared atop the ramp. It moved mechanically, flywheels spinning and pistons hammering away in the spaces between its plates. Steam puffed out from a small exhaust pipe behind the right pauldron next to the slung barrels of a complicated firearm, which was something like a heavy pepperbox musket.

The armored knight descended as another appeared behind it. And then another. In moments a whole platoon of the things had tromped down onto the *Colossus*, bending and bowing the boarding ramp until it looked like the thing would crack into flinders. Wintermourn's officers fell back at their approach, but the machines ignored them, splitting off to stand two to a side, forming a two columns leading away from the airship. In all, Admiral Wintermourn counted twenty of the mechanical, inhuman things.

A man appeared atop the ramp, hands folded behind him. He was young and handsome in a richly cut uniform of red, black, and gold. The boots he wore were so well polished that they gleamed in the light of the shipboard lanterns. A blade was sheathed at his hip, a longsword in the old style. Admiral Wintermourn had never met the youth but recognized him immediately: Crown Prince Gwydion, whose image was pressed into every silver sovereign minted in the Kingdom.

The prince descended to the deck, followed by three others. Two were servants, who split away to join the guards, while the third was a bearded fellow in something *almost* like proper naval uniform. He followed the Crown Prince Gwydion as the prince strode down between the mechanical knights, his cold grey eyes focused intently upon Wintermourn's own. He stopped before the admiral, just far away enough for propriety's sake.

Admiral Wintermourn felt suddenly wary. *Wolf's eyes, cold and grey.* Such a thing was rare in the Kingdom. He bent down to one knee. All about the deck came the rustle of uniforms as his officers and crew followed suit. "My liege," he said.

The prince abruptly laughed. His voice was rich and mellifluous, clearly used to easy jesting. "A hundred-gun salute? That's a bit obvious, isn't it? Though the pirates are apparently deaf and blind both not to notice us so far." He reached down and grabbed Wintermourn's hand, yanking him up. The admiral spluttered; such contact was entirely improper.

"On your feet, on your feet. Enough groveling like some damned peasant who thinks the sun shines out my arse. So! You must be Wintermourn. Lord High Admiral of the Sea, commanding this fine fleet of my royal father's, yes?"

Wintermourn stood, feeling moderately affronted at the contact. The youth lacked a sense of propriety, that was readily apparent. *Who does this young pup*—he checked himself. This young pup would be his king one day. "Yes, Your Royal Highness," he said. "The assembled entirety of the navy is here, every ship capable of fighting and not needed at Arquam Bay. Force enough to smash whatever defense the pirates can muster and burn them out of these islands entire. We've been ready and waiting for battle all day."

"Excellent!" said Gwydion. He clapped his hands together. "My royal father will be pleased. And this will be a perfect test for the *Glory,* commanded by Captain Broadlow here, the first officer in our new aerial corps."

Gwydion gestured to the man behind him, who gave a polite nod. "Admiral," said Broadlow.

Wintermourn only narrowed his eyes at the man. He felt the instant disdain all navy personnel possessed for other branches of service.

"And," continued the crown prince, "this will be an excellent opportunity to try out these Brass Paladins."

The admiral paused. His dispatches had mentioned the prince's arrival in an experimental airship. But nothing had been said of the armored machines. "Pray you, sir, what are these … devices?"

The crown prince turned to face the nearest one. "The Paladins? Why, I'm glad you asked! These are the stout and redoubtable wave of the future. I've a small platoon of marines back aboard the *Glory,* but these are Perinault's newest soldiers. My father may have his Order Gallant, but here I have my Brass Paladins, redesigned from the horses of Triskelion and improved by our guest back at the palace. With my own modest input, of course."

Crown Prince Gwydion reached out and slapped the nearest automaton on the back. At that moment a wave shifted the deck of the *Colossus.* The officers and crew alike adjusted. Even the Brass Paladins shifted their stance with a sudden, alarming internal whirr of clockwork.

The prince's blow proved a bit too much, however. It sent the Paladin toppling over, arms flailing for balance. The mechanical warrior slammed into the deck and slid towards the portside railing as sailors and marines alike scrambled to get out of its way. One failed to move fast enough. The Brass Paladin slammed into him, bowling him over and pinning him up against the rails. He screamed as the deck settled again, legs crushed underneath the weight of the automaton.

Sailors rushed to assist their crewmate as the bosun blew with alarm into his whistle. They surrounded the Paladin, which flailed around like an overturned beetle, clockwork whirring inside its carapace as it attempted to rise. Its gyrations only compounded the agony of the sailor beneath it, who cried desperately for help.

As twelve pairs of hands grabbed at the automaton, it suddenly went berserk. The Brass Paladin flung four men away with one arm, sending them sprawling across the deck. Then it balled up a gauntleted fist and swung out as it kicked at those near to its feet. Both blows missed, but the surprised sailors had barely any chance to recover before it was rolling aside, reaching for the heavy pepperbox musket at its back.

Crown Prince Gwydion ran past, a blur of red and gold. Admiral Wintermourn felt his eyes bug out as the prince leaped onto the heaving chest of the automaton. It slammed back down to the deck, and Captain Broadlow, the marines, royal guards, and officers all echoed the screams of the wounded sailor with their own shouts of alarm, struck out of their surprise by the sudden danger to their liege lord. They scrambled forward into a tight mob before Wintermourn could open his mouth to bellow commands. He watched in horror as the Brass Paladin pulled back its arm for a blow aimed at Gwydion's head.

The prince neatly ducked the armored fist, though it caught his tricorn hat and flung it away. He reached up to grab something hidden up underneath the chin of the automaton and twisted. The Brass Paladin froze, then went limp as the steam puffing from its exhaust slowly died. In moments it stilled, and the only noises were those of the belated scrambling of the crew and the agonized groans of the wounded sailor.

Gwydion laughed aloud and slapped the now-inanimate helmet. The sailor beside him gave a long, barely conscious moan. Gwydion twisted around as if noticing the man for the first time. He grabbed the fellow by the lapels and shook him hard.

"Oh, don't be such a child. You'll have *such* a tale to tell the grandchildren!"

Then the royal guard were there, gently reaching down to support the crown prince and raise him back up. Gwydion stepped away from the lifeless automaton, shaking them off. His two attendants appeared and knelt by the machine, directing the sailors in moving it away.

"Off," said the prince to his guards. "Off! I'm not some high-society socialite, to faint at a bit of excitement. I came out here for a bit of action, and by the Goddess, I'll have it!"

One of the royal guardsman stammered an apology while Captain Broadlow looked on, white as a sheet. Admiral Wintermourn considered his own reaction. Having the son of the king himself die on his ship, on his watch, would have been a career-ending debacle of the highest order. However, the king was not here at the moment. Gwydion was.

He surprised himself by deciding on tact. "That was deftly done, sir. But perhaps such a threat should be left to your subordinates? It's what they're here for, after all." Admiral Wintermourn flicked a glance at the crippled sailor being carried away. It was obvious he wouldn't survive the night. "And we might have saved that fellow." The words felt awkward in his mouth. Sailors were cogs; one was replaceable as any other. Still, it felt a bit off to lose anyone before the battle had even begun.

The crown prince waved nonchalantly. "Bah. I've seen designs that will make that fellow obsolete in two years' time. The Paladins will do the same for your Bluecoats—and my royal guard, even."

One of the guards flanking Gwydion stared at him in dismay.

"The Paladin was merely reacting to perceived hostility," continued the prince. "They are meant to be soldiers, after all. These are simply early days yet for them." He turned and gestured to the airship docked beside the *Colossus*. "The future is coming, my good admiral. These silly sky pirates have had one thing right all these years. Look you there. The *Glory of Perinault*, first of her kind. She's an amazing craft, Admiral. Simply amazing. Don't you agree?"

"It is certainly impressive," agreed Wintermourn with a hesitant nod—this talk of replacing men with machines did not sit well with him. "And the tactical advantages are immediately apparent—advanced intelligence for fleet engagements, increased courier speed. I'm sure that there are some civilian applications to which it could be applied as well."

Crown Prince Gwydion turned back to stare at him. Then he elbowed Captain Broadlow in the ribs and laughed aloud. "My dear admiral, would you have the *Glory* be no more than some overinflated crow's nest? No, no, no. She's a *warship*. Why slug things out on the open seas when you can rain destruction down from above? Thanks to our new guest back at the palace, we'll soon have a whole fleet of such vessels, some even with their own weaponry aboard, though that's a bit of a problem at the moment. Think of it, though—the whole of the Perinese Royal Navy replaced in only five years' time!"

Admiral Wintermourn stared. *Realms Below, he cannot be serious ... can he?* A dozen rebuttals crashed together on his tongue.

"Poppycock," he replied finally, puffing up in spite of himself. "The Royal Navy has guarded the shores of the Kingdom for three hundred years. We've proven ourselves better and more able than any other branch, and our traditions have stood against all adversity. Victory is wrought with the blood of sailors, many sailors, and a broadside of a hundred guns. Not clockwork. These new toys may prove useful, but they will not change how things are and have always been."

He froze as he realized his unforgiveable breach in protocol. But the crown prince only laughed. "Well said! But oh, my dear admiral, just wait until you see her in action." Gwydion turned again to face him, his eyes serious. "Now. Let us turn our talk to matters of more import."

"Of course, Your Highness," Wintermourn replied, feeling relieved. The change in topic provided a timely escape from his gaffe. "Every active-duty ship to be spared is here at anchor, primed and ready to crush the pirates. We'd expected the action to begin today, but apparently, the curs have somehow missed our presence. Thus, the action will begin on the morrow, and when they come to meet us, we will be ready."

"Yes, yes. So you said. I *do* have ears, you know." The prince shook his head. "But really, that hundred-gun salute you gave. Cease such foolishness in the future."

Wintermourn paused, uncertain. "I beg your pardon?"

Gwydion clapped his hands together and gestured out at the deck. "Well, it's loud, isn't it? Anyone paying any attention at all ought to have heard it. Certainly, a fleet of warships at anchor isn't exactly inconspicuous, but by some miracle we've gone unnoticed until now. We really should take whatever measures we can to keep that advantage."

Wintermourn blinked in confusion. "Your Royal Highness. The salute is a tradition going back more than a hundred years. You are our liege lord—of the blood royal. Who cares if a bunch of damned rogues *finally* notice their impending doom? We'll smash them all the same and honor your house, as is only right and proper."

"It is a matter of effectiveness, my good admiral. The only thing that matters is the result, not how you got there. Looking a man in the eye as you stab him might be rightly honorable, and certainly good fun, but it also gives him a pretty chance to skewer you in return. No, a blade in the back is preferable. We should try to remain hidden now, until tomorrow's assault."

Admiral Wintermourn stared in dismay. Tradition was the foundation for His Majesty's Royal Navy and the bedrock upon which he had built his career. All necessary tactics and actions of command had been appropriately analyzed and tested, requiring only moderate adjustment to an individual situation. If a failing was ever found, it was due to a lack of individual mettle. Courage, honor, and skill could fail. The course itself was always clear.

Yet the crown prince stood before him, on his very flagship, presuming to dictate that this was incorrect. Worse, he was espousing a completely dishonorable alternative. Admiral Wintermourn realized he did not like the crown prince so very much.

"Sir," he said with condescension. "I must object in the strongest manner possible. To the layman it may seem as if there are inefficiencies in the service, but trust me when I say that there are reasons for such traditions. A variety of them."

Gwydion waved nonchalantly. "Nevertheless, desist with such pomp in the future. I've already made my will clear in this matter, I should think. Oh. And it's kind of shot for now, but we'll also keep all deck lamps at half capacity, with night gathering such as it is. Now! With that settled, I will be taking direct command at this moment as well."

Admiral Wintermourn blinked. *I can't have heard that right.*

"My royal father has given me dispensation for this minor action," continued the crown prince. "Says I should 'get my feet wet,' and frankly, I agree. Dueling in the capital is an amusing diversion, but I mean to control a *real* military conflict. See some action. It's time we crushed these annoying sky pirates, which should be an adequate test of my abilities."

Wintermourn felt as if his world were crashing down around him. *What? He cannot ... what?* He had known the prince was arriving, of course, but had thought him merely here in an observatory capacity, bringing along the new airship. This gross disrespect for his office was galling in a way he found difficult to express.

"Sir...you cannot be serious. I am Lord High Admiral of the Sea. Command is mine—"

Gwydion stepped in close, pinning Wintermourn with his own wolf-like gaze. "And I will be your king," he said, low and dangerous. The flippant young man of a minute before was gone as if he had never existed.

Wintermourn worked his jaw as bitter words welled up like black bile. Having to practice such restraint was ... difficult. He was unused to it. *You are not king yet.* Wintermourn ducked his head in a deferential nod.

Crewmen and marines both had been directed back to their tasks by his lieutenants during this exchange. They worked as silently as possible, clearly trying to avoid the attention of both the highborn and the murderous mechanical Paladins where they still stood. To Wintermourn's surprise, though, one sailor moved up to kneel just beside them. It was the ex-officer of the *Goliath*, Able Seaman Hayes.

The former officer dared to glance up, not at him, but to the crown prince. Wintermourn would have been stunned at the breach in protocol were it any other fellow. But Hayes was a toadying worm of a man. *You didn't learn your lesson after Almhazlik, did you?* He was pleased to find such a ready outlet for his frustrations. Hayes would have lashes for this. Oh yes. He would see the fellow broken.

"Hayes!" he barked. "What are you doing here? Get back to your post until your betters call for you."

A spasm of worry crossed Hayes's features, pale and sickly in the twilight gloom. He knew what he was risking. "Sir, yes, sir. It's just, the launch is ready."

Wintermourn flushed with anger. "You dog! How dare you talk back—"

"Hold." Gwydion held up a hand. "What are you about, man?"

Hayes ducked his head. "The special mission, Your Highness. We are prepared and ready to depart."

Gwydion cocked his head, curious. "What special mission?" he asked Wintermourn. "I was not briefed on any such action."

This was the last thing Wintermourn wanted to talk about. He regretted ever agreeing to it. "It's a last-minute thing put together by my subordinate," replied Wintermourn impatiently. "Sergeant Adjutant Lanters!" he called.

The sergeant crossed the deck from where he'd been inspecting the longboat. Belatedly, he remembered the prince's station and dropped down to kneel awkwardly. "Sir? Yer Royal Highness?"

"Explain this idea of yours to the prince."

"Ah, sir." Lanters nodded and licked his lips and laboriously chose his words. "Well, th' invasion plan calls fer us to meet the pirates in a fleet action, like usual. Except they haven't come out yet—or even noticed us. So, we've got one o' these sky pirates, a traitor. We've maps off him that say the isles are shot through with all sort o' twisty waterways. So's I wondered, why not try a bit o' sabotage first? A longboat full o' powder, bombs, and desperate men with nothin' to lose. They're to sneak into the pirate port after full dark and do as much damage as they can to the airships there. That'll alert the pirates, so's they'll finally come and face us, and also confirm our route to move the fleet in overland afterward."

The sergeant fell silent. Wintermourn watched the crown prince, waiting for appropriate disapproval. Instead, Gwydion smiled and clapped the kneeling man on the back.

"Excellent!" he cried, wheeling about to face Wintermourn. "I can see that at least some of you here have your minds in the right place. Don't look so glum, my good admiral. We'll make a proper scoundrel of you yet!" He turned to Able Seaman Hayes. "You there, fellow. Get on with your mission, and Goddess speed you."

Hayes ducked his head, backing away as he returned to the longboat. Wintermourn watched him go with grinding teeth.

"Wonderful initiative you've got, man," said the crown prince to Lanters. "Keep it up."

"Thank you, Yer Highness." The sergeant blushed, then saw Wintermourn's freezing glare. He ducked his head and stepped back, subservient. Wintermourn decided there would be punishment later.

"I mean," said the prince, "they're all quite dead, assuredly."

"Indeed," promised Wintermourn.

"Still, wonderful! I apologize for my earlier chastisement, Admiral. It occurs to me that this is even better than trying, probably in vain, to keep ourselves under cover until the morrow. A small distraction even such as this will prove far more useful. And if there *is* a waterway we can take straight to Haventown … yes, they'll never see us coming." The prince paused suddenly. He looked to the airship, then the fleet, and again at the cliffs to the east as they were rapidly becoming shrouded by night. "In fact …" Then he snapped his fingers and turned fiercely. "I have an idea. Broadlow! We're returning now to the *Glory*. Admiral Wintermourn, have some of those maps of yours sent up. After a turn of the glass, I will have the ship back aloft to act as lookout, just as you suggested. We'll confirm a few things—advance intelligence and all that."

Wintermourn did not feel congenial anymore. "It will also allow you to get closer to the action," he said flatly. At the moment he didn't much care if the youth endangered himself.

Gwydion laughed and slapped him on the back. Wintermourn flinched at the contact. "Ha! You know me so well already, Admiral. But I do have an idea for something more. Proceed as you'd planned, waiting in vain out here for a fight. Oh, we're going to have such a wonderful time working together—I can already tell."

With that, the crown prince of Perinault turned on his heel and strode back down between the Brass Paladins with Captain Broadlow following behind, uncertain. The automatons jerked into hissing and clanking life, peeling off from their formation to follow him back aboard the airship. His retainers and royal guard hurried after.

Admiral Wintermourn stood in the middle of his flagship as the officers and his sergeant adjutant waited on his orders. He ignored them, watching Gwydion's departure. As they went, he felt strangely unbalanced. The swaggering peacock was going to be his king, but he brought with him a vision of the future which had very little place for the Kingdom that Wintermourn knew. Indeed, very little room for men at all, it seemed.

He snorted. The boy was a fool youth. There was still plenty of time to educate him.

Wintermourn turned back to his cringing officers and barked a series of terse orders. All drama aside, the crown prince was at least in agreement with him about one thing: it was high time the sky pirates of the Copper Isles were dealt with properly. Admiral Wintermourn intended to see that every last man, woman, and child under their anarchic banner swung from a noose.

CHAPTER THREE

Captain Fengel was finding it difficult to enjoy his drink.

"Listen," hissed Omari. She held Cubbins, her tabby cat, above the small table between them. "I have to build a new life for myself here. I cannot be taking care of this flea-bitten sack of fur."

She shoved the cat into Fengel's face, and he pushed it back with his free hand. "Come now," he replied, pausing to take a swig of warm, sour ale. "Everyone knows that cats bring good luck." He stopped to pull a long, orange hair from between his lips, then grimaced at Cubbins. The feline purred happily at the attention.

They sat on the small balcony of Garvey's Hole, tavern of choice for the crew of the *Dawnhawk* when in port. It wasn't too raucous a place, at least not at this point in the evening. The dry, woody scent of fresh sawdust filled the air, and Garvey's waitresses came quickly with drinks. At the moment Fengel's crew took up most of the taproom; the newcomers from Almhazlik mixed with the others, lounging and chatting among themselves.

A few stood out, as always. His first mate and steward sat near the bar, exaggerating tales of their latest adventure, Lucian occasionally glancing over his shoulder to eye Omari. Crewmates and rival pirates both sat rapt, uttering occasional guffaws of disbelief. In the center of the room, Gunney Lome challenged all comers to arm wrestle. Fengel watched her crush Nate Wiley with a mighty yell and then take up the tankard beside her with frayed exuberance. Somehow, she'd completed the task of relocating all the Revenants aboard the *Dawnhawk* down to a Waterdock warehouse.

Michael Hockton and Allen the apprentice Mechanist had also been assigned to that unpleasant job, and both now sat disheveled and stinking at a table nearby. The young men were frantically attempting to drink each other under the table. It wasn't *entirely* their fault—Miss Stone sat nearby, egging them on while she consoled her vile and ill-tempered pet.

Natasha, as always, held court near the unlit fireplace. His wife never lacked for an audience when in town.

"If it is good luck," insisted Omari, "then *you* can take care of it." She shoved Cubbins back across the table, forcing Fengel to pull back.

Fengel usually drank alone, more for image's sake than anything else. He would spend the evening looking out upon Haventown after nightfall, the stoic and mysterious captain. To be fair, it was a picturesque scene, if a little boring. The lights of the Waterdocks glowed brightly from here, reflecting from the great bundled chimney of the Gasworks on the second terrace and the wide platform it supported. Far up above hung the Skydocks and its airships, likewise reflecting the glow of the Yellow Lantern Terrace from their great, soft gas-bag envelopes. Tropical birds called in the distance, and the occasional breeze brought earthy jungle scents.

"Omari," sighed Fengel. "I already have far too many animals aboard my ship to take care of, including a scryn, a bird, numerous diverse pirates, and a wife. You were in such a hurry to be rid of us. I can't be held accountable that this animal decided to follow you." He looked up as a shadow fell across the table. "Yes, what is it?"

One of the waitresses had appeared, a tankard of ale in hand. "Here ya go, captain."

Fengel shoved the cat away again and took the drink with a frown. "Obliged. But I don't remember ordering another."

She jerked her head back inside. "Compliments of Captain Blackheart, who'd like you to join her."

"Oh." Fengel glanced back to where Natasha sat, surrounded by a gaggle of hapless local admirers. "Tell her I'm just fine out here, but thanks."

The waitress raised her eyebrows. "Not unless you're tipping in diamonds, Captain. Everyone who gets caught between the two of you gets shot or set on fire."

Fengel watched her leave in mild vexation. The complaint wasn't entirely true. *No one's been set on fire since the wedding.*

He returned to his drink while Omari harangued him, trying to appeal to his reason in vain. Fengel ignored her to watch a flickering light up along the Skydocks. Someone was either playing with a lantern or sending covert signals back down to the town below. The latter was more likely. Some skullduggery was always going on in Haventown—shipboard politics, say, or some crewman trying to slip their doxy aboard. Fengel rather looked forward to hearing about it later.

A shadow fell across the table. Glancing up, he saw his wife glaring malevolently down at him. Butterbeak squatted on her shoulder, mirroring her black gaze.

"Leave," she said without looking at Omari.

"But I've got to do something with this cat—"

Natasha grabbed the animal roughly. Then she turned and threw it across the taproom. Cubbins sailed through the air with a yowl and landed on the surprised face of Allen the apprentice Mechanist, who shrieked in surprise and pain. He collapsed beside the bar as the cat savaged him while Lina Stone and Michael Hockton both stared.

Natasha turned back to face Omari. "Leave," she repeated.

The other woman took the hint this time. She slunk away from her seat, which Natasha promptly occupied. Her parrot took flight, more interested in the chaos near the bar.

"I bought you a drink," she snarled at him. "I was being nice. It doesn't happen often. You were *supposed* to pay me back by coming over and joining me."

Fengel gave this a distracted shrug. "I … don't usually drink with anyone, here."

His wife gave him a look that would have set sailcloth aflame. Then she relaxed abruptly, the fight going out of her, leaving her looking weary. "Horseshit," she sighed. "You're still hung up on that meeting with my father." Natasha took his mug and quaffed from it. Then her eyes popped wide. Gingerly, she removed a long orange cat hair from between her lips. "You think that wasn't awful for me too?" she asked sourly. "Two weeks ago I killed a man with his own trousers. Yet my father still treats me like I'm five years old, with a head full of dragons and dashing princes." She shook her head. "You can at least admit you're still troubled over it."

A piercing screech startled them both. Fengel glanced back to see Butterbeak fly past Lucian's table. The malevolent, absurdly colored little thing defecated in Lucian's tankard just as Fengel's first mate was about to take a drink. Lucian cursed and dropped his tankard, then took a swing at the parrot. It dodged, screeching again as it flew up into the rafters.

The taproom burst out into laughter. Natasha smiled. Long, painful hours had gone into training the parrot.

Captain Fengel gestured at the scene. "That fairly much sums it up," he admitted.

Natasha only rolled her eyes. She glanced at the airships and the evening sky above them. "You'll live," she said. "Which means that you can damned well come over and keep me company with all the horny bastards who think they've still … got …" She trailed off with a frown. Then her eyes widened in surprise. "Goddess's hairy arms!"

Fengel followed her gaze. The flickering glimmer he'd seen a moment ago was larger now. A cold thrill of fear shot through his belly—what he'd taken to be a lantern was now several blazing fires, each as large as a man.

He shot to his feet. "Fire on the Skydocks!" he bellowed aloud.

Garvey's Hole evacuated. Some pirates ran off to fetch their captains, others to spread the word. Fengel led his crew towards the stair up to the upper terraces, with Natasha right beside him. Visions of the *Dawnhawk* aflame hung foremost in his mind.

Not again. Oh Goddess, not again. His last ship had died burning, eaten by a living magical fire. He'd got almost all of his crew safely away, but the final eruptive blast that ended her still haunted his dreams.

The gaudy structures of the Yellow Lantern Terrace flashed by. Whores, sots, and sailors looked up from dim alleys, or poked their heads out the windows as the pirates raced past. Fengel ignored them all, intent on the walkways that provided the fastest way through the ramshackle warren that was night-shrouded Haventown.

Fengel rounded the last corner before the stair to the terrace above and slammed into someone. Natasha ran into him in turn, followed by their crew, colliding into a confused knot of people rushing for the stair from the other direction. Fengel shoved his way free, until he could clearly see the hirsute man he'd collided with. It was James Glastos, captain of the airship *Powderheart.* He was not on congenial terms with the fellow.

"Fengel!" cried Glastos, reaching for his cutlass. "Set me adrift at sea, will you? Well, damn you to the farthest Realm Below. I'll gut you like the whoreson dog you are!"

Natasha appeared with a dagger tight against the man's throat. "You'll do nothing of the sort," she snarled, low and dangerous.

Blades and truncheons appeared in the hands of the pirates around them, Natasha's and Glastos's both. Fengel frantically threw up his hands. "There's no time for this! The Skydocks are ablaze!"

Captain Glastos stepped back and pushed Natasha's dagger away. "I've a pair of eyes myself. Where do you think I was going before you and your buffoons tripped into me?"

Off to catch the pox, most like. Outwardly, Fengel only glared at the pirate. He was insulting, irascible, and ultimately intolerable. There was a reason Fengel had abandoned him to die once. But there were more important considerations at the moment.

He stepped back, bowed low, and gestured at the stair hugging the cliffside with exaggerated theatricality. "*Please,* my good captain. Do go first, so long as you and your men *move.*"

Ugly glares were shot back and forth among the crewmen, but Glastos only nodded and bolted for the stair, climbing with Natasha and Fengel just behind.

They ascended to Nob Terrace, where crowds were already forming. A few of the more quick-witted were pounding desperately against the compound wall of the Brotherhood Yard, shouting for help with the strange, explosive gasses that lifted the airships, which only the Mechanists knew how to handle.

Fengel raced alongside his fellow captains, bellowing with all the practice of long years at sea, shouting at the bystanders to clear the way. Past the taverns and costly homes of Haventown's elite, the Skydocks were a beacon, its airship gas bags reflecting the infernal blaze of the decks below.

Not again! He turned a corner past the Sindicato mansion where Mr. Grey did his business—and felt his heart drop into his belly.

The Skydocks were a stair-step structure, complete with landings and a rail, surmounting a small hillock at the far end of Nob Terrace opposite the Brotherhood Yards. Otherwise, it was built much the same as the Waterdocks so far below, composed of a series of piers jutting out into space above the rest of the pirate township, buttressed against the cliff face.

Flames licked the gunwales of the two nearest airships. Fengel recognized them: Captain Glastos's own *Powderheart* and Captain Duvale's *Windhaunter.* Fortunately, the flames were contained to the wooden hulls and had not reached the gasbags themselves. Which meant they only had a little time, as opposed to none at all. The *Powderheart* was aptly named— Glastos preferred to smash his prey with bombs dropped from above, thus requiring a black-powder magazine aboard his ship. Should the flames reach that, it would be just as catastrophic as if the flammable envelope caught ablaze.

"My ship!" cried Captain Glastos. He darted up the stair to the first Skydock landing where the *Powderheart* was moored, with Fengel and Natasha just behind. Cranes for unloading cargo stood beside bins of sand along the pier, the latter for emergencies just such as this.

Up close, the fires were burning along the bow, the gunwales, and the stern of the *Powderheart,* their conflagrations all strangely separate. The sweet char scent of burning wood surrounded them—but not the acrid stink of light-air gas about to ignite. What Fengel could see of the *Windhaunter* on the next pier above was the same. *We can still save both of them, but we've got to work fast.* Fengel offered up a prayer that the flames hadn't started belowdecks.

"Lucian! Gunney Lome!" he cried, gesturing. "Get up to the next pier and form a brigade. Henry! Grab Cumbers and Nate Wiley and get some hands started down—"

"To the Realms Below with Duvale's ship!" yelled Glastos. The pirate captain charged halfway down the first pier to the *Powderheart's* boarding ramp. "We've got to save mine first!"

"You squid-arsed sack of bilgewater!" snarled Natasha. "If we don't save them both, they're all going to go—"

An explosion cut her short. Fengel acted reflexively, throwing himself at his wife and falling with her to the wooden platform at their feet. He crouched above her, heart in his throat, waiting for the deadly rain of burning debris to shower them. He might be damned and gone, but she had to survive.

None of it came. Fengel opened his eyes to see Natasha, frozen and expectant just as he was. He glanced up to see that the rest of the assembled pirates had crouched as well. But both airships were still intact and ablaze.

A figure stood on the deck of the *Powderheart* between two of the fires. It was a Bluecoat Marine of the Kingdom of Perinault, unmistakable in his uniform and round black hat, holding a smoking musket. Behind him stood a man with another firearm, passing it up. Incredibly, Fengel recognized him; it was Hayes, the ambitious but incompetent first mate of the *H.M.S. Goliath*.

The raging fires were no coincidence.

"Take cover!" Fengel cried. "We're under attack!"

More men appeared on the deck of the *Powderheart,* who were soon joined by others against the gunwales of the *Windhaunter* above. They were a mix of naval sailors and Bluecoats, but the muskets in their hands were no less deadly for that.

Fengel crawled behind the nearest wooden sand bin, trusting his wife to do the same. Out the corner of his eye, he saw the other pirates likewise scattering for cover. Captain Glastos himself appeared to be the only casualty so far; he hunkered behind a crane ahead, clutching a bleeding arm.

"Kill them!" shouted Hayes from the deck of the airship. "Kill them all! Especially that one with the monocle!"

The Perinese fired just as Natasha scrabbled up against the bin beside him. The reports sounded like a chain of holiday fireworks. Hot lead hissed all around Fengel, splintering wood and perforating clothing. The chain of a crane on his right snapped, sending the rest of the assembly crashing to the Skydock pier. Pirates everywhere cried aloud in pain.

Fengel felt his arm jerk as a glancing shot took off his left cufflink. He stared at his sleeve, incensed. Then he leapt to his feet, brandishing his saber. "Pirates of Haventown," he cried, "to me!"

He vaulted over the bin and ran down the pier for the *Powderheart's* boarding ramp. Behind him the assembled pirates roared their defiance, and the wood of the pier rumbled with the hammer of their bootsteps as they followed his charge. Somewhere above he heard Lucian and Gunney Lome direct a similar action against the *Windhaunter.*

The Perinese worked frantically at reloading from their place along the gunwales. A few of them fell back with cries of pain as some of the pirates fired back with pistols. At their back stood Hayes, shouting incoherent orders that were promptly ignored.

A trio of Bluecoats with smallswords moved to keep Fengel from boarding the *Powderheart.* Two took flanking positions along the gunwale opening while the third descended the ramp halfway. He was a brute, ugly and scarred. Fengel had known the type well during his own years in the service—he probably had more scars across his shoulders from the bite of the cat than a shark had teeth.

Fengel flicked out a feint to force the man on the defensive, then curled the tip of his saber down into a vicious hack at his blue-trousered shins. The Bluecoat hissed in pain and sagged as the blade bit, yet he still managed a vicious swing for Fengel's head with his own blade. He had both strength and the higher ground of the ramp but lacked speed and skill, too eager by half for a killing blow. Fengel parried and hacked again at the injured leg. This time the man screamed, dropping his sword as he collapsed. Fengel stepped aside as he rolled off the ramp, falling between the hull of the *Powderheart* and the Skydock pier.

The marines at the top of the ramp were a more difficult obstacle, covered as they were by the gunwales and each other's blades. Fengel threw himself against the one on the left, forcing him into a distracted parry, from which Fengel immediately withdrew to strike against the soldier on the right. But that man was already dying, slipping down to the deck of the airship with Natasha's thrown dagger buried in his eye. Fengel gave a curt nod of approval and returned his attention to the lone soldier still standing, beating against his smallsword in a furious assault until the marine's defenses were broken, leaving him wide open for a lunge that left him transfixed upon Fengel's saber. As he slumped to the deck, Fengel withdrew his blade, stepping onto the *Powderheart* with Natasha and the Haventown pirates at his back.

Only a dozen Perinese soldiers remained aboard the airship. The majority moved to contain Fengel's advance, with just two still wielding loaded muskets. They fired wild shots, one going wide and the other dropping one of Captain Glastos's men to the deck. Then the melee was joined in a press of clashing blades.

Fengel deftly sidestepped a wild lunge and slashed the face of the man behind it, folding his free hand tight behind his back as he turned to face another assailant. It was Hayes, surprisingly. The pale, sunken-eyed sailor hacked at him with a smallsword, a grimace of hate twisting his features.

"You!" snarled Hayes. "You're the one. You're responsible for everything that happened to me!"

Fengel parried each blow with ease. "Mr. Hayes—for I cannot believe you have kept an officer's rank—trust me when I say that you have always been at the root of your own problems." He sidestepped a lunge and punched the man with the bell guard of his saber. "Were you born someone completely different, then perhaps your deficiencies could be resolved."

"Shut up!" Hayes threw a feint that Fengel ignored. "I'm going to kill you here and burn your ships and take your damned wife back in *chains,* you—"

Fengel hacked down, lopping off Hayes's hand. It fell to the deck with the clatter of the smallsword it held. Hayes stared at the stump, spurting with blood, and opened his mouth to scream. Fengel buried his saber in the man's chest up to the hilt.

"No," he said simply, "you will not."

The dying man stared up at him hatefully as he slumped to his knees. Fengel put a boot to Hayes and kicked him off the blade, flicking it once to clean the gore covering its length. He turned away and joined in the rest of the struggle raging across the deck.

It would be finished in a matter of moments. The Perinese saboteurs had a few skilled men with them but worked poorly together. In comparison, the pirates had united to fend off their attackers, knowing that every moment spent was time lost to the flames spreading about them.

His wife teamed with Reaver Jane and Andrea Holt to surround two navy men with boarding hatchets while Lina Stone flung her cantankerous pet into the face of a marine trying to reload a musket. Farouk and Etarin teamed together, new on the *Dawnhawk*'s crew but old hands at this kind of work. The little Draykin Rastalak was a reptilian terror, leaping and hissing about. Captain Glastos fought arguably the hardest of all, cursing his own men as he skewered two marines at once with his cutlass. Fengel watched Allen the Mechanist and the ex-soldier Michael Hockton compete to shove a hapless marine over the side of the airship.

I do not like him, mused Fengel as he leaped about the fray, feeling the heat on his face from the flames. Once, a man named Hockton had tried to kill him. Young Michael wasn't the same fellow, but Fengel didn't really care.

The last of the Perinese assailants fell, but there was no time to relish the victory. Fires raged about the deck now, almost out of control. Fengel sheathed his saber and organized a bucket brigade from the sand bins, half blinded by the thick smoke, while Glastos screamed at his men to try to control the spread of the blaze.

Fengel grabbed a bucket of sand from Reaver Jane and heaved it out at a blaze along the port-side deck. The flames danced and curled as the grit rained down on them but did not go out. Frowning, he passed the bucket back and reached out for the next one.

Someone shoved him roughly out of the way. Fengel turned with a curse on his lips and froze. It was a Mechanist, leather greatcoat shut tight, goggles down, and wearing a respirator mask. The man carried a cannon-shaped mechanism of brass and steel in both hands, attached by a hose to a tank on his back. Wasting no time, the Brother of the Cog pointed his device at the flames before Fengel and fired. A torrent of white mist erupted at the flames, which seemed to resist for a moment before guttering and dying.

Other Mechanists pushed past, similarly equipped. With quick, almost ant-like focus, they spread out in a pattern across the wounded *Powderheart*, neatly extinguishing the fires. More arrived on deck, these with tethers and axes. One stopped in front of Fengel.

"We have the situation under control," he said in a muffled voice. "Please exit the airship."

Fengel wanted to complain; they had just spent their own blood, after all. But the Mechanist moved away, leaving a pair of Brothers to escort him clear. Captain Glastos loudly protested but went all the same. No one was better equipped than the Mechanists to repair the airships they had built.

He left the *Powderheart*, descending down the ramp to the pier. A glance up past the pirates, now milling about aimlessly, told him that the assault upon the *Windhaunter* must have gone similarly well—Mechanists were moving about the deck, spreading their strange white mist, which fell over the sides of the injured airship.

Natasha stepped up beside him, covered in blood. "S'not mine," she said, answering his unspoken question with a wicked grin.

"Of course not," he replied, pulling her close for a kiss.

Someone coughed beside them.

Fengel looked up to see Lucian Thorne and Sarah Lome. His officers wore a few new cuts and bruises, but nothing seemed serious. The rest of the *Dawnhawk's* crew were gathering as well.

"Captains," Lucian said somberly. "*Windhaunter* is going to be all right. But I've got a spot o' news for you."

"Yes," replied Natasha, sounding mildly irked. "Those were Bluecoats. We saw."

Their first mate shook his head. "It's not just that. There was a smaller contingent aboard the other airship, and Oscar Pleasant was among them."

A murmur of surprise went out among the assembled crew. Fengel raised an eyebrow in surprise. Oscar had never been his favorite pirate, but the man had been with him for a long time. Though come to think of it, he hadn't seen the fellow in a while.

"Lucian," he said. "How could that be?"

His first mate looked away embarrassedly. "Well … we sort of lost track of him, during your recent … holiday … on Almhazlik Isle. And then … uh … never really went looking for him."

"It wasn't a holiday," said Natasha flatly, glaring at Lucian. Butterbeak mimicked the motion from her shoulder. Fengel noticed, disconcertingly, that its beak was covered in blood.

"I'm surprised at you, Lucian," said Fengel, emphasizing the disappointment in his voice. "We've never left anyone behind before, no matter how obnoxious their personal odor."

"I know, sir," replied his first mate with a wince. "We'd always meant to go back. There were always just more important things going on. He's not dead, though—fellow slipped away in the fight. So he's somewhere in Haventown."

"But what was he doing with the Perinese in the first place?" asked Lina Stone.

Sarah Lome stepped forward, halting all discussion. "Look. There. What's that?"

The huge gunnery mistress pointed out beyond the pier. There, in the night sky above the distant jungles beyond Haventown, floated an airship.

It was like none Fengel had seen. Armored plates covered both the gondola and the gasbag itself. Great propeller assemblies were spaced evenly along the gondola hull, not just at the rear. A sigil was painted on the gas bag, and though he couldn't see it completely in the dark, Fengel knew it would be in black, blue, and gold: the suburst insignia of Perinault. The strange airship lifted away from Haventown, turning with far more grace than Fengel would have thought possible.

"Get a message down to the Bleeding Teeth," he said. "Raise the alarm throughout the town."

Everyone looked to him. "Sir?" asked Henry Smalls.

"This wasn't a lone band of saboteurs," he said. "Haventown is under attack."

From the lights on the deck of the retreating vessel, Fengel thought he spied a single figure standing against the stern gunwales, watching.

CHAPTER FOUR

It sat at the end of the alley, between a barber and a fortified distillery, with the night-clad jungles beyond Haventown at its back. Misshapen walls sagged under a sloping roof; the whole outhouse had been weakened by wood rot and neglect. No one had used it in quite some time—old planks boarded up the door.

"All right," Lina said, gesturing at the other end of the alley with her dagger. "We've searched every other crevice and hidey-hole in Nob Terrace. Oscar Pleasant has got to be here."

"It's an outhouse," replied Michael Hockton, his voice tired, a cutlass slack in his hand. "Why would anyone hide there? I mean, how would he even get in? The door's all boarded—"

Lina rounded on him, one hand up to keep a squirming, unhappy Runt in place. Hockton appeared adorably confused, and even the corpse-stink from his earlier task had faded. Without a word, he'd joined her search for Oscar Pleasant. Her little game with him was *working*. But that wasn't important. She was going to find that traitor Oscar and string him up by his toes. *Bastard. Thinks he can attack the captain? Thinks he can burn us out of here?* They'd been enemies, but to throw in with the Perinese? Unthinkable.

Behind the captivating ex-soldier stood Allen, hefting a boarding hatchet in both hands, his shoulders likewise drooping. Rastalak crouched behind them, peering at the outhouse. Fengel had sent them to scout the Skydocks for any sign of their wayward crewman. So far they'd found none. This alley was the last place Oscar could have hidden before the manhunt started. Lina was certain that he was here.

"Well, if you want to go back and tell the captains that we *almost* finished the search, go right ahead."

Allen stepped forward, boarding hatchet in hand. "Of course not," he said with quavering conviction, apparently glad to one-up Michael. "Show yourself, coward! Or we're coming in after you!"

Michael glared at him. "Damned straight we are!" he added. Cutlass in hand, he pushed past Allen to pound on the outhouse door with his fist. "Open up, you rogue! I don't care how you even got in there."

Allen glared at Michael and hefted his hatchet. Behind them, Rastalak sighed. Lina grinned. It probably wasn't fair to keep doing this to the young Mechanist, especially now, of all times, but Allen's crush just made Hockton jump so *eagerly*, where she was involved. And if it drove them to find that bastard Oscar, so much the better.

The young Mechanist strode up to the door and took a swing with his hatchet. The awkward blow sent a shiver through the ramshackle structure. "Enough waiting!" said Allen. "That bastard tried to help burn down the Skydocks! He's had his chance to cooperate."

Michael narrowed his eyes. He pushed up beside Allen and hacked with his sword. Egging each other on, both young men raced to rip apart the outhouse door.

The popping chop of steel against wood echoed back down the alleyway. Runt raised his head from her shoulder to hiss in irritation at the noise. Lina comforted him. In a way, tonight's excitement had been a good thing; the fighting had allowed her pet to vent his aggression. The little scryn had been growing more and more irritable of late, and she did not know why. *Probably just all the damned Revenants walking around. Goddess knows they've got everyone on edge.*

"Lina," hissed Rastalak. Her crewmate poked his reptilian head forward, twisting it in a curious, inquisitive way. "Mr. Hockton makes a fair point. Why should Oscar come here? There is a whole jungle beyond the town."

Lina raised an eyebrow at him. "So? Why would anyone ever go out there? It's full of awful things, like spiders and whatnot." Rastalak had been with the crew almost a year now. He'd spent most of it in a state of befuddlement but had otherwise adapted well. Obviously, there were still things for him to learn.

The outhouse door collapsed with a crash of rotting wood, sending up a cloud of dust and spores. Hockton shielded his face, then raised his cutlass and peered into the gloom of the interior. "All right, Oscar! We're coming in there for you!"

Allen finished coughing and looked at his competitor in alarm. "Yeah!" he cried.

Both men glared at each other. Then they leaped forward, hands outstretched as they forced themselves into the darkened shack with bloodthirsty shouts.

The shouts turned to cries of alarm. Lina saw a confusion of flailing limbs from both men, now stuck half inside the outhouse. The structure shook and the roof fell in, and then the walls buckled and shuddered. Michael was yelling at the top of his voice, and Allen screamed like a little girl.

They forced themselves free as the outhouse finally collapsed, weapons gone, dancing, hopping, and skipping about as they slapped at themselves.

Both men were covered in spiders.

Thick, hairy, and black, some as large as a man's hand, there were hundreds of them, skittering about frantically across the meters of webbing that now clung to Michael and Allen like the sheets of someone playacting a ghost.

"Get them off, get them off!" yelled Michael. Allen just screamed.

Lina stared. Revulsion and horror roiled in her stomach. She raised a hand and then pulled it back. Out of the corner of her eye, she saw Rastalak recoil.

Allen looked to Lina, one eye visible through a shifting mess of hairy, chitinous bodies. He raised his arms and tottered her way. "Help me!" he cried in a high-pitched wail.

Lina turned and ran. She was down the alley and back out onto lantern-lit Nob Terrace in a heartbeat, crossing it to slam into the boardwalk rail. Haventown fell away before her, its lanterns and lamps glimmering like a thousand lazy fireflies, all reflecting from the network of brass pipes spreading out from the great bundled chimney of the Gasworks. Lina ignored the sheer drop and twisted back about, dagger at the ready, her skin shuddering with the crawling of a thousand phantom legs. Rastalak appeared out of the mouth of the alley only moments ahead of Allen.

"There!" Lina said, pointing frantically with her dagger at an open rain barrel just beside the mouth of the alley. "In the water, in the water—put him in the water!"

Rastalak stepped forward gingerly, then grabbed up the moaning, flailing, web-covered Mechanist in two hands. A quick shove, and Allen was dunked upside down into the barrel, sinking up to the waist. Rastalak leaped back, flicking arachnids away from his arms as Allen flailed madly and the barrel toppled over. It landed with a crash and shattered into flinders, sending out a great gush of water and spiders that left a moaning, sodden apprentice Mechanist behind.

Lina stared at him, heart in her chest as her tongue tried to crawl down her throat. *Wait. Where's Michael?*

The tromp of many boots against the boardwalk interrupted her. Lina turned to see an assorted gaggle of pirates and townsfolk approaching. Most held lanterns high and weapons bared, as if they expected imminent attack. A few of her crewmates from the *Dawnhawk* walked with the crowd.

Fengel moved at the head of the pack, quelling concerns and giving orders. Her captain always had a commanding presence, but it struck Lina then that she'd never seen him so positively *in control* as he was now. Though the eye-patch-shaped monocle was still ridiculous.

"Ah," he said, focusing on Lina. "Miss Stone. There you are." He held up a hand, forcing the group to a stop. "Have you completed your sweep around the Skydocks?"

A long, singular groan echoed up from where Allen lay across the alley mouth. Lina managed a nod. "Y-yes, sir," she replied, taking a step back as a huge, hairy spider crawled across the boardwalk between them. "From the top of the Skydocks to the bottom, around the Sindicato manor and through this area."

Fengel rubbed his beard. "Oscar can't have gotten too far. Oh." He snapped his fingers and gestured to the alley. "Back behind the distillery here, have you looked? There's an old outhouse. He may have taken up inside."

Lina blinked at him.

"No one uses it anymore," continued Fengel. "We had to have it boarded up."

Lina opened her mouth, then shut it.

"A nest of Black Wrigglers settled in it. Nasty, vicious sort of local spider. Ah, there's one now."

Lina hung her head with a sigh.

A figure appeared in the alley mouth. It was Michael Hockton. He was very pale, except for the bright inflammation of hundreds of spider bites covering his skin. His shirt was gone, and one trouser leg was torn up the side.

Lina made to run to him, but Fengel's voice checked her short.

"Crewman Hockton!" barked Fengel. "What are you doing in such disarray?"

Michael Hockton turned his gaze at Fengel but seemed not to see him. The ex-soldier's pupils were very wide.

Lina turned to try and deflect some of the hostility. "We, ah, checked inside the outhouse, sir," she said. "Found the spiders." Allen punctuated the statement with a groan.

"Nevertheless," replied Fengel, not really speaking to her. "Other ships may allow such disarray, but so long as you remain with the *Dawnhawk*, you'll comport yourself to a higher standard. Am I clear?"

Michael Hockton frowned in venom-induced confusion. Then he spoke in a hollow, distant voice. "Yes?"

"Good." Fengel nodded in satisfaction, then turned back to face the mob at his back. "Now, everyone, listen up. We need eyes down at the Graveway Lagoon and the old fort there. If one of our own was helping these bastards, he'll know that's the only safe waterway into Haventown—and the closest route, even by airship. Phred! Did I see you lurking around? I know you're not on my crew, but you and your friends know the jungle pathways better than most. If you could get moving, I'll see if I can find someone to give you a lift once we finish rousing the other captains."

Phred was suntanned and shockingly hairy, an ex-pirate and local hunter who looked as hard as old oak. "Sure thing, Fengel," he replied, pausing to run his fingers through his salt-and-pepper hair. "And can I say that you're looking wonderfully rakish this evening?"

"Why, thank you, Phred." Lina's captain peered at the group. "Geoffrey Lords? Go with him. I need Lucian here, but you're a stealthy sort of fellow as well."

The red-haired, terrifying *Dawnhawk's* cook appeared. He nodded sharply, then grinned to reveal teeth filed down to a point.

"Good. We've got until the morning to prepare. The Perinese are traditional to a fault, and naval doctrine holds that all engagements happen at dawn at the very earliest. So we've that much time. Now send word to the other captains; we'll need people and materials carried to the Graveway fort, but to be honest, lads, I think we need to consider a back-up plan. Maybe even evac—"

"Belay all that, Captain." Lucian Thorne pushed his way through the crowd. The *Dawnhawk's* first mate looked disheveled, both from the fight as well as the errands he'd been dispatched upon. "Word's gone out. Pirate King Blackheart is calling a town meeting. Everyone's required to attend, captains especially. At the Bleeding Teeth, as usual. Natasha's already there."

Everyone froze. They turned to Fengel, who paused to consider. "Well, then. We'd best make our way."

The group disbanded, moving in ones and twos towards Euron's court. Captain Fengel held back, though, making a small gesture for Phred and his crewmen to remain. Lina gingerly rounded up a sopping Allen and a stiff, venom-shocked Michael, pressing them in tight with the others.

"All right," said Fengel, "to the Bleeding Teeth it is. But time is of the essence. Phred? I'd like you, if you would, to ignore what Lucian said and get on to the Graveway; that's more important. Geoffrey, you too. Hockton? You're not coming. Get you back up to the Skydocks. I had some of the lads round up all those Perinese corpses. With that woman Omari still walking around, you need to get them down to that Waterdock warehouse that Gunney Lome picked out before they start walking again. I suggest finding a wheelbarrow."

This seemed to penetrate the venom-induced stupor affecting the ex-soldier. Michael Hockton stared at the captain, mouth opening in protest. Fengel cut him short.

"Come now, Mr. Hockton. No one likes a *whiner*. You've been given your orders—now get to them. The rest of you, come along. We've got places to be."

Lina winced. She tried to cast one last glance over her shoulder at Michael as they walked down the boardwalk, but Lucian got in her way. *Oh, Michael.* She closed her eyes. Lina really hadn't meant to get him into such a mess.

Still, she would have to do what she could for him later. At the moment she had her own skin to worry about. Watching Fengel and Natasha's earlier meeting with Euron had been downright painful. Putting them all together again so soon would be a spark for a powderkeg. *And I don't fancy getting caught in the blast.*

Her captain led their party down the curving boardwalk and around a corner to where Euron held his court. There they stopped. In front of the tavern stood hundreds in a tightly packed mob. They were the assembled folk of Haventown, growing in size with every passing moment, each newcomer adding to the gabble of conversation until it became an inchoate roar in the night. Again and again Lina heard fearful questions about the attack. Where were the Perinese? How much time did they have? How many airships had been lost? What was anyone going to *do* about all this?

Lina considered. Maybe this could even be a good thing. In the face of invasion, Fengel and old Euron might even set aside their disdain for each other and work for the common good.

She sighed. *Yeah. And I'm the Sheik of Salomca.*

Fengel coughed loudly, and her crewmates moved forward. Shoving, tripping, and yelling, they made a path through the crowd for Fengel. Lina followed behind, letting Runt snap at townsfolk as her captain reached the tavern.

Two dour guards stood before the door: Euron's men, a pair of old and hardened killers past their prime but tough like hardened leather. They drew cutlasses at the sight of Fengel, glaring. Slowly, they pulled aside, allowing him alone to pass. One moved to bar Lina's way and she let Runt snap at him, forcing the older pirate back with a curse, giving her and the rest of her friends enough time to push on through the door.

If the Bleeding Teeth had been uncomfortable before, it was now downright infernal. The blazing lanterns illuminated a mob just as thick as the one outside, though this one was more prestigious and wealthy. Fengel took the lead now, pushing through to the fireplace along the far wall where a cluster of pirate captains stood in a rough circle, arguing fiercely.

Lina recognized most of them from their descriptions or time spent in port. There was Natasha, of course, her puffy blouse spattered with blood. She glowered at James Glastos, who was standing across from her and cradling his bandaged shoulder. Beside him was a woman wearing goggles and a tight, double-breasted jacket, with short, close-cropped, copper-colored hair: Captain Tooley, of the *Sky Serpent*. Winston Duvale, the captain of the *Windhaunter,* was an older gentleman, who looked more like a clerk to Lina's eyes than anything else. At the moment he hung back from the discussion, trying and failing to seem aloof.

Beside Natasha stood Captain Weatherby, of the *Moonchaser.* He had come into port just after the end of the earlier incident. Lina avoided the man whenever possible; he was older, experienced, and charming. Yet beneath that veneer was someone ugly and murderous. Weatherby was smiling with disdain at the hulking, ill-tempered Salomcani, a man who went by Khalid al-Murdawzi. Brunehilde, mistress of *Solrun's Hammer* and Khalid's wife, had a hand against her husband's arm, holding him in check. From what Lina gathered, Fengel and the rest of the *Dawnhawk* crew had prior history with the pair, though no one would ever say what it was.

Last were those pirates who still sailed upon the ocean waves. They were less glamorous than their skyborne associates but still respected. The dour Cadmus, originally hailing from Greisheim, commanded *Fortune's Loss.* His long blond hair starkly contrasted the half suit of plate armor he wore, which extended down to the iron gauntlet clutching a tankard of ale. His counterpart was Matice, captain of the *Saltspray.* She was well known around Haventown as an eccentric; her outrageous explosion of hair was dyed all the colors of the rainbow, complemented with an eyepatch and skirts sewn from the remnants of three others.

Beside the fire rose the imposing bulk of Euron's throne-like chair. There the pirate king slouched, for all the world seemingly asleep. Lina swore she could hear him snoring.

"We should take to the skies," said Captain Glastos. "Hunt those bastards down and burn them off the ocean." He shook his injured arm at the assembly, then winced.

"That is just an excellent idea," replied Weatherby, his voice dripping with sarcasm. "Let's just jaunt on out and show those fellows in the powdered wigs what for, eh? That armada I spied out west is only composed of dozens of warships, filled with thousands of soldiers equipped with the finest weaponry the Kingdom can afford." He took a drink from his tankard and wiped the foam away from his handlebar mustachios. "Idiot."

Khalid Al-Murdawzi stepped forward as Glastos's eyes popped wide in outrage. "Captain Glastos has the truth of it," said Khalid, his voice thickly accented. "These pasty people of Perinault think to attack us here? In our home?" The huge pirate slammed a fist into a meaty palm, his eyes eager. "We will fall from above and make an example of them before all the world."

"We cannot fight the whole Perinese navy," replied Brunehilde. She crossed her arms and shook her head, her thick blond braid swinging. "We are reavers, not soldiers. Every last one of us relies upon the element of surprise to hit fast and hard and fly away before anyone can do anything about it. A pitched battle would be the end of us, even if we can fly. No amount of bloodthirst will change that."

Captain Tooley raised one gloved hand. "The fact remains, dear, that we were attacked. Here. In Haventown. If we'd all been more in our cups, the whole damned Skydock would have gone up and our airships along with it. How did they even get in here without anyone noticing?"

"Is *Dawnhawk's* fault!" said Cadmus in his broken Perinese. His armor clanked as he pointed accusingly at Captain Fengel. "I am hearing rumor. Was one of the men on that ship, Oscar Pleasant, who led Bluecoats to Haventown."

Natasha strode over and shoved her face into his. "I will cut off your lips and eat them with minty jam," she snarled.

Cadmus jerked away. He opened his mouth to reply, then thought better of it. Natasha whirled to face the rest of the captains.

"Aye," she said. "An old crewmen was with the raiders. But he jumped ship three months ago. Turns out he threw in his lot with the damned Perinese."

Fengel held up a hand for attention. "And those saboteurs arrived here," he added "on an airship. Which was not one of ours."

Murmurs of consternation erupted across the room, spreading among the pirate officers and noteworthy townsfolk like flames on dry kindling.

"Impossible!" said Captain Duvale.

"What are you talking about?" demanded Glastos. "I didn't see any damned airship in that fight."

"If you pulled your head out of yer arse more often, you couldn't have missed it," shot back Natasha.

"It's true," said Weatherby. "Saw a ship I didn't recognize making speed westward. Was going to ask who it was. After I'd finished worrying about the damned naval fleet on our doorstep, of course."

"How?" asked Brunehilde in utter bewilderment. Beside her, Khalid stood with a stunned expression on his face, his eyebrows almost climbing back over his bald, dark head.

The tromp of heavy leather boots silenced the discussion. "We believe that we can provide an answer," said a muffled, resonant voice.

Lina stepped aside along with the rest of the crowd as a troupe of Mechanists pressed through. They all wore their heavy goggles and gas-mask rebreathers, looking as if they had come straight from fighting the fires aboard the Skydocks. It was impossible to tell them apart, whether they were short, tall, thin, or fat. She could not even tell their rank within the Brotherhood. Allen had once mentioned that a shadowy cabal ran the Brotherhood, these days. For all she knew, this group of Mechanists was them.

They moved into the open space in a triangle wedge. The speaker was at their head, his gait made mechanical by the skeletal metal foot poking out from where his right boot should have been. "The secret of powered flight is no longer only our own," he said bluntly, stopping stiffly before the assembled captains.

Gasps echoed about the tavern walls. Fengel and Natasha shared a look. Even old Euron jerked in his chair before settling back down to snore faintly. Lina held very still, working through her own shock and wondering at the ramifications. *How could it have even come to pass?*

She wasn't the only one. Questions shot about the room, so many they became an indistinct, muted roar. The lead Mechanist held up a hand for silence and was ignored.

"*Quiet!*" roared Khalid, glaring death about the tavern and dropping a hand to the scimitar at his hip. One by one, people obeyed. The big pirate captain had a violent reputation and looked more than a little wild at the moment. Lina shrank back herself, and Runt hunched low against her shoulders.

The metal-footed Mechanist glanced about the room, turning his goggles this way and that, verifying that all eyes were on him. Everyone still watched Khalid, but this apparently seemed good enough.

"We are the Mechanist faction of the Brotherhood of the Cog," intoned the man. "For a little over a year now, we have been without our leader, First Mechanist Atherion Helmsin."

Captain Fengel looked at him sharply. "That explains it. I remember you lot wouldn't take new ship orders after I lost the *Flittergrasp*. This is why?"

The Mechanist nodded. "First Mechanist Helmsin alone possessed the skill to weave the skysails used to ride the aetherlines of the world. Yet he disappeared during a conference of the Brotherhood back on Edrus. Our efforts since have been directed towards discerning his location while maintaining the Haventown infrastructure. It is obvious now that the Perinese have him captive."

Captain Glastos stared at the man in dismay. "There's a Mechanist working for the Kingdom?"

"No," replied the Mechanist, emphatically shaking his head. "Helmsin would not willingly share the secrets we have developed."

"Yet he obviously has," drawled Weatherby.

"The key word here is 'willingly.'"

"From a practical point of view," asked Weatherby, "what's the difference? The fact of the matter is that we no longer own the skies."

Every pirate in the room traded worried glances.

"It is doubtful that the Perinese possess more than the one ship," continued the Mechanist before anyone else could speak up. "Airship construction requires significant resources, and even if First Mechanist Helmsin revealed the secret of light-air, acquiring enough to lift a vessel is no miniscule feat. With the recent Salomcani war, we surmise the sighted vessel may be the only Perinese airship in existence."

"Surmise?" Captain Duvale stepped forward, pulling at his mustache in worry. "You can't know. If Weatherby's right, the whole damned fleet is outside our door. They've built an airship to boot, subverted one of our own, and sent in saboteurs as the opening act. The Kingdom means to crush us, burn us out for good. This isn't some spur-of-the-moment action, gentlemen. Who knows what mad tricks they've got up their sleeve?"

"Good."

Everyone turned at the whisper, so hoarse and unexpected that it carried across the room. Old Euron Blackheart sat up now, leaning forward in his throne. Excitement glimmered in his eyes, and a cruel smile played across his lips.

"Years," he said. "Years and years and Goddess-be-damned years I been pillagin' their merchants and slayin' their people. Finally, *finally*, they're going to do something about it." The pirate king made a fist with one liver-spotted hand. "I always knew this day would come. Well, they haven't found me idle. I'll be sendin' those kneelin' dogs back to their decrepit master with their tails between their legs. They do not control the skies." He thumped his chest. "*I* do."

Lina watched the pirate king uneasily. He seemed more … focused … now than she'd ever seen him before, sitting on the edge of his throne, gripping the arm with his free hand beside the broken tankard that symbolized his rule. *He's been waiting for this attack.*

Fengel gestured impatiently. "Euron, we can't fight the whole damned navy all at once. Even bombardment from above is only going to be so effective. We've a little time to prepare; they'll expect us to meet in a pitched battle tomorrow that won't be coming. But we're still outnumbered a hundred to one here."

The pirate king narrowed his eyes at Fengel. "I always knew ye be weak."

Fengel flushed. He went very still, but he appeared to master himself and continued on. "They know where Haventown is. If they didn't, we could perhaps harry them, weaken them enough to make the cost of taking us not worth it. They won't try the waterways for days, and only one ship at a time, at that. But they're already *here*. Even if they just use that airship of theirs to ferry men, they could have thousands of Bluecoats walking Nob Terrace in days. We can start reinforcing the Graveway fortress now—"

"*I do not care!*" roared Euron. "This be *my* town, and these be *my* islands! I built you up from a bunch of squabbling scallywags into something even the Perinese king must acknowledge! And now they think that sauntering in with a few new toys will cow me? No! I mock them, an' I'll kill them an' leave their entrails hangin' from the yardarm!"

Lina winced. The others in the room didn't look any more comfortable. Fengel was right. She was all for gutting a Bluecoatie now and then, but if the whole fleet was here? *I had enough of that back in Breachtown.*

Fengel wasn't cowed. "Damn it, Euron. There's the townsfolk here to think of as well. Not everyone can fight. We've got to at least think about evacua—"

"Don't ye finish that word," snarled Euron Blackheart. He leaned forward on his seat, his eyes dangerous and spittle flecking his great grey beard. "Don't ye finish that word ye, yellow-bellied coward."

Fengel froze. His hand dropped to rest on the pommel of his saber as the room went deathly silent. Natasha glanced back and forth, obviously torn. For once, Lina felt for the woman.

The muscles in Fengel's jaw worked furiously. But slowly, deliberately, he moved his hand away from his blade. The tension in the room eased palpably.

Euron leaned back with a smile. "That's right. Remember who be in charge here." He looked to the room at large, to the Mechanists and apothecaries, the tavern-owners and well-to-do pimps in the crowd. "This be my town. Ye *all* fight.

"Oh yes," continued the pirate king with a relish. "I've been waiting for this day. I have not been idle, whatever ye dogs be thinkin.' Natasha."

Lina's other captain turned to him with no hint of reticence. "Yes, Father?"

"Take yer ship and half yer crew. On the very northern tip of the Copper Isles is an island, the one I have forbidden ye all on pain o' death. Be there before dusk tomorrow."

Natasha stared at him, stunned. "What? No! The *Dawnhawk* will stay here and fight! I'm not going into hiding—"

"I never said ye were!" roared Euron. "Don't ye dare be interruptin' me again!"

Natasha shut her mouth with an audible, angry clack of her teeth.

Euron leaned forward. "Outnumbered? Of course we be! It don't matter so much as one spilled tankard's worth o' ale. There's a weapon on that isle, old. Voornish. I found it decades ago, back when Haventown still be a rude collection of shacks an' starving Salomcani outcasts. I've kept it hidden ever since, with some of me best men watching over it. *They* be why none go there an' return. They guard me Stormhammer. Yer going to go and get it, girl, activate it, and turn it on me foes." He slammed a hand against the arm of his chair, knocking the old broken wooden tankard to the tavern floor. "That will show those Perinese worms. *That* will teach them to challenge the rule of Blackheart!"

A weapon? A Voornish weapon? Lina didn't like the thought of that. It was always dangerous to deal with the artifacts that the old race had left behind. But what choice did they have? The weapons of the Voorn were certainly powerful. *I need to find Rastalak.* The pygmy Draykin was knowledgeable in such relics.

The news surprised the rest of the room as well. Murmurs shot back and forth. Then Euron slammed his fist against the chair again.

"Quiet! Natasha, get ye to the northern isle. The rest of ye! Prepare fer war! Weatherby, Tooley, and Glastos, I want ye an' yer men at the Graveway Lagoon immediately. Brunehilde, yer gonna carry anyone who can hold a blade to the fort. The rest of ye load up on bombs, incendiaries, musket shot. Oh, this'll be just like the old days! Back when I vanquished Reddon, that dog, and Black Alice." The eyes of the pirate king shone with remembered bloodshed. "Like the day I sank the Free Traders Association and burned their forts to the ground …"

Men and women moved to follow Euron's orders, but Lina saw Natasha press close to Fengel and whisper in his ear. Lina couldn't spare more than a glance for either of them, though. Instead, she watched the pirate king. He wasn't even looking at them anymore. Instead he gazed off blankly, reliving glories long gone.

Lina felt cold.

CHAPTER FIVE

"Lanters, serve the pudding now, if you please."

Admiral Wintermourn felt jovial, his mood buoyed by both impending victory and what had proved an exceptionally fine repast. The others present for the dinner party—all favored captains in the fleet and gentlemen of breeding—were not quite so cowed as his own officers. Still, Caldwell, Thomasen, and the others knew just well enough to reflect his attitude, resulting in pleasant conversation that echoed about his cabin all throughout the meal.

His burly sergeant adjutant leaped into action from his place along the wall. Lanters appeared grossly out of place in his ill-fitting footman's jacket, like some sweating farmer's livestock brought inside to escape a chill. He was properly subservient, though, and moved with a lively step towards the sideboard.

"Gentlemen," said Wintermourn to the table at large. "A toast to our success over that ill-washed rabble—and to the glory of the Kingdom ascendant." He held up a snifter of brandy, watching the amber liquid slosh about the glass as the assembly raised their own drinks in unison.

"Sir," said Chesterly, the captain of the *Juggernaut*. "Let me be the first to congratulate you; by this time tomorrow, those airborne vermin will be nothing more than a bad memory."

Wintermourn glanced at the ambitious young man. "Your praise is utterly misplaced," he said, lowering his glass. "For that, the *Juggernaut* shall deploy to the rearguard." He felt a small, vindictive amusement as the other captain paled. Such a position in any upcoming fight meant little chance of glory.

"No," Wintermourn continued to the table at large. "I meant the Salomcani. Mongrel savages though they are, at least the sheik's men lasted long enough to give us a few real fights. These island pirates are scarcely more than a nuisance, at best. Though they do need taking care of." He raised his glass again. "Now, gentlemen. To the glory of the Kingdom!"

"For the Kingdom!" came the shout in unison.

Wintermourn drank deep, taking pleasure in the warmth that spread down his throat and through his chest. The liquor was ruinously expensive, as was the magically preserved fruit littering the table. Wartime rationing had left short commons all around, both in the Kingdom and even the rest of the Royal Navy. Command, however, did have its perquisites. The common sailors might have to sup on weevil-infested biscuit, but he'd be damned if *his* table wouldn't be sumptuously set. *After all, things are done a certain way. Tradition is important.*

The door to the cabin banged open as Crown Prince Gwydion strode in. Wearing his dark raiment, the prince was almost invisible against the night-clad outer deck, his pale skin making him seem a kind of night-gaunt bogeyman. Gwydion seemed jovial, however, with a wide smile on his lips.

"No toast for *me*, my good admiral?"

Wintermourn felt a moment's panic as he stood, kicking his chair back so hard that it toppled over. "Your Royal Highness—"

Gwydion waved airily. "Worry not, my good admiral. Worry not. We're all comrades here, eh? Soldiers at war? No need to stand overmuch upon formality."

The assembled captains all shot to their feet as the crown prince turned to close the door. Shock and surprise had frozen them into immobility. That was no excuse, however, and Wintermourn glared death at the rest of the table. At least Lanters possessed the presence of mind to drop to one knee.

Gwydion ignored them all. He moved straight to the sideboard and examined the fare there arrayed. "Watercress soup, oysters on the half shell with mignonette sauce, braised hare with an apple garnish and almond-cranberry pilaf, along with an assortment of cheeses, jellies, wines, brandy and, ah! Even a pudding." The crown prince grabbed a plate and began to heap it full. "Magically preserved, no less. Well, there's certainly no danger of starvation around here."

Gasps echoed around the table as the crown prince served himself. Wintermourn flushed in acute embarrassment and shot a glare at Sergeant Adjutant Lanters. "Sir, let my man—"

"Pish," said the prince, turning back to face the assembly. "I've a pair of hands, and we're far from the palace now. Soldiers all together, remember?"

He looked to the table for a place to sit. It was full, of course, the setting carefully designed for those naval men that the admiral had wanted to reward, test, or entrap. Chesterly was the first to respond, with what Wintermourn had to admit was admirable alacrity; the man had an eye for currying favor. The young captain grabbed up his plates in one smooth motion and stood back from the cabin table with them, bowing low.

"It would be my pleasure to offer my place to Your Royal Highness," he said.

Gwydion smiled. "Ah, excellent. My thanks …?"

"Chesterly, Your Highness. Of the *Juggernaut*."

"Excellent. You've just won yourself a place in the vanguard."

The crown prince tucked a napkin into his collar as Chesterly beamed. Adjusting the longsword at his hip, he sat. Admiral Wintermourn frowned.

No. Later for Chesterly. There are more important things here. The admiral felt a moment's unease; it was rare that he had to be on his guard, socially speaking. He took a calming breath and waited for Lanters to right his chair. Then he adjusted his wig and sat, which was only appropriate now that the crown prince had seated himself. The other captains waited a judicious moment before returning to their seats as well.

"Sir," said Wintermourn after a moment. "Let me apologize. If I'd known you were coming, I would have set a—"

"Mrgh," replied the Crown Prince, his mouth full. "Not your fault, my good admiral. The action in Haventown took a goodly bit longer than I'd expected. I also took the opportunity to perform some aerial mapping of the waterway channels on the way back."

Wintermourn paused, curious in spite of himself. "And how did that … sabotage … fare?" He already knew the answer that he wanted, that *had* to be given.

"Oh, miserably," said Gwydion, spearing another slice of braised rabbit. "The fools took all damned evening to slip into the lagoon of that pirate town. Then they climbed the cliffs and snuck into the airship docks via the jungles. That all went well enough, I suppose, as not a single alarm was tripped, but they'd barely gotten any fires started before they were noticed and promptly slaughtered to a man." The crown prince paused to shrug. "Was entertaining enough, in its own way."

I knew it would fail. Damned cowardly way of doing things. Wintermourn adjusted his neckerchief and cleared his throat. "Well, the cost was low enough," he said. "Though it must be said that such skulking about has never advanced the cause of Kingdom. Victory is won by glorious battle, at a great cost of sweat and blood."

"Yes, yes," replied the Crown Prince distractedly, raising up an oyster. "You told me so, and whatnot. Worry not, my good admiral. The pirates are certainly stirred into a tizzy over our opening poke. They'll come looking for a fight tomorrow—if we let them."

Vindication mixed with the brandy to leave Wintermourn feeling heady. "Excellent. We will be ready for a proper fight, full of thunder and triumph—the sea at our back, our guns roaring. Our fleet is a hammer, and we shall crush those curs against the anvil of these isles. Let the pirates assemble and meet our lines. Nothing will save them then."

The assembled captains shouted their agreement and pounded at the table, setting silver tableware clattering against fine porcelain. That everyone was so quick to agree proved heartening. Not only did it show a fine sense of purpose, it was clear that they knew which side their bread was buttered on.

His face froze, though, upon seeing the crown prince. Gwydion stared at him, frozen in midchew. Swallowing, he set down an oyster shell.

Then he laughed—great shuddering belly laughs that shook his slight frame and resounded throughout the cabin. The crown prince laughed until tears came from his eyes.

"Are you … are you all jesting?" he asked. "I swear, you're all fossils, the lot of you. Though not *quite* so bad as my father's Order Gallant."

Wintermourn flushed. As Lord High Admiral of the Sea, *he* was a member of the Order Gallant. "I do not jest," he replied after a calming breath. In his lap, his hands were folded tightly into fists.

"Then I shall be charitable and blame the lack of thought on the hour." He leaned forward towards Wintermourn, hands steepled together. "Tell me, my good admiral. Do you think that a bunch of *flying pirates* are going to just line up for you to shoot them? No. They'll drop from the skies and bombard us with all sorts of incendiaries and suchlike. Most of their airships are unarmed, though I've seen designs for things that I know their Mechanists to possess. Once they're ready for us, they'll fall on our fleet like a pack of starving wolves upon a lamb."

"We've the new guns," snapped Wintermourn, "and ours is the pride of Perinault. I remain confident that we will trounce the pirates."

The crown prince sighed. "Your dedication is admirable. But no. Once they're fully prepared, cleansing these isles is going to be significantly more difficult. Even if we drove the pirates back, what then? A slow, follow-through advance with overwhelming force, the usual tactic, is insufficient. Those damnable waterways thread through everything. Calling this place the Copper *Isles* is appropriate—it's a collection of a hundred little islets. Sending any kind of overland force is going to be nigh impossible. And the path we found? It's the only real way to Haventown, proceeding through a natural series of bottlenecks which are deathtraps, should any properly prepared defenders hold the high ground."

"I assume Your Royal Highness is going somewhere with this," said Wintermourn flatly.

"Of course." Gwydion leaned back with a glass of brandy. "We will treat this action like a duel; we're not going to let them prepare. We need to keep the pirates off-balance." He took a drink, savoring it, and then held the admiral with his sharp, wolfish gaze. "I've had time to mull over that idea I mentioned earlier. After watching the progress of the earlier sabotage, I am convinced that it is a sound one. Speed is better than stealth, any day. Return to your ships. Send word to the rest of the fleet. I've changed my mind about tomorrow. The pirates are certainly distracted at the moment, just as I said they would be. So we begin the invasion in three hours' time."

A flurry of complaints echoed about the walls.

"What? That's not nearly enough time—"

"It's not quite midnight!"

"The men are all asleep. *Or* drunk—"

"We won't be able to see a thing—"

Admiral Wintermourn held up a hand for quiet. The captains quieted.

"Doctrine dictates that, when possible, any fleet action should be initiated at high noon," he said, "dawn at the earliest, for visibility and tactical advantage. If nothing else, navigating those waterways you so worry about, in the dark, will be impossible."

"Not impossible," replied the prince calmly. "The *Glory* will provide lighting from above. The galvanic lanterns are quite powerful enough. Send in twenty of the newest paddlewheel steamships, with the rest of the fleet held in reserve out here. They'll have the easiest time of it and bring as much force to bear as we can, for the moment. Why send only men when we can have warships? I know for a fact that mooring anchors were built by bright lads back in Darrenway for attaching to these sheer coastal cliffs in order to offload the marines. They'll be invaluable in those ravines—break them out. As for the men, rotate shifts as we prepare and get them awake after they've rested a bit." He stopped to chew another bite of hare, meeting the admiral's gaze as he swallowed. "Tell me, my good admiral, how wise would it be to wait for noon when fighting an enemy who flits about the sky?"

"Nevertheless," said Wintermourn in tones of iron. "Attacking before dawn—"

"Will leave the enemy far more vulnerable when we do cross blades. If our boys were to try hopping from islet to islet, or worse, were we to send one ship at a time up those channels, we would get picked off and swarmed, even with the *Glory* to assist. If they're ready when we send in a column, the pirates will bomb at their leisure, stopping up our whole advance and turning the waterways into a graveyard. No, we're not going to give them that kind of chance. I mean to get the drop on them and be in that pirate town when the sun rises, if possible—that or this Graveway Lagoon, at the worst. Oh. A standing order: any Mechanists encountered are not to be harmed. Capture or cripple them, but do not kill them."

"I cannot—"

"I do not care," hissed the crown prince, his voice suddenly low and dangerous. "Admiral, you seem to forget yourself. *I* am in command of this fleet action. *You* are my subordinate. Do not think to test me upon that. Do not think it at all."

He dropped his fork and grabbed the hilt of the longsword at his side. It slid an inch from the sheath, shedding soft golden light that illuminated the room.

Wintermourn stared. "Danlann ..." he whispered, recognizing the Blade of the Kingdom itself. The sword wasn't just Worked, it was a powerful and priceless object, the subject of countless legends through five hundred years of Perinese history.

The silence that followed was absolute. Wintermourn looked to the crown prince and held his gaze. The assembled captains of the fleet watched on. Wintermourn knew his face was flushed. He felt enraged that someone would dare speak to him so.

But what was to be done? Higher authority could only come from the king himself. And if Gwydion's royal father had given him *that* blade ... Wintermourn looked away. He reached up and straightened his wig. "Very well," he said at last. "We attack in three turns of the glass."

"Excellent," said Crown Prince Gwydion, lifting his glass for another drink. "I will go aloft again shortly to rest and prepare. The rest of you, be about it. Really, though, I must say that you serve quite a table; the food this evening has been excellent."

He looked away, leaning back in his chair with a satisfied smile. Wintermourn jerked his head towards the cabin door, and the assembled captains quietly left. Sergeant Adjutant Lanters moved to clean the table. None of them dared to catch the admiral's eye.

Wintermourn pushed past them all, storming out onto the deck of the *Colossus* to give his own orders. He ignored the pair of royal guards bracing the doorway, fully ready to vent his frustrations on the crew.

You are not king yet, pup. Do not forget that.

Rousing the crew of the *Colossus* at such an hour was irksome. Expecting the attack on the morrow, none were in any state of readiness. He snarled at Lebam, his first lieutenant, who transferred orders frantically, and all his other officers moved to chivy the men awake or away from their grog. Once so ordered, all moved with alacrity. Any malcontents had long ago been made examples of. None wished to provoke the admiral's wrath, from the first lieutenant to the lowest seaman. Wintermourn kept a keen watch from his perch upon the rear deck. The crown prince may have been beyond his reach, but he could damned well punish with impunity any slacking or shirking upon his own ship.

Other ships came to life as their captains returned. Men raced to and fro along other decks, shouting orders that echoed across the water until the whole fleet seemed alive, like a hive of ants stirred into readiness. The spreading bloom of oil lanterns revealed the might and power of the Perinese Royal Navy, quickly made ready in even the darkest hours.

The sight was comforting. It was a show of strength, of righteous efficiency. There was no chaos here, no fires blazing out of control. Certainly, there were no murderous corpses tottering about in a hideous, counterfeit version of life.

Wintermourn shook the memory away. "Sergeant Adjutant Lanters," he said stiffly.

"Sir?" The burly sergeant stepped forward, having discreetly replaced his serving jacket with the blue jacket and trousers of marine dress uniform.

"His Highness's commands were clear. Let's give some order to this mess. I want Lebam back up here with the signalman on the double. Send to the *Behemoth* that she's to form ranks ahead of us. The *Ogre* and the *Giantess* will tail us, along with the rest of the fleet. Oh, and signal the *Juggernaut* that she is to have the vanguard." Wintermourn felt darkly pleased. That pup Chesterly might get his wish for glory, but Admiral Wintermourn would make damned sure that he got the danger that went along with it.

"Aye, sir," replied the sergeant, who touched his forelock and ran off.

His lieutenants appeared almost as if by magic, and Wintermourn was surrounded by a clutch of golden braid that issued further commands and gabbled among themselves about wind speed, heading, and other such trifling concerns. He ignored them, watching instead as anchors were raised and great paddlewheels started to turn, shining wetly in the oil-lit night. The mooring anchors—long pikes attached to stout chain—were lifted up from cargo, should the *Colossus* need to anchor itself to the island cliffs ahead.

Minutes ticked by as the fleet changed shape. The crown prince returned to the *Glory of Perinault*, and then the airship ascended aloft. Those vessels

Wintermourn had specified churned the water until they were in position, aimed like an arrow at the dark mass of the isles.

Then came time to wait. The long hours would be rough on some, but Wintermourn had never really slept all that much and did not care—his officers had learned long ago to adapt. The rest of the crew were more bluntly animalistic in their needs, so he ordered a skeleton staff to keep his ship in formation while the others took their rest. The *Colossus's* company of marines would perform the brunt of the fighting to come, but men were tools, and it was never wise to dull one's tools without a modicum of reason, even if most of them would be discarded.

At last Lieutenant Lebam turned the hourglass one final time. As he rang the bell, light bloomed up above. It was the *Glory*, shining a powerful galvanic lantern down upon the bow of the *Colossus*. As Wintermourn watched, the single beam split into three, swinging back and forth among the ships in the lead formation. Calls sounded across the water as paddlewheels began to turn. Lieutenant Lebam gave the order, and the *Colossus* leaped into activity. Ahead, the *Juggernaut* took the lead as the whole formation followed, crawling through the waves of the Atalian Sea.

The invasion of Haventown had begun.

Their destination was difficult to make out in the dark. The Copper Isles were a stark mass that grew with every passing moment. In a handful of minutes, Wintermourn discerned the crash of waves upon the cliffs of her shores, resounding throughout the night. The lanterns of the *Glory* revealed turbulent waters crowned with shifting foam. Beside the vanguard ship, spires of rock appeared, smoothed and chipped by the passage of so many pirate vessels over the years. Gwydion's airship shifted a light, illuminating the chosen waterway ahead: a ravine between two rocky cliffs leading into the interior of the isle.

The walls of the passage yawned wide, swallowing the *Juggernaut*. Wintermourn felt a moment's relief—there was more room here than he had allowed, though certainly not enough for comfort. Two ships could not have gone abreast, and the crow's nest barely poked level with the top of the cliffs.

Then came their turn. The shadowed waterway held them close, amplifying the cries of the sounding-men as they called status from the bow. Visibility ahead was lower than anyone could like, and Wintermourn felt an unusual moment's sympathy for the *Juggernaut*. Fortunately, Lieutenant Lebam was possibly the best sailor in the fleet. The man knew his craft, well enough that Wintermourn had purposely sabotaged the fellow's chances at advancement, simply to keep him aboard the *Colossus*.

Behind them, the third ship in the formation followed, then the fourth. One by one the fleet made ingress into the isles, with not a single enemy resisting them. Which was a disappointment. Crown Prince Gwydion's plan was working, Wintermourn supposed, but why all this dangerous fuss just to avoid a pitched battle? What was the point? Dying in the fray was what men were *for.* Putting the ships at such risk was almost unconscionable.

Cries of alarm yanked him from his reverie. Ahead, the *Juggernaut* shifted alarmingly to port. Her crew assembled with poles, pressing out to prevent the warship from crashing entirely into the cliff wall. Wooden spars scraped and squealed, a few snapped, and the port-side paddlewheel housing skidded along the rock, shedding sparks that were bright even in the light from the *Glory* above.

"Hidden current!" yelled Lieutenant Lebam from back at the helm. "Wheels to half speed! Men, to the port-side railing—and take up spars!"

The steam engine buried in the guts of the ship gave a mighty rumble, and the *Colossus's* wheels shifted. White steam blew from the stacks in great gouts as men ran across the deck to prevent the collision the *Juggernaut* had suffered.

It was enough, barely. Wintermourn felt his ship shift as a current grabbed ahold of them. Lebam swore to the Goddess as he and the second lieutenant threw their weight against the ship's wheel to compensate. They veered dangerously close to the rock walls of the port-side cliff but slid past without colliding.

The vanguard warship recovered, Chesterly proving not entirely incompetent. But just as the way seemed clear, the *Juggernaut* lurched again with the shifting current. For the next hour, the column fought treacherous waters; the *Juggernaut's* warnings were barely enough to protect the *Colossus* from further damage, with First Lieutenant Lebam yelling almost constant changes in heading. If the *Glory of Perinault* had not been at hand, this advance would have proven not only impossible but a costly waste.

Then the current slowed. The way became easier, providing a reprieve. Wintermourn released his grip on the rail ahead of the helm and took a deep breath. It seemed as if the worst was over, for the moment.

The current faded away almost completely, forcing them to engage the paddlewheels. Ahead, the channel walls widened. Wintermourn shook himself and glanced about. Had they reached the Graveway Lagoon already?

He called over the navigating lieutenant and consulted. No. According to Crown Prince Gwydion's reconnaissance—and the traitor pirate Oscar's maps—there was a smaller, nameless collection of several waterway channels before the Graveway. This had to be it, then.

Still, the place was ideal for assessing the column. *And if we've lost a ship to this damned nighttime escapade, I'll have more than a few choice words for that pup.* Wintermourn paused at the seditious thought. *Possibly.*

Gentle waters lapped the channel, which was just wide enough for the *Juggernaut* and the *Colossus* to fit comfortably abreast. Tawny light illuminated the vessels as the airship above played its lamps across the cliff walls, causing veins of ore to peek back at them through masses of jungle vines draping from above.

"Lieutenant Lebam," said Wintermourn, "full stop, if you please. Sergeant Lanters, pass me my telesco—"

A musket shot echoed out across the water. One of the seamen along the starboard gunwales jerked and fell to the deck. Wintermourn looked to the source, a cloud of expanding gunsmoke along the cliff top fifty yards distant.

"To arms!" shouted Sergeant Adjutant Lanters, rushing to the rail beside the admiral. "Marines to arms! Enemy fire to port!"

Crewmen and marines alike leaped into frantic activity as the *Glory* illuminated the cliff. "Really, Sergeant," drawled Wintermourn dismissively, "a single sniper is nothing to be overly concerned about. In fact, it's about time these pirates showed themselves."

A staccato ripple of musket fire exploded from the cliff top, and lead shot ripped across the deck of the *Colossus*, splintering wood and eliciting cries from the men who were hit. One ball whipped past only inches above Wintermourn's face, tearing through the brim of his hat and flinging it from the powdered curls of his wig. He stared at his fallen hat as the fusillade fell quiet. Then Wintermourn felt a surge of righteous anger.

"I don't care who is on that cliff," he snarled aloud, straightening his wig. "I want them dead! Bring up the new guns! Get those cannons aimed and loaded! Marines, form a damned proper line and fire as you will!"

Officers, marines, and sailors all moved to carry out his orders. The Bluecoats raked the cliff top with their muskets, dropping down to reload and allow their fellows clean shots. Sailors unlocked the new eighteen-pounders from their moorings and elevated them; the carriages of these guns had been designed specifically to fire at a high angle to counter airship bombings from above. They fired thunderously, shattering the draping foliage and coppery rock of the cliff face with grapeshot.

Still, it wasn't good enough. Wintermourn caught sight of disheveled pirates in colorful bandanas recoiling from the attack, but the angle to hit them was too steep, covered by the cliff against the worst of the onslaught. In moments they recovered, returning fire of their own.

Clattering ripples of gunfire called out from above, raking the top of the cliff. It was the *Glory of Perinault*, with twenty Brass Paladins standing at attention along its starboard gunwales, firing their heavy pepperbox muskets. They unleashed more shots than should have been possible, reloading quickly and efficiently when they finally had to, not a movement wasted.

In moments it was over. There seemed to have been only a handful of pirates, with no cover against the airship. Lanters's Bluecoats continued their useless fusillade a few moments longer while Wintermourn furiously accepted his fallen hat from Lieutenant Lebam.

"So that is it," he snarled. "Sneaking, skulking ambush in the night. Well, we've seen how well that works out, eh? On both sides." He stalked back to the signalman while his officers hurried to keep up. "Send a message back up the column. I want the *Behemoth* and her marines up here just behind the *Juggernaut*. We're on full alert. Push through to the Graveway Lagoon, expecting resistance. Keep squads of marines at the ready. I want them ready to *scale* these wretched cliffs next time if they have to. Prepare those mooring anchors." He glanced at the *Glory* above, bright and shining against the rapidly lightening sky. "Send acknowledgement ... and thanks ... to His Royal Highness. For his timely assistance."

His orders were carried out with all the alacrity of men used to both battle and avoiding the admiral's displeasure. The *Behemoth* came up the line as directed, her marines thick along the gunwales. Before long the column of ships was underway again, paddlewheels churning the water and smokestacks puffing steam past the reefed sails, their airship hanging from the rosy predawn sky.

The current returned, pushing them along, though not so fast this time as through the near rapids they had encountered before. Wintermourn paced as his officers and helmsmen ran the ship, with Sergeant Adjutant Lanters at his heels as always. They needed to be moving faster. His blood was up. And the first taste so far of combat had been unsatisfying. He wanted battle on the open seas, not this skulking about.

The lookout called from the crow's nest; a wide lagoon lay dead ahead. Wintermourn descended the deck in a hurry and made his way forward to the bow, his entourage following behind.

There, just past the vanguard ships, he could see it. The waterway channel opened again, this time into a wide lagoon that could have only been the Graveway. A few other minor channels ended here, but the only exit was a single waterway leading farther east. Carved into the cliff wall above it on the southern side was an old Salomcani fort.

The Graveway was not empty. Three pirate airships drifted overhead, their crew at attention along their gondola gunwales, muskets at the ready. A fourth flew just into view, lowering itself down behind the fort. The pirates of Haventown had not been idle since last night's attack. They were now ready—and waiting for a fight.

Admiral Wintermourn slammed a fist into his palm. "Sergeant Adjutant Lanters? Lieutenant Lebam? Sound the attack."

CHAPTER SIX

Captain Fengel ignored the rising sun.

There was simply too much to do. He worked with Rastalak, Henry Smalls, Lucian, and the others, hauling away at a pulley to raise a crate from the depths of the *Dawnhawk's* cargo bay.

Damnable Mechanists, he swore to himself as he heaved on the rope. *They built trap doors into the bottom of the* Windhaunter, *but couldn't they have done the same for the ship I stole?*

His hat was off, and his sleeves were rolled up. Fengel felt the lack of propriety keenly; he had certain standards to maintain, after all. But the sun had risen, and the airship needed to be off, and there was just no damned *time.*

"That's it!" cried Lucian from behind him. "It's up!"

Gunney Lome leaped into action, grabbing the netting around the heavy crate and hauling it over to rest on the deck. Fengel and the others released the rope, letting the last of their plundered cargo slam onto the planks of the deck.

"That's it," said Henry Smalls. "Hold's empty but for that smell."

Fengel grimaced as he rubbed one aching shoulder. Unfortunately, there hadn't been nearly enough time to scrub the interior of his beautiful airship. Errant scraps of Revenant littered the bottom of the hold, making it redolent with the fume of old corpse.

"Coming through," called Reaver Jane. She pushed between Henry and Lucian, trailed by Andrea Holt and a panting Ryan Gae. They hauled mesh sacks filled with round iron bombs from a pile Natasha was inspecting a short distance away.

"We're running low," said Natasha, the parrot on her shoulder eyeing the things as if it might make off with one. "Captain Glastos nicked most of the lot already, so these need to count."

She cinched up the sack and held it up for Gunney Lome, who threw it over one shoulder and marched after Reaver Jane to the equipment lockers amidships. The huge woman stumbled over a jagged plank but caught her balance by grabbing a bit of torn canvas dangling from the gas bag above.

Fengel eyed the ragged patch with disdain. *No rest for my poor ship. Or myself.* He removed his monocle to rub his eye; he'd barely managed to steal two hours sleep last night. He sighed, replaced the eyepiece, walked over to his wife, and offered a hand to help her up.

"I'd feel better if you were staying," he said.

Natasha grimaced. "So would I. I don't care if we're not ready for a fight."

All around them the *Dawnhawk* was a messy furor of activity. The pirates tested hawsers, checked rigging, and looked over all the makeshift fixes that had been hurriedly reapplied during the night. Old Euron had wanted his daughter gone hours ago, but some tasks simply could not be ignored, even for a short trip. The airship was still a mess of dangling cordage and half-assembled machinery, though they'd managed to resew the worst of the gaping patches along the envelope and replace the propeller linkages, the Mechanist complaining all the while.

The rest of Haventown was no different. Euron's commands had spread through the night. Now the terraces drummed with the bootsteps of experienced retirees, eager young bloods, and anyone else willing and able to carry a cutlass. Mechanists ran about, overseeing the deployment of barricades and seeing to more arcane preparations that they refused to elaborate upon.

Not everything had come together quickly. There had been confusion, then rumor, and not a little score settling in the chaos. The denizens of Haventown weren't an organized military. A worryingly large number of folk were seeing only to themselves.

The skies were clear and blue—a beautiful morning on any other day. The only oddities were three airships floating a mile to the west; the *Powderheart*, the *Sky Serpent*, and the *Moonchaser.* They circled the Graveway Lagoon while *Solrun's Hammer* returned at speed for more men and materials.

Fengel shook his head. "Damn Euron," he said. "This errand of his is the longest of shots, and there's every possible chance of catastrophe. Voornish weapons … they never end well. The Governor's Lantern was just a gemstone, and it was cursed. Then there was the Dray Engine on Almhazlik."

Natasha puffed out her cheeks. "Don't I know it. Explains why the northern islands were forbidden, though. I'd have gone looking long ago if it wasn't so inconveniently out of the way. But if this 'Stormhammer' can fry a whole fleet from a distance, why hasn't he used it before now?"

Fengel rubbed his beard. "I don't know. It may not even be *real*. He was acting strange last night, more so than usual."

"No. He lies all the time, but not about things like that. He's not creative enough." She shook her head. "Damn my father's hide to the Realms Below. I want to stay and fight. It's not fair—"

"Captain Blackheart!"

The call came from past the starboard gunwales. Natasha stalked angrily over, with Fengel following her.

A pirate glowered up at them from the Skydock pier below. He was old, so grizzled and spare that he seemed wholly made out of hardened leather and knothole wood. His clothes were straight from some bygone era. Nevertheless, his stare was that of a hardened killer. Fengel recognized him as one of Euron's men.

Natasha, of course, knew all of her father's old crewmen. She glared down as if she could turn the old pirate to ash on a whim. "Grant! What in the Realms Below do you want?"

"Captain Blackheart," said Grant. "The pirate king wants to know why ye be still in port."

"Because I'm not ready to go yet!" she yelled back. "You can't spend months fighting and flitting about, then expect to be off again after a few hours in port!"

Grant was unimpressed. "Yer father wants ye after the Stormhammer. So get a move on!"

Natasha gripped the gunwales with both hands until her knuckles were white. "I'll leave when I'm good and ready, you washed up old—"

Thunder rippled from the west. Everyone quieted, pausing to look towards the Graveway and the airships floating there. Fengel spied a minute fireball burst in midair, a prematurely exploded bomb.

Can we be at it, then? It's too soon.

Grant cursed aloud and ran down the pier. "Get yer scow in the air and get going!" he called back over his shoulder.

Natasha shook her fist after him with a wordless snarl. Fengel reached out and touched her arm.

"He's right. The fight's begun. Time to go."

His wife gripped his wrist. "To the Realms Below with him. You need me. You need every ship you can get. Here and fighting."

Fengel looked past her, beyond the unkempt deck of *Dawnhawk*, the Haventown Lagoon, and the jungles beyond. "That I do ... but I'm not sure one more ship will make a difference. The Graveway is a natural chokepoint—it would have been mad of the Perinese to send more than a single ship down it. Two, at most. No, they're only scouting. Though that still only buys us time. With a whole fleet out there ... I don't know." He shook his head. "I don't trust it one bit, but relying on this Stormhammer might be our only hope. You need to go find it. Failing that, we're going to have to evacuate. Sooner or later."

Natasha grimaced, looking away. "Never. But ... fine. Fine, damn yer eyes. Let's risk everything on a bit of Voorn trash that my father has let rot for forty years."

"Take Rastalak," said Fengel. "And Lina Stone; she's clever in a pinch. Our Mechanist says he's been ordered to stay, but I talked him into leaving Allen to run the engines. The Hockton lad—I don't want him here. Reaver Jane. Nate Wiley. Etarin, Jahmal, Farouk. Best keep Ryan Gae out of the fight—he's not doing well. So Andrea will join you as well. Oh! And young Paine too. I'll take Henry, Lucian, and Sarah, of course. And both aetherites, along with everyone else."

A shadow fell over them: *Solrun's Hammer,* maneuvering to dock. Pirates clustered along the piers, cheering as the airship descended, ready for a fight.

He reached out and took her hand gently. "We'll go with Brunehilde, to do what we can." Fengel smiled sadly. "I want to say that this will turn out, but—"

Butterbeak screeched. The sound cut across his thoughts and set his ears to ringing painfully. Natasha grabbed her pet and threw it across the deck. The bird caught itself in midair, flying out past the ship before circling back to dive-bomb Lucian. Fengel turned back to Natasha, and she grabbed his face with both hands, silencing what he was about to say with a kiss. Her hands wrapped themselves around the back of his head, an action just as violent and passionate as she herself was. Fengel dealt with it the only way he could: by giving as good as he got.

When they broke away, both were panting, and Fengel saw little stars flickering across his vision.

"You talk too much," said Natasha with a lazy smile. "Now get off my ship."

"Try not to get mutinied against," he said.

Natasha patted the straining bosom of her puffy white shirt. "I've got your little book, don't I?"

She turned away with a smile and shouted down the deck. Fengel watched her go with a sudden pang in his chest. He made his way to the boarding ramp and then down onto the Skydock pier beside the *Dawnhawk*.

Most of the Skydock piers were empty, but those around the *Dawnhawk* were still frantic with activity. In the berth below scurried the crew of the *Windhaunter*, overseeing repairs and loading a hastily acquired collection of spare cannons aboard the airship. A single figure stood out, leaning lazily against the railing. Fengel knew her in passing. She was Shannon MacKinnon, Captain Duvale's first mate, and possibly the laziest pirate he'd ever met.

Back along the Skydocks stair climbed a steady stream of people. Unaligned pirates and townie thugs, they tromped to the pier above the Dawnhawk, their bootsteps drumming in counterpoint to their outrageous boasting. Atop the pier they waited, nerving themselves up for the fight as *Solrun's Hammer* came ever closer, ready to dock and take them away to the fight at the Graveway. Otherwise, the rest of the Skydocks were empty, dangling scaffolds propped up against the early morning sky.

The *Hammer* was Fengel's destination as well. Turning to the *Dawnhawk*, he waited for the rest of the crew, now being ejected by Natasha. Henry Smalls, Lucian Thorne, and Sarah Lome moved to attend to him first.

"We're ready, sir," said Henry, shoulders slumped. He glanced sadly at the worn airship beside them.

"Why so glum, Mr. Smalls?"

Henry shrugged. "Dunno, sir. I just feel like we might not see her again."

The rumbling thunder of cannon fire echoed in the distance.

Fengel frowned. He looked to the *Dawnhawk*, her hull scuffed and her envelope roughly patched. The last year had not been kind to the vessel. *Wait. Does he mean the ship or my wife?* Fengel decided that he didn't like thinking about either.

"Rubbish," he snorted. "You know exactly how tough Natasha is. None of you need worry—nothing is going to keep her from coming back to us."

His officers shared a look.

"Of course, Captain," said Lucian. "That's exactly what we meant." He jerked his head towards the great shadow of *Solrun's Hammer*, docking now in the pier above them. "Shall we go see what Brunehilde is up to?"

Fengel gazed at the trio suspiciously for a moment before nodding. Then he faced the rest of his assembled crew.

"Listen up!" he called. "Our lovely ship is going elsewhere, but we've still got a job ahead. The fighting's begun at the old fort—we're going to go lend our arms and see what can be done. So get your pig stickers ready! We might be riding *Solrun's Hammer* over to the fray, but let's show those Perinese bastards what the men and women of the *Dawnhawk* can do!"

His crew all cheered. Fengel drew his saber, and they tromped off with righteous bravado, though more than a few glanced back at the airship they were leaving behind.

Movement in the wrong direction caught Fengel's eye. It was Omari, slipping out of the crowd and back up the *Dawnhawk's* boarding ramp to disappear from sight. He scratched his beard, considering. Natasha wouldn't take kindly to stowaways, and she especially disliked the Yulani woman. *No. Best place for her, most likely.* The last thing Haventown needed was the chaos brought on by a horde of Revenants. *And there're going to be a lot of corpses soon.* He shrugged, sheathing his blade before following after his crew.

Solrun's Hammer was an older ship, neither as new as the *Dawnhawk* nor as old as his lost *Flittergrasp.* The hull bowed down towards its keel, reminiscent of the sailing ships that had so obviously inspired it. Old, weatherworn rigging connected the gas-bag envelope, a great semirigid egg of leather and canvas.

Fengel pushed his way to the front of his crew, holding them back with an upraised hand until all others had gone. Then he straightened his jacket and led the way onto *Solrun's Hammer* with measured dignity.

The captain of *Solrun's Hammer* stood just past the ramp, waiting for Fengel. Brunehilde was as tall as he was but looked tougher by far. Torques of gold encircled her bare, well-muscled arms, and her ice-blue eyes shined within a face brought to life by the scars and laugh lines around her lips. One hand rested on the pommel of a heavy broadsword at her side. The other rested on her hip, her thumb hooking her sword belt. A thick golden braid trailed down past her shoulders.

Beside her stood her husband Khalid, a hulking slab of muscle towering above both his wife and Fengel. He was Salomcani, with coffee-colored skin and golden eyes. Fengel had never quite gotten along with the man. On occasion, they had clashed blades.

"There you are, Fengel," said Brunehilde. "Thought you were going to have to swim to the fight."

"What?" he asked, imperious. "And miss the chance to inspect this old hulk of yours? Perish the thought."

She laughed and leaned forward to punch him in the upper arm, hard. Fengel grunted, though he managed to refrain from rubbing at the spot. Brunehilde knew how to hit.

"You supercilious bastard. I heard what happened to you and your crew a few months ago."

Fengel frowned, glaring back at his officers, who had the decency to look away in embarrassment. "Yes," he said. "It worked out all right in the end."

"Good." Brunehilde nodded. "We need as many swords as you've got."

Cannon fire rumbled in the distance. Everyone looked back out the stern of the airship, towards the jungle and the Graveway. The fighting there sounded worse than a single enemy warship would warrant.

"How bad is it?" asked Fengel.

"Bad," muttered Brunehilde distractedly. She turned away to yell at her crew. "Cast off! Let's get in the air!"

She stalked back to the helm at the rear of the ship, and Khalid followed without glancing back. Fengel thought to follow but walked instead to the front of the airship. *No. I have to see.* Lucian, Henry, and all the others trailed behind him.

Anxiety filled Fengel as *Solrun's Hammer* took flight once more. He ignored the shouts of the crew and the bravado of the locals, his eyes alighting one last time on the top of the *Dawnhawk*, where the White Ape was yanking at the canvas skin of the envelope. He was struck then by Henry's fear: that he might not see the airship again.

The trip to the Graveway went quickly as they flew out from Haventown and followed the waterway straight to the old Salomcani fort. Cannon fire and bomb blasts, growing in strength with every passing moment, heralded their coming. Before long, the green jungle canopy fell away to reveal a gun-smoke-shrouded struggle being fought.

It was pandemonium. Sheer cliff walls surrounded the roughly circular lagoon, broken by waterway ravines. Two were large enough to allow a ship to pass. The closest was empty, passing just beneath the fort built into the southeastern cliff wall, where pirates fired muskets from behind crumbling Salomcani crenellations. The farthest was directly opposite, to the west, and was clogged by a procession of steam-powered warships, with the foreign airship hovering protectively above. Perinese Bluecoat Marines were disembarking as well, scaling ropes up the cliffs like a militarized collection of spiders in blue jackets and round black caps. Some had already made the trip and looked to be setting up heavy equipment, with two even raising a great pole; the flag hanging from it bore the golden sunburst of Perinault on a field of blue.

Fengel stared in amazed despair. He had been wrong earlier. *They didn't send a scout—they brought the whole damned fleet inside the isles! But how?*

The enemy was too quick by far. Too strong.

Two warships sailed about in the lagoon: the *Juggernaut* and the *Behemoth*. They maneuvered skillfully in the tight space, paddlewheels churning and smokestacks puffing as they tried to bring their broadsides to bear upon the fort. Above, the three pirate airships here—the *Powderheart*, *Sky Serpent*, and *Moonchaser*—foiled the effort. His comrades bombarded the warships with hand-thrown bombs and musket fire.

Brunehilde brought her airship down at the rear of the fort, where a patch of jungle had been cleared down to bare earth. As soon as the airship was low enough, Brunehilde's men ran out the boarding ramp, disgorging eager, bloodthirsty passengers.

"We're here," called the pirate captain, coming up to the gunwales from back near the stern. "Get yerselves off my ship so I can make another run back to town."

Fengel led his own crew off onto the sunbaked earth. The ramp was immediately hauled back, the airship's rear propellers spinning up again as it rose.

"I'll be back anon," said Brunehilde from along the gunwales to no one in particular. Behind her and unseen, Khalid roared commands up and down the deck.

"Wait!" called Fengel back at her. "Who's running things here? Euron's still back in town, and the others are in the air!"

Brunehilde smirked down at him. "I guess you are, Fengel!"

And then they were aloft, the airship turning away at speed.

Fengel's retort died on his lips. *That's as good an answer as any, I suppose.* He looked to his crew. Gunney Lome was glaring after the retreating *Hammer*, while Lucian watched the other airships, frowning. Henry Smalls waited, patient as always. Without Omari distracting them, Konrad and Maxim stood together like brothers, cracking knuckles and looking about for enemies to hex. Cumbers, Simon, and all the rest stood warily, weapons in hand as they waited for direction.

Past them stood those who had charged so riotously off the ship. They milled about uncertainly. It seemed that Fengel wasn't the only one who'd been confused.

Fengel adjusted his monocle. "Well," he said. "If I'm in charge, let's get this fight run properly, then."

"Aye, sir," said Henry. The steward jerked his head towards the arch leading inside the old brick wall of the fort. "Probably best start there."

"The Perinese are here, all right," added Lucian. He turned back to frown at Fengel. "But they're in a bad spot. Captain, how did they even get so many damned ships here in the first place? And so fast? That little conga line of theirs should have been dashed to pieces in the waterway channels."

I dearly want to know that myself. But anything less than confidence would not do at the moment. "It doesn't matter. We're hideously outclassed, but we've no choice now but to fight. Come, let's—" He quieted at the faces of Cumbers and Simon, his newest crewmen, both staring out past the fort. "Something amiss, lads?"

The ex-sergeant started. "Nay, Captain. Nothing. It's just … those are our countrymen out there. I never signed up to fight them."

Fengel nodded in sympathy, something he didn't entirely feel. "The Goddess makes fools of us all at times," he quoted. "Best keep it in mind that those fellows would hang us all, given the chance."

Cumbers and Simon shared an unhappy look. "I know, sir," said the ex-sergeant. "I know."

"Good!" Fengel clapped him on the back. "This way, then."

The others fell in behind him as he marched into the rear of the fort. Within was a simple room of four walls, the side facing the lagoon open through a series of arches, like an arcade. Beyond stretched a short paved walk, protected by a crenellated wall holding emplacements for fifteen cannons, all empty at the moment. Back inside, a single wide stair descended to the lower levels. Beside it lay a pyramid of old cannonballs stacked four high.

Pirates, brawlers, and hunters all packed the fort. They stood in cliques, glaring at their rivals, hefting cutlasses and muskets thoughtfully, or otherwise just milling about. A few fired their weapons from the crenellations at the ships in the water below.

Fengel frowned. *No. This won't do at all.*

Order was needed, and fast. Fengel stepped aside and jerked his head towards the walk; Gunney Lome moved into action, bulling forward and plowing a path through the crowd. He followed in her wake, stepping outside into the sun before turning back to face those assembled.

"All right, you lot! I want everyone with a musket to assemble on the left and those with pistols and blades on the right. Anyone who knows how to work a cannon, in the middle—I don't see any here, but the *Windhaunter* should be arriving with a load of spares any minute now."

A conflicting chorus answered him.

"What? Who's that?"

"My left or yours?"

"I've got a pistol *and* a musket!"

"That's Fengel, that is. Where's his nasty wife?"

"Shouldn't he be on the *Dawnhawk*?"

"Why should we listen to you?"

"Lookit that fop! I bet he's working with the damned Perinese—"

"*Enough*," roared Gunney Lome, and her voice seemed to shake the fort more than the bombs exploding beyond it. Lucian, Henry, and all the rest spread out beside Fengel, facing the crowd in a show of strength.

"You'll listen to me," said Fengel, "because out there are a bunch of greedy bastards who want you dead. Now, form up so we can properly draw a bit of Perinese blood!"

The crowd didn't cheer, but they at least shuffled about as directed. As Gunney Lome and Lucian moved to take control, two bloodied, bedraggled figures stumbled out of the press: the Haventown tracker Phred, leaning heavily on the arm of Geoffrey Lords, the *Dawnhawk's* own terrifying cook.

Phred was covered head to toe in makeshift bandages, all crusty with blood. Geoffrey Lords didn't look much better. He sagged with exhaustion, not even offering a greeting.

"Hullo, Captain," said Phred. "Was hoping you'd show up."

Fengel moved to assist them, and crewman Cumbers helped set the men down against one side of an arch.

"Good Goddess above," said Fengel. "Whatever happened to you two?"

Henry passed a waterskin, which both men took up eagerly. After finishing, Phred leaned back with a weary sigh. "Thanks," he said before looking again to Fengel. "Captain, you were right to send us out last night. Most of my lads thought you were crazy—until we saw all those warships racing down the waterways in the middle of the night. Tried to needle them a bit, slow 'em before they got to the Graveway. They gave a bit better than they got, though."

"How *did* they get all those—"

"It's that airship of theirs," replied Phred. "It knew the right path somehow, and it's got these big galvanic lamps like the Mechanists make. Might as well have been noon. And each one of those warships is that new kind, armored, with steam-powered paddlewheelers. They got knocked about something fierce—thought a few might even sink and ruin their whole advance, but in the end they didn't even have the kind of trouble old Cadmus has getting that whale of his into port."

Fengel leaned back, thinking furiously. *So that's how they did it.* "Still," he muttered. "Damned reckless of them. Doctrine should have kept them at anchor until daybreak. What could have made them move so early?"

Shaking his head, he reached out to clasp Phred on the shoulder. "Take it easy, man. You risked quite a bit, on just my asking. You too, Geoffrey."

Geoffrey Lords gave a weak smile, then reached for his waterskin again.

Phred reached up to clasp Fengel's hand on his shoulder. "Oh, Captain. I was happy to do it." He frowned. "Rest of the lads probably have a bit of regret, though, seeing as they're dead."

The old tracker leaned back against the arch to rest. Fengel stood, turning to see Henry and the others watching him expectedly. "All right," he said. "Lucian, get everyone with longarms to watch the Haventown waterway; they won't hit anything where they are now, and I don't want anything slipping past unscathed. Gunney Lome? Assemble and assign teams for each emplacement—Duvale should be here soon with cannons. Maxim, Konrad, neither of you have anything that'll make a difference at this range, so hold your spells in case we need to fall back. If there are any other aetherites in the lot, get them to do the same. Henry, I want anyone with a blade out into the bush; Bluecoats are climbing up the far cliffs. They might try to flank overland. The rest of you, split up and help out."

A shadow passed over the fort. It was Duvale's airship, the *Windhaunter*, lowering itself down behind the fort.

Finally. Cannons would give the old fort some teeth—and might make all the difference.

Fengel crossed through the fort and ran back outside, where the *Windhaunter* was just running out its boarding ramp. "About time, Duvale!" he called. "I've got teams sorted and waiting to run those guns you've brought."

"Of course ye'd be up here, arranging such nonsense!"

Euron Blackheart stepped into view against the gunwales, strangely small and hunched in the daylight. He glared down at Fengel, his bushy grey eyebrows coming together in disapproval. "If'n ye were any kind o' man at all, ye'd be down there fightin'!"

Fengel stumbled, his surprise transmuting into anger as if by magic. *Damnable relic! Contrarian old fool!* A hundred and one retorts came to mind, and he opened his mouth to give voice to them, but Euron wasn't even looking at him anymore, gesturing instead to someone just out of sight.

"Get it all off-loaded! Can't be goin' into battle weighed down like a pregnant sow."

Three of his old crew appeared atop the ramp. They were dressed for a fight but looked older than ever. Grunting, swearing, and creaking, they manhandled a light six-pound cannon complete with carriage, rolling it down to the ground before heading back aboard. Three more appeared, their task the same. Fengel watched as cannon after cannon was hastily unloaded and left in a pile at the bottom of the ramp. A pair of powder kegs were dropped in a hurry, followed by a man with an armload of swabs, wadding, and fuses. Fengel cursed under his breath and gestured sharply to Gunney Lome, who rushed over with a number of Haventowners. "You could at least move these things inside!"

"Whyfor?" replied Euron. "Going to be damned useless until Brunehilde arrives with the rest o' the powder and shot."

Fengel stared at the lone pair of kegs. "What? This is all you brought?"

"Aye!" said Euron, watching the work eagerly. "This be the last of it? Good!" He turned to face the stern of the airship. "Let's be off, damn the Goddess's eyes fer making me wait!"

Wait, what? Fengel took a step towards the ramp, but Duvale's crewmen pulled it back aboard. "Hold on now! Where are you off to in such a hurry?"

Euron glared back down at Fengel like he were a yapping puppy. "Because there's fightin' to be had! Hairy armpits of the Goddess above, are ye senseless as well as cowardly?" He looked out past Fengel and the fort to the lagoon beyond. "Oh, I'm going to teach them a lesson, these Perinese bastards. Personally! Enough o' this bombing and sniping with muskets that can't hit a damned thing. Waste of powder! No, we'll do it th' old way, with sword an' fire an' blood." He drew his cutlass, raised it high on a shaking, unsteady arm. "It'll be glorious! Just like the time I vanquished Red Margaret Cray!" He glared down at Fengel. "So cower up here while I show ye how things be done."

The old pirate turned away, his strident demands echoing down to where Fengel stood. He realized he was shaking, but whether it was from rage or exasperation he did not know. *Cowardly? You old fart, you hide there in your too-hot tavern and live vicariously through the glories your* daughter *accumulates!*

"You're going to be the death of us all," he said as the *Windhaunter* lifted off, twisting to face the lagoon.

It hit him then, what the old pirate had been saying. Euron was taking the fight straight to the Perinese. He was going to *board* one of the warships down in the lagoon.

"Oh, for the love of the Goddess," whispered Fengel. A boarding action in such close confines, with experienced soldiers on the defense? Madness. It would be a bloodbath on both sides. And Euron was the only one who commanded enough respect to bind together all the fractious people of Haventown with any kind of speed. If he fell now ...

Fengel twisted violently about. "Sarah! Drop that thing and get more of the men from inside! We need these cannons placed! Grab up all the fuses and swabs! Hurry, damn it, hurry!"

He knelt and grabbed the barrel of a twelve-pounder still in its original frame. He pushed it towards the fort, growling in effort. On a deck of wooden planks, it would have slid easily. Here, though, each foot it was pushed cut deep furrows into the earth.

Two pairs of hands appeared to assist: Phred's and Cumbers's. Between the three of them they shoved the cannon to the rear of the fort, hauling, grunting, and swearing. Before long they had it set into the midmost port overlooking the lagoon. Others arrived with their own cannons, directed by Sarah.

"That's right, lads," he cried over the sound of musket shot and bomb blast. "Get these things positioned! I want an even spread, to cover the lagoon. Who has that powder? Get it up here!" He glanced at the stack of old cannonballs, each a different size. "Where're my loaders? Get those balls over here!

Fengel turned his attention to the lagoon below, ignoring his officers as they executed his wishes. The *Windhaunter* was already below the lip of the cliff, falling towards its prey. The enemy warship *Juggernaut* sat squarely in the middle of the lagoon while its sister ship circled about, paddlewheels churning as it tried to bring a broadside to bear on the fort. Captain Duvale, likely under Euron's strident direction, aimed dead for it. From the far end of the lagoon—where Bluecoats climbed and the Perinese vessel *Colossus* was anchored in the waterway mouth—came shouts of surprise. Floating serenely above them was the strange Perinese airship, the golden sunburst on her envelope bright and clear.

The other Haventown captains adjusted to Euron's mad charge. Their airships frantically turned aside, ceasing bombardment as they moved through a haze of stinking gunsmoke that obscured the blue morning skies above.

Captain Duvale's vessel came in low, boarding tethers flung out with expert skill to land in the masts and rigging of the *Juggernaut*. They snagged ahold and stretched taut, the airship's inertia pitching the *Juggernaut* violently and jerking her through the water. The *Windhaunter* shook with the strain, herself suspended at an odd angle, but ropes were dropped and pirates with them, while those still aboard up above fired muskets to keep pressure on the startled defenders.

Fengel pressed his lips together. One way or another, the glory-mad old fool was committed now.

Well. I'll have to do what I can. Fengel looked to the other cannons. Only five of the nine weapons inside were ready for the fight. They had teams of four men and women at the ready, lighting slow-burning matches and cleaning long-handled swabs.

"Gunnery crews!" Fengel shouted. "Aim for the *Behemoth* as she comes into range. We need to keep her from assisting the *Juggernaut!* Load—and be ready to fire on my mark."

Sarah had done just as he'd asked. Pairs of pirates tottered over to each gun, hauling rusty cannonballs from the stack inside. Henry Smalls and Lucian appeared at each with a keg of powder. The cannons seemed to swallow the powder, poured like shining black sand down a bottomless throat. There was going to be barely enough for a handfull of volleys.

Fengel glanced back at the lagoon. The *Behemoth* was coming around, moving to help her sister ship. Of Euron's attack, he could make out nothing; the shadow of the *Windhaunter* hung too deep. All he could see was the flashing of blades and the flare of pistol-shot.

The cannon beside him slammed forward into the brick wall. Phred had a long match lit, and Cumbers stood to one side, visage troubled.

Fengel recalled the first time he'd fired on a Perinese ship. *He'll live. I certainly did.*

A quick look around told him that the other crews were similarly ready, that their timing would never be better. Fengel drew his saber, stepped back, and hacked down through the air.

"Fire!"

The pirates obeyed. As matches lit to touch holes, the cannons leaped back, erupting in a blast of staggered thunder. Fengel rushed to the wall and peered out at the warship below.

Three waterspouts burst from the lagoon near the *Behemoth*. The last two shots were more on target. Fengel watched the starboard railing explode into splinters as a ball struck it, the foresail stretching taut and tearing away, taking the spars connecting it to the mast. He laughed and rang the pommel of his saber against the low brick wall before turning back.

"Again!" he cried, sheathing his blade. Fengel grabbed up a long-handled swab and rammed it down the barrel of Phred's cannon. Gunney Lome appeared with the powder. Cumbers wasn't far behind, an iron ball in his hands and tears on his cheeks.

The *Behemoth* tried to return fire, but its angle was off. Cannon fire dug holes in the cliff below, harmlessly. Twice more the cannons atop the fort sounded in response, wreaking increasingly accurate damage upon the warship.

Henry Smalls appeared beside Fengel, his fingers in his ears. "We're dry, sir!" shouted the steward. "Powder's all gone!"

Fengel made a fist and slammed it against the crenellations. They'd been doing so well! He gazed down into the lagoon, where the *Behemoth* was floundering her way towards the far end of the channel. The *Moonchaser* and the *Powderheart* were already moving in to bombard her from above. To his surprise, the *Windhaunter* was already lifting away from the *Juggernaut*. As her shadow shrank, Fengel saw no movement on the Perinese decks—and much blood.

"It's no matter," he said to those nearby. "We've done our job, even with what little we had. And Euron actually won, somehow."

An idea occurred to him then. He brightened and turned to his steward. "Henry, get a rough crew together. As soon as Duvale touches back down, let's get them ferried to the *Juggernaut*; we can use it as a forward defense of the lagoon. Why Euron hasn't done it already, I don't pretend to—"

A cataclysmic report ripped up from the lagoon below. Fengel ducked reflexively, then turned back to stare over the crenellations. The Perinese warship in the water below had exploded, sending shards of her ruptured hull and rigging across the Graveway. Fengel could only stare as bits of ship rained down about them.

"That psychopathic old fool!" he howled. "He lit off the powder magazine! We could have used that!"

The pirates only cheered and applauded the devastation. As the *Windhaunter* approached the fort, Fengel glared black hatred at it.

By the time the airship touched down on the landing field, he was waiting, a small crowd of Haventown defenders behind him. Past the airship, over the treetops, *Solrun's Hammer* was returning from their home port with more supplies. Fengel realized he didn't care. Instead, he waited for Euron to appear atop the *Windhaunter's* boarding ramp. The pirate king leaned on his sheathed cutlass like a cane as he descended, but in his other hand held a severed head up by the hair. Behind him came a number of his old crew, in far worse shape than the pirate king himself.

"Ha!" cried Euron at the foot of the ramp. "Let this be a warnin' to any who dare stand in me—"

"What did you *do* down there?" shouted Fengel.

Euron stopped in surprise. A sneer worked its way across his features as he focused on Fengel. "I brought death to our foes, popinjay. Even someone with yer eyesight should see that. Captain fell overboard, but I slew the crew, cut off her lieutenant's head, an' fired her magazine!"

"Exactly!" replied Fengel, gesticulating violently. "You went through all that trouble and fired the powder magazine! We could have used that ship to fend off the rest of the navy! And my eyesight is fine!"

"Don't get yer knickers all bunched up. We'll kill that other ship an' get close enough to bomb the rest. They're sittin' ducks in that channel right, Grant?" He elbowed one of his men in the side. Grant grimaced, then smiled weakly.

"That's not the point," snapped Fengel. "It was something we could have used. We're so damned outnumbered and outclassed here—"

The pirate king curled his lip and stepped up to Fengel. Once he'd been tall, but now he barely came to Fengel's chin. "Glory be everythin,' popinjay. A real pirate would know that."

Euron shoved the bloodied head at him, forcing Fengel to grab it. Then the pirate king pushed past him into the crowd. An unsteady line of his old crewmen trailed along after.

Fengel threw the head hard at the ground and glared death after the pirate king. *If the Perinese don't kill him, I just might myself. Natasha wouldn't blame me.*

Someone touched him on the arm. Fengel whirled, ready to chew the fellow's face off with his teeth. "What?" he snarled before stopping in surprise.

A Mechanist stood before him. Even stranger, it was a young woman. She was squat and short, with shoulder-length hair, her gender barely noticeable under the leather greatcoat and goggles. Behind her, beside the *Windhaunter*, sat Brunehilde's airship, anchored and unloading.

"Captain Fengel?" she asked in a muffled voice.

"Aye?" he replied.

"You are wanted in Haventown. Please return with me aboard *Solrun's Hammer*. The Mechanist Cabal would speak with you, and you alone."

Fengel frowned, uncertain. Behind him, the battle in the lagoon began again.

CHAPTER SEVEN

THE IRREGULAR BLAST OF CANNON FIRE GREW LOUDER WITH EVERY PASSING MOMENT.

Lina struggled with the *Dawnhawk's* wheel. It had mechanisms to ease steering of the airship, though a certain degree of sheer brawn was still required—something she very much lacked. Runt coiled around her neck, heavy and irritable, which certainly didn't help.

The *Dawnhawk* flew ponderously just above the jungle canopy. Her battered deck felt strangely empty for so late in the morning. Only a handful of the crew had been picked for Natasha's mission, as the rest had gone with Fengel to fight at the Graveway. Those remaining rushed about, trying to finish all the makeshift repairs that had not been completed before takeoff, like carnival entertainers spinning plates. Reaver Jane moved quickly down the deck, hastily examining each of the hawsers connecting the two halves of the *Dawnhawk*. Etarin and his big friend Farouk greased the whirring gear trains near the stern propellers with unseemly haste. The ex-twin Nate Wiley worked sullenly at dismantling a piece of the port-side exhaust pipe, damaged in a storm and awaiting proper repair. Rastalak and Ryan Gae clung to the underside of the envelope frame, roughly sewing a canvas patch back into place while lengths of rope dangled down about them like hempen vines.

Lina had been ordered to stand in as navigator and pilot. She didn't mind at first. Anything that took her away from the Graveway battle, she'd cheerfully volunteer for. A fight was a fight, but she'd tasted enough real warfare during the Almhazlik incident. Lina had not liked it one bit.

But when they'd lifted off, with only just the barest preparations finally complete, Natasha had ordered them west, to the Graveway. The brief pops of bomb blasts grew to sharp thumps, filling her with dread. At times she swore she could smell the smoke and sulfur on the wind.

A gust blew across the airship's rudder, twisting the wheel. Lina fought it, her feet barely touching the deck as the gondola gave a deep, troubled groan. At the same time, Runt tightened his coils about her neck. Lina gasped, letting go with one hand to slap at him, and the wheel slipped. *Damned fat cranky scryn!*

Someone reached roughly past her, seizing the wheel. Lina looked up into the scarred, unsmiling face of Reaver Jane. The pirate woman wasn't even looking at her, gazing instead at the front of the airship.

"I've got this," she said, jerking her head towards the bow. "Go find out why we're heading west. We shouldn't be going anywhere *near* that fight."

Lina hauled at Runt's coils with both hands and moved to obey. *About time someone else wondered what was going on.*

Though she *was* sending Lina over to do the asking.

Natasha stood near the bow, framed by clouds of growing gun smoke against the soft blue sky. She stood with arms crossed, Butterbeak on her shoulder, obviously irritated at the two crewmen squabbling before her. They were Allen and Michael Hockton, and the sight of their feuding cheered Lina.

"I'm the one that needs Lina's help!" Michael Hockton all but shouted. The ex-Bluecoat looked even more rugged than usual, covered in grime and sweat. "I hauled all those muskets up to the lookout's nest, but the ape won't leave them alone. It always takes two to handle him, and he's afraid of Runt. Oh, and someone left the gas-bag hatch open earlier, and things looked all shifted around in there."

"You can deal with the ape just fine," said Allen. "I'm the one who needs Lina's help!" He dropped one end of a heavy brass pipe to clang on the deck, then leaned against it. Allen was covered in soot. "Someone was digging around where they shouldn't and left the coal stores open belowdecks. There's a terrible mess down there—you'd think someone crawled inside to hide. We need it cleaned up to feed the engines. But before I can do that, the dented part of the port-side exhaust needs replacement." The young Mechanist narrowed his eyes. "Besides, I'm sure that Lina wouldn't want to spend half an hour freezing atop the gas bag while watching you get thrashed by the stinking White Ape."

Hockton glared at him. "Why would she be any better off with a little grease monkey like you?"

"*Enough*," roared Natasha, punctuated by a staccato blast of cannonfire. Butterbeak added an ear-shattering screech that made everyone wince, only to fly into the air when Natasha slapped him off of her shoulder. "You," she said, rounding on Allen. "Get aloft and help Hockton secure those guns against the ape. When you're done, the both of you go fix that damned pipe. No arguments, or I'll string you up by your toes."

A midair bomb blast flashed off in the distance, cutting short the threat. Both men moved to obey, expressions sour. You could never tell when Natasha would choose to follow through.

I should say something to Michael. Before Lina could catch his eye, Natasha spoke up again.

"Wait," she said thoughtfully. Then she retrieved a small tome from out of her puffy white shirt and flipped it open to a dog-eared page. "Before you two little idiots go, know that I val ... value? Damned smudge. I value your efforts aboard this ship."

Allen and Michael Hockton stared a long moment, then stammered mumbled replies and fled. Natasha ignored them, turning her attention again to the book.

Curiosity won out over Lina's disappointment. She bent low and peered at the cover, where *How to Pillage Friends and Intimidate People* was printed in heavy gold lettering. *What? A self-help book?*

"Fengel got it for me," said Natasha dryly, finally noticing her. "Figured that it might help with all the mutiny." She jerked her head back at Allen and Michael, who were climbing to the gas bag. Past them flew another airship, *Solrun's Hammer*, heading back to Haventown. "Also, don't tell me you're encouraging that stupidity."

Lina met Natasha's cold gaze. The wind changed, though, distracting her with the gunsmoke smell of sulfur. "I ... ah—"

"Never mind." Her captain shut her book and jammed it back down in her cleavage. "I left you at the helm. What are you doing up here?"

Lina forced herself to face Natasha squarely. "We're all wonderin' at the course, Captain. We were supposed to head north. You've got us going for the Graveway." She glanced past her mad captain to the airships flitting about the sky ahead.

Butterbeak screeched overhead at her insubordination. Runt, who had finally had enough, rose up and chirred angrily. Lina grabbed him with both hands, fighting with his weight. Now wasn't the time for such squabbling.

Natasha turned away, looking towards the bow. "Damned right I am. We should be almost on top of it. 'Just a scout,' he says." She slammed a fist into her palm. "We should be fighting, gutting those witless Perinese for daring to show their powdered wigs on these isles. But my father says that there's something more important to do, and damn him for it, Fengel agrees." She turned her gaze to Lina. "But I'm not going to fly off without even *seeing* if we're needed."

She stalked up to the bow, with Lina hurrying after. They passed the young boy, Paine, looking sour as he helped Andrea Holt sand away at a jagged deck plank. Both of them paused to stare at the commotion off the bow. A cloud of dingy yellow smoke blew across the deck then, enveloping them all in the stink of fired gunpowder. Lina felt her way blindly, running into a hanging rope several times, until she ran into the gunwales beside her captain. Natasha was standing angrily, hands clenched into fists so tight her knuckles were white. "We should be down in that," she said, gesturing violently as the cloud blew past.

A slow conflict was being waged below in the Graveway Lagoon. The pirates of Haventown manned the old Salomcani fort, with perimeter lines spread out to either side. Gun-crews manned an assortment of cannons, firing with almost mechanical efficiency at the command of a huge red-haired woman who could only be Sarah Lome. Across the lagoon were the Perinese, their warships snug in the lagoon mouth and beyond, anchored against one cliff of the ravine. Several companies of bluecoated marines clambered about the clifftops, erecting defenses. A battery of heavy guns was already in place, lobbing artillery fire back at the fort and falling just short. Above them floated the strange airship from last night's attack on the Skydocks, guarding against the pirate vessels. Lina could just make out the golden letters along her bow, which read *Glory of Perinault*.

Above the Graveway floated the pirate airships. The *Powderheart*, *Windhaunter*, and *Moonchaser* were all bombarding a single warship in the waters below. She was a battered thing, barely held together as she dodged her impending doom. To her captain's credit, the ship maneuvered with skill and grace, minimizing what the defenders could do. The only thing truly saving her, however, was the Perinese gun battery. Lighter cannons not aimed at the fort lobbed shots high into the air—they'd been specially built, it seemed, for shooting down airships. The pirates were forced back above the fort, attacking only when opportunity presented itself.

"Feh," Natasha sighed. "Fengel was wrong; they're here in force somehow. But things aren't a complete catastrophe—more's the pity." She yelled over her shoulder back to the helm. "Bring us about three points north! Skirt the lagoon, and let's get to work. I guess."

Relief washed over Lina. Getting mixed in with the struggle below was the last thing she wanted to do. The *Dawnhawk* had taken cannon fire during the Almhazlik affair after stumbling onto parts of this very fleet. It had been a surprise, though, and they'd run away from it as far and fast as they could. Now it would be different. Staying to fight would be something else entirely.

Lina knew she was not a soldier.

Natasha turned away from the bow. "Stone, stay up here. I want you—what are *you* doing here?"

Lina blinked in confusion, then followed her captain's gaze. Natasha was staring at the foreward entry hatch to the lower decks. There a dark face smudged by coal peeked up from over the edge.

It was Omari.

She started at Natasha's cry and tried to duck down belowdecks. The *Dawnhawk's* captain proved quicker. Natasha was there in a heartbeat, hauling Omari up by her blond hair.

"Ow!" yelped Omari. "Let go, you madwoman!"

She slapped at Natasha's arm, trying to keep her balance as the airship changed direction. Her clothes were a disheveled mishmash of several different outfits, an obvious attempt at the impromptu dress of Haventown. She was filthy all over, streaked with coal dust.

"Chapter two of my little book says it's rude to throw stowaways over the side," said Natasha idly. "So I'm going to simply ask you again—though I'll be louder this time, of course." She paused for a breath. "What are you doing here, you twisted corpse-puppeteer?!"

She dropped Omari to the deck, who glared back up at Natasha angrily. "It's not my *fault*, what happens to the dead. And I was trying to get *away* from the fighting, so that I wouldn't be a problem!"

Natasha planted her hands on her hips. Butterbeak mimicked the action, hunching low to peer down at the woman. "Really. By somehow stowing away back aboard my ship?"

"Well, yes." Omari looked embarrassed. "It was either that or run off into the jungle."

Lina felt a rumbling vibration through the deck—the engines kicking into higher gear. Hot steam shot from the partially dismantled port-side exhaust, causing a passing Nate Wiley to dive away with a yell. At the stern, the great propellers spun back up to a steady buzz. Reaver Jane was wasting no time in getting them away, which Lina approved of. *No one wanted to come out here but you, Natasha.* She rubbed at Runt's slightly oily scales. He chirred unhappily but squeezed her tighter.

"I heard that the *Dawnhawk* was not going to the battle," said Omari. "So I came back aboard and hid in the coal stores. It was only when I heard the sounds of fighting growing closer that I came out to see." She climbed back to her feet. "The Perinese will conquer Haventown. Even you have to see that."

Out of the corner of her eye, Lina saw Michael Hockton appear, descending the port-side rigging. She started to smile at him, but stopped at the look of utter panic on his face.

"That's not going to happen," replied Natasha flatly.

"They will." Omari shook her head. "You were not there for the pacification of Breachtown. You did not see. It is not possible for you to win. Not with a handful of airships crewed by swarthy miscreants."

Michael Hockton cut off any reply. "Captain!" he cried. "We're being pursued!"

Natasha frowned and turned about. "Hockton? What do you mean?"

The ex-Bluecoat clambered farther down. "It's that Perinese airship! The White Ape was dangling me over the side of the gas bag when we noticed. She's broken off from the Graveway to follow after us!"

Natasha pushed past the stowaway. Lina followed her back down the deck to the stern, past dangling cables, past Reaver Jane at the helm, to where the propellers spun and the exhaust stacks spit steam out behind the airship.

Hairy arms of the Goddess. Michael was right. The enemy airship had broken away from the fight, leaving its position above the Perinese to chase directly after them. On her gas bag, the golden sunburst sigil of Perinault gleamed in the sunlight.

The *Windhaunter* moved to intercept her, but she was too slow to react; the only path quick enough to match the *Glory of Perinault* took her straight into the fire from the cliff top battery opposite, and the cannon blasts drove her back. The *Glory* continued on unopposed. Natasha had thought to play tourist with battle, but now the battle was coming to them.

"Damn the luck," whispered Natasha. But she smiled as she said it, and her eyes were fixed like a raptor upon their pursuer.

She turned back to the deck at large. "Break out the guns and sharpen your blades! Anyone not at the helm, stand by and prepare to repel boarders!"

Lina met Omari's eyes. The Yulani woman was downright frightened. Lina forced herself to composure, though the same uneasiness wormed its way through her guts, like a scryn through the corpse of a cow. She'd been in plenty of scrapes before, but as she glanced at the empty deck and the bedraggled appearance of her airship, she couldn't help but feel apprehension. *This time feels different.*

It didn't take long for the crew to prepare. Lina lined up along the port-side exhaust with the others; Reaver Jane, Farouk, Rastalak, Jahmal, Andrea

Holt, Ryan Gae, Nate Wiley, and Natasha, of course, standing fiercely. Michael Hockton and Allen clustered near Lina, while Paine hung back, uncertain. Everyone had cutlasses and fresh muskets. Etarin was at the helm. Butterbeak chirped in excitement at the impending violence, while Runt chirred irritably.

The Glory of Perinault still closed the distance between them, coming up along the port side. It was smaller than the *Dawnhawk*, more trim. Thick, armored plates covered the gondola, as well as the gasbag itself. Along the hull were an array of propellers, three to a side, smaller than the two great spinning blades whirling at the stern of the vessel. The sigil painted on the gas bag was even more gaudy, up close.

Lina was aghast. How could such an ugly thing move so quickly? She glanced back around her own deck for reassurance. The *Dawnhawk* was the latest of the Mechanist's airships, fast and strong. Surely they'd pull ahead.

Though when Lina took in the well-patched gas bag, the splintered deck, and the cracked exhaust stack hissing steam, she felt no confidence. The airship was bedraggled and worn down. She needed repairs and refitting. A haphazard curtain of rope dangling down from the top of the gas bag to starboard seemed particularly out of place.

The enemy airship closed in. A thousand meters, then five hundred, then a hundred. Lina lifted a musket, but Natasha hissed at her, at them all; they'd never hit a thing at that range. It would still feel good, though, to fire. She glanced to Michael standing beside her, confidently gripping a musket. *My soldier.* He noticed her watching, smiled bravely, and stood a little straighter. Lina felt butterflies in her stomach, but then she winced. She shouldn't have been toying with him. Her little test seemed foolish right now.

The airships were parallel now, close enough to see the enemy standing behind the armored sides of the airship gondola. Lina blinked in confusion. The Bluecoat marines she had expected, but spaced evenly along the gunwales were a score of tall men in heavy brazen armor, holding massive, pepperbox muskets. *Who are they? Are those knights? That's … that's ridiculous. Who wears plate armor in this day and—*

Someone yelled a command over on the other ship. The brass knights raised their weapons in unison, took aim, and fired. Flames blossomed and thunder roared out from the barrels of their overlarge guns, sounding more like cannons than muskets.

Death flew past Lina with a cracking whip-hiss that sent her ducking frantically. Other shots proved more lethal. The gunwales in front of the assembled pirates exploded into jagged shards at the impact of heavy musket balls, clearing the path for their brethren to hammer into the exhaust pipe.

Lina watched dimples appear in the skin of the pipe from those shots that pierced it, which then rung about inside as the whole piece ruptured and cracked in front of her eyes. Scalding heat washed over her as steam shot out in great hissing gouts that added a teakettle whistle to the cacophony of the bombardment.

Her ears were ringing, and blood spilled down her face. Something made her cheek stiff. Lina ignored it, praying that whatever wound she'd taken wasn't too serious. Adrenaline numbed the pain for now. But when had she fallen to her back? *Got to get up. Get up and draw my knives—there isn't any time—*

A branching metal hook flew through the steam and landed on the deck just beside her. An attached rope pulled taut, yanking back to catch on the ruin of the exhaust pipe. Others followed just behind it, running down the length of the ship in front of the beleaguered pirates. The boarding hooks all pulled tight, and Lina shouted a wordless warning as she realized what was coming next.

Light from above dimmed as the *Glory of Perinault* pulled tight against the *Dawnhawk*. The brass knights held the boarding grapnels, and Bluecoat marines stood between them now in odd harnesses; they took smallswords and bayonet-tipped muskets to hand as they leaped aboard the pirate airship.

Lina scrabbled to her feat, drawing both of the daggers at her hips. On her shoulder Runt arched up, hissing violently. She tried to yell another warning as she saw Natasha on her feet with cutlass upraised, her puffy sleeve torn and bloody, long splinters sticking out from her shoulder. Rastalak was snarling, fingers spread in claws, looking for all the world like some monstrous beast. Nate Wiley lay facedown, and Michael Hockton was taking aim with his musket as Allen clutched the spurting stump of a missing finger. Then the Perinese were flying through the steam and there wasn't time to do anything but fight.

She fell back at the charge of a bull-necked man with a smallsword trailing a rope tether back to the *Glory* from his leather harness. He blinked in confusion as he saw her, expecting something other than a hundred-pound waif with a weird creature on her shoulders. Lina recognized the gift for what it was and threw herself forward. She slashed at his wrist, then aimed for his throat with the other dagger. Runt snapped forward, hissing poisonous spittle at his face. The soldier fell back with an inarticulate cry, only for another to replace him, eyes narrow with determination.

Her new opponent was hampered by his harness and tether but still dangerous. He thrust for her head with his blade, forcing her to bring both daggers up in an X-shaped block. The blow stumbled her backwards. Then he was on her again, hammering his smallsword at her like he was pounding nails.

"I've got him!" screamed Allen. The young Mechanist appeared with a long pike he'd found who knew where, goggles down, his wounded hand clumsily wrapped. He jabbed her assailant in the side. The Bluecoat grunted and knocked the pike away, sending the butt of the polearm straight back into Lina's chest.

Her air whooshed out as she staggered back again. The shine of another Bluecoat's smallsword flickered in the corner of her eye, and she made to duck away, only to be knocked sprawling as Michael Hockton crashed into her, sword upraised to block the blow she would have easily dodged. Lina lost her grip on a dagger and watched it clatter to the deck. She barely kept ahold of the second.

"I'll save you," Michael cried dramatically.

"Stop helping!" Lina reached for her other dagger. Its hilt was in her fingers when Michael stepped on her wrist. She yelled, and he stumbled, falling back into the soldier attacking Allen, forcing the man forward with a scream onto the pike.

She threw her arm up at the melee from where she lay, not quite caring at whom she pointed. "Runt! *Kill!*"

Her pet eeled from her shoulders and took wing, hissing and spitting and filling the air with lurid red light. Hoarse yells and curses rose up over the roar of the battle.

Lina scrabbled out from between the furiously stamping feet and twisting, knotting Bluecoat tethers only to find herself caught in yet another melee. She rose up and swiped at a marine, then dodged past Andrea Holt as the other woman charged into the fight. Lina swung wildly as she ran, taking as many opportunities to attack as she could—until she slammed into the exhaust pipe running along the starboard gunwales and there wasn't anyone else to hit. Lina breathed great gasping breaths and used the pause to take in the battle before her.

The Perinese boarding action had been successful. Though there were fewer marines than she'd initially expected, their charge had worked perfectly, following just on the heels of the brass knights' fusillade. Her crewmates had fallen back, allowing even more soldiers to board. Now individual melees raged up and down the deck, the defenders outnumbered two to one. Their only advantage was the mess of Bluecoat boarding tethers that stretched back to the enemy airship, hampering the invaders.

Past the struggle lay the *Glory of Perinault*, masked by a constant spray of steam. Through the cloud she thought she could see the knights. They hadn't moved at all to join the attack, frozen like statues as they held the boarding grappels tying both ships together. Lina realized that they weren't knights at all. They weren't even alive.

Clockwork automata. Like the Brass Horses back in Triskelion. Or some kind of Voornish machine.

A figure leaped out of the steam to the port side of the *Dawnhawk's* deck. Not a Bluecoat, he landed adroitly to stand with his hands on his hips, pompous and excited and very well dressed in tasteful scarlet and sable. He wore a boarding harness like the rest of the Perinese and was barely older than Lina herself, both thin and handsome. Instead of a smallsword, he wore an honest-to-the-Goddess longsword, like something straight from a penny-tale of knights and dragons.

"Avast, ye scallywags!" he said in a rich, cultured voice. "The day of yer doom be—" He abruptly broke into laughter. "I'm sorry. I always wanted to *say* that, but it sounds so *silly* out loud." The fellow shook his head and looked about the deck. "Now, what have we ... ah!"

He looked to Natasha, who was fighting in the middle of the deck. Putting a hand to the hilt of his longsword, he sauntered in her direction with polite calm, like a spectator at a sporting exhibit.

A soldier collapsed in front of him with Rastalak crouched upon his bloodied chest. The little Draykin looked up, saw the newcomer, and leaped.

The man moved like a serpent. He twisted and ducked, coming back up to catch the little Draykin with the palm of his free hand. Rastalak flew past, slamming against Reaver Jane and big Farouk, who stood back to back against four soldiers.

"My word," said the newcomer, "there's all manner of strange beasts aboard this vessel."

He made a little pirouette behind Natasha, who was noisily sawing open the throat of a soldier with her cutlass. She seemed to see the movement and dropped her toy, twisting to swing her blade in a great, head-chopping arc. The newcomer laughed and stepped away, his longsword leaping from scabbard to hand in a parry like it was a living thing.

His blade flared with soft golden light. The metal positively glowed. When it met Natasha's cutlass, sparks flew, as if from a blacksmith's anvil. As she pulled back to strike again, Lina saw the blade was badly chipped.

A Worked blade. Oh no.

Aetherite magic was uncommon enough. A Worked object was an order of magnitude more rare. To bind a permanent enchantment to a tool that anyone could use was difficult—and costly. Any aetherite willing and able to do so charged dearly for the service. But the results were worth almost any price: blades made of flame or charms that provided unparalleled protection.

Natasha was a skilled and vicious fighter. But the dandy seemed capable as well, and a magic sword put the odds firmly in his favor. Lina took a breath and ducked back into the fight; the captain was going to need her help.

"Natasha Blackheart!" crowed the fellow, cutting at her face. "Captain of the airship *Dawnhawk* and ravager of the Atalian Sea. I've read so much about you! It is an honor to finally meet you."

Natasha parried the blow, more sparks flying. She bound his blade and held it, glaring at him between the cross of their swords. "And who are you, you damned peacock?"

The newcomer gave a nod. "Forgive me. You have the pleasure of speaking with Crown Prince Gwydion, heir apparent to the Kingdom of Perinault."

Lina faltered as she ducked past another fight. *The Crown Prince? Here? But that's insane, impossible.*

Natasha apparently came to a different conclusion. Her eyes widened in surprise, and she smiled cruelly. "Well now, if that's true, you're worth this trouble and then some. You should have stayed on your ship, peacock! Now I'm going to ransom you for all the gold in the Kingdom while my allies bomb your boats into flotsam!"

Gwydion laughed. "Oh, don't blame me. I was *bored!* Besides, they'll deal with it. We're so completely superior to you silly pirates, after all. I even gave my royal guards the slip for a moment—left them behind to make this a bit more fair." He looked away, at the *Glory*. "Do you like my airship? It's *very* modern. Full of all sorts of clever mechanical improvements to this old rattletrap vessel of y—"

Natasha tried to take advantage of his distraction with a vicious cut at his head. The golden blade parried it neatly. "Come now," he mocked, turning back to face her, "you're going to have to do better than that. I wield Danlann, the Ruling Blade itself."

"It's a pretty thing," snapped Natasha. "It'll look perfect on my hip."

Lina reached the two of them and moved to circle around behind Gwydion. As she watched, Natasha feinted with a sweeping overhand cut that fooled the crown prince. He raised his longsword to parry. Natasha suddenly drew a pistol with her free hand and aimed at his thigh. The plume of gunsmoke obscured Lina's view, but the whine of a ricochet was all too familiar to her ears. When the smoke cleared Gwydion was standing nonchalantly, an eyebrow raised.

"Really now," he said. "I'm the heir to the greatest kingdom in the world. Did you think I wouldn't have all manner of rare and expensive protection at hand?"

Natasha hissed. "A bullet-warding Worked charm?" She looked directly to Lina. "Leave off—you'll just get in the way. Fengel said you're clever; go cut that damned armored whale from us!" Then she renewed her attack upon Gwydion with a flurry of blows so furious the prince was forced on the defensive.

Lina fell back. Natasha was right; there wasn't much she could do against the prince. The question was, could Natasha?

Lina backed away, glancing to the struggle surrounding her. It was going poorly for the defenders. No one was laid out yet, but everyone was wounded. And if those automaton knights came aboard as reinforcements, it would be all over. She had to get the *Glory* separated from the *Dawnhawk*, just as ordered.

But how am I going to do that? A Bluecoat ran past her, screaming as Butterbeak and Runt swooped together at his head. Behind him trailed the rope tether of his boarding harness, slithering back to the *Glory* like a lazy serpent. It hit her then, what to do.

Rope. That's the answer.

She turned away, sheathed her blade, and ran for the starboard gunwales. Arms and heads and the plumes of gun smoke all tugged at the corner of her vision, but she ignored them; success might be measured in moments now.

The exhaust pipe was hot under her hands as she clambered atop it. Lina quickstepped among the skysail linkages with the ease of long practice and leaped up onto the rigging leading to the gas bag above. It was all she could do to climb. Her back itched at the thought of a smallsword or even just stray musket shot.

Nothing stopped her, though. Lina clambered up to the gas bag and higher along the canvas skin of the upper airship. The sky was blue, sharply contrasting the dark green jungle below, interspersed by the watery ravines threading the Copper Isles. The fight below was muted, secondary to the sounds of the wind and the whir of propellers.

Her goal was one of the half-dozen ropes dangling down from atop the gas bag. Normally they were neatly coiled near the lookout's nest for when they were needed to haul things up above, such as light-air cells or provisions for the lookout. They'd been in heavy use these last few days, however, and no one had bothered to put them away. Lina had thought them unsightly. Now they might just save the ship.

Lina sidled over to grab the nearest one. She coiled it once around her neck and continued her climb, coming up over the curve of the *Dawnhawk's* roof. It was empty up here save for the White Ape, sitting in the lookout's nest at the peak of the airship as usual, playing idly with the boots of two Bluecoat marines who'd attempted to board from up above.

The ape bared his fangs reflexively, then grunted in apprehension as he saw who she was and looked about for Runt. Lina ignored the beast and gathered more of the rope. She followed it back to the thin wooden deck running the length of the airship, to the metal ring where it was attached. Past it, the gas bag sloped back down to meet the curve of the *Glory*—from up here, the airships were a pair of canvas eggs floating through the sky.

A trick of the wind carried the sounds of battle up to her. Lina knelt by the ring and took up her dagger again. *Faster. I've got to move faster.* She sawed at the end until the fibers split and frayed. It seemed to take an eternity, but at last the rope came free.

Lina didn't waste time. She jammed the dagger roughly back into its sheathe and almost ran down the planks to the stern end of the ship. Almost. Even sure-footed as she was, the top of the airship wasn't a place to go dancing. More than one pirate had slipped to his doom up here.

Caution paid off. The rear of the *Dawnhawk's* envelope attenuated to an ovoid point; the propellers were down beneath. But the *Glory* was built differently. In addition to those along the sides of her hull, two great propellers spun side by side at her stern—but up above, from the rear of the armored gas bag.

Now came the hard part of her plan. Lina took a breath. She made a quick prayer to the Goddess. Then she ran down the port-side canvas slope of the *Dawnhawk* and jumped.

For a moment she hung in space. Then she realized that she hadn't leaped nearly hard enough. The hundred-foot coil of rope hung around her shoulder and in her arms, awkward and sickeningly heavy. But no, she landed on the armored plate of the other airship.

Armor plate that was too damned slick. She slid downward, scrabbling frantically for purchase, the golden paint of the painted sunburst sigil scratching away in the process. Her fingertips bit painfully into the crack between two plates, threatening to jerk her arms right off as she came to a stop. Lina groaned with the pain. If she fell now, she'd be chewed up by the hull propellers of the *Glory*—or drop straight down into the jungle below.

So there wasn't any choice. She pulled herself up, inch by inch, until her weight shifted and she could reach another handhold. *How do those idiots ... even get up here?*

Her arms ached and her fingertips were bloody by the time she climbed up to the pinnacle of the airship, but there wasn't time to feel it. She rose to her feet and made for the rear of the envelope, sliding and slipping on unsteady footing until the propellers loomed just below.

Lina swallowed. *Here goes … everything.* She unshouldered the rough coil of rope and pitched it towards the far, port-side propeller. It flew through the air in a lazy mess, straight for the spinning blades. Her breath caught in her throat as the propeller smacked the coil aside, but then it was drawn neatly along the shaft like a ball of twine onto a loom.

The whole contraption slammed to a halt. Metal groaned, and something snapped loudly down below. The wind brought up the smell of burning grease.

She smiled, and then the ship pitched hard to the left, pushed away from the *Dawnhawk* by the one remaining propeller. *Oops. Not done yet.* Worse, she was on enemy ground.

Air tinged with a whiff of gunpowder and the jungle smells of the isles filled her lungs as she ran back for the side of the airship. The *Glory* pitched beneath her feet, almost as if it were angry at what she'd done. Then the downward slope of the gas bag held her footing no more and Lina leaped back aboard the *Dawnhawk*.

Rough rigging caught her hands and feet. She grabbed on and held as momentum threw her about until she was safe again. *Seriously. How do they climb atop that beast?*

Lina glanced down between the two airships. The armored automatons stood all in a row on the deck of the *Glory*, twenty strong, gauntlets clamped tight on the ropes binding both airships together. She ignored the whirling propellers spinning down below them in the space between the airship hulls. Those ropes were next—she had to figure some way to cut them free. But they were braided, thick and tough, too big a job for her little dagger.

Sunlight glinted from the armored carapace of the knights. An epiphany struck her. *I don't have to cut them free.*

She just had to get the clockwork knights to let go.

Another dangling rope caught her eye, one of those tied forward atop the gas bag. Lina skittered over and gathered it up, coiling it until she had the lower end, which she tied around her waist. Then she returned to the rear of the envelope. Taking a breath, she aimed for the brass automaton at the end of the row and threw herself again over the side.

Lina fell, down between both envelopes and the rigging that kept them attached to their lower decks. The rope jerked taut, knocking the air out of her and swinging her in a low arc, straight along the gunwales of the *Glory*. Lina lifted her legs and kicked out as a knight rose up hugely.

She hammered into the thing so hard that she thought her legs would break. The machine was *heavy*. But her daredevil act worked. It rocked back slowly, then toppled over, clumsily flailing for balance. The rope it held fell free. Behind it, four soldiers with halberds and rich uniforms ceased trying to don boarding harnesses, staring at the commotion in surprise.

Lina landed precariously, kneeling in a balanced crouch upon the gunwales. Fortunately, they were thick and rather wide, meant to facilitate boarding attempts. She stood again, ignoring the four soldiers, running straight at the next automaton in the row, jumping over the numerous boarding harness tethers draping across both airships.

Sopping wet, she weighed maybe a hundred and ten pounds. Budging this machine with just her own weight was impossible. It didn't matter, though. The clockwork knights were turning towards her, responding with whatever programming filled their mechanical heads. The nearest reached out to grab at her, letting go of its rope.

Lina ducked the clumsy grip and charged past for the next. It took a swing that she likewise avoided. As she made her way up towards the bow, the machines tried for her, letting go of their straining ropes until the short gap between the two airships rapidly became a wide gulf, pushed on by the uneven propellers back above.

Then she was past them all. Lina took a breath, made a prayer to the Goddess, and jumped free. Her tether to the *Dawnhawk* carried her back across the span between both hulls, close enough to the whirling propellers of the hull of the *Glory* that she felt sucked towards them, only to swing past and land neatly feetfirst between the port-side skysails on her own airship.

Lina gasped for breath, glancing back aboard to check on her crewmates. The struggle had become a violent mess. Everyone was wounded. Ryan Gae was at his knees, gasping, as Andrea Holt fended off three men at once. Rastalak moved like a short but monstrous shadow, crouching down only to leap up and hiss, claws outspread, his mouth bloodied and a fang broken. Reaver Jane brutally hacked at the eyes of a man with a broken musket, who screamed, clawing at her face and leaving great jagged fingernail rents in her skin. The boy Paine hunkered against the starboard gunwales, tears in his eyes and a hatchet in both hands as he warded away anyone who came near, Bluecoat or pirate. In the middle of it all stood Natasha, still fending off the crown prince. Her sword was jagged like a saw blade, chipped and thin from the blows it had parried. She was bloodied as well, covered in a hundred thin cuts that had slipped past her defenses. The Perinese prince stood uninjured, though sweat slicked his brow.

"You're better than I expected," crowed Gwydion. "Skilled and vicious! I thought I'd have hacked you down in moments. The news reports don't lie, overmuch."

"Expensive toys you may have," hissed Natasha as she parried again. "They're not going to stop me clawing your eyes out and pissing in the sockets. I've beaten far better men than you, you little shit, including my husband."

Gwydion drew back in surprise. "What's this? The great Natasha Blackheart is *married*? Well, will wonders never cease." He drew his glowing sword up in guard and wrapped both hands around the hilt. "That poor bastard will be thankful, I'm certain, once I make a widow of him."

Natasha snarled. There was worry in her eyes, though. The notched cutlass she bore couldn't take much more punishment, and Gwydion laughed at pistol balls.

A chorus of startled cries sounded about the deck. Both Natasha and Gwydion flinched in surprise, but neither looked away from the other. Then a boarding tether snapped taut between them and a Bluecoat flew past, forcing them apart.

Gwydion blinked. "What …?"

It was happening all over. Confused marines were falling back, tumbling and toppling as their harnesses yanked them towards the *Glory*, now rapidly pulling away. Their boarding tethers had become a knotted mess during the fight, and now it was all that Lina's crewmates could do to duck out of the way.

"No!" shouted Gwydion. He twisted to hack at the rope upon his own back. "This is my victory! I won't lose it to something so absolutely ridicu—"

His tether went taut. Over the deck he tumbled, slamming against the ruined portside exhaust, then the gunwales past Lina. His eyes met hers, the outrage comical and plain upon his face. He aimed a rough cut at her legs, but she nimbly kicked away.

The soldiers of the *Glory* went flying through the air to dangle below their airship as it veered away—or to fall with a scream as their ropes snapped apart. Black smoke trailed from the rear propeller assembly Lina had sabotaged, which noticeably slowed the enemy airship.

"Curse you!" screamed Crown Prince Gwydion of Perinault as he swung down below the *Glory*, just missing the propellers along his hull, unlike some of the hapless Bluecoat marines. The sword Danlann waved back and forth in his hands, brilliant even in clear daylight. "This isn't over! I'm going to sack that ridiculous pirate town of yours. I'm going to burn everything you've ever loved! Broadlow! Get us back over there! *Get us back over there!*"

Then his ranting faded, dopplering into incoherent buzz as he dangled below the airship. The four richly uniformed men still aboard frantically pulled him up.

Lina looked back to the deck of her own airship. The defenders stood, too weary for surprise, all injured. Some were grievously so. Nate Wiley lay crumpled on the deck. Ryan Gae was grey faced, wrapping a bandage around the leg of a furiously swearing Reaver Jane. Andrea mechanically loaded a pistol. Rastalak was tearing strips of cloth off a dead Bluecoat to wrap his hand with. The Salomcani, Jahmal, clutched a hideous belly wound. Etarin slumped against the helm wheel and held his neck, while Allen clutched the blood-soaked rags around his hand and was now weeping openly. But Lina's heart went to her throat as she spied Michael Hockton, sitting on the deck with his head in his hands, covered in blood.

Natasha looked furious, like she wanted to give chase. Then she looked to her ruined sword and dropped it down to the deck. The impact snapped the blade neatly in two.

"Enough," she said. "Stone, get aboard. Help Etarin at the helm. North, at all speed."

Relief washed over her. Lina had half expected the captain to order pursuit. She ached and wanted a rest but nodded instead and wearily climbed back aboard. She couldn't help but feel frustrated. *None of this would have happened if you hadn't wanted a fight, Natasha.*

But if old Euron Blackheart was wrong—if the Stormhammer wasn't real—then this was just a taste of what was to come. Lina shook her head and raised her arm for Runt, who circled angrily up above near the ragged bottom of the gas bag. Then she limped over to help Etarin keep them flying north.

CHAPTER EIGHT

THE CANNONBALL FLEW LIKE A BLACK COMET TOWARDS THE BOW OF THE *COLOSSUS*. It whipped over the churning waters of the lagoon, a ricochet shot that had already hammered the floundering *Behemoth,* continuing freakishly straight for the naval flagship sitting anchored.

Admiral Wintermourn stood watching at the edge of the poop deck. His crew ran about at the command of Lieutenant Lebam, tending the damage taken so far. The Bluecoats were lined up along the starboard side of the ship, muskets slung as they waited to ascend the rope lines dropped from the cliff above. Stray bits of rigging and shattered wood decorated the deck, accented with the occasional spray of blood. It would disappear soon enough. Everyone aboard knew to keep the ship trim and tidy. Though that didn't mean they were safe.

The *Colossus* sat in the mouth of the Graveway, jostled constantly by the waterway current. Mooring anchors secured her to the cliff walls on their right—specialized spikes attached to chains forged just for such a purpose. Still, the current banged them about, setting the deck to shifting abruptly, ringing the starboard paddlewheel housing like a gong. Wintermourn did not trust the arrangement to hold them fast and had ordered power kept to the engines all throughout the morning.

Dead ahead lay the Graveway—the bowsprit of the *Colossus* aimed like an arrow at the heart of the old Salomcani fort atop the far cliff. The pirates there nested like termites, watched over by their accursed airships, which drifted back and forth like wolves waiting to pounce.

Wintermourn's own forces now had a fort of their own situated on the cliff top above. It was admittedly somewhat makeshift, but the cannons they'd lifted there were doing an admirable job of warding away the pirate airships, for which they'd been specially designed.

Behind him waited the rest of the warship column. All were similarly anchored against the current as their crews raised both men and materials up the cliff. The reports that had reached him were enough to give pause; every ship so far had sustained some form of damage traversing the ravines. Worse, the incidents continued to pile up with each passing hour they held this ridiculous position. Fortunately, the damage was largely superficial, though the pirates had given the *Ogre* a beating—everyone could, and would, still fight.

Their own airship, the *Glory of Perinault*, had taken to the skies without warning, and now was nowhere to be seen. Admiral Wintermourn had said quite a lot about that earlier, as pirates rained down their bombs and the cliff battery fought to drive them back.

Lieutenant Lebam shouted a warning as the rogue cannonball careened out of the Graveway Lagoon. It skipped against the water and rose to hammer straight into the bowsprit of the *Colossus*. The great wooden spar shattered, raining debris on the crew as the cannonball continued along, tearing rigging and falling back down to clip the capstan before rolling to a stop against the mizzenmast. The vessel's superior construction spoke well by it, but the damage wasn't negligible.

"Clean that mess up!" roared Wintermourn. He straightened his wig, not even caring if it was mussed. "Get this under control. I want the ship's carpenter up here on the double. Replace that spar in two bells, or by the Goddess I'll have every last man jack of you strung along the bow to stop the *next* cannonball."

An image came to mind then: a string of sailors torn apart, falling dead to the deck but still moving, awfully. Clawing and moaning and reaching as they rose again.

Wintermourn turned away with a snarl, forcing his useless officers to clear out of his way. Normally, their haste would have mollified him a little. But not now. His mood was too foul, he had to admit. And it was growing blacker by the minute.

The offensive was … stuck. Both of the vanguard ships had failed to take the Graveway Lagoon, and the rest of the invasion force was stopped behind them. The *Juggernaut* had let herself be boarded, of all damnable things, failing to fight off the pirates before they'd fired her powder magazine. Captain Chesterly had been spotted in the waters near the ravine, having somehow survived. Her sister ship, the *Behemoth,* had survived the few hours since then, but now she was being pounded piecemeal into a slowly sinking wreck, the pirate airships darting in and out of range from the cliff battery above. Worse, while the guns there had the angle and distance, the shells they fired were too damned light to do more than irritate the old Salomcani fort across the lagoon. As well, the *Colossus* was too distant to give any aid to the fight, though protected enough by the cliffs that only the odd enemy cannonball proved threatening.

Wintermourn put a hand to the stern railing, looking at the ships stationed back along the channel to the rear. All considered, things were in stalemate. Any advantage they'd had with numbers and equipment was countered by the ridiculous terrain of the Copper Isles. Pushing in might still have been possible, if the crown prince hadn't taken their air cover with him on whatever ill-considered errand he'd sought out.

No, any progress they were to make now would be along the clifftops around the lagoon. It would have to be made slowly. On foot. But if there was one resource the assembled fleet possessed, it was men. Inch by inch they could take these isles, for king and country, and to the Realms Below with the cost in marines.

The thought made him want to smile.

That's how things are done. With pride and courage and the spilled blood of stalwart soldiers.

He would go above shortly. To make sure that a proper beachhead was being built, with an eye on an advance to the Salomcani fort. Once enough marines had been off-loaded from the warships, they could pursue assault along that route.

Someone coughed for his attention. Admiral Wintermourn turned, raising an eyebrow fiercely. It was Sergeant Adjutant Lanters, standing at attention with Lebam and the other officers behind him, who looked thankful that someone else had presented himself as a target for their admiral's ire.

"Sir," said the burly sergeant. "Captain Chesterly has been recovered from the waters below. And a launch has just arrived bearing the captains of the *Titan, Ogre,* and the *Giantess.*"

The ships so named were those most immediately behind the *Colossus.* As such, their captains were some of the most senior in the fleet. Wintermourn was modestly pleased; he'd expected them to make their way over a goodly bit later.

Not that it would do to let that be seen. "About time," he growled. Wintermourn turned away and descended to the lower deck. There the commanders were just coming aboard, a cluster of embroidered blue jackets and golden epaulets. All of them wore wigs, a habit of the older, more distinguished gentleman—one didn't advance in the fleet without the requisite amount of years *or* connections, after all. The crown prince might look at them and see a bunch of conservative stuffed shirts, but Wintermourn saw them for what they were: paragons of tradition and service. A collection of long years of experience hammered into the only worthwhile class of men, commanding the most powerful vessels of the greatest kingdom alive.

And they're mine.

"Well, gentlemen," he said condescendingly. "If you're done taking your leisure, please join me in my cabin."

Sergeant Adjutant Lanters was already standing by, holding the door. Which was pleasing. *Fellow is worth more than half of my own officers.* Not that he'd ever progress any farther than his current, temporary station. Lanters was noncommissioned—and lowborn to boot. Wintermourn had hinted at the promise of a real navy promotion after the pirates were crushed, but it would never happen. Marines weren't capable of any *real* initiative; they were only weapons. Even their ranks were mostly honorary, after all.

The ship's carpenter had replaced the setting of the previous evening. Gone were the extra chairs and the credenza. Wooden paneling had been put back into place, giving the room a small, closed-in feeling. His bunk and chest had been put away, leaving only the heavy table to dominate the space. Atop it were numerous charts and maps, along with a Worked bucket chilling a bottle of wine, because he wasn't a savage. Through the stern windows could be seen the prow of the *Ogre*, frenetic with repairs.

Wintermourn took his customary place behind the table, at the only chair. "This has rather turned into a pig's ear now," he said. Lanters came around with wine, serving him first. "Not my plan, of course. But we do what we must. Chesterly! Do I see you lurking in the rear there?"

The ex-captain of the *Juggernaut* looked up at him from the rear of the assembly, numb with shock. He was still sopping wet and covered in numerous small injuries. His jacket was tattered and torn. Appropriately, he'd lost his epaulets. Still, the fellow seemed to have some sense of propriety about him, because he gave a sharp salute. "Sir," he replied, voice hollow.

"Dashed luck," said Wintermourn, warming to the topic. A captain without a ship lost his commission and was reduced to a mere first lieutenant again. Only the admiralty were safe from such an eventuality; they controlled the disbursement of new vessels, after all. Not that *he* would have ever let his ship get blown out from under him. "Losing your ship. Whatever happened?"

Chesterly stared past Wintermourn, looking haunted. "It was the pirate king himself. Dropped down on us like a bolt from the blue. Just old men, we thought at first, but by the Goddess, they were mad. They lit off our *powder stores*, for Her sake. Blew me overboard when it went. I … I don't know why I'm alive … "

Wintermourn raised an eyebrow at him. "Captain Euron Blackheart? In the flesh? That fellow has to be pushing seventy, if he's even really still alive. You mean to tell me your ship was taken by a bunch of geriatric old criminals?" He shook his head. "That's the saddest excuse for losing one's command I have ever heard. I should just hang you, you incompetent." He snorted disdainfully, then turned away. "Now, Captain Thomasen, the *Ogre* seems to be a bit out of sorts. How go her repairs?"

The burly, muttonchopped Thomasen sneered contemptuously at Chesterly, who was served last, as Wintermourn had intended. "Had a dashed bad blow," he said, shaking his head and setting the curls of his wig to swaying. "I'm ashamed to say. That pirate airship—*Moonchaser,* I think it was—dropped a whole load of bombs upon us before the cliff guns drove her off. I've lost most of my mainsail and starboard deck cannon." He paused to make a flippant gesture. "Oh. Quite a few dead crewmen too. Lookout got smeared all over the inside of the crow's nest, I think I heard. These are tough new vessels, though—no one builds a ship better than the Darrenway Yard boys. We'll be back on our feet before too long."

Wintermourn nodded in commiseration. "Well, see what you can do about the guns. I—"

The cry of the *Colossus's* bosun and the tromp of assembling boots cut him short. Wintermourn looked to the cabin door in confusion. *What in the Realms Below?*

The door banged open as Crown Prince Gwydion strode through, and his royal guards took up position just outside. Bruises colored his features, and he walked with a limp. His clothing was torn, and he had lost his hat somewhere. He smiled, though, and his eyes were like that of a young child on his birthing-day. Wintermourn rose and bent the knee, as did the rest of the room.

"Oh, get up, get up," said Gwydion, gesturing dismissively. The sable glove he wore was torn, missing two of the fingers. He shrugged upon noticing this, pulled it off, and threw it over his shoulder. "By the Goddess! You've all got wine—where is a glass?"

Panic at the impropriety checked all the irritated things that Wintermourn wanted to shout at him. "Of course, Your Highness—"

But Chesterly was there, passing his own glass over. The crown prince took it with a nod and drained it in one go. "Ah, that's the stuff. My thanks … Chesterly, wasn't it? *Juggernaut* was your ship?"

"Yes, Your Royal Highness."

"Ha! Saw what happened down there in the lagoon. Bad bit of luck, that."

A pained look crept over the ex-captain. He opened his mouth to reply, but Gwydion had turned away already. "Now, I expected to find my good admiral so cloistered, but what are the rest of you old fossils doing in here?"

Wintermourn felt all his irritation at the crown prince rising again. "We were convening over the aftermath of this morning's action." He shook his head. "Quite a pity. Two ships lost and a third severely damaged."

"Those damned pirates made a run at us after the *Juggernaut* blew," said Thomasen irritably. "Bypassed the *Behemoth* entirely. We'd no proper air cover at that point." He looked pointedly at the crown prince.

Wintermourn blinked in surprise. Thomasen was an old hand at politicking, and needling Gwydion was far from a rational move for such an old soldier. He must have been more upset than he appeared. *Not that our princeling doesn't deserve it.* It was possible for a man to serve another and not respect him personally. So far, that seemed like it would be the case with most of the fleet's commanders and the heir apparent.

"Oho," laughed Gwydion. "Found your spine now, have you?" He shook his head. "Yes, yes. My apologies for leaving you all in the lurch. I just got so sick of you lot getting all the glory. And with such an opportunity presenting itself, how could I resist?"

Wintermourn frowned. He looked to the rest of the assembled captains, who appeared just as confused.

"What opportunity was that, sir?" asked Chesterly.

Gwydion gestured dismissively with his wineglass. "Oh, I spied an airship out of formation just north of the lagoon. The *Dawnhawk*, under Natasha Blackheart. All on her own, she was. Which meant that I just *had* to have Captain Broadlow try to chase her down. I'd have tried to pick off one of the other pirate vessels earlier, but numbers do still matter, alas."

A dropped pin could have been heard in the cabin. The assembled officers, even boot-licking Chesterly, all stared at the Crown Prince of the Kingdom in astonished horror. Wintermourn himself was appalled.

"You hared off away from the conflict here on nothing more than a whim?" Wintermourn all but shouted. He felt his wig hanging acutely askew. "You could have been killed!"

"Oh, I do certainly hope so," replied Gwydion dryly. "Otherwise, it would somewhat have defeated the point of risking life and limb."

Wintermourn felt a red rage rise up, eradicating caution. "You little fool!" he shouted. "You exposed the fleet for some doomed errand that you couldn't even bring to completion!"

The crown prince met his outrage coolly. "Have a care with how you speak, my good admiral."

The room fell silent then, with everyone present trying very hard to become invisible. Wintermourn realized the precipice he stood on and forced himself to calm. Abruptly Gwydion gave a sigh.

"In this instance, however," he said, "you may be correct. I've little enough to show for my adventure but sore ribs and a limp, in spite of all these expensive, arcane accoutrements I carry. Someone take a note: those boarding harnesses are a terrible idea. Cost me my victory and hampered my platoon of marines. Who are mostly dead now. We'll do without them in the future. The harnesses, that is."

He held out his empty glass, which Lanters raced to fill, and then he made an apologetic shrug to the room at large. "Natasha Blackheart is made of sterner stuff than I thought," he continued. "And she mentioned a husband." He looked around the room. "I hadn't read of that. Has anyone else?"

A chorus of coughed negatives echoed about the cabin, until Chesterly raised a tentative hand. "Captain Fengel, of the *Flittergrasp*," he said quietly. "Or so I've heard it said."

Gwydion frowned. "Really? The traitor and mutineer?" He tapped his chin with his free hand and smiled. "The man is supposed to be a master with a blade; I'll look forward to finding him. But wherever did you hear he was married to her? I've made extensive study of all the dossiers and reports."

The sodden ex-captain coughed in embarrassment. "Ah. I … ah, one of my crewmen picked up a few of those penny-papers they publish in Triskelion about the pirates. Silly stuff," he continued, flushing red, "boys' stories and whatnot."

"Well," said Gwydion. "I'll have to consider going over those. I do so hate to be uninformed."

"Be that as it may," said Wintermourn, fixing Chesterly with a fierce glare, "it is beside the point. We are in a costly, untenable, damnable position. The *Ogre* has taken severe damage, with those pirates ready to bomb us again if we should relax our vigilance for even a moment. We're sitting ducks here in this ravine, just like you'd wanted to avoid. I see no other alternative now than to take the fort by committing the marines to an overland assault."

Crown Prince Gwydion laughed. "What? Why, that's ridiculous. I mean, do you realize how many of those men we'll lose to such an action?" He shook his head. "No, no. We'll do no such thing."

"That is what they're *for*—"

Gwydion cut him off with a glance. "Do not forget who is in charge here, Admiral. I made a misstep, 'tis true. But our larger action is going just fine. And we're not going to waste our resources on some grand assault."

Wintermourn opened his mouth to reply again, but Gwydion cut him off. "Fast and efficient, gentleman. Speed, as I said last evening. New days are upon us, and that's the name of the game. Now. I'll be returning aloft shortly, and you'll have your orders. But first. Chesterly? You've lost your commission?"

"Yes," replied the man, miserable.

"Good. You're with me then, as royal adjutant. At least for the duration of this invasion."

Chesterly looked up in surprise as everyone else in the room made cries of consternation. Wintermourn stared. The upstart youth he'd sought to destroy had just gained a royal posting, something he'd not accomplished in fifty years at sea.

"But Your Highness," he protested, "Chesterly just got kicked off his own damned ship—and has barely a decade at the post!"

"I don't care, overmuch," replied the crown prince. "I don't especially care how things *have* been done, but I do care how they *will* be going forward. Haven't I mentioned that enough by now? New days, gentlemen. New days. Fellow here has experience fighting these pirates and saw the pirate king in the flesh. I want to wring it all from him. Also, he's quick with a wineglass and a chair when needed."

Gwydion drained his glass and passed it to his new adjutant, who handed it to Lanters in turn. Then the prince turned to the door. "The key is the pirate captains," he said, less conversational now. "They're only a loose coalition. That makes them vulnerable. We can pull them away from the pack. And if we take the right ones, the defense here will fall."

Wintermourn was unable to choke down the retort. "You already tried that," he said, voice bitter.

Gwydion raised an eyebrow. "It's still a viable tactic. And it's going to get us out of this 'damnable position' that you're so worried over, my good admiral. Enough. I return to the *Glory*. I have a plan to win the Graveway. If we're lucky, we'll get Euron Blackheart with it. If not, it'll do for at least one of these reaving bastards. Remember, though: I want any Mechanists we come across captured—do not kill them."

Harsh daylight and the stink of fired powder flooded the cabin as the crown prince left, accompanied by his new adjutant. Wintermourn watched them leave, feeling like there was very little under his control at all.

CHAPTER NINE

FENGEL KEPT GLANCING AT THE MECHANIST AS THEY WAITED TO DEPART SOLRUN'S HAMMER.

Short and stocky, she'd removed her mask during the flight back to Haventown, revealing plain features and quick, intelligent eyes. Fengel thought her young, in her midteens. An apprentice still, he surmised, though she'd said little beyond the summons to speak with the Mechanist Cabal.

He wanted to be back at the Graveway. The fight there needed his attention. A summons by the Brotherhood of the Cog was not to be ignored, though, even if their timing could be better. Why now, of all possible moments, did they feel the need to chat with him?

The question rattled around inside his head as Brunehilde's crew ran out the boarding ramp to the Skydocks. Was it a new weapon? Something they'd whipped up to help thwart the invaders? *If so, why me? Brunehilde is the one taking everything to the Graveway.*

He'd meant to further interrogate the young Mechanist, an enigma herself—as he understood it, there were no women in the Brotherhood of the Cog. That plan had been forgotten as soon as they'd passed the *Dawnhawk* on their way back to Haventown. His ship was flying west, straight for the Graveway battle. Just as a small part of him feared, Natasha had rebelled and come to join the fight. He'd ranted and cursed and run about the deck until Khalid Al-Murdawzi threatened to pitch him overboard, calming only once the *Dawnhawk* turned herself northward again. The rest of the journey had been split between worrying over his wife's crazy antics and why the Mechanist Cabal wanted to see him.

Fengel disembarked as *Solrun's Hammer* finished docking. *It can't be about my bills, can it? I mean, there's a war on at the moment. And my tab isn't … that big. Not really.* He forced the thought aside. No. It was ridiculous. *Unless … unless they want to make sure I'm settled up before we all die.* Fengel scowled and left the airship.

Local dockhands were waiting on the pier beyond, ready with a load of black powder and other supplies. Fengel pushed past, and his Mechanist escort rushed to catch up as he reached the Skydock stair, panting with exertion as she fell in behind him.

"We're heading to the Brotherhood Yards, then?" he asked.

The apprentice Mechanist nodded. "Yes."

Fengel felt encouraged. "Well enough, then—I know the way. I do hope, though, that there's a good reason for hauling me all the way back here?"

She only shook her head. "I do not know."

He gave a sigh of exasperation. "Do you at least have a name, girl?"

She looked at him sharply. There was something in her gaze … did she think the question a taunt? He shrugged and looked away.

Nob Terrace spread itself before them as they reached the base of the stair. The boardwalk stretched like a crescent moon atop the clifftop, bounded by jungle behind it and a precipitous drop to the terraces below. The furious activity of earlier had been replaced by something more sedate now, though people still ran to and fro, boarding over windows and erecting makeshift barricades in their yards. It was a chaotic mess, with little cooperation or guidance. Fengel watched the distillery lads race the barber next door in using up a stack of spare lumber, the both of them forgetting the undefended alley between their buildings in their haste. At the Sindicato manor, Mr. Grey was shouting at his thugs as they built an impromptu cannon emplacement near the front door. Everywhere Fengel saw people working at cross-purposes. With Euron's crew and all the other real fighters out at the Graveway, there wasn't any authority strong enough left here to provide order.

Some seemed intent on avoiding the conflict entirely. A few of Nob Terrace's more wealthy folk were packing valuable objects into carts, apparently intending to hide in the jungle interior.

Fools. All of them. But he felt more dismay than scorn. A creeping sense came over him that the chances of the pirate township were worse than ever before. He hung his head and stalked down the boardwalk, aiming for the fortified walls of the Brotherhood Yards that dominated the far end of Nob Terrace's boardwalk crescent.

"It's Imogen," said his Mechanist escort suddenly. "Mechanist-Aspirant Imogen."

Fengel glanced back at her with one raised eyebrow. "Well, good to finally meet you, Mechanist-Aspirant Imogen—"

"And I don't *actually* know why the Cabal wants you, but it's fairly obvious from just the smallest bit of deduction. Though I should be charitable, as you pirates aren't really known for your cleverness."

Fengel stared at her, coming to a stop.

"I beg your pardon?"

"Pardoned," she said. "It's got to be because you're the least useful captain at the moment. Order in Haventown operates on two principles: the rule of Euron Blackheart, as carried out by his own old crew and subordinate pirate captains, and the Brotherhood of the Cog, Mechanist Faction, keeping basic utilities running along with the airships. The *Dawnhawk* is elsewhere at the moment, and the rest of the airships are fighting the Perinese. That leaves you—possessed of a modicum of respectability but not too occupied."

Fengel blinked. He started walking again, pointedly looking away from her. "I'll have you know that I was commanding the fort battery, which was the only thing that prevented Euron from getting his damned fool self killed." Probably, at least. The old man had boarded and destroyed the Perinese vessel on his own. But there were limits to Fengel's charity.

Imogen hadn't seemed to notice the rebuttal. "I saw the big woman, Sarah Lome, ordering the guns. As your subordinate, I'm sure that she's more practiced at the actual task of gunnery. Also, she's likely familiar enough with your desires to predict your preferences in a pinch. In fact, when I consider how much time you spent playing with that weird monocle on just the flight back, I expect your officers and crew more than practiced at making spot decisions."

Fengel yanked his hand from his eyepiece. It had only needed a little adjustment. Glancing back in disdain, he noted that Imogen was panting now, troubled at keeping up with his long-legged stride. Intentionally, he lengthened it.

By the time they reached the fortified gates of the Brotherhood Yards, Imogen had managed to criticize how he dressed, his manner of speech, his failure to keep the *Dawnhawk* in good repair, and his choice of co-captain. She also told him how he *really* should have infiltrated the Tower of Mad Doctor Invigg.

"By the Goddess's hairy arms," he yelled at her, "that never happened! It's made-up! A starving author back in Triskelion makes all those penny-stories. I haven't received any royalties from him in close to a year."

"Still," replied Imogen, "he should have had you order Sarah Lome to pry open the drain entrances on the south side of the tower. Then you could have slipped inside without raising the alarm. That would have given you plenty of time to plunder the vaults—and coincidentally prevent Invigg from finishing his Aetherbeast."

Fengel glared at her as he pounded on the gate. "I told you that I don't write them!"

A metal slit snapped open at eye level. Through it peered the goggles of a Mechanist. "What is this racket—Imogen, that you?"

"I've brought Captain Fengel for the Cabal," she said simply.

The eyeslit shut. There were several mechanical clicks, and then a postern door opened in the gate. Behind it stood a tall Mechanist, hidden beneath a greatcoat and goggles like all the rest. His only defining features were the distasteful glower he directed at his younger colleague, his unkempt hair, and the complicated-looking musket he gripped in one hand.

"You really should oil those hinges every two days," said Imogen to the gate guard. "And the proper way to hold a musket at all times is with both hands on the weapon—or secured over your shoulder via the stra—"

"Get inside!" growled the guard.

Imogen shut up and scurried through the portal. Fengel tipped his hat to the man, favoring him with a smile before stepping into the Brotherhood Yards.

The Mechanists were an insular lot who treasured their privacy. To the average townsman, the Yard was a place of wonders. They were right, but this place held little mystique for Fengel. Like most pirate captains, he had been here before.

The Yard was just that, a wide open space bounded on all sides by fortified walls, with numerous storage huts and workshops built up against them. Running across the great space were the omnipresent brass pipes that threaded through the rest of the town and terminated here, interspersed by piles of coal and raw ore. At the heart of the enclave loomed the Great Hall, a long structure where the arcane construction of airships and other great wonders were completed.

Fengel strode off for the Great Hall as the guard slammed the postern shut. Imogen ran to keep up with him.

"That's Montrey," she said, breathless. "He never listens to my advice. No matter how many times I tell him."

Fengel glanced back over his shoulder at her, even as he tried to leave her behind. "That, Miss Imogen, is because your 'advice' is—"

An orange blur shot out from beneath a raised brass pipe and slammed into his ankle. Fengel lurched, staggered, and pirouetted as he tried to avoid pitching face-first into a man-high stack of coal. He succeeded, barely, regaining his balance as a fat orange ball of fur did figure eights in between his ankles, purring loudly. It was Cubbins, the orange tabby cat that Omari had tried so fervently to foist off on him.

"What are you doing here, you flea-bitten mongrel?" asked Fengel in distaste. The tabby cat only bumped his head against Fengel's boot.

"Oh," said Imogen. "A cat. That really shouldn't be in here."

Fengel looked up at the dismay in her voice. "Something wrong?"

The young Mechanist covered her face with a gauntlet. "None of us are allowed pets. Hair and feathers and whatnot in the mechanisms … terrible. Also, I'm allergic."

Fengel looked down at the furry orange feline, then at Imogen, then back to Cubbins. He stooped to gather up the cat, rubbing its head with his fingertips. "Well. I certainly can't leave it here, then. Just have to take it along. We don't want fur in the mechanisms, of course. Come now, young Miss Imogen! Take me to your masters."

Imogen stared at the cat. She edged around him carefully, then led the way to the Great Hall at a goodly pace, actively keeping distance between them. Fengel smiled to himself, then to Cubbins, following along at leisure.

The interior of the Great Hall was one huge and cavernous space. It smelled of oil, leather, and burned metal. An unfinished airship hull sprawled down its length, draped by gantries, chain conveyors, and walkways hanging from the ceiling high above. Shadows ruled the room, as not a single window allowed any light from the outside world. Instead, great galvanic lanterns shed small pools of radiance over the work spaces littering the floor. There were only a few Mechanists here, scurrying about as they frantically worked strange machineries. The room echoed with the sounds of industry.

"Now," mused Fengel, "where are we to go?" On previous visits, some nameless Mechanist functionary would appear as if by magic.

Imogen sneezed in reply. "Ober dere," she said a moment later, her voice muffled and thick. Fengel glanced back to see her wiping her nose, standing as far away from him as she politely could. Imogen gestured with her other hand towards the prow of the airship hull. Below it, Fengel spied a small platform raised up to provide a vantage point over the rest of the floor. Five figures in leather greatcoats stood there arguing.

Fengel rubbed Cubbins on the forehead with his thumb, eliciting a deep, rumbling purr. "Well then, Miss Imogen. Let's not keep them waiting. I've a fight to be about."

He set off before she could reply, taking the most direct path between work spaces. Those few Mechanists he passed seemed absorbed in their work on racks of complicated muskets, fold-up barricades, and what looked for all the world like a rotary cannon. Other, stranger things loomed out of the gloom: an inert Brass Horse from Triskelion, dripping oil from its maw, and a column of brass with a collection of crystals at its peak that hurt the eye to look upon.

The platform loomed before him then, with a single stair climbing ten feet to its top. Fengel released Cubbins and ascended with Imogen in tow. Unfortunately, the tabby cat bounded up after him.

Fengel folded his arms as he reached the top. "All right, then," he said. "What's so important that you had to drag me all the way back here?" He tried to ignore Cubbins ramming his ankles, purring into the sudden silence.

The members of the Cabal made a semicircle around the edge of the platform, roughly twenty feet in diameter. Between them stood a small table with a miniature diorama of some kind atop it. The Mechanists turned to face him, their discussion interrupted. They were dumpy and shapeless in their greatcoats and goggles, as expected. There were a few differences, however, marking them out as senior members of the Brotherhood faction.

The one on the left wore a complicated mask of hoses and piping, through which he gasped audibly every few moments. His neighbor wore no mask, though his goggles were surrounded by six smaller lenses that could click into place on tiny armatures. Next in line stood a very stiff Mechanist, the leather of his jacket scarred and scorched by flame. The fourth brother had six timepieces strapped to his left arm, which he constantly checked. And at the far end stood the last Mechanist, who otherwise appeared normal enough, save for the prosthetic mechanical foot poking out from beneath his greatcoat, which Fengel recognized from the delegation sent to Euron's court last evening. Fengel knew they wouldn't bother with names, so he mentally assigned them designations: Wheezer, Eight-Eyes, Scorch, Timekeeper, and Clangfoot.

As one, the Cabal peered suspiciously down at Cubbins the tabby cat.

"What is that animal … doing in here?" said Wheezer, his voice raspy and thick behind his mask.

"Pets are not allowed in the Great Hall," added Timekeeper in disdain.

"They disrupt delicate instrumentation," said Eight-Eyes.

"Besides," said Wheezer, "we are … mostly allergic."

Fengel wanted to smile. Instead he made a sharp, cutting gesture with one hand. "That is a trifling concern. Every second you waste is gifted to the Perinese. Now, why in the Realms Below did you call me all the way back here?"

Behind him, Imogen sneezed.

"Quite," said Clangfoot unemotionally. "Captain Fengel of the *Dawnhawk*, we have summoned you because you are needed, and you can serve the struggle better here than at the Graveway. Haventown … is doomed."

The statement echoed about the platform. The finality of it rankled Fengel. He glared at the Mechanist. "That isn't certain. Not yet. Are we in trouble? Of course. But—"

"It *is* certain," intoned Eight-Eyes. "Our prognostication engines are far more accurate than you can imagine. We have seen that the current conflict will amount to little more than a spirited defense. The numbers do not lie."

Fengel put his arms behind him angrily. "Well, numbers can certainly stretch the truth, when it pleases them." Who were these men, to tell him what the future would be? Cubbins rubbed against his boot, and he tried to force the cat away.

Two of the Cabal Mechanists paused to look at each other. "No," said Wheezer. "That's … that's the exact opposite of what we just said."

"The point," continued Clangfoot before Fengel could retort, "is that evacuation must be considered our prime response to this invasion, going forward."

"Yes," agreed Timekeeper. "You convinced us yourself last evening at the Bleeding Teeth."

Fengel blinked, taken aback. *Strange, that I find myself so reversed.* For all the arguing he'd done with Euron, he didn't want to consider retreat now. They'd actually done well at the Graveway, albeit in a messy, disorganized, skin-of-their-teeth sort of way.

"Now, hold on," he said. "The whole damned Perinese navy is assembled against us, but I was only attempting to get Euron to consider the option of retreat. Not calling for it. Not just yet." The argument sounded hollow, even to his own ears.

"Yes. But it was not just your words that swayed us. It was Euron's."

"We came not just to inform you of the missing First Mechanist," continued Clangfoot, "but to assess the pirate king's handling of the situation. As we feared, Euron Blackheart will not prove a capable wartime administrator." The Mechanist held Fengel's gaze. However, the effect was ruined by Cubbins, whose purr seemed to pull at his attention.

"He hungers for little other than old glory," said Eight-Eyes.

Clangfoot shook his head, returning to the discussion. "His only real solution to the invasion is impractical—reliance upon an ancient and unlikely Voorn superweapon. Such devices are unreliable at best and positively suicidal at worst. We are not certain this Stormhammer even exists. How could he have hidden it all these years? But if it does … such a past should stay buried."

Wheezer shook his head. "These factors … combined with the numerical and qualitative superiority of the invaders … only confirm the output of our prognostication engines."

Fengel looked away with a sour frown. He had to admit that they had a point. Even Wheezer. Not a few hours past, he had commiserated with Natasha about how mad Euron's solution was. And no one needed to convince him that the pirate king was a doddering old fool who'd get them all killed trying to relive his past victories.

Wheezer wasn't finished. "Since Haventown is so heavily outnumbered …" Here he paused to glare at Fengel, "And because *math does not lie* … there is only one possible recourse open to us. Haventown should be evacuated."

Fengel sighed. It was true and he knew it. He'd always known it. His blood had been up at the Graveway, but that long line of navy warships, their airship and Bluecoat marines … In the cold light of reason, there had only ever been one solution. The Perinese knew where Haventown was and were committed to destroying it. Those two simple facts meant downfall more than anything else.

He shook his head. "We can pull the captains back here to load the citizenry, food, and water. Scuttle one of the waterborn ships in the mouth of Haventown Lagoon to act as an obstacle. Cadmus's, most likely—it's the biggest, and he was always an ass. A token group can stay behind to harry the invaders long enough to get the majority of the populace to safety." He paused to rub at his beard. "It *might* work. But even if that buys us enough time and we've enough transportation, where to go? The Yulan is our best bet, but it's too damned far away. And there would need to be several trips." He rubbed at his beard, thinking furiously. "Maybe build temporary rafts to drag along? No, the fleet would catch up in a day …"

Clangfoot held up a gauntlet. "Such supposition is unnecessary. We already have a plan. Emptying the township in enough time would be impossible, at any rate. We have only a handful of days, at best."

So soon. Fengel blinked in confusion. "Then what in the Realms Above are we to do?"

"Captain Fengel," said Eight-Eyes. The Mechanist paused to sneeze. "We already told you. We're not going to empty the town … .but to *evacuate* it." He gestured at the table before him. "Look. See."

Perturbed, Fengel stepped closer, forcing Cubbins out of the way. The table was simple and bare but for the miniature in its center. Upon closer inspection, it was a collection of buildings, terraces, and structures all rendered in tiny detail—a perfect replica of Haventown. Everything from the Gasworks to the Skydocks to the brothels of the Yellow Lantern Terrace and more were represented.

"Oh, that's just fabulous," marveled Fengel. "Look, someone's even painted tiny airships!"

"Mechanist Second Class Thaddeus is a deft hand with a brush," agreed Eight-Eyes, gesturing to the stiff, fire-scarred brother beside him. "But look at how elegant the solution is."

Fengel looked up at him. "So you've said. But I still don't see anything. Other than this pretty diorama, that is."

Cubbins, hungering for a leg to rub against, turned and trotted towards Clangfoot. The Mechanist hurriedly stepped out of the way, turning the motion into a purposeful approach of the table. There he flipped a hidden switch on the backside of the diorama. "That's because you have to turn it on first."

There was a faint whirring, then a hiss. Fengel watched as the tiers of the miniature Haventown all shifted … and rose up off the cliffsides upon which it rested, supported by tiny gasbags built into the underside of each terrace. His jaw dropped open as he understood.

That's … impossible. Isn't it? You can't … "You don't mean to tell me that we're going to fly the town away from here?"

"That is exactly what we mean to do," said Eight-Eyes, pausing to sneeze again. "There is no need to locate a new home, Captain Fengel, because we will be taking it with us."

His watch-clad brother reached over and poked the floating miniature, sending it back to hover in the center of the table. "Everyone knows of the agreement made between First Mechanist Helmsin and the pirate king, yes?"

"Of course," replied Fengel. "He let you stay here and gave you a spot for these yards. In return, you oversee the town's infrastructure and keep it all running." Behind him, Imogen sneezed again.

"That is the common interpretation. Though it is not technically accurate. For one thing, Euron Blackheart never asked us to oversee the infrastructure of Haventown. We've taken up that task up ourselves."

"Another … reason," interjected Wheezer, "that … we have so little faith … in his ability to protect the town."

"Why?" asked Fengel, confused.

"Because what we asked of the pirate king wasn't land," added Eight-Eyes. "It was mining rights." He stepped back warily as Cubbins dropped to the platform and rolled over to his back, presenting his belly, looking up hopefully at them all.

Clangfoot gestured to the miniature cliffface below the floating Haventown. "The Copper Isles are a special place," he said. "Until very recently, they were the sole locale from which light-air gas could be gathered. Raising an airship without it is an expensive and time-consuming process."

So that's the secret. Everyone in Haventown knew what kept a Brotherhood airship afloat. But where the gas was generated, or how, was unknown. "All the piping running through the town. From the Gasworks down on the Craftwright's Terrace, up to here. That's what it's for."

Eight-Eyes cocked his head. "You didn't think they were for pumping hot water?"

"Of course not," Fengel lied. "But why are you telling me this?"

Clangfoot gestured again to the miniature floating township. "Because you are needed. But first you must understand. We came to Haventown because it is the source of the light-air gas we need. And we took care of the township's infrastructure not just to harvest it but for Atherion Helmsin's greatest experiment: to make a city fly."

"And now ... it is time to ... test it," wheezed his fellow Mechanist.

"The Perinese are at our doorstep," said Timekeeper. "They will not stop. And there are many, many preparations to make before we can lift away. Two of which have bearing upon this discussion."

"Fortunately," added Clangfoot, "all the light-air gas we need has been harvested from the mining tunnels below the town. It simply needs to be released into the Gasworks. That will be your task, Captain Fengel. Mechanist-Aspirant Imogen will lead you. The rest of us will be leading four teams to break the great mooring shackles that keep each terrace tethered to the clifffaces of this lagoon."

Fengel raised a hand. "All right. But again ... why me? This sounds like something any one of you could do."

"Because we are short ... of time and manpower ... both," said Wheezer, somewhat irritably. "And because you are the only ... trustworthy captain who can be spared ... from the Graveway at the moment. Natasha has taken ... your ship north on Euron's foolish ... errand."

Behind him, Imogen made a self-righteous noise. Then she sneezed again.

"Maybe a quarter of the populace of Haventown is fighting at the Graveway," said Clangfoot. "The rest are all here. The citizens look to the pirate captains to lead them. Our misgivings of Euron Blackheart aside, someone is still needed on hand to keep order once we are afloat. That will be you."

"My crew need me at the Graveway," said Fengel.

"Everyone else needs you here more," replied the Mechanist. "We are raising a city. You must be the one to captain it."

Fengel looked away at the half-finished hull of the airship behind them. It all seemed mad. The Mechanists kept repeating that he was needed, but to captain the city? The *flying* city?

Insanity.

The Mechanists were deadly serious, however. And they were right. The people of the town were all independents and free-thinkers. When crisis hit, they looked to Fengel and his fellow captains for leadership. Euron was spiraling out of control with every passing moment, the glory-mad old fool. *Realms Below, he might already be dead.*

Fine, then. He had never been one to shirk from duty. Looking back to the assembled Mechanist Cabal, he nodded. "Very well. Let's get to work, then."

Timekeeper nodded. "Good. Mechanist-Aspirant Imogen? Approach."

Imogen stepped up past the table, though on the opposite side from where Cubbins wriggled on the platform, still waiting for attention. She wore her full mask and goggles now, and her voice was muffled. "Sirs?"

"Take Captain Fengel down to the mines below the Gasworks—the entrance behind the Smuggler's Warehouse, which I am sure you know. Activate the pumps. The Gasworks team will fire signal flares once light-air gas is distributed throughout the system, and the rest of us will release the mooring shackles for each terrace."

Pounding feet and a ringing clatter echoed up to them atop the platform, cutting short Imogen's reply. Fengel glanced back to see another Mechanist barreling down the pathway towards them, his bulky leather greatcoat catching on all manner of trays, tools, and devices on the workbenches he passed, spilling them to the ground in his haste. The Brother of the Cog did not stop until he had ascended to their level, startling Cubbins back to his feet.

"Sirs!" he cried, gasping. The fellow wore no gas mask, but did, of course, have his goggles. "The Graveway has been lost!"

What? Fengel felt his monocle fall free as the Cabal made varying noises of shock and surprise. Fengel grabbed the newcomer by the shoulder. "How?" he demanded. "What happened?"

The Mechanist looked startled by the contact, but Fengel held his gaze until the man answered. "It was the *Powderheart*. The Perinese, they sent a lone ship, the *Ogre*, into the lagoon. Captain Glastos tried to board her, just like Euron did. But it was a trap. A fire ship. The invaders detonated her, which killed the *Powderheart*. The others moved to assist and got shelled by the *Glory of Perinault* and the enemy gun batteries atop the Graveway. Everyone's falling back. We've been routed!"

Fengel paused to think. He let go the messenger and turned back to the Cabal. "The pirate captains will make a fighting retreat, to save face if nothing else. And I know my men will harry any ships from the cliffs above. The Perinese will keep up the pressure, but securing the old fort will take time, and that entrenchment of theirs will take time to move as well. We've a few hours, at least. Is that enough time?"

Clangfoot nodded slowly. "It will have to be." He turned to face the rest of the Cabal. "To work, then!"

Fengel grabbed Imogen and hauled her after him as he descended the platform. The others likewise scattered. As she flailed, Cubbins ran down the steps ahead of them, purring loudly. The fat orange tabby cat seemed far too enthusiastic for what was to come.

CHAPTER TEN

LINA LIFTED THE CORPSE BY HIS SHOULDERS. Young Paine grabbed the feet. Grunting, they prepared to sling the dead man into the open cargo hatch of the *Dawnhawk's* holds.

One more gone. In the chaos of the fight, she hadn't even seen how Nate Wiley had died. Now she just wasn't sure what to think of it. Nate and his dead twin brother Jonas had come from Natasha's crew originally. They had been crude and violent but not terribly malicious. Now he stank of dried blood and the great gash in his stomach that had killed him. Lina couldn't help but think that he smelled only a *little* worse now than he did in life.

"On three," she gasped. Across from her, Paine nodded, red in the face. Nate Wiley had not been a small man. "One … two … thr—"

The corpse of Nate Wiley opened its mouth and moaned, hands and feet twitching violently. Lina and Paine both yelled in surprise. They released the newly arisen Revenant to fall back to the deck.

"In the hold, in the hold!" shouted Lina.

"I don't want to touch it! You touch it!"

The thought made her skin crawl. If they didn't move it now, though, the thing that was Nate Wiley would be more or less back in control of itself.

"Both of us together," she said. "Quickly now, while it's confused!"

She forced herself to kneel beside the twitching corpse, trying not to focus on its entrails flopping about. It reached for her head, forcing her to duck aside. Out the corner of her eye, Lina spied Paine, still standing, his boyish face twisted up in horror.

"Now!" she yelled at him.

Paine fought with himself a moment, then knelt beside her. No coordinated effort this time. They shoved at the reanimated corpse haphazardly, pushing until it flopped over the side of the hatchway and fell out of sight. There was silence—and then a wet thump.

Lina climbed to her feet, panting. She felt nauseous. The deck around them was clear now, if stained. Nate was the last of the half dozen corpses they'd thrown hurriedly into the holds before they could become Revenants. Of the *Dawnhawk's* crew, only Nate and the newcomer Jahmal had been casualties, with the rest composed of Bluecoat invaders cut free of their boarding tethers. Not all of the latter had been beyond saving, but Natasha gave no quarter. That had been … conflicting. Lina had expected better, for some reason. At least they weren't just dumping the corpses over the side, though, leaving the walking dead to haunt the jungles of the Copper Isles.

She'd wanted to get away from the war, but the war had come along after them. The deck of the airship had been a mess before the attack. Now it was a downright shambles. Dangling cordage, torn sailcloth, and a great rent in the starboard exhaust belching steam made the *Dawnhawk* seem just as ruined as the Revenants within her hold. There was also blood—a lot of blood, smeared across deck planks gouged by blade and ball. The wide blue skies and green jungle beyond the gunwales stood in stark, peaceful contrast.

Natasha herself stood at the wheel, shouting questions of heading and speed to Reaver Jane where she limped about the bow. Omari had been banished to the lookout's nest and the care of the White Ape. Michael Hockton ran up and down the ship on a number of tasks, freed from Revenant handling by virtue of light injury. Amidships sat the rest of the diminished pirate crew. Big Farouk tended to his friend Etarin, who had taken a nasty blow to the neck. Ryan Gae wrapped Rastalak's arm, looking himself uninjured, though exhausted and aged. Andrea Holt sat cross-legged in front of a whimpering Allen, finishing the stitches on his hand. The apprentice Mechanist was now short a finger.

Lina watched Michael Hockton as he ran back to Natasha. She really wanted to hear his voice at the moment, wanted him to tell her that everything would be all right. It was a small, selfish desire, and she knew it. Realms Below, she should probably go say something to Allen about his missing finger. But in the aftermath of the fight with the Bluecoats, everything just felt like it was falling apart. She'd never wanted to fight a war.

Maybe Paine would do, if she could get the ball rolling. She wiped the half-crusted blood off on her pants and then put a hand on the youth's shoulder. The towheaded boy was staring at the cargo hatch with his characteristic sulk. "Good job on that," she said, hoping the praise sounded sisterly.

"Captain said to help," he muttered, not looking up at her.

His voice quavered. Lina realized he was more upset than she'd thought. A memory came to mind of the last fight, of Paine hunkering against the gunwales, trying to escape the fight, if not actively to hide.

"Hey," she said, rubbing his shoulder. "Hey, it's all right. Everyone freezes up their first time in a fight. I sure did."

An ugly memory, that. She'd been even younger than Paine was now. Caught in an alley by some of the Bundle Street Gang, her only weapon a broken bottle, against their ugly leers and grasping hands.

"I don't want to be here," said the boy. He stared into the black pit of the cargo hold. Weak groans from the restless dead within rose up to them both. "I don't wanna be a pirate. I didn't want to even be in the navy! Father sent me, because that's what Paines do. But Granduncle is an industrialist in Triskelion. Why couldn't I have gone *there?*"

"I came from Triskelion," said Lina, fighting off awful memories that only sank her mood further. *Goddess. Paine, this wasn't* really *supposed to be about you, of all people.* She gave the boy a brittle smile and gestured beyond the airship, where distant white clouds puffed along through a blue midafternoon sky. "Oh, come on. This is so much better than that smelly old coalsmoke city."

Paine looked up at her flatly. "Of *course* you'd say that," he replied. "Everyone knows you were a whore."

Spoiled little shit. This was what she got for trying to be comforting. Lina whacked the boy upside the head. "Get that hatch closed, then report to the captain," she growled. Great. Now she was angry as well as melancholy and depressed.

Her eyes alighted on Allen. *Yes!* The young Mechanist always wanted to please her—he'd be good for some comfort. Besides, she really should say something nice to him. *I mean, a finger. That can't be easy.*

She walked over to where her friend sat next to one of the equipment lockers amidships. Andrea Holt was beside him, using the locker as a low table, holding Allen's hand firmly against the wood while she swathed it in bandages.

"Can't we find it and sew it back on?" wheedled the apprentice Mechanist. His voice was frantic, tight with pain as he pleaded. Tears leaked through eyes scrunched up tight, carving channels through the blood and dirt caked onto his face.

Andrea didn't look up. She kept her focus on the bandages. "Do you know how to do that?" she asked.

"N-no ..."

"Neither do I." She gave him a tight smile. "Buck up, lad. You Mechanists lose bits all the time."

He looked like he would break down. "But I never thought it would happen to me."

"I've cleaned it and stanched the bleeding. We'll have a proper sawbones take a look when we get back to town. Find Lina; that Cure-All she keeps for Runt will put paid to yer hurt, for now." She glanced over as Lina approached. "There she is. You injured, Lina?"

She shook her head. "Just sore."

The other woman nodded. She gathered up the surgeon's kit and stood. "Give 'im a pull off that flask o' yours. I've got to see to Ryan and the others."

Lina waffled a bit. The Cure-All was for Runt. Still, there was plenty— her pet hadn't been drinking it of late. Yet another worry on her mind.

She pulled the flask from her pocket and uncorked it, releasing the overpowering stink of apples into the air between them. "Careful with this," she said, passing it over.

Allen whimpered but accepted the flask. He knew all about the Cure-All by now.

She sighed as his eyes bulged out and he gave a violent cough. Allen thrust the flask back at her and doubled over to pound the blood-spattered deck beneath them with his good hand. When he looked up again, fresh tears streamed anew.

"I can't … I can't feel my finger anymore," he rasped hoarsely. "I can't feel my tongue either."

This wasn't working. It should have been funny, watching Allen flop around. Instead, it just seemed pitiful. "Yeah, that's Cure-All for you." Lina capped the flask and put it away, tempted to take a pull herself.

"Where's Runt?" gasped Allen.

Lina glanced over at the exhaust pipe where she'd last seen her pet. The scryn was there, a little farther down from where he usually relaxed. He hunkered in tight, angry coils, glaring out at the world. With the steam from the rent in the pipe washing over him, Runt looked like some infernal daemon ascended from the Realms Below to harry them all.

Lina didn't understand what had come over him. Usually Runt was downright affectionate after a fight. But at the moment he was so cranky she'd decided he was better off alone. Though it wasn't just now, either. He had been ill-tempered for weeks now, and he was growing more irritable with every passing day. What was going on?

Her mood was blacker by the minute. Maybe she could get him started, like with Paine. "That was brave," she said to Allen, "in the fighting."

"Tried to help where I could," he whispered. Allen forced a weak smile for her, but the Cure-All was making him flush violently—his face was as red as a beet. "Saw you in trouble, I thought. So I came to help." His shoulders slumped. "Now I've lost a finger."

Great. Lina realized she was actually fairly bad at this. Now she felt guilty. She fumbled wordlessly for a response.

Heavy boot steps sounded behind her on the deck. It was Michael Hockton, jogging furiously from the stern of the airship back up to the bow. Lina's heart rose at seeing him. Why had she sought sympathy from Paine? And *Allen?* No, her ex-Bluecoatie soldier would do the trick.

"Hey, yeah, don't worry," she said to Allen distractedly. "Should be fine. I need to go … see to something." She turned away to follow after Hockton. Out of the corner of her eye, she dimly saw Allen staring after her like an abandoned puppy.

Lina jogged up the deck after Michael. She called his name several times, but he did not stop, didn't seem to hear her. She reached him just before the bow and reached out to grab his arm. Michael stopped and spun at the contact. His eyes were wide and his face pale. A fresh cut oozed wetly across his cheek.

Lina pulled back in surprise. "Hey," she said, forcing some girlish excitement into her voice. "How are you doing?"

"I just killed six of my own countrymen," he whispered.

Lina blinked. "What?" He wasn't even looking at her, she realized, just staring past her shoulder.

"I didn't know any of them, but they were just soldiers, like I was."

"They were trying to kill us all," she said, aggravated.

"A year ago, I would have been one of them."

That does it. Her depression and melancholy evaporated, replaced in an instant by irritation. It felt like there were hot burrs under her skin. *Him? Him too? Is anyone on this boat not absorbed in their own little miseries at the moment? Can't they pay attention to* me, *for once, when I need them? Well, to the Realms Below with it. They can all wallow, then. Oh no, I got a finger lopped off. Oh, I killed a bunch of stupid Bluecoats.* She folded her arms angrily.

Hockton blinked and glanced down, seeming to notice her for the first time. "Lina? I—"

A shout from the port-side rigging cut him short. It was Omari, pointing north beyond the bow. "Your stupid island is up ahead!" she shouted.

The island. The one with the Voorn superweapon on it. The point of this stupid trip.

Lina pushed past Michael and strode to the bow. His boot steps echoed up behind her. She ignored them, peering out beyond the confines of the airship. Captain Blackheart and the rest of the crew arrived also, crowding up beside her.

Beneath them stretched the uninhabited portion of the Copper Isles, which were more broken and fragmented here than to the south. No one ever came up this way. The waterways between the islets were wider, almost completely open to the Atalian Sea.

One island lay dead ahead, a round chunk of land maybe a mile across. It was ringed by a fringe of sandy beach that rose up to sharp slopes of brittle rock a few hundred feet above the water. There the slope cut off abruptly, revealing that the island was cratered, like the caldera of a long-dead volcano. Thick jungle growth filled the interior, growing sharply sparse towards the center, where a great golden pyramid poked up. The structure was fanciful and strange, its angles odd to look upon. Lina knew at a glance that it had not been crafted by the hands of men.

"I am *not* going back up where that ape is," said Omari. "How can you even keep such a—"

"Shut up, Omari," said Natasha. She retrieved a spyglass from her hip and peered around the island. "This is the place," she said after a moment. "But where are ... ah!" The pirate captain closed the glass and pointed. "Down there."

Lina followed her gesture, along with everyone else. Natasha pointed at a series of rooftops poking up through the jungle, not too far from the closest part of the southern-facing cliff of the crater. Ramshackle, the buildings were definitely man-made.

"That's where my father's men will be." Natasha turned to stalk back down the deck. "Everyone, get ready—we're putting down there. Maybe we can get this over with quickly and get back to the fight."

Lina watched her go. At her side, Michael leaned down to whisper at her. "Lina ... do you think it's true? That there's some old Voorn weapon here?"

"Whatever," she replied, still angry at him. She threw up her hands and walked away. Why didn't anyone ever care how *she* felt? Well, to the Realms Below with it. She was Lina Stone, of the *Dawnhawk*, and everyone else could go hang.

The trip to the tree houses would have taken hours on foot. The *Dawnhawk* crossed in minutes, descending past the cliff-top boundary of the crater. Natasha brought them down until the airship floated just above an opening in the jungle canopy, through which other buildings could be seen.

Up at the bow, Reaver Jane hoisted the land anchor. It was a heavy, hook-shaped device meant to keep the ship somewhat moored to one place. She let it fall overboard, then unrolled a rope ladder after it.

Beneath Lina's feet the steam engine belowdecks rumbled, downshifting. Natasha had disengaged the propellers. She locked the helm in place and stalked up to Reaver Jane, gesturing for everyone else to attend her. Lina pressed in along with the others.

"All right," said Natasha quietly. "I don't like surprises, but this place looks like it's got more than a priest's bedsheets. Somehow my father has kept that golden pyramid here a secret for the last forty years. Probably because he's got a whole pack of his old crew murdering anyone who ever came down to check. I want as many blades at my back as I can get, which means all of you. Get ready to go ashore. Omari!"

The accidental necromancer started in surprise from the rigging. "What do you want? I'm not one of your crew."

Natasha's grinding teeth was audible. Lina winced. Her captain may have been polishing her social skills, but there were limits to what could be accomplished.

"You aren't one of my crew," snarled Natasha, "but if you don't want me to pitch you over the side, you'll do as I damned well say." She glared at the other woman until Omari looked away. "Now," Natasha continued, "we're going down there, and you're going to pull up the ladder afterward. Don't let it down for anyone but us. Other than that, just keep out of the way and don't touch anything. Got it?"

Omari nodded in wordless reply. Natasha grunted, then fished out *How to Pillage Friends and Intimidate People,* opening it to a dog-eared page. "Also, I appreciate your ass ... assets? Damned smudge. Assistance! I appreciate your assistance in these dire times."

She shut the book and jammed it back down the front of her puffy shirt, only then realizing that everyone was staring at her, Omari included. Natasha growled and jerked her head towards the side of the ship.

Lina paused as the others moved to disembark. What was she forgetting? *Ah.* She ran over and grabbed up Runt. Cranky or not, she didn't go ashore without him. The scryn chirped grumpily but crawled to his customary place across her shoulders.

The ground below the airship was hard packed and clear of any growth. The tree houses were clearly visible now, three shacks built in the spreading branches of two different banyans. A number of smaller huts sagged against the trunks on the ground below, complete with fire pits and clotheslines. A fume of garbage and burned wood filled the air. Yet the encampment appeared completely empty. Lina didn't like how that felt.

"Ahoy there!" cried Natasha as she stepped down from the ladder. Butterbeak joined in from her shoulder, screaming sharply enough that she winced, along with all the other pirates, prompting a swat from the *Dawnhawk's* captain. Both calls echoed about the encampment, unanswered.

"No one's here, Captain," said Reaver Jane. The pirate woman limped around, a cutlass in her hands, peering at the darkest shadows for any threat.

"It figures," replied Natasha flatly. "Decades? Here? Damned pirates probably left after five months."

"I do not think so."

Lina turned like everyone else. It was Etarin, standing beside a fire pit near one of the huts. A thick bandage swathed his neck, and with difficulty he gestured up past the *Dawnhawk* to the cliff walls of the island through the treetops. "Those are sheer," he said. "Too smooth by far to climb, I think. And here, look. This fire is only a day cold, and it was left in a hurry." He stabbed into the pit with his scimitar, lifting the blade to reveal the charred carcass of a small bird on a spit. "Whoever was here left in a hurry."

Lina glanced about. There were other signs of recent occupation: rags hung on the clothesline and an unceremoniously piled trash heap still stinking of refuse. But where had the inhabitants gone?

Natasha sheathed her cutlass. "Fine. We've more important things to do than track down a bunch of fossilized cutthroats. Come. We're here for the pyramid and that Voornish weapon. If we find Euron's old crew along the way, that's fine. I'm not wasting time on them, though. Rastalak, you can tell me how to work the thing, right?"

The little Draykin turned to her in surprise. He looked suddenly awkward as he lifted his hands up in a wordless shrug. "Maybe?"

"Good enough." Natasha whistled up at the *Dawnhawk* and gestured for Omari to pull up the ladder. Then she turned towards the center of the island and stalked out of the camp. One by one the rest of the crew joined her, leaving Lina standing alone.

There was something unsettling about this place. Where was everyone? And why had they left so abruptly? *We're probably only going to find out when it's way too late.*

Lina sighed. She glanced up at the *Dawnhawk*, where Omari had yet to pull up the ladder. Then she ran to catch up.

The undergrowth proved less dense than it had appeared from above, though still thick. Big Farouk moved at the forefront of their pack, hacking down vines and fronds with his blade, and the others followed along untroubled. Rich jungle smells of damp earth and pungent flowers rose from all around them, tinged by the sea-scent breeze of the ocean. Through the treetops she spied the golden peak of the Voornish pyramid, unvarnished and shining in the afternoon sun.

Ahead, Paine ducked a branch, followed by Reaver Jane, who bent it back to pass it. Lina put up her hand to catch it, but moved too slowly. The limb whipped into her face, a tangle of leaves and overgrown vines.

Runt went berserk.

"Chirr!" screamed the scryn. "Chirr!" He hissed and spat poison, thrashing about from her shoulders as Lina disentangled herself from the branch. His coils tightened about her shoulders, restricting her arms and clamping on her neck.

"Runt!" she gasped, slapping at his coils. "Calm down! What's wrong?"

Her pet only hissed in reply. Lurid red light reflected from the fronds and vines all around them.

Michael Hockton moved up beside her. "What's happening?" he asked, concerned, looking like he'd shaken whatever malaise possessed him back aboard the ship. After a moment Allen appeared beside him, eyes red but somewhat recovered from his own ordeal. Alarm showed plainly on the faces of both young men. They weren't stepping *too* close, however.

"It's Runt!" said Lina, trying to simultaneously calm her pet and retain balance against his flailing. "Something hit him in the face, and he just lost it!"

"Ah," said Allen.

"Right," said Michael.

Neither one of them moved to help.

Her pet was usually ill-tempered at the best of times. Ever since the Almhazlik affair, though, he'd been especially cranky. Lina had meant to visit the disgraced veterinarian back in Haventown again, but there hadn't been enough time before the invasion. A tiny pang of fear shook her for the first time. What if her pet was sick? What if he was dying?

"Get over here and help me out!" she snarled.

Michael looked pained. "But what do you want us to *do*, Lina?" Beside him, Allen ducked a stream of poisonous spittle.

Damnable cowards! Really, Lina didn't know why everyone was so wary around Runt. He was perfectly sweet, normally, especially right after he'd eaten a seagull or had a shot of Cure-All. *The flask!* That was it. Maybe Cure-All would work.

Neither man moved. They warily watched her dance about while Runt thrashed.

"If someone could help me with Runt," she said, trying for what she thought was a demure tone, "I'd be ever so grateful."

Both men looked conflicted. They took a step and stopped, simultaneously noticing each other. Determination flashed across their faces, and they both strode over purposefully. Lina wanted to breath a sigh of relief, but her pet was coiled too tightly now for that.

"What should we do?" asked Michael.

"Allen! Get over here and rub his back. Along the scales, like you would a dog."

The Mechanist just stared. "Runt's going to bite me. I don't want to lose another finger!"

"It'll be fine. Now, do you want to help me or not?"

"Runt's going to *bite* me!"

"Michael," she said, ignoring him. "Grab the flask on my hip. You need to feed it to him, slowly. The Cure-All will calm him right down."

"Runt's going to bite *him*," said Allen.

Her ex-soldier grimaced. Then he deflated. He and Allen shared another look before Michael reached for the flask like a man going towards the gallows.

The next few minutes were unpleasant. But at the end of it, Runt was calm again, chirping in an unhappy, drunken daze against her shoulders. Allen had black-and-blue bruises along his face and good hand, and the side of Michael's neck was swelling from a near-miss of poison spittle. The ex-soldier also shook his hand, covered in red, angry scryn bites.

"There, there," Lina cooed, patting Runt along his scaled, wormy coils.

"Why is he so cantankerous?" asked Michael. "Is he … backed up? Your pet is fat, Lina."

"I've never seen him like this before," said Allen. "Well, except that one time he tried to eat my face. And the time he poisoned my food. And that time you threw him at me."

Lina turned to Michael. Even with a red splotchy mark on his neck, he looked gallant. "*Thank* you," she said to him, heartfelt. "Poor little Runtie appreciates it too, even if he doesn't show it. But we both know you care. You've got a special rapport with him, after all." She winked at him.

Michael blushed. He gave an embarrassed shrug. "Well," he said. "Well."

Out of the corner of her eye she saw Allen stand a little prouder, as if waiting for a compliment in turn. Lina wasn't sure why—it was only Allen, after all. Right now Runt was what was important, and she had to say something to Michael while she remembered. He was just *so* dashing. He'd let himself get bitten no less than three times in calming Runt down, after all.

Allen seemed to freeze suddenly. Then he blinked at Lina, standing there with Runt. He looked odd. Angry. Something changed with the apprentice Mechanist.

What's your problem? Lina ignored him. "Who's a sweet thing? Is it my Runtie? Is it?" She turned to the others. "Oh, I hope he isn't getting sick."

"Chirr," muttered her pet.

"He's fat," said Allen sharply. "Probably got a seagull lodged sideways in there."

Michael Hockton sighed. "We should move on. We're still in a strange place, and the others have gone up ahead."

"Whatever," said Allen. He stared at his bandaged hand with a grimace.

"Yes," said Lina. "We'd best catch up."

The others hadn't gotten far. Natasha glared at them when they arrived, but Farouk was still cutting a trail through the undergrowth. As the minutes passed, though, it thinned out, as palm fronds and creeping vines were replaced by open patches of green, growing grass.

Farouk paused at a particularly thick fern and reared back. He swung, parting the plant with ease, and the follow-through pitched him forward through it. After the others pushed through, Lina followed, stepping out into warm sunlight and blue skies.

They'd reached the edge of the jungle, about halfway to the center of the isle. The underbrush and trees faded away, becoming sparse after only a few hundred feet, replaced by open land covered in green grass. The midafternoon sun shone brightly, reflecting from the golden pyramid squatting at the center of the island, alien and strange.

"Well," said Natasha, stepping aside as Rastalak moved to help Farouk up. "This'll make the going easier—"

A monstrous roar cut her short. It echoed out from somewhere else on the island, bestial and strangely tinny.

Everyone drew weapons, peering around warily. Lina eyed the jungle past the pyramid, where it sounded like it had come from. "I think it came—"

She stopped short, though, at seeing her captain's face. Natasha stood rigid, stone-like. Her knuckles were white where they gripped her cutlass, and her face was a mask of enraged hostility. On her shoulder, Butterbeak peered around with frightened eyes, looking as if it might take flight at any moment. Etarin and Farouk shared an incredulous look. Young Paine looked as if he'd seen a ghost.

"No," she hissed. "Impossible."

"What is it, Captain?" asked Ryan Gae.

"Nothing," she said. "Probably just a … jaguar. Or something." She gestured with her cutlass at the pyramid. "Get over there now," she said. "And run."

Warily, Lina did as she was told. The crew of the *Dawnhawk* moved at a jog across the grassy plain, dodging the occasional fern or short palm tree. It felt good to have the sun on her face and the wind in her hair, even though Natasha hissed at them to go faster.

The golden pyramid containing the Stormhammer grew as they approached. It was Voornish, certainly, a stair-step structure rising a hundred feet above the ground. Etchings and bas-reliefs dotted its sides. She was still too far away to make them out clearly, but Lina knew they would represent a strange, long-limbed people. Beside her, Rastalak hissed in familiar wonder. His people inhabited ruins such as these, still standing after uncounted millennia.

The pyramid was not completely immune to the ravages of time, however. A great golden spire had once stood at its peak, rising up even higher above the crater. It had fallen now, snapped free from its mooring, though the base of it was still propped up across the top of the pyramid. The rest of the spire ran down to the ground, its tip buried beneath the surface of the earth like a needle stuck in a seamstress's thumb.

More details became apparent as they ran towards the building. A rectangular opening appeared in its nearest face. Only eight feet tall or so, it was wide enough for the entire crew to enter its darkened interior abreast. Before the entrance, on the ground, lay a mess of components, both Voornish relics and primitive tools, along with rough-hewn planks and hempen rope. Something very much like a canoe caught Lina's eye, which appeared to be made from cobbled-together pieces of Voornish brass.

The pirate crew slowed as they reached the entryway to the pyramid. "What is all this?" asked Farouk, gesturing with his cutlass.

"Must be the work of Euron's crewmen," said Reaver Jane.

The monstrous roar sounded again, closer this time, as if just around the pyramid. Everyone stilled, raising their weapons and looking about.

"That is no jaguar," said Rastalak.

Lina heard something else now too: heavy footfalls and a mechanical hiss, as of steam escaping. The ground shook.

Etarin turned to Natasha. "Captain," he said, "Goddess strike me down, but that sounds like—"

"No," she replied. "It's just not possible." She turned to the others. "Get inside. *Now!*"

They rushed into the darkened entryway, going about fifty feet before reaching a much greater space, which smelled of ozone and unwashed bodies.

Standing just inside that main chamber was a small group of maybe a dozen people, all somewhat elderly. They were greying, their skin wrinkled and suntanned. Some had long, scraggly beards. A mix of Perinese and Salomcani, it was obvious by the rags they wore and the swords at their sides that they had all been pirates at one time. They looked wary—and more than a little crazed.

Runt hissed drunkenly at them from Lina's shoulder. Her other crewmates spread out, wary. Natasha pushed forward, sheathing her blade. "Hello there, then. Who are you lot?"

They looked uneasily at each other. One man, with a long grey beard and an eye patch made of ancient leather stepped forward to meet her. "We be the Castaways," he said, voice thick with the old Haventown accent. "Euron Blackheart's crew, left behind on this accursed isle. How did ye get here? And how did ye escape the beast?"

Lina relaxed. This was the group they were looking for.

Natasha turned her attention back to the Castaways. She breathed a sigh of relief. The rest of the *Dawnhawk*'s crew lowered their weapons, following her lead. "I got here on an airship," she said. "And you're just the ones I've been looking for."

Outside, the tread of something enormous shook the earth.

CHAPTER ELEVEN

Admiral Wintermourn glanced at the bomb falling towards him.

A grapefruit-sized sphere of black iron with a fuse fizzing merrily away at one end, it was close enough to touch, one of several thrown from the pirate airship *Solrun's Hammer* flying above. He slapped at the thing, sending it bouncing off the forward railing and tumbling down to the main deck of the *Colossus* below.

"Load faster," he roared, turning his attention back to his gunner's mate and the starboard gun crew below. Their firing angles were too sharp here in the Graveway Lagoon. There was only a tiny window when they could hit the old fort above them, even with grapeshot and the elevated cannons. *We need to fire, and it needs to be now!* "Load faster, Goddess damn you—"

The bomb exploded below him. Its blast shivered the stern cabin deck he stood upon and sent lethal metal shards whipping up past his outstretched hand, missing by only inches. The flash of light lit the rear of the warship in a moment of stark illumination, highlighting nearby sailors and the other falling bombs.

Their blasts seemed fiercer, eager to outdo their companion. Two burst up near the bow while the third detonated in the rigging amidships, directly above the port-side gunnery crews. What remained of the pirate salvo splashed into the lagoon off to port between his ship and Captain Caldwell's *Titan*. The damned foolish pirates had let loose too early.

Wintermourn shook his head to clear away the afterimages of the bombs from his vision. Victory was at hand, here in the Graveway Lagoon. His *Colossus* worked together with the *Titan* to rake the Salomcani fort as best they could with cannon fire, circling the burning wreck of the *Ogre* and the

Powderheart, where what remained of both vessels slowly sank in the middle of the lagoon. Along the southern cliff wall, Captain Roderick's *Giantess* sat anchored firmly, his company of Bluecoat marines ascending with the support of their compatriots who had already made the climb.

A few pirates remained at the walls of the fort, firing irregular musket volleys. They did little more than blunt the advance, though. Most of the ruffians were in full retreat, and all their airships save *Solrun's Hammer* lumbered behind the fort down low to the jungle. Dozens of lines and rope ladders dangled from each airship, each thick with pirates desperate to escape.

Crown Prince Gwydion's plan to win the Graveway had been an audacious gamble. Wintermourn had to admit that it had worked, though he still raged at the cost. All repairs had been ceased upon the *Ogre,* and instead Captain Thomasen's beleaguered warship was loaded with as much ordnance as could be spared. Sufficiently full, she was sent to the Graveway alone with a timed fuse in her powder magazine and her sails half-furled to hide the deck from above.

One of the pirates had taken the bait, just as hoped. The *Powderheart* fell on the *Ogre,* ignoring both the cliff guns and the airship's own allies in its eagerness to duplicate Euron Blackheart's earlier success. Then the fuse lit off, killing the pirates and the *Ogre* both. The blast had been apocalyptic, igniting the airship's gas bag and sending a fireball raging up into the sky. Even Wintermourn found himself impressed by the explosion.

Other pirate vessels moved to assist their fallen, but the cliff guns and the score of Brass Paladins aboard the *Glory* pounded them fiercely, causing severe damage and driving them back off. Wintermourn had then ordered the charge. While angered by loss of the navy ship, it would have been foolish not to capitalize on what the sacrifice had bought them.

Of the pirate airships, only *Solrun's Hammer* had tried to drive them back. Now she tried to escape, turning ponderously as shells from the cliff guns burst across her gas bag. The pirate vessel would pay dearly for bombing the *Colossus.*

"Sir!"

Wintermourn glanced over his shoulder. It was Lieutenant Lebam, taking a half step from the helm and reaching out to him.

"Sir!" he repeated. "That blast ... are you all right?

Wintermourn rounded on the man. "Take your other hand away from that wheel, and I'll chop it off myself," he snarled. "Slow us down and keep on heading. I want that round of shots at the fort before we turn aside."

His lieutenant drew back, chastened. Beside him, ex-captain Thomasen stood, stone-faced and angry. The man hadn't been required to captain his ship on its suicide run, though maybe it would have been a kinder fate. Even with his decades of service, he was unlikely to gain another commission. Now he lingered about, just another officer without a ship on which to serve. A small part of Wintermourn recognized the unfairness of it, and perhaps something might be done after the invasion—a small sloop or some such. Still, he felt the ingrained disdain any career naval officer would have of a man who'd been demoted, whatever the reason behind it.

The gunner's mate shouted from the deck below. His guns thundered in response, rocking back, almost toppling completely over from their elevated positions as they spit fire and thunder along the railing. Their shots hammered the old Salomcani fort, the grapeshot gouging into the native stone, collapsing a section of wall, and even skipping up off the roof, past which the majority of the pirates were ascending to their airships. Wintermourn saw a ball sever one rope line completely. The pirates dangling from it screamed as they fell down into the jungle. The shot had been one in a million. Still, he would take it.

Those crewmen not too injured gave a raucous cheer at the volley. Admiral Wintermourn approved of their spirits. It wouldn't have been appropriate to join in or do something so vulgar as pound his fist against the rail. Instead, he pursed his lips, not quite allowing himself to smile.

There wasn't time or room enough to fire again. It did not matter—the guns had done their work. The Bluecoats above were charging, their yells echoing down to the water as the defenders recovered from the cannon volley. Some of them managed to rally, but the answering shots were inadequate, felling just a single marine before his brothers leaped over the walls and into the interior. In minutes it would be over. The Graveway Lagoon belonged to the Kingdom now.

Admiral Wintermourn allowed himself to relax a little. *The scoundrels are routed and their fort taken. That's another victory sorted.* "Bring us back around alongside the *Giantess*," he said to Lebam. "I am going up once the fort is secured."

"Aye, sir," replied the lieutenant.

Thomasen moved up to the rail to stand behind Wintermourn. "Well," he snorted. "At least we've won through. I'd have hated to have sacrificed my ship on some damned boondoggle."

Wintermourn stiffened, feeling the usual affront at such presumed familiarity. While he had actually known Thomasen a goodly time, it still wasn't any excuse. Turning to deliver a sharp chastisement, he paused upon seeing the ex-captain's face. Behind the well-practiced countenance of a stern naval officer hid something raw.

The man had good reason for the emotion. What had been done was downright infuriating. Gwydion had ordered an entire warship sacrificed for the sake of a fleeting tactical advantage. True, the tactic had won them the day, and the *Ogre* had been worst off of all the fleet at the moment. Fire ships weren't anything new in the history of naval warfare. Such things simply weren't *done*, however. A ship might be lost in glorious combat, but to throw it away as if it were worth so little as the men who crewed it? To use it as a … a trap?

Not that it would do to make such thoughts clear, even to his senior captains. "We have managed no less than I expected," Wintermourn lied. "The *Ogre* proved us the superior force. Take heart in that, Thomasen, if nothing else."

"I don't think I'm getting a royal appointment out of it," replied the man in ill humor.

"No," agreed Wintermourn. "Likely not." Chesterly's reassignment as royal adjutant still rankled. Who did the crown prince think he was, to assign such an inexperienced, undeserving minion such a plum of a post?

He turned his attention to the Bluecoat running down the deck. It was Sergeant Adjutant Lanters, his blue uniform bloodied and his round black cap all torn. The man climbed up the stern cabin and made his salute.

"Sir," said the sergeant, a finger-long splinter embedded in the meat of his shoulder. He didn't appear to give it notice, of which Wintermourn approved.

"Yes, Sergeant? Out with it."

"The other lads up top signal that they've taken the fort."

The sergeant adjutant's voice was as subservient as ever, but Wintermourn could tell that he was unhappy. The man had wanted to be part of the charge, where the fighting was thickest and the most glory could be gained.

Wintermourn had refrained from sending his own company of marines into the assault, though. It seemed only prudent. Along with the *Titan*, the *Colossus* had kept up the battle from the water, shelling the fort and braving bombardment from the pirate airships above. He hadn't thought it too unlikely that some of the damned fools would try to board, even after the death of the *Powderheart*. Among their many failings, pirates simply didn't seem to learn. And he hadn't intended to get butchered by some last-ditch show of desperation.

"Very good," he replied. "Signal back that I will be coming ashore personally to inspect the site. I want a cordon set—"The thump of the cliff battery at the western edge of the lagoon interrupted him. Looking up, he watched shells burst in the air all about *Solrun's Hammer*. The now-fleeing airship gave a violent shudder in return. Flames shot from the semirigid gas bag as it ripped out along the stern, a propeller exploded, and men flew screaming from a lucky shot that slipped along her decks. The airship managed to hold together somehow, though, and ponderously moved out of range, flying past the fort and above the channel leading east, straight for port in Haventown with the rest of the retreating foe.

"Aye, sir," said Lanters. He completed his salute and retreated to find the signalman.

Other ships entered the lagoon as First Lieutenant Lebam brought the *Colossus* up alongside the *Giantess,* moored to the southern cliff. With the enemy in full retreat, it was safe to advance the new steamship, which was capable of maneuvers that would have been impossible with an older vessel. The other ships presented a stirring tableaux, their gunports open and at the ready, ranks of marines in blue at her rails. Still, the sinking wreckage in the middle of the lagoon caught his eye.

The *Colossus* pulled up alongside the *Giantess,* sending a shiver through both ships as they touched hulls. Lines were tossed over and made fast. As soon as the boarding ramp had been extended, Wintermourn crossed over, followed by Lanters and a small honor guard of Bluecoats. Captain Roderick, commander of the *Giantess,* was waiting for him, the toady, and began an obviously rehearsed bit of fluff congratulating him on the larger victory. Wintermourn paid him no mind. Instead, he went straight to the far side of the vessel, where a rope ladder and a bosun's chair dangled against the cliff face, each held by a sailor. Wintermourn sat upon the chair, disdainful though it was, and barked a command. In moments he rose in jerky fits up the cliff.

A bosun's chair was a simple bench attached to two ropes, much like a swing. Usually he avoided them. They were perfect for situations like this, though, where the alternative was a hundred-foot climb up a swaying rope ladder. As much as it galled Wintermourn to think on, he wasn't all that young anymore. The chair lacked dignity, but arriving at the top winded and out of sorts would be simply unconscionable.

Two *Giantess* Bluecoats grabbed for him once he'd reached the top. Wintermourn swallowed his disapproval at the contact and let them assist for just long enough to find his feet. He nodded as they made their obeisance, then turned away to view the top of the cliff.

It was much as he'd expected from below. Verdant jungle undergrowth grew thickly, running out from the recessed tree line to spill over the edge of the cliff. The only exceptions were the artillery battery they'd built to the west and the Salomcani fort up ahead. A loose path of sorts had been torn through the foliage by the Bluecoat charge.

The place wasn't much to look at. But this was what he'd come for: to stand on something the enemy had held, something that he'd taken from them.

Wintermourn waited impatiently for Lanters and his men to finish their ascent. "Come along then," he said as they rose over the cliff, and then pushed his way in the direction of the fort. Behind and below, Captain Roderick's voice echoed up, plaintively telling the men to hurry with the chair.

The Salomcani fort wasn't much to look at anymore. If any decoration had improved it at an earlier time, it had long since been wiped away. Now the fort was a simple square of weathered and gun-battered stone, open to the lagoon past a crenellated wall that hid the cannon emplacements. Wintermourn disdained that entrance in favor of a hole blown into one wall by fortuitous cannon fire.

Inside, the place was just as dull as the exterior. Blood and gun smoke fumed the air, but there were surprisingly few pirate bodies. They lay still, all slain in battle or savagely executed by the marines, their faces frozen in rage, fear, or horror. Admiral Wintermourn watched them a long moment, half expecting them to rise up as unholy Revenants seeking revenge.

There were few other exits: an arched opening led out back to the jungle, and a stairway in the floor that led to lower levels. Marines tended minor wounds and stood about chatting idly; the fort was secure.

Sergeant Adjutant Lanters bellowed out, calling attention to their presence. The other squad sergeants stepped to, roaring orders and driving the rest of the men to weary attention. Wintermourn gave a cursory nod, mildly enjoying their respect. He did not smile, though, quickly pressing his way past the men, looking to the walls, the roof, and the walkway with its cannon emplacements. Nothing would make it a proper Perinese fortification. But it could be repaired and fortified—there was still value here. *I'll need to pull masons and carpenters up from the fleet. We'll move the cliff battery here—maybe we can get better facing from the roof?*

The clatter of boots and muttered cursing told him that Captain Roderick had arrived. Surprisingly, First Lieutenant Thomasen was with him as well. Wintermourn raised an eyebrow, though he shouldn't have been surprised. It wasn't like the man had anywhere else to go.

"Sergeant Adjutant," he said, turning back to Lanters. "What do you think about these walls? Should they be reinforced?"

"Don't know, sir," he replied. "Far one looks a bit shoddy."

"Aye," added Roderick, pushing into the conversation. "We'll need to get the masons and carpenters up to take a look. Shouldn't be too hard though, eh?"

The man was an idiot. Wintermourn prepared a withering retort. A shadow fell across the fort exterior, though, cutting him off. It was the *Glory*, crossing the lagoon to the fort. Shouts from marines out back made it clear that the airship was descending. Wintermourn frowned and walked over to the rear exit. He should have expected this. It was inevitable that the crown prince would have wanted to consult after the battle.

That didn't mean that Wintermourn was looking forward to it.

Out back, the airship hung overhead like some ugly mechanical bird. It made its way down, propellers buzzing to hold it somewhat stationary. The hull had barely touched the ground before the ramp shot out and the crown prince stormed down onto the newly claimed Perinese soil, outpacing his ever-present guards while Captain Broadlow watched from along the gunwales.

Gwydion had replaced his torn finery, looking again as he had before haring off on his ill-advised chase after the *Dawnhawk*. The prince seemed far from stately at the moment, though, as his features were screwed up in consternation. One hand was tight on his hip, holding the relic Danlann in place as he stalked over.

"What are you *doing?*" he demanded.

Wintermourn drew himself up stiffly at the tone. The sheer *cheek* of this lad. He may have been the prince, but Wintermourn was still Lord High Admiral of the Sea, one of the Order Gallant. "Surveying the ground we've just taken," he replied, reaching up to straighten his wig. "I would have thought it obvious."

"I can see that," Gwydion said, an edge of irritation to his voice. "But why, in the Goddess's name?"

Wintermourn pursed his lips and gave the crown prince his best condescending look. It was a good one, which he'd worked years at perfecting. "Apparently," he said slowly, "there is still much for you to learn, sir. For all of its shoddy construction, this fort is an immeasurably better spot for entrenchment than what we've got across the lagoon. We'll repurpose it, move the naval banner from the cliff battery, and turn it into an excellent forward base for the rest of the assault."

"Only if we are damned fools." Gwydion gestured behind him, past the *Glory*, at the jungle to the east. "The pirates are injured, on the run. We'll never have a better time to press our advantage than we have now."

"Impossible," said Captain Roderick.

Gwydion looked at him in surprise, one eyebrow upraised. "I wasn't talking to you. Say another word, Captain, if you want to be a midshipman."

Captain Roderick rocked back in surprise. Wintermourn merely sighed. "My prince, Captain Roderick is correct. We may have taken the lagoon for now, but haring off willy-nilly for Haventown will only raise the stakes. Doctrine is clear: a forward base is needed to support the next step of the assault. That way we're not pushed completely out of these islands should we fail. A steady, unstoppable advance. That is how these things are done."

"I don't care a used apple for doctrine, and we both know the pirates aren't going to do any pushing back unless we give them time to lick their wounds! Get back down to those boats and push on to Haventown! Now is the time to make haste."

"Because haste worked so well for you this morning," growled Wintermourn. He looked exaggeratedly about. "Oh. But I don't see that pirate airship you wanted so badly to capture."

The crown prince glared at him with eyes like grey ice. "It worked well enough last night, and got us this far, when your lot would have sat out there on the ocean, content to suffer a bombing that would have sent us packing back to Edrus. I am not reasoning with you, Admiral. This is an order. Get everyone back down aboard the ships and push on through." He pointed a sharp finger at Roderick. "You're in the vanguard, and the *Colossus* is behind, followed by the *Titan*. Now get moving, or I'll see you all broken! And capture any Mechanists you come across!"

Wintermourn bristled. *Insolent, foolish pup. Spoiled rotten princeling.* He grit his teeth to keep from saying any of this. Instead, he gave a short, sharp nod before turning on his heel and walking angrily away.

Lanters shadowed him, as expected. Captain Roderick rushed up to follow, joined by Thomasen. Wintermourn ignored them both, not trusting himself to speak. Fortunately, Thomasen had no such compunctions.

"That boy is a damned fool," said the ex-captain, looking back over his shoulder as he did so. "Who does he think he is, to ignore centuries of tradition?"

"The Crown Prince of the Kingdom of Perinault," snarled Wintermourn in response.

They reached the ladder back down to the *Giantess*, where the Bluecoat guards still stood at attention. Lanters moved to assist with the bosun's chair, but Roderick paid no attention to it. Instead, he glanced furtively back over his shoulder, then reached out and grabbed Wintermourn's sleeve.

Wintermourn rounded on him, outraged. But he held back at the look of earnest furtiveness on Roderick's face. "Sir," he said. "A moment. We do not *have* to listen to his ineffectual chirping. All the others agree: we should have held back offshore and waited for the pirates, battered them at sea, and then sent in the marines as was planned. Luck has held so far, but it's only a matter of time before this fiasco crushes us all. The king surely would understand."

"That is a treasonous line of thinking," snapped Wintermourn. "Whatever we think of him, personally or professionally, the boy will one day be our liege lord." He yanked his arm free, though not as harshly as he could have. "No, we follow his commands, as is our duty." He made to turn away, then stopped. "And by doing so," he continued in a whisper, "we give him just enough rope to hang himself."

Captain Roderick stared a moment before nodding sharply. "Very good, sir," he said, standing up straight. "We'll move our lads back aboard, then prepare to lead the assault."

He stood aside, gesturing for Wintermourn to take the chair. Wintermourn returned the nod, then sat. As the marines lowered him, he watched the naval vessels flowing into the lagoon. *For all that the princeling barks, these ships are mine. I am the Lord High Admiral of the Sea—the navy listens to me, seamen and marines both. He would do well to remember that.*

Once back aboard the *Colossus,* he gave full vent to his ire. The lieutenants were called to order and berated soundly, then allowed to return to the task of repairs and preparations for the assault. They took their own irritation out on the rest of the crew, driving them to speedy progress. The blood on the deck was washed with sand. Debris and broken rigging were removed. Spare powder and ammunition were brought up from the magazine. The elevated cannons were shifted free of their complicated carriages and recalibrated. Quickly, the moans of the injured and the weary complaints of sailors were replaced by the sounds of industrious labor. Wintermourn approved, unsmiling as always. Aboard his ship, men knew their duty. Not that it ever hurt to put the fear of the Goddess into them.

Wintermourn chose the order of battle in accordance with the prince's wishes, then conveyed it to the rest of the invasion force. He ordered the marines back aboard from the clifftop to the ships marked for the vanguard. Quietly, Wintermourn spread word for a small force to remain with the battery of antiairship guns and move them up to the old fort. Even the querulous crown prince couldn't disagree with protecting those weapons still in the field. Or if he did, no word came down from above.

In short order, everything was ready and in position. The order was given, and the *Giantess* led the way into the eastern channel, followed by the *Colossus*, then the *Titan*. After the vanguard came the remaining warships, each chock-full of Bluecoat marines and battle-hardened sailors. The waterway wasn't quite so narrow as those that came before. It still wouldn't allow two ships abreast but lacked the twists and tight turns that threatened to dash them up against the cliff walls of the channel.

Shouts echoed down from the foliage atop the cliffs as pirate stragglers tried to outrace the warships on foot and return home with a warning. A few seemed to find their backbones, as evidenced by the pop and smoke of musket fire among the foliage. They caused only a handful of light wounds, however, and brought a fusillade of return fire from the Brass Paladins aboard the *Glory* above. Wintermourn sharply reissued his commands for the marines to hold fire. It would have been satisfying to annihilate the upstarts, but only the *Glory* had any chance of hitting them now. These few pirates wouldn't be a real threat unless joined from above by their airships.

Which there was no chance of at all. The rest of the enemy was gone. Trails of black smoke hung across the otherwise empty sky; even *Solrun's Hammer* had escaped intact. Those few that could be glimpsed were all directly to the east, fallen back to their home port in search of safety. Which they wouldn't find. With every moment the fleet closed the distance. In the waters below, Wintermourn spied the corpses of pirates that had fallen in the frenetic retreat from the Graveway. *Before we're done, these waters will be choked with Haventown dead.* It was a promise he intended to keep. And then they'd burn the bodies, just to be safe.

The end of the channel appeared past the *Giantess* up ahead. Wintermourn felt the old thrill seize him. Regardless of how they'd gotten here, the real objective was now in sight. He had his officers ready the men. It was a redundant order, but a good one to give all the same.

"Sergeant Adjutant, prepare the marines. First Lieutenant, we push on directly for the nearest dock; beach us if you have to. The rest of you—"

Cries of alarm called back from the *Giantess* as the warship entered the lagoon. Wintermourn looked ahead to see the stern of the vanguard ship veer hard to port, the paddlewheels along her hull suddenly churning. Then the cacophony of twin broadsides erupted from beyond.

Their thunder echoed down the channel, followed a heartbeat later by the sounds of splitting wood and tearing metal. Men in blue coats went flying from the ship and down into the water of the lagoon—or to hammer against the cliff wall.

Wintermourn stared. The pirates had been waiting for them. He slowly nodded in satisfaction. *Good.*

The *Giantess* hadn't quite cleared the channel mouth, but close. Wintermourn rounded to face his first lieutenant, pointing for the gap. "Make to starboard, full steam ahead!"

Lebam nodded, grabbed the speaking tube beside the wheel, and relayed the command down to the engine room. In moments the rumble beneath the deck changed as they were received. The *Colossus* sped down the waterway, veering for the gap between the stern of the injured vanguard warship and the wall of the ravine.

The gap closed from fifty yards away to twenty to none at all. *Too narrow!* Wintermourn had just a moment to brace himself. The bow of the warship slid through easily enough, but the great paddlewheel housings along the hull were too wide. Everyone on deck staggered as the ship collided along its outer edges, the housings ringing against the cliff face and the stern of the *Giantess* like a pair of great brass bells. Metal squealed and tore, but still they slid by, momentum pushing them through. Then it was over, and the *Colossus* was in Haventown Lagoon.

The pirates were indeed ready for them. The lagoon here was as large as the Graveway, fed by a number of smaller waterways. Two ships floated at anchor just inside the mouth, *Fortune's Loss* and the *Saltspray*, canted to present their broadsides straight on to the invaders, their crews busily reloading. The path between them led straight to Haventown on the opposite end of the lagoon, where the pirate township rose from a series of terraces cut out of the cliff wall itself, webbed over by brass pipes. All of the retreating pirate airships were here, floating above, attached to the highest terrace. A single airship, the *Moonchaser*, hovered directly overhead, ready to bombard any Perinese vessel that made it within the lagoon.

Wintermourn considered quickly. It was barest luck that they'd pushed through as they had. They could weather anything the *Moonchaser* dropped, but if those ships fired again ...

He didn't mean to let that happen. "Straight on down their throat," he roared. "Gunnery crews, fire as you bear!" A quick check back revealed that the impact had pushed the injured *Giantess* out of the channel's mouth. The assault could continue, so long as the *Colossus* opened the path for the other ships.

The calls of the gunner's mate rang out as they pulled abreast between the *Saltspray* and *Fortune's Loss,* both older ships lacking in modern steam-driven technology but no less deadly for that. Their crews swore insults and fired muskets. His own cannons gave answer as both port and starboard gun crews fired away. A few of the pirates' own cannon crews had managed to reload, and for a moment everything was a senseless chaos of sulfurous gunsmoke, shattered wood, and the screams of dying men.

Then it was over. The *Colossus* was through. Half-deafened, Wintermourn thought he heard the pop of muskets shot and bomb bursts from the *Moonchaser* above. Most of the Bluecoats and sailors hunkered on the deck below; only a few had been slain by an unlucky cannon shot.

Dead ahead lay the lowest levels of the pirate township, where a series of piers stretched out into the lagoon. Wintermourn picked the nearest, at the far end, then turned back to order Lebam towards it.

The first lieutenant was dead. His corpse slumped against the helm wheel, a hunk of ruined meat. Behind him, Thomasen had been blasted as well, along with the remainder of Wintermourn's own useless lieutenants. Even the sunburst flag flapping from the rear of the ship had been shredded. The sight gave him pause. He had not even felt the blast that killed them all, and only a quirk of positioning had saved him from the same fate.

There but for the grace of the Goddess … well. This hadn't been his first close call, not by far. It certainly wouldn't be the last, and he hadn't gotten to where he was by being useless.

Wintermourn moved to the helm and kicked Lebam's corpse away from it. He grabbed the wheel and threw it, feeling his ship twist them straight for the empty berth at the bottom of the pirate township docks.

Damnation. I'm going to have to find a new helmsman now.

The plumes of cannon fire bloomed along the terraces of the city, flinging iron balls that called up great waterspouts in the waters of the lagoon. It was impossible to see where the guns were hidden—the pirate haven seemed a ramshackle warren of sagging buildings and firetrap alleyways, all stacked one atop the other.

The pirate town grew with every moment. Men cried on the deck and fell still. Wintermourn barely heard himself as he roared commands to hold, to prepare to go ashore, to *hold*, by the Goddess, or he'd see them all dance from the yardarm.

Pirates and townsfolk appeared on the docks ahead. Some were on the ships, some were on the piers, and a few hunkered atop the lower rooftops, muskets and ancient blunderbusses and even crossbows at hand. Wintermourn saw both men and women ready to fight, young and old. He curled his lip at them. The Haventowners couldn't even muster a proper group of defenders. They were uncultured savages.

A musket ball whipped past his head. Wintermourn grimaced and grabbed for the speaking tube as the prow of his warship passed the end of the starboard pier. He shouted down the tube to the engine room, calling for a full stop. Too late. The *Colossus* gave a great shudder as her bow slammed into the boardwalk, which snapped and crunched like kindling as the vessel pushed even farther into a shoddy warehouse, which violently arrested its motion. Wintermourn was flung up against the wheel. Through the spokes he saw the Bluecoats on the deck below topple as well.

Sergeant Adjutant Lanters knew his role, though. The man was on his feet in an instant, shouting for the men to advance ashore, for king and country. They responded by throwing down the boarding ramps and pouring out onto enemy territory with a roar on their lips and weapons in their hands, a blue-backed, black-capped army.

Wintermourn used the wheel to pull himself back up to his feet. He glanced around his ship, battered and broken by the charge, a season's repair in dock by his estimate. Blood pooled around the corpses of sailor and Bluecoat alike, littering the deck like so much debris.

The damage to his ship dismayed him, as did the part his own reckless bit of seamanship had played. But he looked out back across the lagoon to where the other warships followed in his wake, tearing the defender vessels to pieces as they came. He looked up to where Crown Prince Gwydion engaged the *Moonchaser* and Brass Paladins fired from the *Glory of Perinault*. Most of all he looked out at the Bluecoat marines surging onto the piers with muskets and smallswords and the sunburst flag of Perinault at hand, driving back the degenerate pirates, whores, and vagabonds with blade and ball. He decided that the cost to get here had been worth it—any cost would have been.

Finally, Admiral Wintermourn let himself smile.

CHAPTER TWELVE

Captain Fengel ignored the pop of musket fire and considered the question calmly.

He rubbed at his beard as they made their way down the Flophouse Terrace boardwalk. "Aha," he said, snapping his fingers. "Eight-Eyes. That's what I called him."

Beside him, Mechanist-Aspirant Imogen stumbled. Her boots made a staccato tromp as she fought the weight of her satchel for balance. Recovering, she stared up at him, face still somewhat puffy from her allergies. "That's Mechanist Second Class Isaacs," she said, scandalized. "He's responsible for all things involving optics. The goggles he wears are his own invention."

"They still makes him look like a damned prat," Fengel replied in vexation, stepping once more past Cubbins. The fat orange tabby cat was seemingly inexhaustible in his affection and had gamely kept up with their pace.

Haventown's middle terrace was frantic as they threaded their way through the narrow alleys along its southern edge. Townsfolk boarded up windows and passed out weapons while Mechanists ran on orders of the Cabal. The sounds of battle raging down in the lagoon drove them on, their widespread panic only barely checked at the moment.

Fengel had hoped for more time to prepare. He had hoped that Natasha would find Euron's Voorn relic and make all this moot. The sight of the pirate airships returning to port took care of that, though. It seemed their only chance now was the mad scheme of the Mechanist Cabal.

A part of him wanted to join in the panic. The Perinese had moved far more quickly than he would have thought possible. He wanted to rush up to the Skydocks and find out what had happened, to get news of Henry Smalls and the others, to organize the defense. But he had a command again now, and the enemy was at the gates. *Never let them see you stumble.*

Imogen, however, didn't quite have his discipline. Her worry was well-hidden, but Fengel heard the quaver in her voice and the hurry with which she moved. He distracted her as best he could, at least until they could reach the light-air mines beneath the town. So far it seemed to be working.

"What did you call the others?" she asked, adjusting her satchel. Fengel didn't know what was in it, only that she'd retrieved it on their way out from the Brotherhood Yards, refusing to say what it held.

The airship *Moonchaser* flew overhead. Her crew fired muskets with abandon, aiming for something out in the lagoon. Fengel pretended unconcern. "Well, there's the one with all the watches on his sleeve. So, Timekeeper."

Imogen laughed, then hid her mouth, abashed. "That's Mechanist Second Class Granville. He's all about efficiency."

"Then there was the tall, stiff fellow. Never moved much. All burned up?" Fengel gave her a shrug as they walked. "Scorch just seemed to fit."

The young Mechanist snickered. "Mechanist Second Class Thaddeus. Responsible for all welding operations."

"Can't say I liked the fellow much," continued Fengel. "But there was the one with the breathing apparatus? Wheezer."

"It's a mechanical lung," said Imogen, her tone partially chiding. "Mechanist Second Class Merrywether was born one short. He oversees all pumping and exhaust operations."

"And there was that last fellow, with the artificial leg? The rest of your Cabal, they seemed to defer to him. What's he in charge of?"

"That's Mechanist Second Class Harland. He's more or less the leader of the Brotherhood these days. Since he and my fa … I mean, since he and Mechanist First Class Helmsin worked so closely together." She kept only half an eye on the boardwalk ahead, curiosity and dread warring across her features. "What did … what did you call him?"

Fengel stopped at a junction between a fisherman's hut, a black apothecary, and a sailmaker. They were at the southern end of the Flophouse Terrace, near the stair that would take them down to the next part of Haventown. He turned to Imogen squarely, then paused for dramatic effect.

"Clangfoot."

The young woman doubled over with a howl of laughter. Fengel smiled. Even Cubbins purred, catching up and winding figure eights around his boots.

Ear-splitting thunder roared out beyond the town in the lagoon. He'd heard the sound often enough in his time. *A full broadside. Ninety-six guns, by the sound of it—definitely Perinese.* The blast could have been meant for either the *Saltspray* or *Fortune's Loss*. Both ships had been positioned to stop any advance on the town—an excellent idea, though whose precisely, he did not know. If either took a beating, he hoped it was Cadmus's ship. *Still, Matice is a tough bird, if a trifle odd. If worse comes to worst, she'll—*

An eruption of splinters pelted him as the sailmaker's shack burst apart. Fengel had a split-second glimpse of a heavy black cannonball as it passed within inches of Imogen's skull.

A part of him reacted instantly, and reflexes honed over a lifetime came into play as the projectile flew past. He tackled Imogen, and they landed roughly on the boardwalk with his arms up to cover their heads. Bits of board and building rained down about them as other cannonballs ripped through the Flophouse terrace. The thunder and commotion faded after a moment, replaced by yells of panic and the screams of the wounded.

He uncovered a bit, looking at Imogen. The apprentice Mechanist lay stunned, staring wildly about. "Are you all right?" he asked.

She stared at him, eyes wide. "I don't know how to answer that."

Fengel climbed to his feet. He glanced about and held out a hand to lift her up. Devastation surrounded them, as this part of the terrace had shattered. The buildings, so narrow and close only moments ago, were now roofless ruins, gaping up from the boardwalk beneath them like jagged teeth. Midday sunlight washed over them now, impeded only by the smoke and dust hanging in the air. Sailcloth lay heaped with broken glassware from the apothecary, though a few racks were still standing, stocked with noxious medicines. Beyond, the edge of the Flophouse Terrace fell away.

Fengel left Imogen to clamber among the wreckage. A cursory glance told him that there was no one among the ruins. He moved to the rear of the former shops and looked out at the war being fought.

Fengel felt his jaw fall open and his monocle fall free. *I can't believe it.* Natasha's mission to find the Stormhammer was pointless now. Perinese warships were streaming into Haventown Lagoon. The *Saltspray* and *Fortune's Loss* were beleaguered, raked with the deck guns and muskets of the enemy, even as they were held tight by other vessels attempting to board. Above, Captain Weatherby's *Moonchaser* dueled with the *Glory of Perinault*, giving worse than they got in return. In the waters just below floated the *Titan*, her port-side guns smoking from the broadside she'd fired. Fengel vowed quietly to see that ship sink.

There wasn't time for that, though. The enemy wasn't just in the lagoon, which seemed impossible enough. They were already *here*, in the town. Fengel had a perfect view of both the Craftwright's Terrace and the wide crescent of the Waterdocks below it, both stretching northward along the cliff of the lagoon. And at the far northwest end of the bottom terrace, a single warship had rammed itself into port, knocking half a warehouse down after weathering the worst that Cadmus and Matice could offer. The damage was immaterial, though. Bluecoats swarmed the piers and streets near her hull, fighting the immediate defenders in the area. The line of the conflict was only several streets away from the old Smuggler's Warehouse, which he needed to reach.

"They fired on us!" coughed Imogen, climbing beside him. She waved away noxious smoke. "They fired on the town! We're not all pirates here. I mean, not mostly."

"Our friends in blue aren't making much distinction," Fengel replied grimly. "They want us gone, root and stem. Although …" He peered again at the fighting along the far northern end of the Waterdocks. "The *Titan's* captain must be overeager. Why else land men if you're just going to bombard the town?"

"Look!"

Fengel followed her gesture down to the Craftwright's Terrace just below them. Halfway up its length, just a few streets away from the great bundled chimneys of the Gasworks, lay Pillager's Square. The square was a juncture between several streets threading the terrace and a wide stair that hugged the cliff down to the Waterdocks. There, beside a rough bronze statue of Euron Blackheart, the Mechanists were preparing to fight.

Or they were doing something, at least. They'd erected a squat column with a platform offering a vantage point on the streets and alleys of the terrace below. A device sat atop the platform, looking like a cross between a rotary cannon and the equipment the Mechanists used to fight fires with. Behind the assemblage of flywheels and brass pipes, an operator sat in a chair; numerous hoses trailed down past him to heavy-duty canisters. The Mechanists ran all about the thing, making adjustments and calling back status reports to their brother in the chair. Behind the statue stood a crowd of pirates, watching curiously, weapons in hand.

"We've deployed Atherion's Siren," said Imogen, voice rapt.

Fengel replaced his monocle. "What?"

"The siren. My fa—I mean, First Mechanist Helmsin designed it. Harland must have had it built. Watch, they're about to fire."

She suddenly covered both her ears. Fengel frowned, then returned his attention below.

The Mechanists scattered, fleeing from Atherion's Siren, with the sole exception of the operator. He pumped foot pedals and turned flywheels with abandon, causing the whole device to swing about, aiming for the Perinese warship at the north of the city.

At first Fengel felt it more than heard it. A deep, thrumming vibration that seemed to resonate within his chest. The sound grew, climbing in pitch, accompanied by a strange noise that after a moment he realized were the numerous stray dogs in the pirate township all howling at once. Then the siren screamed.

He clapped his hands over his ears to shut out the ear-splitting wail. It felt like his teeth were going to fly out of his head. The pain must have been even worse in the square below—the assembled pirates and townsfolk all dropped to their knees.

On the far edge of the Waterdocks where it was aimed, the effects of the weapon were downright infernal. Bluecoat marines clutched at their heads, round caps falling away, their screams subsumed by the unholy wail of the siren. The invaders writhed on the boardwalk and on their ship, unable to fight, think, or even flee.

The siren quieted, its charge momentarily spent. Fengel gingerly pulled his hands away from his ears and stared.

"What is that … thing?" he asked.

"Weaponized sound," said Imogen. "Technically nonlethal. Until we get the kinks worked out, at least." There was a fervor in her eyes that Fengel hadn't noticed before.

"Awful," said Fengel. "And what about the townsfolk down there! That must have near-jellied their innards!"

A booming, mechanically augmented voice cut short her reply. It echoed down from the Perinese airship above them, the *Glory*, which was breaking away from its duel with Captain Weatherby's *Moonchaser*. Her sunburst sigil shone bright against the sky.

"Admiral Wintermourn! Why don't you capture this mechanist contraption for me? Here, have some soldiers who won't mind a bit of noise!"

A score of bright figures appeared along the side of the airship hull, brazen in the sunlight. As the *Glory* drifted directly over the Waterdocks, they fell, dangling down on long cables that only just slowed their descent, slamming into the boardwalk among the writhing, moaning Bluecoat marines. One punched almost completely through the planks, getting stuck from the waist down.

"What are those?" asked Fengel. "Men in armor?"

"No," said Imogen. "They fell far too fast—a man would break his legs like that."

The brazen figures rose, slowly, mechanically, moving as one to untie the cables around them. Then they unshouldered heavy, complicated muskets and marched forward as if they hadn't even noticed their fall—or their single, stuck compatriot.

Shouts of readiness sounded again from Pillager's Square. The Mechanists fled Atherion's Siren again as the operator fired.

Fengel was better prepared this time. Still, the wail of the siren was overpowering. Again, the pirates clustered at the back of Pillager's Square, huddling. Down on the far edge of the Waterdocks, the Perinese Bluecoats collapsed again, writhing and screaming. The soldiers armored in brass ... marched forward through the sonic blast, completely unaffected. As he watched, they raised their heavy muskets and returned fire of their own.

Great gouts of gun smoke erupted from their volley. Almost every shot seemed to hit its mark, an incredible bit of marksmanship across such a distance. The siren shook with the impacts. The Mechanists hadn't armored the thing, and pieces dented and went shattering off. Steam and more arcane substances sprayed through the air. The operator lurched violently in his seat, injured by gunshot or some fragment of his machine—Fengel knew not which. Slowly, the wail of the siren faded, replaced by the soft background chaos of the battle surrounding them all.

"How did those men resist the siren?" asked Fengel. He unplugged his ears and turned to Imogen. "And those aren't muskets they carry, they're almost damned cannons!"

She stared at the scene below them, intensely focused. "Those aren't men in armor," she said. "Automatons. They have to be. Nothing living could ignore such a blast from my father's siren."

"Well, better and better," he said. "Come. Let's get down there. We've still got to get to the mines and release that gas. I'd hoped the Mechanists would stop the Perinese advance ... but maybe those pirates can escort us— or provide a distraction."

Imogen glared at the brass automatons, far distant. She nodded, then turned away. Fengel made to follow, pausing only at a small noise. He raised an eyebrow as Cubbins popped out from beneath some of the wreckage to chase after them both.

They picked their way to the stair leading down to the next terrace. Fengel itched, wary of another bombardment. But the *Moonchaser*, free from its engagement with the *Glory of Perinault*, was busily wreaking vengeance upon the *Titan*. Bombs fell like little black seeds on the Perinese vessel, unleashing half-second blossoms of fire and force.

It was satisfying to watch, but the *Titan* had done her work better than she knew. As they crossed the Craftwright's Terrace, chaos reigned. The artisans here were in a frenzy, and everyone they passed reacted frantically on their own. A compass maker forced his young daughters to board up their shop from the outside—those worried young women only seemed to realize afterward they'd been shut out from safety. Their neighbor blacksmith ignored their yelling, intent instead on fitting his assistant into outdated, makeshift armor, trying harder with every pop of a fired musket. Fengel saw no one taking charge, no one running messages back and forth, no captains ordering anyone to work together.

We were always going to lose. The thought sat sour in his mind. *The Perinese have discipline and order. Getting anyone to do anything here is like herding cats—unless a captain with a whole crew behind him knocks enough heads together, nothing ever gets done.* He shook his head as they stepped out into Pillager's Square. *Well, enough of that. I'll knock whatever heads I must. Never let them see you stumble.*

In a town where two men couldn't often walk abreast, Pillager's Square was surprisingly spacious. It lay along the western edge of the Craftwright's Terrace, halfway up its length where a stair descended to the Waterdocks. In its center stood a massive bronze statue, depicting old Euron triumphant over Captain Reddon, the last of his old enemies to stand in his way. Fengel remembered that day fairly well; he'd taken advantage of the distraction to marry Natasha.

The team of Mechanists was still here, clustered thickly around the busted hulk of Atherion's Siren. Fengel knew at a glance it would not work again anytime soon. Some of the marines continued to fire upon it, apparently bearing a grudge.

The pirates he'd seen earlier hadn't yet fled. Maybe twenty in all, they clustered still behind the scant cover of Euron's statue. Fengel recognized most of them as Captain Duvale's crew, from the *Windhaunter*. At their head was a red-haired woman in a half cloak and broad-brimmed hat. It was Shannon MacKinnon, Duvale's extraordinarily lazy first mate.

"All right, you rotters," she said, her voice colored by an impressively thick Perinese brogue. "I had a word with some of the Mechanists, and that screaming contraption of theirs isn't going to work again anytime soon. Just as well, really, because it was giving me a headache."

She leaned back against old dead Captain Reddon. The assembled pirates shifted back and forth, waiting. After a moment, it was clear that Shannon wasn't going to continue.

"Was this the weapon that Euron Blackheart talked about?" asked one pirate, worriedly. "It's all busted. Now what are we going to *do?*"

Shannon tapped her chin, revealing a bandolier full of pistols beneath her half cloak. "That's a good pair of questions. But as far as answers, I haven't a clue. Anyone got any ideas?"

That's my cue. Fengel glanced at the crowd. He very much wanted to ask where his own men and women were, but there wasn't time for that now.

"I've got an idea," he called, striding up from behind the crowd. "I save the town, and you help me do it."

Shannon MacKinnon blinked at him in surprise. "Captain Fengel?"

"Of course. Where's Captain Duvale?"

The *Windhaunter's* first mate frowned. "Pleading before the Goddess, I suspect. A lucky blast of Perinese grapeshot rattled us during the retreat. The ship's rudders are a ruin now and so is Duvale. I got us back to the Skydocks, then brought the lads down here to see what good we could do." She shook her head. "Things are a mess up there, Captain. Everyone running around like chickens with their heads cut off. Old Euron made it back, fortunately, though he crabbed about cowardice the whole way. So it's not *complete* chaos. And our Mechanist friends had this little incursion in hand, until those knights showed up."

"They're automatons," said Imogen, appearing beside Fengel. Anger twisted her features, and she fingered her satchel as she stared at the wreck of Atherion's Siren as if it were a personal insult.

A murmur went up among the assembled men and women of the *Windhaunter.* Shannon MacKinnon snorted, setting her red braids to swaying. "Well, that's fancy. Just worsens the odds, though. Things are already falling apart down below—everyone's either fleeing or trying to fight the Bluecoaties on their own. They were getting slaughtered before that toy over there began to sing. How are we supposed to drive the bastards back now?"

"We aren't going to," said Fengel. He walked around the crowd to the statue, then turned to face the assembled pirates, pointedly ignoring Cubbins, who rubbed against his boots. "If we charge straight in, the Perinese will chew us to pieces. Even if my wife finds the Stormhammer, it's too late for that. No. The Mechanists and I have a different plan, one that could save us all, but I've got to get down below to get it started. We just need to buy time to *slow* the Bluecoats. After that, it won't matter."

He looked out into the crowd. A woman with dark, shoulder-length hair caught his eye. Her clothing was as ratty as the next Haventowner's, but her dragonskin belt covered in seashells was unique. "Danica Barker?" he asked. "Is that you?"

The woman fingered the shells on her belt distractedly. "Aye, Captain."

"You're Tooley's aetherite, from the *Sky Serpent*. What are you doing here?"

She gave a shrug and looked past him at the lagoon. "Got lost in the fighting, Captain. Came back aboard the *Windhaunter*."

"Have you Workings left?" She nodded, and he smiled. "Excellent. Stick with me. Now, the rest of you? Come along—"

"Arr! There ye be. What are ye all doin' standing around? Thar be men to kill!"

Fengel felt his heart sink.

Euron Blackheart entered Pillager's Square from the southern boardwalk alley. The old pirate appeared more than a little battered. His outdated finery was shredded and stained, and his beard was singed in places. But his eyes were alive, even as he staggered along, using his ancient, sheathed cutlass as a walking stick.

The same couldn't be said for those following him. Eight old pirates limped into the square at his rear, covered in bandages. They were all of them Euron's old crew, and Fengel had never seen them looking so *old*. The killers were an omnipresent force in town, keeping the peace by busting heads when needed. Now, though, they seemed weary and worn. Had they always been so?

Euron stalked up to the statue at the center of the Square as the *Windhaunter's* crew broke apart for him. He stopped to admire the monument, a faint smile playing at his lips.

"Reddon. Goddess, you were a bastard. Thought to steal my throne, eh? Ha!" He thumped the sheath of his sword against the boardwalk. "Oh, it were a glorious day when I killed ye. A glorious day." The pirate king rounded on Fengel. "Why couldn't ye be more like him, eh? Be someone *worthwhile?*"

Fengel stiffened. "What are you doing down here, Euron?"

"What's it look like I'm doing, ye useless popinjay? I've come to drive the Perinese off me town and out o' me isles!"

"If you're in town, then you're needed back at the Skydocks. If Brunehilde and Tooley can join Weatherby, we can slow the warships—"

"Pah!" Euron shook his head. "They're all lickin' their wounds. They fled when things were lost, cowards all! Not that I saw ye up there! How'd ye get back to town, Fengel?"

Fengel ground his teeth together. The Mechanists, the light-air mines, and the escape plan—none of it was worth explaining. Instead, he gestured back out at the lagoon, where the *Moonchaser* flew, chased by the *Glory of Perinault*. "Everyone follows you. They'll listen if you order them back up! And we need people up there! Brunehilde and Tooley will follow your orders, no matter how injured they are. Weatherby, Cadmus, and Matice are just barely—"

"What? And leave the stinkin' Bluecoats in me town? Not a chance!" Euron drew his cutlass and thrust it into the air, forcing Shannon MacKinnon back with a curse. "We'll drive the dogs back into the sea and then pillage like we've never pillaged before!"

"You and what men?" cried Fengel, exasperated. He gestured to the eight old, tired pirates flanking Euron. "You had fifty before this morning, and now you're down to eight! They've been with you for decades, and you're going to get what's left of them killed!"

"What? Nonsense! And I see a good two dozen hands here sittin' idle with ye." He turned to face the crowd. "Come, all of ye who would see the invaders out, who want to see vengeance and bloody glory!"

A ragged cheer rose from the crew of the *Windhaunter*. Fengel watched, incredulous, as Euron led them, first across the square and then down the Waterdock stair. Shannon MacKinnon swore and ran after them with an apologetic shrug at Fengel. In moments the only ones remaining in the square were Imogen, the Mechanists, and surprisingly, Captain Tooley's aetherite.

Fengel raised an eyebrow at her. "At least you had the good sense to stay behind, Danica."

The aetherite gave another shrug. "You ordered me to stay with you, Captain."

"Does he even know about the automatons?" asked Imogen.

"No," replied Fengel, his voice low and tight. "And he's going to get them all killed." He drew his saber in one smooth motion, taking pleasure in how it felt in his hand. "Come on. We make for the Smuggler's Warehouse." He stumbled over Cubbins with a curse, then reached down and yanked the tabby cat up by the scruff of its neck. Fengel shoved it into the arms of a passing Mechanist. "Take care of this!"

He turned away from the rather surprised young man and stalked towards the stair down to the next terrace. "But what about all the others?" asked Danica Barker worriedly. The shells on her belt jangled as she hurried to keep up with him.

"They made their choice!" he all but shouted back at her.

Cannon blast and musket retort washed over Fengel as he stalked after Euron—the stair he'd taken was the only path down to the Waterdocks. Fengel stomped angrily down the old wooden steps, his saber gripped in a white-knuckled fist.

The man was infuriating. Absolutely infuriating. Here they were, with a dozen warships on their doorstep and hundreds of soldiers in their door, and all Euron could think to do was charge. Worse, everyone listened to him! *Well enough. Enough and more than enough. They can all rot while I do what needs to be done.*

Haventown's lowest terrace was a sprawling collection of warehouses, criminal shipwrights, and all the other diverse structures that needed to be near the water. The Waterdocks sprawled, a third of the entire pirate township by itself and a ramshackle place where structures leaned against each other. Construction wasn't regulated in Haventown. You simply built where you had room, if someone didn't stop you.

A number of years ago, it had half burned down. He'd wed Natasha, and she was trying to kill him, of course, and a simple spark had resulted in an inferno. Looking around, it seemed that no one had really taken the lesson to heart.

The old Smuggler's Warehouse was built near the northern third of the terrace, opposite the lagoon and up tight against the cliffs. Fengel left the pirate king and his followers to their fate, threading his way through streets and alleys that were all but empty. There weren't many people on the Waterdocks at the busiest of times, but it seemed the more permanent residents had either fled the invasion or gone to fight it. Those he saw clustered in the doorways and windows, seemingly oblivious of each other, waiting.

They need to group up. Fengel shook his head. *Everyone is hiding in little gangs, even ready to fight, but we need the strength that comes from numbers.* Euron should have gathered them up, brought them on his mad charge down the throat of the enemy. Maybe … maybe then he might have had a chance. Now it was too late.

He ran through intersections and through alleys, ignoring the sounds of battle. Finally, he stopped at a junction, their destination in view, and Danica and Imogen ran into him. The Smuggler's Warehouse was located down a narrow alley and up against the face of the cliff, all but hidden in the shadow of the Craftwright's Terrace above. To his left the street continued on, twisting past a coal yard and an old warehouse roofed with whale bones. Shouts echoed down to him—the cries of pirates and soldiers just out of sight.

"Here we are," said Fengel. Now up close, he could see several great brass pipes running out from the Smuggler's Warehouse to the rest of the town above. "Imogen, you're sure this is the entrance to the mine?"

The young Mechanist nodded, distractedly. She stared down the street towards the battle raging just out of sight. "Just at the back, behind a fake stack of crates." She looked at him. "Shouldn't we … shouldn't we do something to help?"

"We are," he replied frostily.

Fengel took a step forward just as the nearby conflict reached a crescendo. "By the Goddess," someone shouted, "they're unstoppable! Flee fer yer lives!"

He stopped despite himself as a number of panicked men and women from the *Windhaunter* came into view, fleeing the fight or trying desperately to hold ground. The pirates fought not Bluecoats but the twenty armored and shining automatons he'd spied earlier. They tromped forward, moving in a tight wedge that drove the pirates before them.

These machines were like neither the clumsy, steam-driven Brass Horses of Triskelion nor the ancient and spindly Voornish automatons. They stood taller than a man, armored like the storybook tales of the *old* Order Gallant. Past the plates, though, pistons and flywheels moved, while steam puffed from an exhaust pipe behind the right shoulder. Each held a heavy, complicated musket with several barrels bundled together, like a pepperbox pistol writ large. They pressed the defenders back with an implacable tread and a brutal, inhuman efficiency, their armor shining beneath eaves made of grinning whale skulls and the shadows cast by warring airships.

Euron and his geriatric reavers held firmest, trying to stand their ground against the things. Fengel pointedly looked away, back to the Smuggler's Warehouse.

Damned old fool neither wants nor needs my help. He looked to Imogen and Danica, who stared at the nearby struggle as pirates fled past them. *And so what if he falls? We're better off without that mad old bastard.*

The sharp snap of shattering steel caught his attention. It was Euron, fighting the automaton at the head of their pack, backed up by two of his men. The pirate king had tried a heavy, two-handed chop with his cutlass. Only the automaton had raised its musket and shattered the old, oft-nicked blade. The automaton did not pause; instead, it lowered its weapon and fired to one side. Thunder erupted, obliterating a pirate.

Euron opened his mouth in a shout of rage or denial. But he never got the chance. The automaton swung out with the barrel of his weapon, catching the pirate king full in the chest and sending him flying.

Fengel winced. He looked away, only to see the two women behind him watching. *We're better off without him. Better off!*

A hoarse scream echoed down the street as he took a step for the Smuggler's Warehouse. Fengel turned back in time to see an automaton lift one of Euron's remaining men with one gauntlet and slam him into a brick wall with a sickening crunch. The pirate king himself rose to his feet and limped back into the fray, a bare handful of his former crew and those of the *Windhaunter* still standing.

Damn it all. Damn him to the Realms Below!

Fengel sheathed his saber. "Danica. You said you've still a few Workings?"

She nodded in distraction. "Aye, Captain. Goriot—ah my familiar, is pretty pleased with all the carnage going on."

"Follow me. Use whatever you can to help."

"Wait, what?" asked Imogen. "What about me?"

"Wait here. I'm going to rescue that cantankerous old bastard—and whoever else I can."

The young Mechanist reached for her satchel. "I've got something for this. I can—"

"Wait here!"

Fengel jogged down the boardwalk street. Reaching out, he grabbed an unfired musket from a fleeing pirate, who cursed him but ran on.

No alleys were present, a mixed blessing; while no Bluecoats would be flanking him around behind the other buildings, it also meant he couldn't do the same. Which would have been nice. He needed something, any advantage at all if he was going to pull this off somehow. The gleaming brass of the automatons whirled and twisted, flailing about with their pepperbox muskets like clubs, seemingly impervious to any blows the pirates rained upon them. The machines had even kept their wedge formation, gaining ground steadily.

Behind their automatons crept the Bluecoat invaders. All appeared ragged and injured. They hung back a goodly distance, letting their machines do all the work for them while they recovered from the effects of the siren.

Only eight men and women on his side still stood, holding the thin line of the battle. Fengel came up beside Shannon MacKinnon, who fired pistol after pistol into the head of an automaton before her. The lead balls ricocheted off the armored helm of the thing, ringing it like a bell.

"We're outmatched!" he shouted at her. "Pull everyone back!"

"Oh aye," she yelled back at him. "I'm just standing here for the fun of it! We're dropping like flies in autumn. Euron refuses to leave!"

"Just pull back! I'll take care of him."

An automaton on their left crushed the skull of an old pirate, then lurched their way. Hissing, spitting liquid light slammed into the thing, knocking it back against the wall of the warehouse. The automaton toppled but immediately began righting itself. The chest plate it wore was scored and burned, but otherwise uninjured.

Fengel glanced back to where Danica Barker stood, both hands clenched over a Working that seeped droplets of something that sizzled on the boardwalk planks.

"Hurry!" she said, unleashing another awful blast.

Fengel turned to Shannon. "Just go!"

Then he twisted away, ducking past as another of Euron's men fell to the machines. Arcane light sizzled overhead as Danica unleashing her Working to distract the automaton fighting the pirate king.

Fengel came up behind Euron, down now to a single minion and his own broken sword. As the clockwork knight bludgeoned Euron's man down to the boardwalk, Fengel used the opening, ducking low and thrusting his musket out like a spear, not at the machine's torso, but between its legs. Throwing his weight into it, he rushed past, feeling the barrel catch against the knee of the construct. Swordplay might be useless here, but as he so often told Lina Stone, that just meant he needed to improvise.

His opponent toppled, reaching clumsily for him as he stepped neatly out of the way. Another of the war machines was waiting behind its fellow. Fengel raised the musket and jammed it into the space where its chest plate met the neck, right into the spinning flywheels and twisting pistons. He pulled the trigger, letting go and turning his head away.

The weapon exploded, knocking the automaton back even as it knocked Fengel's monocle free and showered the side of his neck with hot metal. Fengel gave thanks to the Realms Above even through the pain—it could have been much, much worse.

There wasn't time to recover, though. He leaped away, back over the first automaton that was even now climbing to its feet. Euron was frozen, staring, surprised by Fengel's appearance.

Fengel slammed a fist into the pirate king's gut, a blow he'd been waiting *years* to deliver. The old man folded with a whooshing gasp, dropping his broken weapon. Fengel kneeled and lifted his father-in-law up onto his shoulder. The man was lighter than he would have thought.

The pirates beside him didn't even notice. Those few left standing were already turning to flee back, past where Danica Barker threw caustic light and Shannon MacKinnon emptied her bandolier. A figure darted into view from the other direction, on his left.

It was Imogen, the young Mechanist. She pulled something from her satchel, heavy and black and complicated. Fengel didn't need to see the hissing fuse at its top to recognize it as some sort of bomb.

Fengel yelled at her wordlessly, even as he pushed on into a sprint, with the old man flailing on his shoulder and his monocle dangling on its chain. He needn't have bothered. Imogen planted the bomb up against the brick wall of the old warehouse just as an automaton before her lowered its weapon. She ducked aside as it fired, missing her by a handbreadth and gouging a spray of brick dust out of the wall. Imogen twisted about clumsily and joined him as he sprinted away.

The bomb erupted behind him with the force of a thunderclap, lifting and throwing him. He lost Euron and was thrown painfully to the ground.

Slowly, the world ordered itself again. The street was piled high with crumbled brick, old wood, and the bones of long-dead leviathans, all shrouded from the sun by a cloud of dusty ruin. Through the ringing in his ears, he heard the distant din of the battle being fought elsewhere and the hoarse calls of Perinese Bluecoats. None of the automatons were visible. He felt sore, and his leg hurt; the right leg of his trousers was dark with spreading blood. It was only a flesh wound, thank the Goddess, though it bled freely enough.

Others picked themselves up off the boardwalk planks nearby. Imogen stood, unharmed thanks to her heavy Mechanist's garb, though she shook her head, as if her ears were ringing. Shannon MacKinnon was covered in scrapes, her broad-brimmed hat missing. She held Danica Barker in her arms. The aetherite was unmoving, either dead or unconscious, her dark curls matted and wet with blood. Old Euron Blackheart groaned from his hands and knees, looking around blearily. Of any others, Fengel saw no sign.

Euron Blackheart glared at him. "Ye damned, craven peacock! What did you—"

Fengel rose to his feet, driven by frustrated rage. The pain in his leg flared, but he ignored it, grabbing up the pirate king by the shredded lapels of his outdated coat and hoisting him up like a butcher would a side of beef.

"Shut your damned yap," he snarled.

The pirate king's eyes widened. "How dare ye—"

"I dare plenty!" roared Fengel. "Because you've not got the good sense the Goddess gave a scryn!" He gestured about them at the ruined street shrouded in dust and rubble, at the half-seen bulk of the *Moonchaser* fighting with the *Glory* overhead.

"Look!" continued Fengel. "Look around! Where are your men? Where are your loyal crew? They're dead! Half the *Windhaunter's* crew are gone as well—and Goddess knows how many townsfolk. You've led them to their deaths and gained not a damned thing in return!"

"They went with pride," hissed Euron, shaking now, angered himself. "They went with glory, fighting th' enemy, when all ye do is run—"

"There's no glory here! There's no honor! Look around you, Euron. The enemy is here, on your doorstep. Your gambit with the Stormhammer has *failed*, and we are *losing*. You're spending lives pointlessly!"

"I don't expect ye to understand," spat the pirate king. "Yer a peacock, a popinjay."

It came to him then. Fengel threw the old man to the ground, panting with the effort of holding him up. "I understand just fine," he snarled. "You never wanted to win. You're just looking for one last battle to die in. You sent Natasha off to keep her safe. I wonder if the Voorn weapon is even real. Now you'll burn the rest of us just so you can go out in glory."

Euron glared at him hatefully. Slowly, without breaking his gaze, Fengel put his monocle back into place.

"Shannon," he said after a moment.

The *Windhaunter's* first lieutenant looked at him, the aetherite in her arms still unmoving. "Aye, Fengel?"

"I'm going to save what I can of this town. Get this bag of bones back up to the Skydocks. Have him get the other airships moving. I don't care how broken up they are or what it takes. Send whoever can be spared back down here or to the Craftwright's Terrace. I promise them that there's still a chance, so long as we can buy time. If the pirate king here won't give the orders, tell Brunehilde and Tooley that he isn't in charge anymore. *I* am."

Euron Blackheart rocked back in surprise. "Ye mutinous dog! How dare ye?"

"I dare," he snarled at the old man, "because you can't stop me."

He brushed past Euron without another glance, stalking towards the Smuggler's Warehouse and the secret the Mechanists had hidden so cleverly. If he moved quickly, he might even be able to keep that promise.

CHAPTER THIRTEEN

Lina's arm was getting tired.

She hefted her daggers again as violence threatened to erupt for the dozenth time inside the ancient Voornish pyramid. Runt wove threateningly atop her shoulders, further throwing off her balance.

"I'm asking you, again, how do we turn on the Stormhammer?" growled Natasha. Butterbeak punctuated her demand with an angry squawk.

"And I'm askin' ye, again, how ye knew of it!" replied Morgan One-Eye, spokes-pirate for the Castaways.

Euron's old crew hadn't turned out to be as welcoming as they had hoped. The twelve Castaways, as they called themselves, were cantankerous, unhelpful, and downright curmudgeonly. The weapons they brandished seemed frail and weathered, though Lina and her crewmates kept up their guard. Just as they wanted to know about the Stormhammer, the Castaways asked a thousand questions about the crew of the *Dawnhawk*. Natasha was, of course, being utterly contrary, refusing to answer a thing. The air within the ancient Voornish pyramid had been fraught with tension for the last three quarters of a glass.

"Look," said Natasha. She waved her cutlass at the hollow room about them. "It's obvious this is the place. Let's just cut ... cut to ..." A tremor silenced her.

Lina sighed. That was the other thing. Something else was on the island with them, something huge and mechanical. Whatever it was had them trapped. The Castaways grew quiet whenever it drew close, their wrinkled scowls softening with fear. Natasha herself seemed strangely pensive, as if she knew what it was. For Lina's part, the thing had never drawn close enough to the tunnel entrance for her to get a good look.

The pyramid was like other Voorn ruins she'd seen. Hollow, made of some weird gold-brass amalgam, it climbed in an inverse stair-step to a central peak, with just the one passage leading back outside. In the center of the space rose a wide dais with a carved stair. Atop it glimmered incomprehensible machinery; all tubes, pressure canisters, and fragile lattices. A softly shimmering crystal sphere floating in an empty clearing at its heart.

Incongruously, the floor of the pyramid was filthy. Decades worth of dirt had been tracked about. The Castaways had obviously been busy. A mess of primitive tools and pieces of roughly cut wooden planks lay about the floor, as did coils of hempen rope and bright, brassy pieces of Voorn machinery, apparently ripped straight from the construct in the center of the room.

The Castaways themselves were ragged, a hard-bitten band of older pirates. The crew of the *Dawnhawk* faced off against them, forming two rough semicircles just spoiling for a fight.

The mysterious beast outside stomped past, and Natasha dragged her attention back around to Morgan One-Eye. "Let's just cut to the quick of it," she said. "This is an ancient Voorn ruin in the middle of nowhere, with a bunch of Euron's Blackheart's pirates sitting watch. Just tell us how to turn on the Stormhammer—"

Morgan hawked a mighty gob, then spat. "We're not Euron's crew!" he snarled, his grey beard quivering. "We're not his crew, and we're not his guards. We're his damned prisoners!"

"Oh, I don't care!" shouted Natasha. She gestured violently with her cutlass. "I—"

The ground shook again as the monster passed by again. Hissing pistons and the ratcheting clank of clockwork echoed down the tunnel.

Natasha whipped back around with a snarl. "No! I refuse to believe that you're here, you wind-up pile of junk! You outdated piece of slapped-together refuse! Almhazlik is six hundred miles away. You can't be here!" On her shoulder, Butterbeak hunkered low, uncharacteristically cowed.

The thing outside went silent. A great cloud of steam hissed across the mouth of the tunnel, occluding what little sunlight there was. After a tense moment, it began moving again. The tromp of its footsteps faded. Lina released a breath that she didn't know she'd been holding, as did everyone else in the room.

"Enough," growled Morgan One-Eye. He raised his notched cutlass. The rest of the dozen Castaways readied themselves for violence. "Ye'll be takin' us back to yer airship right this moment. We ain't stayin' one more Goddess-damned minute on this poxy island."

Natasha rounded on him, blade up, teeth bared in her usual snarl. Lina's captain wasn't patient at the best of times. In her mind's eye, Lina could see it: the bloody fight that would ruin any chance of achieving their objective.

This is so stupid. She sheathed her daggers and leaped out in front of the two pirate crews. "Wait!" Lina cried, hands outspread. "Just wait, damn us all to the Realms Below. What are we *doing?*"

Michael Hockton took a half step forward, eyes wide in alarm, and she loved him for that. But there wasn't time for that right now. Lina met the eyes of every pirate there, Natasha and Morgan One-Eye in particular. "Listen, just listen a moment," she said. "We've been standing here for more than an hour, dancing around, ready to gut each other, when we can all have what we want and fly off smiling."

She turned to face the Castaways. "Look, Euron Blackheart abandoned you here a couple decades ago, and it's been horrible. You want out. We understand that. But do you know what's happening out there? Haventown is under siege. The Perinese are invading the Copper Isles. If you don't tell us what you know about the Stormhammer, then there ain't gonna be anything to fly home *to.*"

Before Morgan could reply, she rounded on Natasha. Runt rumbled unhappily at the sudden movement. "Captain, we need all the hands we can get, right? Anyone who can hold a sword. Let's just agree to fly them back to Haventown. Is that so hard?"

Lina quieted. She waited, hoping that everyone would see reason. It was stupid to argue when so much was at stake.

Natasha stared at the Castaways. She sheathed her cutlass, then fished out her copy of *How to Pillage Friends and Intimidate People.* The pirate captain consulted a section, grunted to herself, then looked back up at them, face sour. "I guess that's ... acceptable." She jabbed the tiny booklet at Morgan One-Eye. "But get to the damned point and tell us about the Stormhammer." She then gestured behind them all at the tunnel. "And how did that thing outside even get here?"

The leader of the Castaways frowned but lowered his rusty cutlass. He looked to his mates, who all nodded warily. It was as much as Lina had hoped for. The offer of a free ride away from the island seemed to cut through their isolation-induced misanthropy.

Morgan jammed his blade back into the rough hempen loop of his belt. "Aye. A deal it be, then. We'll tell ye everythin', an' ye take us away from this place. Perinese or no, we'll have our vengeance on Euron Blackheart!"

A ragged cheer erupted from the Castaways. Lina blinked. *Have we stood here this long without letting slip who Natasha really is?*

Morgan One-Eye turned back to face her with a grim smile on his lips. Natasha stepped up beside Lina, shoving her booklet back down her shirt. "Well?" she asked.

The pirate jerked a thumb at the huge device behind him. "This be the only Voorn building on th' isle. Yer precious Stormhammer's right there."

Natasha sighed in exasperation. "We figured that out," she said flatly. "How does it work?"

Morgan snorted. "Haven't a clue."

She started, taken aback. "What? You've been here for decades!"

"Oh aye," replied the Castaway, a snarl creeping onto his face. "An' we spent the first few years guardin' it dutifully. We weren't going to play with the damnable thing. Voornish machines? Pah! Could have blown up an' taken us all with it. No, we didn't even touch it until a few years ago, when we were desperate enough for parts. An' then we still lost Gareth. Stank in here like cooked chimp for a week." He shook his head, and the rest of the Castaways muttered rueful confirmation.

Lina felt her heart sink. The Perinese would be stopped up at the Graveway for only so long. *Maybe Rastalak can figure this thing out.*

Natasha was frowning but appeared otherwise unfazed. "Fine. What about the thing outside?"

Morgan shrugged. "Can't help ye much there either, lass. Like a dragon but all machine-like. Voorn brass, just like this place here. Fell over the lip of the isle two days ago, then started rampaging around. Damn near killed us all, 'til we fled here. Now it's got us trapped."

Natasha made a pair of white-knuckled fists. "Everywhere I go. By the hairy arms of the Goddess! I can't get away from that ridiculous, overbuilt—"

Runt chose that moment to have a fit. He rose up higher on Lina's shoulders to wave back and forth, chirping crankily just as he had in the jungles outside the pyramid.

Lina reached up to soothe him. "Runt, calm down. Calm down!"

"Chirr!"

The last thing she needed was to put the Castaways on edge again. Lina gestured to her friends. "Allen, Michael, get over here and help me!"

The two young men looked at each other, then at Lina and Runt. Allen was still mottled black and blue where he showed skin, and Michael's neck was still swollen red. Michael took a step towards her, his trepidation plain. Allen stood frowning in place, then cursed as he ducked a stream of poisonous spittle.

She ignored them both and turned to the Castaways. "Don't mind Runt. Normally, he's really sweet."

But they didn't seem alarmed. Or even that curious. They watched Lina dance about like a particularly weird circus performer. One of them, a bald fellow with a leathery, repeatedly sunburned scalp, scratched his bushy beard.

"Realms Below," he grunted. "O' course it' be cranky. It's bleedin' pregnant."

Silence reigned within the pyramid.

"What?" replied Lina. "No, that's not possible."

"Oh aye. Got all the signs, right? Swollen, cranky, you can even tell by the color of the spittle she's throwin' about."

Lina looked at the noxious streams puddling on the brass floor of the ancient structure. She shook her head. "No, Runt's a boy. I had him checked with a disgraced horse-doctor back in Haventown."

The old pirate snorted. "Well, I guess that shows me then, don't it? Only I spent three years trappin' an' eatin' scryn, 'til there weren't none left on this damned island. Pools o' rum and a heavy stick. Fry enough o' th' little bastards and you eventually figure it out. There aren't any scryn menfolk. They're all born pregnant, an' after enough time an' alcohol, they get all swollen with babes. That one's gonna pop any day now."

Lina looked up at Runt, at a loss for words. Her pet was curling down again, chirping crankily, leaning into her hand. Her scales were warm against Lina's palm.

"But … that's wonderful!" she said aloud. Relief washed through her, and Lina turned to her crewmates. "Guys, Runt's going to be a *mother*. Isn't that great? I mean, things make much more sense now. And think of all the little scrynlings we'll—"

The men and women of the *Dawnhawk* stared in utter horror. Michael Hockton stood frozen in midstep, Allen was cringing, and Farouk chewed on his lip. Ryan Gae paled. Reaver Jane and young Paine joined Rastalak by taking slow steps backward, their distaste plain. Natasha drew her blade, holding it up as if to ward Runt away. Even Butterbeak seemed to share her look of revulsion.

"That be a noxious truth," said Morgan One-Eye. "But it be beside the point. We've told ye 'bout yer artifact and that monstrous machine outside. Now let's get back aboard yer ship an' get out of here!"

Natasha glanced at him, not moving her cutlass an inch. "We need to figure out how to fire the thing first—or to take it back with us, if we can. Don't worry your ugly little heads, though. I won't let it be said that Natasha Blackheart breaks her word."

"You break your word all the time," Lina said, sulking. Why wasn't anyone else happy about the good news?

"Well, yes," replied Natasha, looking back to her. "But not about important things."

"You took us to the Graveway," continued Lina, "when Captain Fengel made you promise not to."

"Because he's a gigantic damned worrywort," she said, exasperated. Natasha turned back to the Castaways. "Anyway, let's turn this thing on and smite the Perinese. Then we can all fly away."

But the old pirates had changed. Morgan and his mates stared at her with unbridled rage. They drew their ragged weapons and raised them up again, promising violence.

"Blackheart. *Blackheart.* Yer his daughter!"

"Uh," said Natasha taken aback.

"Of course Euron sent his daughter to find his toy! Or were ye just plannin' ta use it for yerself?" Morgan took a step forward.

Natasha shifted her stance, raising her cutlass in guard and launching Butterbeak into the air. "Hold now. This hasn't anything to do with my father. Not really."

"Euron Blackheart!" howled Morgan One-Eye, as if he could make the pirate king hear him. "We're going to gut yer daughter an' her crew, steal her ship, an' then come fer yer head!" The Castaways all roared their approval.

"Now hold on a damned—" But it was too late. The Castaways charged, and then the fight was on.

Runt uncoiled from Lina's shoulders and launched herself into the air. It was their usual tactic, but she grabbed after her pet desperately. "No!" she cried. "Runt, come back, you'll get hurt—"

Morgan One-Eye hacked at Lina's head with his notched and rusty cutlass. She ducked back with a curse, then leaped aside as he thrust at her, throwing her off-balance. For all his age and appearance, the man was still deadly with a blade. He pulled back for a final blow, only for Natasha to appear between them.

"I've wanted to kill you for over an hour," she snarled, parrying his blade with her own, raining flakes of rusty steel down on Lina. Morgan met her challenge. Lina took the opportunity to slip away, drawing her daggers as she did so.

She had immediate need of them. Runt flew awkwardly through the air, hissing and spitting and glowing red as she went. A Castaway stepped up in front her, the scryn-eater. He raised up a heavy, makeshift club made out of an old oar.

Lina yelled and threw her dagger. It went end over end before sinking deep into the old pirate's arm. He gave a cry of his own, dropping the club as Runt flew past.

There wasn't time to dispatch the pirate. She had to get Runt back and keep her safe from the bloodshed around them. It was a task easier said than done, however. Runt flew through the melee, lashing out at whoever was closest.

"Here, Runt!" Lina cried, leaping over Rastalak as he grappled with a Castaway. She grabbed for the flask at her hip and uncorked it with her teeth. "Come here! You can't fly around like this—think of your children!"

Runt flew past big Farouk, forcing Lina to duck under his arm as he laid out another pirate. Runt suddenly reached the wall and eeled about, circling back around behind the melee. Lina cursed and tried to anticipate her, moving laterally. Reaver Jane put paid to that, tripping over a stray piece of Voorn machinery and knocking them both to the ground.

Lina scrabbled up to her feet as Paine went running past. She took a wild swing at the Castaway chasing him, and the old pirate cried out, his rusty boat hook falling into view. She ignored them, stepping atop a cursing Jane to push past their assailant in pursuit of her pet.

Runt was just up ahead. She'd half fallen, half landed on the steps of the Stormhammer dais, her bloated, wormy length too heavy to keep aloft anymore. Lina made concerned noises and scurried over the arcane machinery, coming at it from the side.

Things sizzled and hummed about her, releasing brief arcs of galvanic energy to flash in the gloom. Lina hissed as one hit her hand, burning it. Then she was on the stair and kneeling and scooping up her scryn with one arm.

"There, there," she cooed.

"Chirr," said Runt. Her pet was weary and lethargic. Lina could only smile. After months of uncertainty, now she knew why Runt was so out of sorts. She hugged her pet close. *You're going to be a mother soon!* At least, if these bastard Castaways didn't get her.

Lina whirled with renewed purpose, raising her only remaining dagger. *No one is eating you—or your scrynlings.*

But the battle was won. The Castaways could fight, but their failing, feeble weapons betrayed them. They were fleeing even now for the tunnel entrance with Natasha chasing after them, a smile on her blood-covered lips.

The older pirates ran outside yelling. Natasha jerked to a sudden stop behind them and spread her arms to prevent anyone else from passing. A mechanical roar answered Lina's curiosity, as did the tremor of earthshaking footfalls. Lina sheathed her dagger and cradled Runt as she ran down the stairs, crossing to the tunnel entrance.

"Hold," said Natasha as Lina pushed through her crewmates. She stepped up beside Michael Hockton, who wiped sweat away from his brow. He smiled at Lina, though he froze upon seeing Runt.

"They're done for," continued Natasha. "Those poor bastards might as well have been unarmed. Now *that* thing has them." She rested her cutlass on one shoulder, then held out her other arm for Butterbeak to land upon.

"Captain Blackheart," said Allen. "What's … what's making that noise?"

"It's the Dray Engine," she said flatly.

"That can't be!" added Etarin. "We left it behind on Almhazlik."

"Tell it that yourself," she replied. Natasha gestured outside with her gore-slicked cutlass, and the monster came into view.

Memory didn't do the thing justice. It towered over the Castaways it now chased, a reptilian horror rendered in Voornish brass. The thing stood on its hind legs like some ungainly land-bound dragon, reaching and grasping for prey with rending forelimbs. Its inner workings—whirling gears and churning pistons—ticked along between the armored plates of its hide. Every few steps it would raise its coffin-long jaw up at the sky to roar, and a mechanical cacophony echoed from somewhere deep in its chest. Then it began the chase again, its red glass eyes eager.

Away ran the Castaways, fleeing towards the jungle as fast as their geriatric legs could carry them. It wasn't fast enough. Lina watched the Dray Engine reach the slowest of the pirates. The monstrous machine darted forward, leaning suddenly, faster than should have been possible. She thought it was going to snatch him up whole and devour him like a sea serpent eating a shark. Instead, it closed its maw and knocked him over.

The poor fellow yelled in terror, one arthritic hand raised up to ward away the ancient machine. Lina watched with her crewmates, rapt, as the Dray Engine came to a sudden stop. Then it lifted one armored foot above the old pirate and stepped down slowly as the fellow beneath it shrieked. His screams went on for far too long.

Steam gushed forth as the Dray Engine snorted in satisfaction, then turned to face the rest of the Castaways, who had frozen in horror. It roared, and they screamed in kind, fleeing again for the jungle. Almost leisurely now, the Dray Engine pursued them.

No one made a sound within the tunnel about her. Even Runt had quieted in response to the noise and horror taking place outside.

"Captain," said Reaver Jane. "That's a problem." She turned to Natasha. "It's still between us and the *Dawnhawk*."

Paine kicked at the metal floor sullenly. "Pirates and monsters. It's always pirates *and* monsters."

"Oh, don't I know it," replied Natasha to them both. She gave a sour shake of her head. "But we've more important things to worry about right now." She gestured with her cutlass back at the arcane machinery shining behind them. "Let's get that mess figured out," she continued, "and see if we can win a war."

CHAPTER FOURTEEN

ADMIRAL WINTERMOURN JAMMED A HANDKERCHIEF TO HIS BLEEDING NOSE.

The advance had fairly stopped for the moment. Whatever bomb the pirates lit off had packed one impressive wallop. Now rubble and whale bones filled the street in a man-high pile, walling it off more effectively than the sagging walls creaking ominously to either side.

Of the Brass Paladins, there was no sign. The blast and collapse had buried them, just as it had thrown his own men back from the fray. Admiral Wintermourn felt conflicted about that. On the one hand, they had been unarguably effective in the advance. On the other hand, damned good riddance to Gwydion's wind-up toys, and to the Realms Below with how well the inhuman things worked.

Sergeant Adjutant Lanters tottered across the rubble to make a snappy salute. His cerulean jacket and trousers were coated in a fine layer of dust, giving him the appearance of some cheap stage-born ghost. His eyes were bloodshot and dried blood coated his mustache. Wintermourn knew he looked just as much a fright—the legacy of that infernal screaming Mechanist device, as well as the bomb. His nose wouldn't stop bleeding.

"I've reassembled a platoon for immediate duty," said the sergeant.

About damned time. Wintermourn gestured for the man to stand at ease. He turned to see a loose clump of Bluecoats at attention. They were just as ragged and bloodied as their sergeant, but they stood with stiff spines and muskets at the ready. Some even still had their hats.

The invasion of the Waterdocks was proving unexpectedly difficult. At first, things had gone well enough. Crashing his own beautiful *Colossus* into the Waterdocks had certainly taken the locals by surprise. Their disorganized defense had fallen quickly to the marines, and the piers and streets surrounding his beached warship became territory of the expanded Kingdom of Perinault. As the only field officer left in the area, he'd buckled on his saber and taken direct command.

He'd made shockingly little progress since, though. This part of the pirate city was a thickly clustered maze, full of dead-ends and blind alleys. As if that wasn't enough, the pirates had rebounded. Though not led by anyone of note, as Gwydion had seemed to think they would have been, pockets of resistance appeared in the oddest places. Just when Wintermourn thought them finally all crushed, that damnable Mechanist weapon on the second terrace had come into play.

He knew Gwydion wanted it intact. Yet if Wintermourn had his way, it would never work again. The scream it uttered was something more felt than heard, reverberating within the chest and shaking the limbs until one felt they were shattering apart. Men had died all around him, falling to the boardwalk with blood gushing from ears and nostrils. Not even his *Colossus* had been immune. Spars from the mast turned to flinders that rained down about them all, an excessive bit of devastation.

"It will take some time to get the rest of the company going," said Sergeant Lanters.

That's a matter of opinion. Wintermourn gestured at the marines lazing about the street, resting and nursing their injuries. "If they can still walk and hold a smallsword, I want them on their feet. Reinforcements should be due at any moment, and I won't have this honor snatched from—"

A shadow fell over him. It covered the marines, the rubble, and this whole end of the pirate township. Wintermourn glanced up, shading his eyes with the handkerchief.

An airship flew overhead. It wasn't the *Glory*, but rather a Haventown vessel taking off from their Skydocks: the *Sky Serpent*, according to the crude legend across its hull. Another drifted just behind it, the much-battered *Solrun's Hammer*. A third airship, the *Windhaunter*, came lackadaisically up behind, both propellers obviously nonfunctional and tethered to a pier by long lines, but doing what it could for the fight.

The airships bore down on the *Glory* as Wintermourn watched. Prince Gwydion would soon be caught between them and the errant *Moonchaser* he hunted. The pirate vessels opened with rippling musket-fire volleys, and the flow of battle changed up above.

Damnation. So that's where Haventown's leaders were. The pirates had rallied. Soon, they would have aerial advantage once more. It was even conceivable that they might impede the action still raging in the lagoon.

Wintermourn curled his lips in a snarl, even as a coppery tang filled the back of his throat. He spat and pressed the handkerchief back to his nose. *Damnation!* He needed those reinforcements to land.

Someone shouted nearby. Admiral Wintermourn looked to a pair of Bluecoats heaving a massive whalebone away from the rubble in the street ahead, revealing a skin of polished brass. Gwydion's clockwork soldiers had been found.

"Sergeant," said one, turning back, "here's the first—"

The automaton shifted beneath the rubble, a cascade of cheap brick and old bone sliding away as it tried to sit upright. A brazen helm appeared, followed by the shoulder and right arm. But there it stopped, still too buried beneath the detritus to free itself further. The marines stepped away in apprehension.

"Damn yer eyes, Bryant!" snapped Sergeant Adjutant Lanters. "That's valuable Kingdom property! Have more care with it."

Private Bryant and his companion both snapped their salutes, though they looked put-upon.

Admiral Wintermourn sighed. "Very well," he said, forestalling the sergeant. "Go ahead and unearth the things. Our crown prince is going to want them back if they can be recovered." *Besides, the Mechanists doubtless have more surprises to unleash.* And Admiral Wintermourn swore to himself that he wouldn't be taking the brunt of their attentions. To the Realms Below with capturing them, no matter what the crown prince wanted.

The two Bluecoats bent back down to obey. Beneath them, the automaton went suddenly berserk. It lashed out with its free arm, catching Bryant by the leg and toppling him over, then reaching over to grab the other marine by the throat with that jerking, surprising speed that so belied expectation. The Brass Paladin pulled the flailing man in close, metal fingers tightening like a vise.

Sergeant Adjutant Lanters gestured at the assembled men. "Get it off him!" he shouted.

Wintermourn felt his nostrils flare, dried blood cracking. *Damnable malfunctioning contraption!*

Bluecoats rushed forward to pull at their fellow. The dying marine gasped and choked, going red beneath the grit and dust that covered his face. One hand flailed at the mechanical arm that was killing him, even as he tried to pry himself free with the other. Musket strokes battered at the head of the automaton, ringing down the street and echoing off the walls.

The Bluecoat gave a last, guttural rattle, then fell still. His fellows continued to beat the machine, which lashed out at them defensively. Private Bryant was trying furiously to crawl away.

Damn! Damn and blast these things to all the Realms Below. "That's enough!" Wintermourn shouted. "Clear away, you fools, on the double!" He watched the corpse of the marine twitch out his last little bit of life. Wintermourn felt his gorge rise. *Rotting claws, coming through the fire. Reaching up …*

The marines' training took precedence over their anger. They fell back, though their frustration still showed clearly.

"Sir?" asked Lanters.

Wintermourn spat. "Those wind-up toys are more trouble than they're worth. I'll spend good Perinese blood against the foe, but not as sacrifices for these damned infernal machines."

"But sir, the prince—"

"If he wants them back, he can dig them out himself!" snarled Wintermourn, gesticulating wildly. "Now, form up and move out! We find another path forward. Shoot any Mechanists on sight. And any man in the company who can't march will be *dragged*!"

Blood seeped from his nostrils, soaking his mustache and staining his lips. Admiral Wintermourn hurriedly replaced the handkerchief, glaring death at the soldiers. From its place in the rubble, the Brass Paladin continued to flail, flywheels spinning beneath its armor and steam belching from the exhaust pipe behind its shoulder.

Sergeant Lanters formed up the men and made them ready to advance, but finding a way forward turned out to be harder than it appeared. The pirate's bomb had effectively sealed the street they stood upon, and this ridiculous shantytown was built with even less forethought than Wintermourn could have imagined. What started as a boardwalk alleyway would widen into a street before abruptly coming to a dead end. There *might* be a kind of sense to it all. Perhaps if one lived in this place long enough it became clear. Wintermourn did not care. He would see it all burned to the ground.

In the end they had to pull almost all the way back to the *Colossus* and advance along behind the other piers. Even that proved slow going. The pirates had hauled out every crate, barrel, and old table they could lay hands on, it seemed, choking the piers with makeshift barricades. Few defenders stood behind these, though. With good reason.

Haventown Lagoon was a damnable mess. Stray bombs and musket balls flew everywhere, and stinking gun smoke clouds lay over the water like thick fog. Navy warships fought pirate vessels in the tight waterway while the airships dueled above. Incredibly, the *Saltspray* and *Fortune's Loss* still survived near the lagoon entrance, preventing more than a handful of Perinese vessels from entering. They were wrecks, only barely afloat. Still, their crews fought on bitterly, their battle cries loud enough to be heard above the chaos surrounding them.

The *Titan* had managed to slip that gauntlet, even opening fire on the town earlier, damn Captain Caldwell for a fool. The pirate airship *Moonchaser* had wrought vengeance, though, and now the *Titan* struggled to come about, her masts shattered and her paddlewheels stuck within dented housings.

Above, the battle was even more fierce, tilted heavily in the defenders' favor. Now Crown Prince Gwydion's airship was outnumbered three to one, by the *Moonchaser, Sky Serpent,* and *Solrun's Hammer.* The *Windhaunter* hung back, still tethered to the aerial docks. For all of Gwydion's boasting, the heavily armored ship was sorely pressed. Two pirate vessels would move to board the *Glory,* grapnels flying, forcing Gwydion away and giving the third ship enough room to run amok, bombing the Perinese naval vessels below with impunity.

Reinforcements wouldn't be coming any time soon. Wintermourn sighed. *Of course I've got to do every damned thing myself.* He shook his head and climbed past a makeshift barricade. Three old men had been behind it, taking potshots at the Bluecoats and missing every time. Sergeant Adjutant Lanters was about to skewer the third and last defender as his marines spread out to secure this part of the docks.

"Quarter!" cried the pirate, kneeling, one hand outstretched to ward off the sergeant. He was old, with the leathery skin earned by an entire life at sea. Past him, the docks continued on—a pier to the right stretched off into the frothing water of the lagoon, and to the left a dark street wended deeper into the Waterdocks. "Quarter," he repeated. "I beg ye!"

Sergeant Adjutant Lanters paused with his saber upraised. He looked to Admiral Wintermourn.

Admiral Wintermourn smiled at the fellow, genuinely amused. "What a ridiculous consideration," he laughed. The Bluecoats standing nearby knew what was good for them, so they laughed as well. "No, of course not. Sergeant, if you please."

The pirate panicked. He looked back to the man standing above him, but Sergeant Lanters was already thrusting. The pirate scrabbled feebly at Lanters's blade, crying out as he was transfixed on two and a half feet of steel.

Of all the ridiculous things people come up with. Wintermourn chuckled to himself and grinned at the Bluecoats standing nearby, who laughed dutifully. "Quarter! Can you imagine that? I mean really—"

Explosions burst all about them. They staggered Wintermourn and shattered the makeshift barricades, sending a hail of jagged wooden splinters flying through the air.

"Bombs!" shouted Lanters. "Sir, we're in the open. We need cover!"

Wintermourn regained his bearings. The salvo had come from the *Sky Serpent*, opportunistically bombing them while her sister vessels kept the *Glory of Perinault* occupied. "I can see that!" he snarled. Something wet dripped down his chin. Wintermourn wiped away blood with a curse and retrieved his handkerchief. With his other hand, he gestured down the path leading back into the pirate town. "Advance! All of you! For king and country!"

"For king and country!" cried the marines.

They fled the docks, down the twisty street leading back into the Waterdocks' interior. The ramshackle structures loomed overhead, a mishmash of slapdash architecture that hid a hundred different places where pirates might be lurking, just waiting to ambush them.

Which happened almost immediately. Several popping pistol shots rang out in the narrow street, and the first two marines in the column behind Sergeant Lanters crumpled, their hats flying. Wintermourn spotted their assailants: four pirates in an alleyway. He ordered the men forward, relishing the sight as the dastards were cut down. Lanters saw the street secured, then made his way back to the admiral.

"Sir," he said, making his salute. "This place is even twistier than the docks around the *Colossus*. We'll be walking into a hundred such ambushes here."

Wintermourn gingerly pulled his handkerchief away from his nose. The flow seemed to have stopped for now. "Hoary locks of the Goddess," he swore. "I'd thought any pirate with a spine vanquished already, yet they keep popping up on every street we turn down. They're like cockroaches!" He paused to consider. "Very well. We shall treat them as such. Sergeant! We go building by building from here on in, so long as we can keep cover from above. Our objective is to take control of the Waterdocks. Eliminate *all* opposition. Be methodical."

"Aye, sir," he said with a salute, turning back to the Bluecoat column. "Secure that shack! Greene, Bryant, Slain, you're all on point! Batter down the door if you have to."

Wintermourn watched in approval as the men jumped to. Muffled shouts and the clatter of steel sounded within the little building. A few moments later the bedraggled marines emerged, hauling behind two little old ladies wearing bandoliers full of knives. The sergeant put them up against a wall and had them shot.

Wintermourn nodded in approval. They'd been pushed back, yes. They'd been bloodied. But they would not be stopped.

Next came a warehouse with a wide sliding door, just before an intersection. There seemed many such structures down here on the Waterdocks. It made a certain sense—pirates needed *somewhere* to store their loot, after all.

Bluecoats pulled aside the door to reveal a haphazard wall of carts and wooden pallets. Grimy, youthful faces appeared behind them, with swords and makeshift pikes at the ready. It was some gang of filthy hoodlums, without even enough gumption to serve with a pirate's ship. The men dealt with them quickly, subduing resistance and putting them up against the wall as they wept and plead. Wintermourn felt acute satisfaction at the report of muskets, followed by the chain gang slump of fresh corpses collapsing.

Not everyone shared his enthusiasm. A few troubled faces appeared among the soldiery. Private Bryant was prime among them as the column marched to the junction up ahead. Wintermourn decided to have Lanters put him in the lead. One way or another, everyone would be reminded of their duty.

The intersection was dominated by a two-story tavern, a rusty cutlass above the door its only signboard. Wide, smoke-stained windows looked out onto the lane—perfect spots from which to prepare an ambush. The Craftwright's Terrace above cast its shadow over all of it, the cliff wall it sat upon only a short distance away, past the tavern and a low warehouse. Wintermourn realized they'd almost doubled back through the twisty streets, ending up quite near to where the pirate bomb had blunted their initial advance.

Sergeant Adjutant Lanters ordered the men up to the front of the Rusty Cutlass, with Wintermourn observing from the middle of the street. The sergeant tested the latch, then kicked in the door. Bluecoats followed his charge inside, their battle cries mixing with the shouts of defiance from within. The soldiers emerged a few minutes later with captives. There were two older pirates, a middle-aged woman, a girl clutching a doll who couldn't have been more than eight, and surprisingly, a Mechanist in his leather greatcoat.

Wintermourn felt his boredom fade. *Will wonders never cease.* Aside from their awful screaming cannons, the Mechanists had hidden from the battle, preferring to let the pirates do their fighting. Wintermourn considered. Perhaps this one could be of use, if only to avoid more of their infernal weaponry. "Well done, Sergeant Adjutant," exclaimed Wintermourn. "Hold off on shooting them a moment. Bring that fellow over, so that we can have a bit of a chat."

"Right," said Lanters. He gestured at the other captives. "Put the rest of them up against the tavern wall."

One of the marines balked. It was Private Bryant again. "Sir? The girl?"

"Your senses rattled, soldier? Up against the wall with 'er."

Suddenly, the Mechanist dropped to his knees. He freed one arm and shoved a hand into a pouch at his waist. It came back gripping a grapefruit-sized black sphere with a complicated clockwork mechanism atop it. A bomb.

"Go!" he shouted at the girl, his voice muted by his mask. Then he thumbed the mechanical fuse and tossed it into the middle of the street.

The girl grabbed the head of her doll and pulled it free, revealing a stiletto's blade with a plushy handle. This she jammed into the arm of Bryant, who cried out and fell back. The other pirates took advantage as well, biting, kicking, and fighting their way free.

Wintermourn stared in horror as the bomb hit the boardwalk and bounced towards him. *No!* He stepped back and reached for a Bluecoat standing to his right, then pulled the man in front of him.

The blast was a surge of force that slammed into his living shield and bowled the both of them over. Wintermourn fell to the boardwalk, stunned. For what seemed an eternity he struggled to recover; *this* way was up, *these* were his limbs, and *that* was his own saber he was lying uncomfortably atop of. Hearing was a loss, for the moment.

He thrust the soldier atop him aside. The fellow was dead, a ruined and bloody mess who had served with distinction at the end, even if he hadn't meant to.

The Bluecoats lay about the street, similarly thrown back. Windows were shattered and the boardwalk splintered where the blast had gone off. Those closest had been likewise killed, but the bomb had stunned more men than it had done real damage. Sergeant Lanters was climbing to his feet, slapping his ear in confusion, one of his eyes red and bloody. The young girl had survived, along with the Mechanist, amazingly. Both of them ran away down the street, past the tavern and warehouse, headed perplexingly for the cliff wall.

"After them!" roared Wintermourn. His voice sounded weak and tinny in his ears, more felt than heard. "Get those bloody pirates!"

Sergeant Lanters looked to him, then followed his outstretched arm. He roared a command of his own and took off in pursuit. After a moment, a few of the less injured Bluecoats staggered after.

Rough hands helped Wintermourn up. He shoved the marines aside as soon as he could stand, drawing his saber with one hand and straightening his wig with the other. "On your feet!" he snarled at the marines all about him. "Get on your damned feet and get after them. And if any one of you kills that Mechanist before I get to him, you'll hang for high treason!"

He led the remnants of his force down the street. It didn't take long to catch up to the other marines. They clustered at the back of the warehouse, where a number of the thick brass pipes emerged from the solid rock, climbing up to the Craftwright's Terrace and beyond, cleverly hidden by the shadows.

"What are you doing?" demanded Wintermourn.

Lanters turned back, revealing a stack of crates between the warehouse and the wall. The Bluecoats were prying at them with their muskets and smallswords. "There's a hidden door here, sir," he said. "They slipped right through before we could nab 'em"

"Then get it—"

The Bluecoats heaved, and something snapped with a metallic ping. The stack of crates slid out on oiled hinges, all of a cunningly crafted piece. An opening wide enough for two men was revealed, leading down a passage that descended into the bare rock of the terrace wall.

"Hmm," muttered Wintermourn. Lanters and his Bluecoats looked back, awaiting his orders. The opening could lead anywhere, really. Some sort of mine? The Mechanists could have any number of nasty surprises waiting. *I'm certainly not exposing myself to another of those screaming contraptions.*

But he'd be damned to the Realms Below if he'd let those two escape.

"Sergeant Adjutant," he said. "Take a pair of men and go down there. Find the Mechanist. Find out where this goes."

Sergeant Lanters raised his eyebrows in surprise. "Sir? What about the rest of the Waterdocks?"

"I am the ranking navy field officer here," replied Wintermourn in tones of iron. "I will lead the company. Who is your second?"

"The platoon sergeant," said Lanters. "Greene! Get over here!"

Wintermourn glanced back at a marine with a bloodied coat and a battered hat, one of the bomb-battered others running hurriedly over to join them. He stopped to make a salute, and Wintermourn curled his lip. He had little use for tardiness.

Well, any port in a storm, as they say. Though the fellow certainly wouldn't get a promotion out of this.

"Good enough," he said to his adjutant. "Now get below and do your duty. We'll have control of these Waterdocks soon enough."

"Sir!" Lanters made his salute, grabbed two men, and entered the hidden passage with his blade drawn.

Wintermourn watched him disappear. Then he turned to Sergeant Greene and the marines standing nearby. "Back to the intersection!" he barked, sheathing his saber. "Form up and move out. We've still got a job to do!"

Technically, Greene probably should have given the command. Wintermourn was in a hurry, though; there was a lot of ground still to cover. And the man was a marine officer, after all not even possessing a real rank.

The company moved away from the Rusty Cutlass, continuing on to another series of warehouses. He had eighty-some troops left in fighting shape, more or less. It would be enough, if they kept up the momentum. Soon they marched along again, the very picture of efficient conquest.

Progress came slowly, though. The next few buildings were excellently situated for ambush. Under Wintermourn's eye, Sergeant Greene led the men to secure each one, just waiting for a pistol shot or battle cry, followed by a rush of blades. Most were empty. It did prove tedious, nerve-racking work, though.

Still, the men did what they were told. Any reticence had been quashed by the Mechanist's bomb. Anger stiffened their spines. Bit by bit they marched, conquering this ridiculous pirate town, even if the rest of the fleet floundered about in the lagoon just beyond it.

The final warehouse in the area was small, in an out-of-the-way corner of the Waterdocks. It was short and padlocked from the outside. The lock was heavy and well made, better protection than Wintermourn had seen so far on any of the other warehouses. And quizzically, while it seemed that the pirates didn't want anyone getting inside, several brand-new crates were haphazardly stacked up against the wall near the door, as if put there in a hurry. Sergeant Greene and a trio of men moved cautiously over to examine it and listen carefully at the door. They whispered in hushed tones to each other before Wintermourn's new second returned to him.

"Sir," said Greene, snapping a salute. "There're people inside this one. Not saying anything, but there's plenty of shuffling around."

Wintermourn raised a condescending eyebrow at the man. "So? Break the door down, then, and kill them." He didn't care if it was a whole pirate orphanage this time. The men and women inside would die.

Greene licked his lips nervously. "Beg pardon, sir. But those crates are marked. I think the pirates are storing tea in there."

Admiral Wintermourn paused. "Tea, you say?"

The Bluecoat nodded. "Aye, sir. Marks are from Greisheim, Zhong-hei, Capricanto. From all over. They must have hauled a bunch of crates outside to make room, though they had to be in a hurry. Rest of the warehouse has to be filled with it. Can't imagine why it's locked from outside, though."

A whole warehouse full of ill-gotten tea, eh? This was valuable cargo. And it had been positively ages since he'd had a good cup. Wintermourn considered a moment.

"Hmm," he mused. "Let us try to minimize the damage, then. Line the men up in a semicircle around that door, muskets at the ready. Then hack off that lock. Let's give these poor fools a chance to surrender."

Greene nodded, then looked back to him in shock. "Sir? We're taking captives?"

Out the corner of his eye, he saw the marine, Private Bryant, sigh in relief. The man would be dealt with summarily, once this task was finished. "No, of course not. As you were, Sergeant Greene."

The Bluecoat ducked his head and gave the order. As his marines took their places, Wintermourn strode forward with his hands behind his back, just far enough away that he could be heard clearly. Greene moved past, coming up to the door with a drawn pistol before firing at the lock. There was a pop and a flash, and it fell to the boardwalk with a clatter. Green stepped aside, ready to grab the door handle, and nodded to Wintermourn.

"Ruffians and scurrilous knaves!" he began. "I know that you're in there. Come out with your hands up, and you will be treated fairly."

He smirked, turning to share the jest with the rest of the Bluecoats. They joined in with a chorus of snickers, as they well should have.

A long moment passed with no reply. Wintermourn frowned. Surely the pirates heard him? He could hear their rustling now and the shifting of many feet. "Have a care," he continued. "My patience grows very thin, you scallywags. It will not last forever."

Silence, and the distant boom of battle. Near the door Sergeant Greene jerked his head aside and covered his nose with the back of his hand. Wintermourn smelled it too: the faint whiff of old meat. Was someone keeping a dead cow in there?

This is what I get for trying to be reasonable. "Very well, then," he said. Wintermourn turned and marched back behind the first rank of Bluecoats. "None will say that I gave you less than every chance in the world," he said frostily. "Sergeant Greene!"

The Bluecoat nodded. He reached out and grabbed the handle to the warehouse door, then hauled it back, opening it out into the street and taking cover behind it from the muskets of his fellows. No one fired, though. Instead, cries of shock and horror rang out among the marines. Wintermourn himself only stared.

Corpses stood in tight ranks within the warehouse. They were locals, pirates and townsfolk both, all hideously wounded and in varying stages of decay. But they still moved. They shuffled back and forth and bumped into one another, a constantly rustling pack of the living dead. As one, they looked out onto Admiral Wintermourn and the Bluecoats.

Wintermourn smelled phantom smoke. An image flashed in his mind's eye, of flames and dead hands reaching for him. "Goddess of the Realms Above," he yelled in sudden panic. "Fire! Fire, damn you!"

His marines obeyed instantly. They cut loose in a hasty volley, and musket balls slammed into rotting shoulders, sunken chests, and oozing cheeks. Splinters from the wood of the warehouse joined flying offal to fill the air with foul confetti.

The Revenants did not fall. They groaned, arms coming up, talons out and seeking. The living dead surged forth from the warehouse in a wave.

Horror washed over Admiral Wintermourn. He drew his saber and backed farther away. "Fire! Fire again! Fire everything! Kill those damnable monstrosities!"

Discipline held the Bluecoats in front, who dropped to one knee and tried to reload with shaking hands. The second rank stepped up, took aim, and unleashed another volley. Again the air filled with lead shot, and again it failed to stop the oncoming horde. The Revenants groaned angrily, their voices mixing with the panicked shouts of marines to fill the street with unholy song.

More shots rang out. Smallswords were drawn. Wintermourn shouted commands and dire curses. The dead ignored him, however. They came on, unstoppable, until their rotting claws fell on living men, punctuated by the desperate flash of bright Perinese steel.

CHAPTER FIFTEEN

PICKING A LOCK WAS NEVER QUITE AS EASY AS EVERYONE SEEMED TO THINK.

Fengel sat back in his crouch, taking a breath and shifting his grip on the screwdriver. The door before him was massive, an armored portal in a bulwark of steel that stretched across the tunnel from one rough-hewn rock wall to the other. A bundle of wires poked out from the keyhole, his impromptu picks. Beside him stood young Imogen with a Mechanist's galvanic lantern. The light it shed was stark and overbright in the close space.

"Two doors!" he exclaimed. "Two doors *behind* your secret, hidden mine entrance. Really, now. Who does that?"

"The machinery down here is quite dangerous," said Imogen, voice muffled behind her gas mask. She stepped warily aside as Cubbins trotted over from the wall he had spent the last few minutes staring at. "And it was deemed prudent by the Brotherhood, since the most important element for aerial flight happened to be discovered beneath a town full of *pirates*."

Cubbins butted up against Fengel's leg, purring loudly. Fengel sighed. The cat had apparently followed them down to the Waterdocks, having appeared just as they slipped inside this tunnel. "Whatever. Time is wasting. Don't you have a key?"

"I'm only a Mechanist-Aspirant!" replied Imogen. "The Cabal must have forgotten about that. I told you this not ten minutes ago, at the last door. Really, if you're that forgetful, then it isn't any wonder that you have to share your airship with Captain Blackheart. You should carry a journal around and keep notes."

Fengel glared at her witheringly. "Look. Just use that other bomb of yours and blast this thing open."

Imogen stared at him like he was an uneducated simpleton. "You really have no idea of the basic principles behind physics and mineralogy, do you?"

"Of course not," said Fengel, his voice frosty. "I'm a pirate, as you pointed out. Which means I *do* have a grasp on aether-science and flight dynamics."

"It's not just because this is Haventown!" Imogen gesticulated, the light from her lantern whirling wildly. "These bulwarks are here because light-air gas is insanely flammable! An explosion down here would collapse the tunnel, at the least, and could possibly blow up the whole town!"

Fengel glared at her a moment. Then he turned pointedly back to the door. "Light, if you please, Miss Imogen." He bent back to the lock with his makeshift picks. "Though we're wasting precious time while good men and women—"

Tumblers twisted within the door. Something screeched like bending metal, then clicked loudly. "Oh," said Fengel. "Never mind. Got it now."

"You didn't break this lock too, did you?"

"Of course not," Fengel lied. "And anyway, we're in a hurry."

He reached up and pulled at the handle, which twisted satisfyingly. The door didn't budge at first, and Fengel stood to get a proper grip. Imogen leaned over to help him, and together they swung the portal slowly open. It was a foot of solid steel all the way through.

Darkness reigned in the chamber beyond. Through the gloom came the rumbling, hissing, thumping rhythm of great mechanisms hard at work. Imogen aimed her galvanic lantern and strode ahead into the gloom, with reflected light glinting from shining brass and steel. An orange blur rushed past her feet: Cubbins, giving a short trill as he went.

Fengel rose from his feet with a frown. *Where's that flea-bitten thing off to, in such a hurry?*

He recovered his makeshift locksmith's tools—they were Imogen's, but one never knew when such things would be needed. Then he stood and stretched. A choir of bruises, aches, and pains all sang at him, a legacy of today's fighting and the long night before. Fengel wanted little more than rest. There was still much to be done, however. Besides which, Imogen was right there. *Never let them see you stumble.* Wearily, Fengel took a step towards the next part of the Mechanist's mine.

Something echoed down the passage from behind. He paused at the sound, his hand going automatically to the grip of his saber as he glanced back over his shoulder.

The dark at his back deepened as Imogen moved farther away with the lantern. Still Fengel stood, rooted and still as a statue, straining his ears if not his eyes. The sound had been like the clang of metal upon metal, single and sonorous. Or … had it? *Am I just hearing things?* Ahead, the many assembled machines beat to their own stagger-step rhythm. Sound was strange, down here in the mine.

Nothing came screaming out of the gloom at him. Fengel shrugged, then turned to catch up with his young Mechanist guide.

She was waiting a short distance inside, one boot tapping impatiently against diamond-plate metal flooring. Fengel made his way over, staring at the chamber illuminated by her light.

Far from a simple passage of hewn stone roofed by brass pipe, they stood in a great chamber whose borders lay like mist-born phantoms at the edges of the light. Huge iron beams supported the ceiling and the walls, making it seem as if they stood inside the gullet of a great mechanical leviathan. The floor was covered in steel, save great sections bored out of the ground to allow room for fat, riveted pipes to rise up out of them. Egg-shaped rows of metal cylinders sat in between. Steam engines rumbled along beneath them, occasionally venting thick white clouds across the floor.

"Crusty toenails of the Goddess Above," muttered Fengel. "This place has been under Haventown all this time?"

"Oh yes," said Imogen. "And none of you ever knew about it." She frowned. "Until now, that is."

Fengel nodded. "Well. We're not going to make the town fly just by standing around. How do we … turn everything on?" He glanced at a row of pressure gauges, all their needles dancing madly behind the glass.

Imogen shook her head. "Not here. Controls are in the last chamber past this one. We need to release the gas there, then all these pumps will push everything up to the Gasworks on the Craftwright's Terrace. My brothers there will send it on and alert the other teams to unmoor the terraces."

Fengel sighed in exasperation. "*Another* door." He shook his head. "Fine. Let's get—wait." He glanced around, realizing something was amiss. "Where's Cubbins?"

Imogen looked left, then right. "What? The cat?" She shrugged. "I don't know. And aren't we in a hurry?"

"Yes, but …" Fengel frowned. He found himself mildly surprised. "I just … hope he doesn't get crushed under all this machinery."

"That would be absolutely awful," agreed Imogen. It was hard to tell beneath her muffling gas mask, but he could swear she sounded pleased.

"Just …" he shook his head. "You're right. We need to get moving."

Something echoed faintly behind them—a single loud clang, as of metal on metal. Fengel whirled, hand to his saber. He stared into the dark.

"What—" began Imogen.

"Shh!" He hissed, holding up his free hand. "Shine your lantern back towards the door."

She obeyed, illuminating the bulwark entryway with harsh white light. The open portal was a black, gaping maw against the polished steel.

Fengel waited. He counted to ten—and then to twenty. *Did I imagine it?* It had been a long night and a longer day. He wasn't entirely uninjured from the fighting, either.

The rattle and clang of the machines all about them beat on. It echoed about the chamber, down to the open entryway.

Fengel shook his head. "It's nothing. Let's move on."

They continued on through the pump chamber, with Fengel occasionally looking over his shoulder, for what he did not know. The fat orange tabby, Cubbins, did not reappear. Imogen seemed untroubled by this, marching stolidly along as always. She led them on a twisting path through the forest of grinding, twisting, churning machinery.

While the young Mechanist may not have had the keys they needed, she was certainly familiar enough with this place. Even with a lantern, Fengel would have gotten lost in minutes. Imogen led him around a wall of fat, wagon-wheel-sized gears grinding away, to reveal a section of wall dug out to create another passage, twisting away into darkness.

"Wait, a side passage?" said Fengel. "Not another bulkhead wall?" He was hopelessly turned around.

Imogen pointed away with the lantern. "No, that is off to the side. We keep going past."

Fengel peered into the passage. "Where does this go?"

"The secret path was never meant to be permanent. This excavation leads back out to the Waterdocks, to a place more suitable for a large entrance. Goes right up to the cliff wall behind that old tannery that the Brotherhood keeps trying to move." Her gauntleted fingers clutched greedily. "There should still be a lot of explosives left there for the final work, if we need them for the Perinese."

"I'm certain we will," he said. "But let's move on to that last chamber."

"It's just around these camshafts," said Imogen, gesturing with her lantern and stepping past a series of rotating metal rods.

Fengel followed and found her at the armored rear wall of the chamber. "I don't suppose this one's unlocked?" he asked.

Imogen just looked at him through her goggles. Not for the first time, he wondered how she saw through them in this gloom. "Fine," he said with a sigh, retrieving his makeshift lockpicks. "But when this is all said and done, you're going to go demand all the keys in your weird, secret club of—"

A loud, singular clang echoed from the opposite end of the chamber, like metal striking metal.

Fengel dropped the wires and whipped about, drawing his saber in one smooth motion.

"What?" asked Imogen. "What do—"

He held a hand up for quiet. It didn't help. Even with both of them silent, Fengel couldn't hear anything over the clangor of the machines filling the chamber.

"We've been followed," he said. "Shine the light back towards the way we came."

Imogen aimed her lantern past him. Its cone of light reflected from the polished skin of the pumping and whirling machines. Nothing jumped out at him or scurried frantically away. Fengel didn't need such a confirmation. He *had* heard something. This time he was certain of it. *And it's not the damned cat, either.*

No, he had it now. Past the mechanical noise lay a rough, dragging clatter punctuated by an irregular thump against the steel flooring. Fengel raised his saber into guard, feeling that old there-not-there feeling, his nerves and senses and instincts all ready and waiting to act. His only warning might be the flash of a pistol—or the hiss of a blowgun.

It was neither. A hulking figure staggered from out behind the wall of large sprockets. Fengel paused at the leather greatcoat and respirator gas mask he wore. It was a Mechanist, leaning heavily on a young girl with long, dirty hair who couldn't have been more than eight. Her eyes went straight to Fengel, and in her free hand she raised a stiletto with a plush doll's head for a handle.

Fengel knew her. "Molly Mayhap?" he asked, lowering his blade. "What are you doing down here?"

"Who?" asked Imogen.

"She's the kitchen-girl over at the Rusty Cutlass," said Fengel. "Hasn't ever said much, but she's got a real talent for knives."

The Mechanist lifted his head at Fengel's voice. "Who's there?" he asked. "Captain Fengel?"

"The very same," answered Fengel. He sheathed his saber and strode over. Behind him, Imogen lowered her lantern a bit. "And I've one of your unbelievably critical brethren-aspirants here with me as well.

The Mechanist looked past him. "Imogen? What are you doing down here?"

"Hello, Brother Barlett," she said, making a small wave. "If you're injured, you really shouldn't be walking around down here. The protocols against injured Brothers here in the mines are very clear."

Mechanist Barlett gingerly stood on his own, allowing Molly Mayhap to step away. The leather along the right side of his greatcoat was gashed and wet with the slick of his own blood. Fengel eyed it critically, wondering for the hundredth time how the Mechanists could tell each other apart. Barlett might survive if they found a physician soon. He retrieved a handkerchief and passed it to the fellow, who took it gratefully and pressed it to his side. The girl, Molly, turned away from them both, peering back into the dark towards the front of the chamber, her secret stiletto never wavering.

"Don't quote protocol at me," said Barlett wearily. "We were driven inside by the fighting. The Perinese have conquered half the Waterdocks now … and they're on their way to take the rest."

Fengel cursed. He turned back to Imogen. "We have to hurry."

Barlett peered at them critically. "A Mechanist-Aspirant and the captain of the *Dawnhawk*. The Cabal want to raise the city, don't they?"

"Aye," said Fengel. He tried not to think too much about Natasha. "It's about the only chance we've got left at this point."

"We need to hurry, then. A squad of soldiers followed us down here. I've done what I could to jury-rig the doors behind us, but someone broke the locks."

Imogen glared witheringly at Fengel. "You said—"

He coughed loudly. "Yes, speed is essential. Only there's this last door in the way. Do you have the key?"

"Of course," replied Barlett. "Every full Brother has one." He fished a complicated skeleton key from one of his innumerable pockets and suddenly doubled over with his free hand to his wounded side. Molly Mayhap ran over to support him, quiet as always, one hand tightly clutching her knife.

Fengel took the key from his outstretched hand. "Here, fellow. I've got it."

"You can't just jam it in," hissed the Brother in pain. "Press this in slowly, only about—"

"Three-quarters of the way, then a quarter-turn to the right, followed by a seven degree reverse rotation. Yes, I've got it down by now."

Barlett looked up oddly at him. "You didn't try *picking* the locks, did you?" he groaned. "Imogen, you know how sensitive they are!"

"We didn't have any other choice!"

Fengel let them argue and turned to the door. He carefully inserted the key in the proscribed method, working the tumblers and shifting them around until a great click sounded somewhere within the armored lock. Brother Barlett wasn't joking. Even with the key, this was still tricky.

So much faster this way. Having the key was always best, though a part of him did want to go back to work with the wires and the screwdriver. It was good to keep such skills polished—one never quite knew when one would need to tease a lock. *Maybe some other time.* Fengel grabbed the handle with both hands and twisted it, hauling back and slowly opening the armored portal to their destination.

The others quit arguing and joined him. Imogen shone her galvanic torch into the darkened vault, revealing another chamber just as large as the one they stood in. Most of the floor was gone, tumbling away into a dark pit filled with bundles of brass pipe rising up to fill it like the branches of some overgrown bush. Directly ahead, diamond-plate steel steps led down a wide platform. It hung out over the pit, supporting arcane panels of wood and glass from which the Mechanists could do their work. A faint odor filled the space, more than just stale air. Fengel recognized the flammable stink of light-air gas.

"There," said Fengel. "Imogen, do you know what to do?"

"Of course," she replied. The Mechanist-Aspirant pushed past him and tromped down the stairs.

Fengel stepped aside and let Barlett stagger past. The Mechanist stood a little straighter and moved on his own, leaving Molly behind. He clutched his side still, though, and his breath was ragged behind the mask. "Don't forget that you're still just an *aspirant*, Imogen. Observe the protocols. This isn't something that can be rushed."

"Of course I'll observe the protocols. I've studied this system since I was little!"

"Well, I helped build the Goddess-damned thing, so you'll listen and listen well."

Fengel let them argue. He glanced at Molly, who stood just inside the door with him, then cocked his head after the Mechanists with a smile. She shrugged, returning a smile of her own.

"Is that blood I see on your stiletto, Molly dear? Stab yourself a soldier, did you?"

The little girl nodded enthusiastically in the gloom.

"That's a good girl. Well, let's go on down, and you can tell me all about it."

A clatter and a curse from the chamber behind them stopped him cold. Fengel whirled and drew his saber. The machinery ratcheted and whirred as usual, but past the big wall of turning gears, he spied a splash of light. Not cold and constant like Imogen's torch, but the flickering yellow of an oil lantern. Barlett's pursuers had caught up to them.

Three men stepped out from behind the gears. The one in the lead held the lantern, while the other two raised pistols and smallswords. They wore the blue jackets and round black caps of the marines and moved cautiously, staring at the room about them like it would come to life at any moment and devour them.

Bluecoats. Damnation. Apparently Barlett hadn't secured the doors as well as he'd thought.

Fengel quickly moved to the right, behind one side of the doorway. "Molly girl," he whispered. "Get down there to the platform." She shook her head and he sighed. "I can take three Bluecoats, but I need you down there in case one gets past, all right?"

The little girl glared at him with narrow eyes, then nodded slowly. She turned and ran, her shoes clattering on the metal stairs.

Yellow lantern light flashed up after her. "There!" cried one of the marines. "It's the girl!"

"Pistols up!" ordered the sergeant at their head. "Don't let 'er close!"

A shaft of lantern light flashed past Fengel for the stair and the platform below it. Barlett and Imogen turned in surprise, while Molly dove behind a heavy pipe. "The Bluecoats!" cried Barlett. "Captain Fengel, you can't let them fire in here!"

Two stubby pistol noses poked through the doorway as the light behind them brightened. Fengel rolled away from the wall and lashed out at the nearest soldier, aiming carefully. The blade bit, cutting away the pistol and the hand holding it at the wrist. Blood spurted from the stump, and the Bluecoat froze in shock and pain. Fengel didn't wait for his reaction. He pushed past, ramming the bell guard of his blade into the face of the other soldier, feeling the crunch of breaking teeth through his weapon.

Faster, faster. The soldier dropped his pistol and fell back with the start of a muffled scream, the twin to the hoarse shriek just erupting from Fengel's first victim. He pushed between the two Bluecoats, aiming a backswing hack at the head of the third and final soldier, the one holding the lamp.

The man was too quick, though, too wary. At Fengel's appearance, he'd already started falling back with his smallsword raised in a block. It was enough, barely. Fengel's blade rang off the hasty guard, forcing the man to retreat even farther with a curse.

"Hurry up down there!" Fengel yelled back over his shoulder.

"I'm trying!" shouted Imogen.

"Follow the damnable protocols!" ordered Barlett, his voice like a leaking balloon.

The two soldiers collapsed behind Fengel, one shrieking and clutching at his severed hand, the other off-balance and flailing. Fengel drove ahead with an experimental slash at the third man. He blocked the blow with confidence, neither overeager nor unskilled, and gave enough ground that Fengel had to step out away from the cover of the door and into the vaulted space before it.

The man set the lantern down and moved aside, watching Fengel warily the whole time. By the chevrons on his sleeve, he was a sergeant and, given the battered nature of his face and the men he'd sent forward as bait, an experienced one.

"That was cowardly of ya," said the sergeant. "But well done."

"The wrist is especially vulnerable to a sharp blade," replied Fengel. He eyed the distance between them and the angle of the lighting. "A dagger can sever tendons and arteries. While a sword ..." He raised his own up into guard. "A sword can do so much worse."

They circled. Out of the corner of his eye, Fengel saw the machinery all about them in a new light. The massive gears could catch and grind. Chain linkages could twist and trip. He had to be wary.

The sergeant hefted his blade. His dry, scarred lips were pursed in calculation, and his eyes narrow above an oft-broken nose.

Something about that face gave Fengel pause. *Do I know him? He seems ... familiar.*

The sergeant jerked back in surprise. His eyes widened, and then a crazy, cruel grin stretched itself across his features.

"Ashley Fengel," breathed the man.

A galvanic shock shot straight through Fengel. It traveled from his boots to his brain and left white-hot rage in its wake. "I don't know how you know my name," he hissed, "but you will not die cleanly for using it."

His opponent gave a deep belly laugh. "By the Goddess Above. Little Ashley Fengel. Here, of all places! Now, ain't that just something."

"I would have your name before I kill you," snarled Fengel. "Have we met somewhere, sir?"

The Bluecoat sergeant touched his chest with his free hand, mockingly shocked. "You dunno me, Ashley? After all the fun we had back in Darrenway? All the running you did from me an' my Coal Street Boys?"

Fengel stilled. He felt his jaw drop open. Memories long forgotten washed over him: Filthy alleys and firetrap tenements. Helping Da with his prad-rolling, trying to stay a step ahead of the aristocrats. Getting flattened every single day by the Coal Street Boys, until he learned to fight back against them and their leader: big, mean Jacob Lanters.

"Jacob," he breathed. "How? How can you, of all people, be here now?"

"How else?" said the sergeant. He started circling again, forcing Fengel to keep up. "Last time we met, you cheated yer little arse off—hit me with a damned cat and knocked me out cold. I lost control o' the old gang. You had 'em then. After that, all I had left was going home to be beaten by my drunkard pa every night. So I nicked every penny he had on 'im and ran off to join the navy." He smiled. "Now I serve Admiral Wintermourn 'imself. Adjutant with command of a whole company of marines! And you're just a damned traitor and pirate. I'm gonna take my time killing you, you little shit."

Fengel recovered. He brought his saber back up in guard. "I never dropped a cat on you, Jacob. If you hadn't been torturing the thing, it wouldn't have attacked. But that's beside the point. You wouldn't have won that day, and you're not going to win now." He smiled a grim smile of his own, relishing the moment. "I'm going to kill you, Jacob Lanters. For everything you did to me back then, everything you've done today, and all the things in between that I'm so sure you richly deserve."

He lunged, aiming the tip of his blade square for the heart of his onetime nemesis. Jacob's eyes widened at his speed. The sergeant just barely parried his blow, sending Fengel's blade skidding up to tear across his right breast before continuing on up past his shoulder.

A more skilled swordsman would have taken advantage of Fengel's overextension. Lanters only cursed in pain and clutched at the cut with his free hand. He fell back, giving Fengel all the time he needed to recover.

Fengel raised his blade back into guard. "Remember, Jacob? I found a sword to fend you off with, an old arming blade." He feinted, slipping his saber up past the sergeant's guard to slash his thigh. "Watched the guards as they practiced, to learn how to use it." He beat Lanters's blade aside, pushing past to nick the upper arm. "I've come a long way since then. Fighting for my life, first in the navy, then for myself. *Years* spent practicing, with my life on the line every time." He casually parried a slash at his head. "I'm sure that you're capable in a brawl, but here and now, that's not going to save you."

The sergeant backed up with a curse to a set of man-sized pumping pistons. He was a bulky shadow now in the dim light shed by the lantern at their feet—his sergeant's uniform was soaked with blood.

Somewhere in the chamber overhead a thunderous hissing began. Someone shouted in triumph. Imogen, likely. She'd managed to get the light-air gas pumping.

Fengel returned his attention to his victim. *Time to make an end of this.*

Jacob Lanters met his eyes and gave a shallow nod. He hawked and spat phlegm. "Oh aye," he said, glancing aside. "I'm no fencer. Then again, I don't need ta be."

A flash and a thunderclap erupted from the doorway, where the Bluecoat who still had both hands had recovered enough to fire a musket. The ball whipped just past Fengel's cheek, impacted against a piston, and ricocheted back. It caught Fengel's hat, taking it off and away. He turned to take in the new threat, raising his saber to ward off Lanters from any desperate action.

The Bluecoat sergeant barreled forward with his smallsword upraised above his head. He swung down in a two-handed chop that knocked Fengel's sword aside. Fengel automatically turned it into a binding disarm, but Lanters let go, lifting up one hoary fist to catch Fengel squarely across the jaw.

Stars bloomed across Fengel's vision, and he felt his monocle fly free to dangle on its chain. He brought his free hand up to block, but Lanters caught it with his own and hauled it out of the way. The sergeant hit him again with another tooth-loosening blow, knocking him down and back off balance. Fengel fell to his knees while the other man held him half-up and pummeled away. He couldn't think, couldn't react, couldn't do anything but try to get away.

"Now this ... is more like it," roared Jacob Lanters. "Just like old times ... eh, *Ashley?*"

The sergeant paused for breath and reared back with one bloody-knuckled fist. Fengel only stared at him, trying to focus through the pain, trying to react.

Something fell out from the dark up above. It landed squarely on the burly sergeant's head, a hissing and spitting ball of furious orange fur, like some daemon out of the dark.

Jacob Lanters let go of Fengel instantly, both hands going for Cubbins where he bit and scratched. The sergeant screamed, high and hoarse, and beat at the furious feline.

Fengel felt the strangest thing, not unlike nostalgia, or deja vu. Then he looked down at the saber he still gripped. Amazingly, his reflexes had kept him from letting go. He grit his teeth, lifted the tip of his blade, and thrust up. The blade entered Lanters's belly and slid up past his ribs to his heart.

Sergeant Lanters choked, then went strangely still. He batted weakly at Cubbins, his other hand now seeking gingerly for the length of steel buried in his guts. Then he collapsed forward onto Fengel as his fat orange savior leaped off the corpse with a final hiss.

Blood from the sergeant's ruined face poured onto Fengel's, and the man's limbs twitched reflexively. Fengel cursed, struggled, and finally rolled the dying body aside. He sat up, soaked in the gore of the man, to look at the other Bluecoats near the door. One of them should be just about to fall upon him.

But they weren't coming to the aid of their dead fellow. They wouldn't be helping anyone ever again. Mechanist Barlett knelt over their crumpled corpses, leaning on a heavy two-handed wrench. Molly Mayhap stood beside him, blood on her doll's-head stiletto shining wetly in the light from Imogen's galvanic lantern.

Cubbins trotted over to butt his head up against Fengel's leg. Fengel wearily reached over and petted him.

"We got the gas reserves engaged," said Imogen. "Everything's pumping up to the Gasworks. Our brothers stationed there should be seeing it right this second."

"That's … that's good," said Fengel. He felt tired, and his lips were swelling up. Still petting the cat, he reached up and wiped the blood away from his face with his sleeve. Then he gingerly felt at his teeth. "We should look at getting out of here now."

"The entrance … is being watched," gasped Brother Barlett. "Can't go back out that way."

Fengel frowned. His head hurt. He'd had worse beatings in his time, but not *that* many. "We're trapped, then. That's the only other exit, isn't it? The other isn't finished yet. We can't get through."

The light shifted as Imogen wrestled with something. Then it steadied as she lifted a heavy black bomb in her other hand.

"I beg to differ," she said.

The mask muffled her voice, but Fengel was absolutely certain that she had spoken with eager glee. Beside him Cubbins purred, oblivious, yet happy as could be.

CHAPTER SIXTEEN

Lina watched the earth burn.

She stood in the mouth of the pyramid tunnel, peering at the devastation outside. The ground was scorched and blackened, and all nearby vegetation had been obliterated by the blast they'd triggered. Smoke rose up in lazy streamers stinking of char to occlude her view. Through them she could just make out the spreading banyans and tall green palm trees of the distant jungle. Not everything had been destroyed, then.

Runt chirruped unhappily, squirming in her arms as she leaned out the tunnel entryway to get a better look. Her scalp prickled suddenly, and the air felt greasy on her face. There was a charge in the air. Lina ignored it, looking instead to the enormous broken spire that had toppled who knew how long ago from the peak of the pyramid. Apparently, it was still somewhat attached. Or at least enough to be a functional part of the installation. It had done more than just cook everything outside the pyramid; Lina spied a line of devastation running out straight from the broken spire along the ground, stretching beyond the clearing to carve a burning path all the way to the distant cliffs at the edge of the island.

Lina whistled, long and low. The Stormhammer had certainly packed a bit of a punch, and then some. Through the smoke-streamers Lina spied the flash-cooked corpses of gulls and other flying things littering the earth. The blast had reached into the sky as well, then.

An ear-shattering screech echoed out from inside the pyramid, startling her. *If only you'd been outside too, Butterbeak.*

"Well?" yelled Natasha. "What happened out there? Is it dead?"

Lina turned back and jogged down the tunnel. For all the devastation it had wrought, the pyramid's interior was safe enough. Her crewmates still resided within. Reaver Jane, Paine, Farouk, and Etarin all rested against the machinery the Castaways had been working on, battered but otherwise all right, eying the structure about them suspiciously. Captain Natasha stood on the steps of the central dais, thumbs hooked into her sword belt, with Butterbeak hunkering on her shoulder. Behind her, Allen and Rastalak examined the shimmering, brazen machinery of the Stormhammer. The little Draykin touched it with reverence, while the apprentice Mechanist poked and prodded in a decidedly careless manner. Michael Hockton stood off to one side of the tunnel, waiting for her to return, a helpful expression on his face.

The ancient machine was an enigma. Between Natasha, Rastalak, Allen, and Lina herself, they all had varying degrees of experience with Voorn relics. But the Stormhammer proved resistant to their meddling. They'd spent almost an hour trying to figure it out before Natasha leaned back against a lever by accident. Then everything was pumping and hissing and the crystal sphere floating at the center of it all shot a beam of crackling, scintillating light up at the ceiling. The thunderclap that followed outside had been titanic.

"Everything's cooked, Captain," said Lina, jogging past Michael and the others to come to a stop just below the dais. Runt chirruped unhappily, and Lina turned her attention back to her pet, cooing and rubbing the smooth scales around her swollen middle.

"Stone? Hey." Natasha snapped her fingers. "Look at me. What do you mean by 'everything?' Did we get it? Did I kill the Dray Engine?"

Lina looked up at her captain, surprised. "Oh, sorry, Captain. Looks like everything in the clearing surrounding the pyramid. The blast only touched a small piece of the jungle, though it scorched a path straight up to the ridgeline. I couldn't see the Dray Engine anywhere. So … maybe?"

"It must be a focusing device of some sort," said Allen. He tromped over sulkily to stand just above Natasha. "With the spire broken, I don't think this installation is going to work."

Rastalak rose from his crouch near a series of sputtering glass vials. "Indeed. The artifact of the Great Masters can be triggered, but we have yet to find a way to aim it. It may not be possible, damaged as it is."

Allen wheeled on him. "I just said that!" he cried.

The little Draykin jerked back in surprise. Even Lina was taken aback. Allen *never* raised his voice.

"What's your problem?" asked Natasha. She turned away to stare outside, smacking one fist into her palm. "Of course it's still alive. But I *will* kill that thing. I swear it by the paunchy gut of the Goddess herself."

"My hand hurts!" said the apprentice Mechanist. He held it up, swathed in makeshift bandages. "I lost a finger back on the ship, and all anyone's done is bind it up, and by the Realms Below, it *hurts*, and I'll never play the piano now and I'm stuck on *another* damned island with a bunch of monsters and cutthroats, and Runt is just downright awful!"

He stopped to pant. Lina cradled her writhing pet and glared up at Allen. She was going to have a talk with him, later, about the feelings of others.

Natasha blinked in surprise, having evidently forgotten the apprentice Mechanist. "Oh, quit *whining*," she said. "Stone's pet has always been awful. And I lost a damned nipple once, but you don't hear me squalling like some brat who dropped her favorite musket."

Allen blinked at her. Even Lina was taken aback. The chamber was quiet for a moment, save only the hiss and hum of the Stormhammer.

"How did you ..." Michael Hockton quieted, appearing to consider for a moment. "Did ... did you play with loaded muskets as a child?"

Natasha was nonplussed. "What? Of course. Look, I didn't come all this way to get stuck on an island with a giant clockwork lizard." She shook a fist at the pyramid entrance vigorously, forcing Butterbeak to flap for his balance on her shoulder. "Fengel said you geniuses could get this thing working, so do it! There's a whole damned invasion going on to the south, if you hadn't noticed."

"Captain."

Lina glanced back to where Reaver Jane was climbing wearily to her feet. The older woman looked battered and bruised, covered as she was with numerous scabbed-over cuts. But she seemed ready for a fight, as always. "Captain, we can't make it work."

Natasha looked affronted. "What? Of course we can."

Reaver Jane shook her head. "Captain, we don't even know what this thing was meant to do, way back when. The pirate king said it's a weapon, but we don't even know that for sure. And it's *broken*. We could spend a month here and never get it working right."

Runt let out a hiss, then bit Lina on the arm. She yelped and barely managed not to drop her pet. The fat scryn writhed, and Lina felt her heart go out to the little mother. "Shh," she cooed. *Yowch, that stings.* The spittle was already raising an angry rash on her skin.

She looked back up to see that the others weren't even looking at her. Well, Michael was, with a faint smile. She returned it, then noticed Allen glaring down at them both. The rest of the crew, though, was watching their captain. Natasha was uncharacteristically silent, weighing the options.

Oh no. Lina wasn't thrilled with the idea of being stuck inside the Stormhammer, but at least in here they were safe. And Runt would give birth any day now. The fight to the south would be a *terrible* place for that to happen.

"But Captain Fengel said you should listen to your father," she said, not thinking.

As soon as the words were out of her mouth, Lina realized her mistake. Natasha Blackheart glared down at her, eyes suddenly furious. "You're right, Jane. To the Realms Below with this crazy scheme. We're going back to Haventown! We're going to win this fight, and then we're going to haul every damned cannon back up here that I can lay my hands on and pummel that clockwork monster until it's scrap!"

She stalked down the stair, pushing past them all, and crossed the floor of the chamber to the entryway tunnel. Lina shared a look with Reaver Jane, then scurried after.

Their captain came to a stop at the exit mouth of the tunnel, staring out at the charred earth and the jungle beyond. Lina stopped just behind her as the rest of the crew tromped after them. Michael Hockton pushed through to stand next to Lina. Runt abruptly spat, forcing him to dodge aside.

Somewhere distant, the Dray Engine roared. Natasha bared her teeth angrily. "I knew it," she muttered.

"Kalyon?" asked Farouk. "How do we get past it to reach the ship?"

"It's not going to be easy," she admitted. "That dumb mechanical lizard is fast, and so far unstoppable. It sleeps, sort of. But we can't count on that. We'll have to be quick—and quiet. We'll have to avoid its notice with all the low cunning we possess."

A great crack echoed out from the distant jungle, as of trees being uprooted and snapped in half. Lina heard a faint manlike scream, which was followed by the roar of the Dray Engine on the hunt. The sun flashed through the canopy, reflecting against ancient Voornish bronze. The Dray Engine was moving quickly, directly away from the southern part of the island, where the *Dawnhawk* was moored above the village of the Castaways.

"Or we could just run for it," said Natasha flatly. She turned to face the crew and gestured violently outside. "What are you waiting for? Go! Go like yer arses are on fire!"

Lina opened her mouth to protest. Didn't anyone remember that her lovely pet was *pregnant?* But Reaver Jane pushed past, followed by the others. Then there wasn't anything to do but move or get run over.

Her boots jarred against the charred earth outside the pyramid. It was baked hard, and running on it was like running across broken pottery. The stinking air was hot and greasy, and it prickled her scalp and skin. Lina tried to keep from jostling Runt too much, letting Farouk and Etarin take the lead as she fell back to the middle of the pack. Her pet still chirped unhappily, and Lina felt a pang of worry.

"Look at all this!" cried Michael Hockton. "Everything's cooked for a thousand feet in any direction!"

"Less yapping and more running!" snapped Natasha.

The jungle ahead grew closer. Lina focused on running and not jostling Runt, but a small part of her still had to marvel. The blast from the Stormhammer stopped cleanly at the tree line. Everything up to that point had been reduced to charred cinders, but the old-growth palms and banyans hadn't lost anything more than a stray vine.

Midafternoon sunlight turned to shade as they passed beneath the canopy. The stink of char and ozone faded, replaced by humid jungle air. Amazingly, they'd reached the trail that they'd forged earlier, and Farouk's hurried passing this time had only widened it. Still, Lina cursed to herself as the clear ground became a tangle of ferns, vines, and mazelike banyan roots. She hopped and skipped along, trying desperately not to fall.

The race back to the *Dawnhawk* proved a frantic mirror of their earlier trip. Leafy vegetation pressed in on all sides as she ran, illuminated by shafts of brilliant sunlight spearing down into the gloom from above. Save for the panting of her crewmates, it was eerily silent. No gibbons hooted in the distance. The only parrot squawking in the branches above was Butterbeak, flapping and falling forward in his own unique, ungainly way.

Runt let out a strange groan and writhed in Lina's arms. She looked down at her pet in alarm, catching a bent-back branch that almost knocked her over. Lina kept her balance, spitting out leaves, and continued to run. Her pet was swollen about the middle, distended enough now that she could see the skin in between the scales, stretched tighter than a drum.

"Shhh," she soothed. *We're almost back to the ship. Just a little farther.*

She didn't think about what they'd do then. Lina had thought her pet sick for weeks now. But pregnant? It was a wonderful thing, and frightening. Could Runt hold out long enough for them to get back to Haventown? Could she find that horse-doctor with all the fighting going on to deliver the scrynlings?

I've got to calm Runt down. Maybe the others could help with that. She looked up again at her crewmates, almost tripping as she did so. Lina had fallen even farther behind now. Michael Hockton ran just a little ahead. And Allen was right beside her and a little off.

"Michael!" she panted. "Michael, I need you to help calm Runt!"

He glanced back at her, caught a branch in the face, then stumbled. Michael Hockton staggered but found his balance and ran on. "It's gotta wait!" he called back over his shoulder. "We've got to get to the airship, love."

Lina blinked. She opened her mouth to snap at him, then closed it to avoid a low-hanging vine. *But I need you now!*

Allen. Allen was always desperate to help. That's why he was so ideal in testing Michael. She glanced over to where he tromped clumsily along, sweating like mad and gasping great huge breaths as he struggled to keep up.

"Allen! Get over here and help me with Runt—"

The look he shot her was cold. Cold and angry and hurt. At least until he slammed into a palm trunk and fell behind her.

Shouts of triumph echoed from up ahead. Lina pushed through a pair of ferns and found the even, open ground of the Castaways' village. Something heavy had come through in a hurry, flattening and shattering the buildings here, snapping the long branches high up clean from the canopy. Huge, taloned footprints were stamped into the dirt. But the Dray Engine was nowhere to be seen. And gloriously, the *Dawnhawk* still hung up above, tethered in place with its rope ladder hanging down. Lina put all thought of Allen out of her mind and dashed across the dirt to her airship home.

"Hold!" shouted Natasha. She held out a hand and drew her cutlass, forcing Lina to a stop along with everyone else. Natasha glared warily about them, looking to the village suspiciously. "The Dray Engine came this way, which means that the Castaways were ahead of it. Where are they?"

"Maybe it killed them?" asked Andrea Holt.

"No," said Natasha. "There isn't enough blood spread around here. And there—damn it all to the Realms Below!" She spat, focusing on the rope ladder dangling down from their airship. "Omari left the ladder down! Just like I *told* her not to! I'm going to gouge her eyes out and ram them so far up her backside she'll have to open her mouth to see where she's going!" Her grip on her cutlass went white-knuckled, even as she continued to mutter curses and dark promises under her breath.

Everyone paused. After a moment Reaver Jane cautiously stepped forward. "Captain ... the Dray Engine was chasing something when we saw it last. Those Castaways didn't have any weapons—they likely kept on running. That aside ... does it, or the aetherite, really matter right now?"

A distant roar echoed over the jungle canopy at them, brazen and mechanical. Natasha shoved her blade back into its sheath. "No," she said. "No, it doesn't. Though I'm still going to wring that witch-woman's neck when I see her. No one ignores my orders! Now get back aboard the ship!"

A queue quickly formed. Lina took her place behind the young boy Paine, shifting Runt to her shoulders as she did so. "There, there," she soothed her scryn. "There, there. We'll be home in just a moment."

Her pet chirped miserably, wobbling as she tried to coil herself into her usual position. She was too round to easily find balance, though, and slipped off continuously. Lina put up a hand to help, holding her pet in place by the smooth, drum-tight skin of her belly. Runt rolled into place more easily, and Lina smiled. Then she felt something twitch beneath the skin of her pet.

She stared at Runt in shock and amazement. *Was that a kick?*

"Stone!" snapped Natasha from the back of the line. "Get a move on! That thing could be coming back!"

Lina started. She looked up to see the rope ladder dangling ahead of her. Paine had scrabbled on up, and now Allen, Michael, and the captain herself were waiting on her. Her soldier started to smile at her but froze as Runt let out a growl. "Aye, Captain." she replied. "It's … it's just amazing. I felt Runt's *babies*—"

"*Now*," snarled Natasha.

Her excitement shriveled at the look on her captain's face. Lina sprinted to the rope ladder and climbed awkwardly, using only one hand. The other she kept up to hold her miserable scryn in place.

The ascent seemed to take forever. But it was important that she go slow, even though the village inched past and the others groused at her from below. Why didn't any of them understand? There was a *new mother* on her shoulders!

At last the old, familiar gunwales appeared above her, along with Etarin reaching out to help her aboard. She took his hand and swung carefully over. Runt abruptly lifted her head and hissed, spraying poisonous spittle at the older Salomcani man. He cursed and fell back while Lina put boots back upon the deck with a sigh. Then she pushed past him, making for an out-of-the-way place toward the middle of the deck.

Her airship home looked … ragged. The damage from the earlier fighting had compounded the wear and tear of their long voyage before coming back to port. Now the vessel looked like something from an old sailor's ghost story. All the others milled about as they came aboard, seeing the ship with fresh eyes as well. Lina swore she heard faint groans echoing up from somewhere beneath the deck.

Oh. Right. The Revenants. Lina wrinkled her nose. *This is no place to bring newborns into the world, with the lot of those things shambling around below.*

"You!" snarled Natasha.

Lina glanced back to see Captain Blackheart come up over the gunwales. She shoved past Allen and Michael Hockton, knocking them both to the deck, and charged straight for Omari. The Yulani aetherite was just climbing down from the ratlines leading up to the gas bag, her clothing disheveled and torn. She flinched at the shout and looked frantically about.

Too late. Natasha was there, slamming a fist into the aetherite's gut and doubling her over. Runt gave a low moan as most of the crew flinched sympathetically.

"I told you to raise the damned ladder!" she snarled.

"I—"

Natasha kicked her legs out from under her, dropping Omari to the deck. "When I give an order, you obey!"

Runt made a weird trill and started to writhe on Lina's shoulders.

"I forgot!" gasped Omari. "That monster started roaring out there, and I climbed up to get a better look!"

"At least tell me you saw where the damned Castaways went!"

Omari looked up at the furious captain from between her shielding arms. "Wh-who? I saw some men run into the clearing, chased by the monster …"

Runt chirred, waving her head back and forth oddly.

"Never mind that! I've about had it with you, woman. First you stow away on my ship, then you *raise Revenants*, and then disobey when I was clear—"

"Well, I wouldn't have," Omari snapped back, "if that damned great ape hadn't insisted on playing cards! I tried to get away six times! It was only when that mechanical monster chased those men down below that it lost interest and let me go!"

"Um, everyone?" asked Lina.

"Hey," said Paine. "That's blood on the deck."

"Yes, lad," said Reaver Jane. "We were in a battle, you know."

"No, it's fresh blood, I think. Near the forward hatch."

"Everyone!" shouted Lina. "Hey! Runt's giving birth!"

Her crewmates fell completely silent.

"Not … not right now?" asked Allen, tentatively. The cold glare from earlier had been replaced by his more normal look of uncertain worry.

Lina quickly worked the writhing scryn down off her shoulders. Runt was hissing and curling and uncoiling her manta-like wings. Her belly pulsed soft red bioluminescent light. And her lower regions were positively swollen.

"Yes, right now!" she snapped. "Get over here and help!"

Everyone stared at her. Etarin and Farouk appeared horrified. Young Paine was wide-eyed. Natasha had her sword out, and utter revulsion was etched across her face. Omari scrabbled away from Natasha's feet, taking the opportunity of the distraction to escape. Reaver Jane looked pale beneath her tan. Michael Hockton seemed conflicted, and Allen chewed on his lip. Rastalak watched curiously from the ratlines that lead up to the gasbag, having scampered up when no one was looking. Even Andrea Holt and Ryan Gae, her friends since the beginning, were at the far end of the deck, grimacing and trying not to be noticed.

"Michael? Allen? Both of you get over here right damned now, or by the Goddess Above, I'm going to dangle you from the ship by your stones and make you sing patter songs!" The tremor in her voice surprised her.

Both young men shared a sickly look. Then, as one, they inched their way forward, like two men condemned to the grave. The rest of the crew watched them go, horrified, but making no move of their own to help.

Panic warred with excitement in Lina's gut, all underscored by a current of dread. What did they need to do? What if something went wrong? She soothed her pet and glared at the two young men, who held the squirming scryn down and were bitten, repeatedly, for their efforts.

Fortunately, Runt seemed to know instinctively what was needed. She moaned and yowled as she gave birth, writhing in pain. But her young emerged into the world.

They didn't come like Lina had expected, as eggs. It seemed scryn gave live birth. The scrynlings were blind, stubby, and only a little longer than her fingers. They looked like miniature eels, and seven of them writhed in Lina's cupped palms when the delivery was finished, slick with afterbirth.

A chorus of disgust echoed across the deck. Allen and Michael were white as sheets—where their skin wasn't rash-red from exposure to poisoned spittle. Lina didn't care. Her eyes were blurry and her cheeks wet. "Runtie," she said, bending down with the wriggling scrynlings. "Look. Your children."

Her pet raised her head wearily. "Chirr," she said before thumping back down to the deck in exhaustion.

Lina sniffed. She turned to Michael. Holding up the scrynlings as they slithered across her hands, she tried for words, but her throat was too choked with emotion.

Allen and Michael both stood up abruptly, their bodies tight with tension and faces pale as sheets. The apprentice Mechanist abruptly turned and ran for the starboard gunwales. He shoved past the horrified Natasha, then clambered past the wreck of the exhaust pipe to vomit explosively over the side. Michael Hockton just stood there, still as a statue, obviously at war with himself.

"Aren't they beautiful?" she managed at last.

The scrynlings stopped writhing about. They opened miniature mandibles and began to devour the wet afterbirth still clinging to their hides. Michael Hockton convulsed once, and then he covered his mouth with his hand, turning to flee for gunwales beside Allen.

"That … is … the third worst thing I have ever seen," said Natasha. The pirate captain's voice was appalled, and the tip of her cutlass never wavered.

"Oh, Goddess," said Paine. "They look like worms covered in sick!"

The scrynlings all paused at his voice. They raised themselves up, shiny black heads waving back and forth.

"Hey," said Paine. "What's that? What're they doing?"

The scrynlings all looked his way. Then they unfurled themselves, revealing tiny wings and pulsing red bellies. They hissed and launched themselves into the air, straight for the unfortunate youth.

He screamed and fled down the end of he deck, a swarm of miniature horrors trailing after him. The crew dove out of the way, swearing and cursing. Lina laughed—they were just like their mother.

"Don't hurt them!" she called after the shrieking youth. "They just want to play!"

She wiped the mess on her hands absently on her pant legs. Then she froze.

An idea crept over her as she watched the ex-midshipman run in terror from the newborn monsters. The way he ran and yelled. She turned to Natasha, who shifted her cutlass defensively at her approach.

"Take another step, and I'll kill you, Stone," she said. "You wash those hands and burn those clothes before you come any closer."

"I've got it!" she said. "I know how we can beat the Perinese!"

Her captain narrowed her eyes. "What?"

"The Stormhammer is broken and useless. There's still something here, though, a weapon we can use."

Natasha lowered her cutlass, a little. "Tell me."

Lina laid out her plan as Runt chirped wearily from where she lay on the deck. Somewhere nearby, the Dray Engine roared.

CHAPTER SEVENTEEN

"STAND!" SCREAMED ADMIRAL WINTERMOURN. "STAND FIRM, YOU SONS OF WHORES!"

The Revenants advanced with rotting claws upraised. They moaned as they came on, hungry for his flesh and thirsty for his blood. Neither musket balls nor the cut of flashing blades stopped them. The alley filled with their stink, just as it resounded with the echo of their infernal moaning, drowning out the battle raging elsewhere. The horrors seemed unstoppable, tearing at the desperate ranks of Bluecoats with abandon, which was the only thing standing between Admiral Wintermourn and a vile end at the hands of those unholy abominations.

Every inch of his skin crawled in revulsion. "The first man to let one pass will spend a year in gaol!" he almost shrieked, gesturing with his saber as if he could drive the monsters back through sheer force of will.

"Sir! Sir, it's all right. We've got them now."

Wintermourn whirled to face him. The Bluecoat officer, Sergeant Greene, jerked back as Wintermourn whipped his blade about. The man was scuffed and bloodied but otherwise uninjured.

"They're … not that mean, actually. Sir. They're tough, but we've got 'em licked, for now."

Wintermourn frowned. He lowered his saber, taking another look at the fight raging in the alley ahead.

It was true. While they clawed and moaned, the Revenants weren't actually doing much damage. His soldiers worked in tandem, shoving them back with musket strokes before using smallswords to hack off their rotting heads. That seemed to stop the things. A few of the men had fallen back here and there, tending to a worrisome gash, but they recovered quickly enough. Whereas the ranks of the dead were being quickly transmuted to a pile on the boardwalk. The fighting would be over in moments.

Still, Wintermourn held his saber, so hard that his knuckles were white around the grip. "Are … are you certain?" he asked, peering ahead.

"Yes, sir."

By the Goddess in her Realm Above, I give thanks. Wintermourn took a deep breath, and the air in the alley made him immediately regret it. Slowly he relaxed back into a more normal posture: spine stiff and chin thrust out. His relief proved only temporary, though. Sergeant Greene stood there, watching. Judging him. Seeing him at his weakest. Embarrassed anger washed over Admiral Wintermourn.

"Very good, then," he snapped. "Finish hacking up these misbegotten corpses, and let us get a move on."

The sergeant snapped a salute. He turned back to the men, raising his sword and barking out orders. Wintermourn watched him with narrow eyes.

So what if he detested the undead? Not a one of the thousand differing denominations back on Edrus could agree on which way to best please the Goddess. But every single one preached that Revenants were an unholy horror best purged by righteous fire. Even the heathen Salomcani of the Sheikdom understood *that* much.

Yet an officer couldn't afford such weaknesses. The Lord High Admiral of the Sea and a member of the Order Gallant, even less so. Only Sergeant Lanters was aware of his horror, and Wintermourn weighed that knowledge against his value every time he saw the man. Fortunately, the sergeant was loyal and dull. Could the same be said of this Greene?

No. No. Best not take the risk. Wintermourn smiled with thin lips. Glory was always in the advance. Soon Greene would take his prying eyes to the grave. Where they'd damned well stay, if they knew what was good for them.

The last three Revenants toppled over. Even then the Bluecoats kept at it, hacking away until they were just another pile of rotting meat. Greene shouted an order, and they stopped, weapons out, waiting and expectant. What was left of the Revenants did not move.

The men let loose a victorious cheer. It wouldn't have been appropriate to join in, but Wintermourn felt relieved all the same. He sheathed his sword and folded his hands behind his back, waiting for the noise to die down.

Sergeant Greene turned to him, and the rest of the men followed his lead. Wintermourn looked to each in turn, holding their eyes a moment.

The rippling pop of musket fire and bomb blasts from the battle in the lagoon echoed down past the ramshackle buildings they stood between.

"So," he said. "Now you see. Pirates, whores, smugglers. And worse than that." He curled his lip in a sneer. "Necromancy. Abomination. While you wear that uniform, you are a soldier of our great nation. The church doesn't enter into it. But if any of you had any doubts ..." He gestured at the rotting carcasses in the middle of the street. "This is holy work we're about."

Wintermourn snapped his head up to glare at them each in turn. "There'll be no rest while even an *inch* of this wretched soil remains unclaimed. If even one perfidious pirate can raise his sword against us, then the price of mercy is too high. Greene!"

The man made his salute. "Sir!"

"Assemble the men and move out. This part of the town *will* be mine by nightfall."

The sergeant nodded sharply. He turned to the men and barked orders. The Bluecoats moved wearily but moved all the same. Not a few glared with disgust at the remains lying about the street before falling back into columns for the march.

And march they did. Fear was better, to Admiral Wintermourn's mind, than inspiration. So long as they followed, though, what did it matter? But whether because of his speech or their own righteous disgust, the column moved with purpose back through the pirate township.

It wasn't long before another ambush occurred.

The march through the streets went unopposed at first. Doors were kicked in and windows shattered, but no one appeared to fight back. Wintermourn was wondering if the knaves had evacuated completely to the higher terraces when the street widened to a small fish market. It was an impoverished affair, filled with poorly built driftwood stalls and leftover canvas. Crates containing last evening's catch rotted in the sun, their stink mixing with the gunpowder haze that hung in the sky above. An airship flew past, returning to the battle raging just beyond the city.

What is taking those laggards so long? How hard could it be to mop up that ridiculous pirate force? The lagoon should be positively *filled* with their own ships by now. *Is it the crown prince? Has he come up with some other contrivance of a plan? Or has he just gone haring off again—*

"Sir! Look out!"

It was Private Bryant, who slammed into him, tackling him down behind a stall just as the crates atop it exploded into flinders and scraps of fish.

Debris rained down about him as the men shouted cries of alarm. Wintermourn lay in stunned surprise before shoving the marine aside and clambering to his feet. He'd forgotten about the man. Maybe he was of *some* use, then.

Some of his Bluecoats returned fire blindly, and the pop of their muskets echoed about the market while those more perceptive charged a cart at one end. It had been overturned, spilling rickety crates everywhere. These shifted and shook as someone beneath tried to escape, but it was too late. The marines kicked the detritus aside and hauled out two men, one clutching an ancient and smoking blunderbuss.

Both were thrown roughly up against their cart, seconds away from being skewered by Perinese smallswords. One was a grizzled old man with a peg leg, obviously once a pirate. The other was younger, of fighting age, and Wintermourn wondered why he was here in town until he spied the fellow's clubfoot.

"Pirate scum!" shouted Sergeant Greene at the top of his voice.

"No!" begged the young man. "Please, we're just hiding! I didn't mean for it to go off!"

"Oh aye we did!" belted out the older pirate.

"Sneaking curs," said Sergeant Greene. "Can't beat us in a fair fight, so you snipe and skulk." He turned to the other Bluecoats. "Cut their Goddess-damned throats!"

An angry murmur arose from the assembled soldiers. Wintermourn held up a hand. "Wait," he snapped.

The marines froze, their bloodlust checked by their training. All eyes turned to him, including those of the pirates. Wintermourn stepped forward, and the men moved aside as he pushed through to face his would-be ambushers.

"Please, sir," said the younger pirate. He struggled against the Bluecoats holding him to raise his arms in supplication. "I didn't mean it, really! We were just hiding, and that thing went off!"

"Pity it didn't take yer head," snarled the older man. He spat at the marine holding him.

"Oh, I believe you," said Wintermourn to the younger man.

"You do?" he replied in surprise.

"You do?" said the older pirate.

"Of course," replied Wintermourn. He reached out to a marine standing to one side and took the blunderbuss. It was indeed ancient, the stock weathered like driftwood and the bell-shaped barrel dented and smoking. "Goddess above. I haven't seen one of these since I was a lad."

"Sir," began Private Bryant. "They—"

"It was obviously a mistake," he continued, ignoring the man. "Even this old salt had to know that the two of them alone against us was folly."

The younger man relaxed visibly.

"Because that's not how they fight, is it?" snapped Wintermourn. Both men looked up at him in surprise, and he held their panicked stares with a glare of his own. "You're scoundrels, daemons, the worst scum of the world. You drop bombs from overhead. You hole up in these miserable islands, thinking yourselves safe. And when we come anyway, you unleash *abominations*, falling back to hide and cower while undead monstrosities do your dirty work!"

"What? What are ye going—"

"I don't know what you—"

"Enough!" shouted Wintermourn. "Enough and more! Cut their throats and move on! It's fire and the sword for this miserable pirate town, and if we have to do it door by door, street by street, we will!"

He threw the blunderbuss down and turned away as the Bluecoats moved to obey. Wintermourn froze as the panicked protests of the Haventowners turned into grisly gurgles, so similar to the calls of the unquiet dead.

Sergeant Greene shouted a series of orders before moving up beside him. "Sir? Are you all right?"

"What?" said Wintermourn, starting in surprise.

"From the shot. I only meant—"

"I know what you meant," he snapped. "Get the men moving. Your overfamiliarity is unwarranted, Sergeant. And no, I am not fine. I will not be until every man, woman, and child in this place shares the peace of the grave! Now get back to the column, and you, personally, lead us forth!"

The sergeant gave his salute, took his place again and ordered the men onward. They marched with weapons in hand and eager, grim looks upon their faces. Wintermourn approved. They marched with a natural, military rhythm completely unlike the shuffling gait of a Revenant.

Yes. Soldier on. For king and country. Not even the walking dead can blunt our purpose. And next time it'll be you on the wrong end of a blunderbuss, Greene.

The fish market exited onto a short street between a pair of warehouses before curving sharply past a thin, two-story building. Past its rooftop and on through the gun smoke haze, Wintermourn spied the stair leading up to the next terrace, up against the curve of the lagoon cliff itself. They'd almost swept these Waterdocks clean entirely, he realized.

Wintermourn allowed himself satisfaction. *And where are you, Crown Prince Gwydion? Hmm? Or all the rest of you laggards in the fleet? Still fencing with a bunch of worthless scallywags!* It made him want to despair. All these mechanical men and flashy airships that couldn't even take advantage of the beachhead he'd given them. The others were only playing at warfare, while *he* fought the rotting claws of *real* monsters.

His Bluecoats advanced down the street to its far end, eyes eager and weapons held tight. No warehouse rooftops collapsed on them, and no hidden ambushers opened fire. They reached the tall building at the end of the street, and Sergeant Greene called a halt, rubbing his injured leg and panting wearily. The Bluecoats fanned out to cover the front door, as Wintermourn stalked over to stand beside the sergeant.

The building looked on the verge of collapse. It seemed to sag, weary and worn, the two shuttered windows like heavy-lidded eyes. Bright, violently red paint coated the door, almost a vulgarity. There were other attempts to spruce up the place, including a flower box beneath each window. No sign hung out front, but a lady's weatherworn corset dangled from a gaff hook on a pole above the door.

"What is this place?" asked the sergeant.

"It's a bordello," said Wintermourn dryly.

"Oh." Sergeant Greene blushed. Then he gave a resolute nod. "Rainely, Bryant! Knock down that door."

The two Bluecoats stepped up and slammed their shoulders into the bright red door. It cracked but did not otherwise open. Girlish shouts came from somewhere inside.

Private Bryant turned back to face the lieutenant. "It's blocked shut, sir," he said.

"Of course it's barricaded," snapped Wintermourn. "Now put your backs into it and bust it down! The cause of the Kingdom will not be stopped by perfidious tarts and their animate corpses!"

The Bluecoat paled. He turned back to the door and threw his weight against it, joined by his fellow. With each blow it cracked more and more. The shouts from inside took on an edge of panic.

At last the door split from the latch. It popped inward a foot, checked by a stack of dark furniture. A woman's hoarse shout called for order.

Rainely and Bryant worked further at the door, widening the space behind it until they could wrestle with the furniture itself. Rainely hauled free a chair and passed it back to a waiting marine as Bryant reached for an ottoman that had been wedged beneath it.

A pointed metal spear shot out through a crack in the pile. It slipped past Bryant, knocking free his cap, burying itself into his companion's gut. Rainely shrieked in pain, hands grabbing for the haft. Whoever held the other end fought him, jabbing back and forth.

"Muskets forward!" shouted Sergeant Greene.

Bluecoats surged to Rainely's aid, half a dozen shoving their muskets past the screaming soldier into the makeshift barricade. Bryant dodged aside as the men fired, turning the doorway into a chaotic cloud of gun smoke, muzzle fire, and exploding wooden splinters.

Shrieks echoed out past the barricade. Bryant withdrew, pulling the wounded Rainely with him back behind the lines as another group of soldiers stepped forward. They were ready, stepping in to tear down the barricade. They worked quickly and efficiently until finally it was disassembled enough to allow men to pass through.

Wintermourn tapped an impatient foot as more Bluecoats barged into the brothel. A cacophony of shouts, gunshots, and the clatter of steel on steel erupted only moments later. Wintermourn sighed. Weren't there *any* common peasants in this ridiculous pirate nest? It seemed that even the whores here could fight. He almost admired them for it, though not nearly enough to overcome his disgust. *On top of everything else, women fighting.* He shook his head, then paused. *Though it's not as if they're ladies.*

The soldiers emerged a few moments later, hauling a dozen struggling captives along with them. They were all women, and their makeup and jewelry denoted them as common dockside whores, though all wore boots and trousers and were otherwise dressed for a fight. They appeared to have not gone without one, either. The Bluecoats yanked at them angrily, bearing fresh bruises and cuts or clutching more serious wounds.

"You Bluecoatie bastards!" shrieked a heavyset woman with a face like a bulldog. "We've got nothin' to do with ye, so leave us be!"

Sergeant Greene opened his mouth to retort, but Wintermourn cut him off. "On the contrary. Not that I believe in leniency, but your fate was sealed the moment you raised those unholy abominations and sent them to fight us."

The matron seemed taken aback. "What?"

"We're just whores!" shouted a woman with wild, dyed hair. She struggled against the marine who held her. "Please, we beg quarter. We'll do anything you want!"

Wintermourn smirked. "Quarter," he said, turning to the lieutenant. "Why do they always ask for that? Put the first six up against the wall."

His soldiers split the group in half and put them up against the front of the brothel, along with the sobbing younger woman who'd spoken up. A dozen of their fellows formed a firing squad a dozen paces away. They worked to load muskets, the first six kneeling in a rank.

"Ready!" barked Sergeant Greene.

The marines finished loading and raised their weapons.

"Take aim!"

The marines lifted their muskets to their shoulders.

"Please," begged the young woman with the wild-dyed hair. Wintermourn ignored her, watching instead the frozen grimaces of each soldier waiting to fire. They might as well have been carved from stone. He approved.

"Fire!"

A rippling pop rang out along the street. The women jerked, and the wooden front of the brothel splintered as the musket balls tore through them. Mixed wails of anguish rose from those still standing. "Reload," said Sergeant Greene, voice suddenly soft.

Wintermourn raised an eyebrow at him. The man was pale. *Is that weakness I see?* It would have made him despair if he hadn't decided to end the fellow already.

"Get the rest of them up there," said Wintermourn, already bored. "I want to clear this street in the next half a glass."

His soldiers shoved the remaining captives up against their brothel. They swore and fought and wailed helplessly. The ugly older woman just glared at him, murder in her eyes.

"I'm no aetherite, but I curse ye all the same," she spat.

"That reminds me," said Wintermourn. "Sergeant, make sure to cut off their heads before we leave. No need to give more resources to the filthy necromancers that hide here."

The older whore blinked. "What?"

"Of course, sir," said Sergeant Greene. "Ranks ready!"

The soldiers put away their powder horns and hefted their muskets again.

"Take aim!"

They raised the weapons to their shoulders.

"Avast, ye scallywags!"

Wintermourn blinked in surprise and turned at the shout, which echoed to him from down the street. Then he stared.

A small knot of pirates stood a good fifty paces away. Wintermourn knew in an instant that they were real pirates: a red-haired woman in a half cloak, another with a belt of jangling seashells and a bandage upon her head, even more men and women bearing cutlasses and pistols and assorted mismatched weaponry. At their head stood a bent-backed old reaver with a greying beard and fierce eyes. He held up a much-worn cutlass while leaning on the sheath with this other hand for balance.

Admiral Wintermourn recognized him from description. "Pirate King Euron Blackheart," he said. "So you finally decided to show your face, eh? About time you found your spine."

"Ye dogs! How dare ye set foot in me kingdom? The people here be mine! No matter what that blasted popinjay says. Th' airships be aloft again, so to the Realms Below wit' him an' his!"

Admiral Wintermourn blinked in confusion at the rant. Behind him, Sergeant Greene ordered the men to form ranks.

"Sir," said Bryant. "What about the whores?"

"Shoot the damned whores and then form ranks!" snapped Wintermourn back over his shoulder.

"Yer fight be wit' me, ye bluecoated bastards!"

"Yes, yes," said Wintermourn, waving nonchalantly at him. "We'll crush you insects in a moment. I'm not going to chase a bunch of escapees through all the ground I've already covered today."

"Danica," said the red-haired pirate woman in a half cloak. "Now."

The bandaged woman in the seashell belt lifted her hands up high and cupped them together. Oily darkness bloomed between her palms, swelling and streaking towards the Bluecoats. It moved strangely through the air, like ink poured into a mug of water.

Then it fell on them. It was like the aetherite had given birth to night itself. Wintermourn couldn't see his own hands in front of his face; he was blind. Hoarse shouts of alarm echoed from the men about him, along with the pop of muskets fired in panic.

"It's sorcery!" Wintermourn yelled. He had a horrible epiphany. "It's damned aetherite sorcery! Beware the corpses, she's calling up Revenants. Beware the Goddess-damned corpses!"

They were coming for him—he could feel it. The dead women would already be clambering to their feet as they sought him out of the crowd for revenge. Something brushed up against him, and Wintermourn yelled. He drew his saber and swung, eliciting a shriek of pain from what only could have been a Bluecoat soldier.

It didn't matter. Wintermourn cursed the man for getting in the way, ruining a good swing. They could be behind him now, reaching for him with their rotting claws …

The darkness lifted. It evaporated like smoke blown on the wind. Wintermourn once again saw the street, the brothel, and the Bluecoat marines frantic with panic. No one was seriously injured—they weren't under attack. He looked to the brothel wall. The corpses were there, still and unmoving. Wintermourn breathed a sigh of relief.

But the other whores were gone.

The pirates! He whirled to face Euron, shoving aside Private Bryant, who gasped and clutched at a saber slash on one arm.

The pirate king wasn't bearing down on them, though. He wasn't even on the street anymore. The pirates were disappearing down a side alley, a pair of coattails and a flashing boot the only sign of them.

Wintermourn snarled. "They're getting away! After them! Get the damned pirate king!"

A trio of Bluecoats responded by running down the street. Wintermourn grabbed the useless Sergeant Greene and shoved him forward. He yelled for the Bluecoats to follow, then ran for the alley as the other marines shook off their confusion. Wintermourn let a few pass by, glancing back one last time at the corpses lying in the street.

The alleyway was narrow, more a coincidental crack between the bordello and an adjacent warehouse. Bryant, Greene, and the others crammed themselves down it, and Wintermourn cursed their slowness. Finally, he too wedged himself within it, panting and gasping at the exertion.

"Up ahead!" yelled a marine.

Wintermourn shoved himself along, prodding his useless sergeant. A jagged board caught his sleeve, and he cursed, shoving past and forcing away the pain of an inch-long splinter in his wrist. The tip of his saber caught the low-hanging gutter, causing old tiles and debris to rain down on them. Then Admiral Wintermourn pushed out of the alley into the street beyond.

It was narrow, like everything else in the pirate town. Buildings leaned in on either side, racing each other to collapse. Behind his marines the street trailed away, disappearing into darkness like the tail of a lazy snake. Ahead, the pirates stood in a group at the far end of the street.

Clustered around a cannon.

"To the ground!" shrieked Wintermourn.

Euron Blackheart slashed at them with his cutlass. "That usurping peacock thinks he'll be the one savin' the day?" he shouted. "Him an' his clever plans? I'll show him. Fire!"

A pirate lowered a long match to the touchhole at the rear of the weapon. Fire bloomed from it in a thunderous eruption, shattering windows along the street. Wintermourn glimpsed black iron death hurtling towards them before a marine was picked up off his feet by the cannonball and thrown back, killed in a heartbeat along with three other men.

The pirates fled down an alley, though a few hung back long enough to make obscene gestures. Wintermourn closed his eyes and wiped blood from his face. He fought aside visions of blood dripping from a Revenant's rotting jaws and gestured with the saber in his other hand. "After them!" he cried. "Get those damned pirates!"

Bluecoats poured from the alley behind him, angrily rushing to obey. Wintermourn paused to catch his breath before joining them, only to find himself stuck in yet another tight alley leading Goddess knew where. The walls to either side groaned as he shoved himself through, making him uncomfortably aware of his gut. Even with the brief rest, his wind was all but gone as well.

Damn these unholy pirates and their tricks! Damn their deathtrap construction! And damn all those rich dinners!

The alley disgorged him onto another boardwalk street, this one wide and airy and opening on the docks at the far end. Euron Blackheart and his pirates were out in the open, heading for another alleyway. Past them, on the water, everything was a fog of gun smoke and magically conjured mist. Bombs burst and muskets flashed in the gloom while the spars and rigging of at least a dozen masts drifted by.

"Get them!" snarled Admiral Wintermourn.

The pirate king turned to face them, only fifty feet away. "That treasonous dog thinks he can steal me daughter—and me town to boot? Well, I've a lesson or two left, just as soon as I wipe ye mangy curs from me boots!"

Six marines raced forward eagerly with blades in hand. Wintermourn followed, but abruptly fell back as the boardwalk gave way with a great splintering crash that swallowed the men whole. Euron belted out a hearty laugh, then disappeared down another alley.

Rage washed over Wintermourn. It swelled up in his throat like a black ball so large he couldn't breath. He shouted a wordless command at the marines who were already in pursuit, gingerly traversing the part of the boardwalk that hadn't been sawn completely through.

Hands reached down to help him up. Admiral Wintermourn fought Sergeant Greene off with a snarl, pointing weakly at the escaping pirates.

Ambushes, traps, necromancy! You wretches don't deserve the clean death of battle! I'll see you hung from the wreckage of your own airships!

He gasped his way forward, shoving himself into the alley and quickly running into the backs of the hesitantly advancing Bluecoats. Black spots appeared in his vision, and the close air was hard to breath. Anger and spite and decades of training pushed him on, until the soldiers stumbled out into another street. Feeling lightheaded, Wintermourn followed.

Another street. Behind him it curved out of view, but ahead, it terminated in a dead-end cluster of three low buildings. A makeshift barricade rose up before them, walling off the end of the street with overturned carts, old crates, and ratty furniture. There was nowhere else to run. On the next street over rose the stair to the Craftwright's Terrace. Wintermourn could just see the top half of a large brass statue beyond the clifftop.

Pirate King Euron Blackheart stood behind the barricade, his thieves and cutthroats arrayed out beside him with weapons in hand. Wintermourn noted a huge, red-haired piratess as well as the woman in the half cloak.

"Come forward, ye men of Perinault!" he cried. Euron paused to gasp a breath before lifting his cutlass up with one wavering hand. "No more tricks! I be here, ready to send ye off to the Goddess!"

Wintermourn gasped for air. He half knelt, supporting himself with one hand on his knee, the other gesturing violently with his now too-heavy saber. The words wouldn't come. His side burned. Somewhere, he had lost his hat.

More Bluecoats poured into the street. They formed ranks, angry but wary of approaching the barricade after so many traps. Sergeant Greene appeared, seeming torn between the threat ahead and his gasping admiral.

"Get ... get ..." tried Wintermourn.

"Come forward, ye dogs!" snarled Euron. "I'll have the measure of real men before I hunt down that peacock popinjay!"

A tremor shook the boardwalk, giving everyone pause. Wintermourn struggled to look up as it came again, followed by a metallic, mechanical rhythm from down the street behind him. A Brass Paladin rounded the corner, brilliant even in the muted sunlight shining down through the haze above the town.

Cries of dismay came from behind the barricade. Wintermourn stared at the automaton, confused.

"But ... how are they here?" asked Sergeant Greene.

A pair of Brass Paladins appeared behind the first, followed by two more. They marched onto the street in a column, a score in all, looking only mildly scuffed and dinged. A single figure followed behind. He wore a ragged navy officer's jacket, though without the golden epaulets that denoted a command.

"Column halt!" ordered Royal Adjutant Chesterly. The Brass Paladins stopped abruptly, shaking the whole boardwalk street.

"What's this?" called Euron Blackheart. "You bring yer wind-up toys again to do the job of flesh an' blood men? Come forward, I say, an' I'll make quick work o' ye!"

Adjutant Chesterly strolled up beside the column. He stopped at its head, reviewing Wintermourn's forces as well as those of the pirate king beyond his barricade. Though his clothing was torn and rumpled, he stood with confidence.

"Chesterly?" gasped Wintermourn. "What in the Realms Below are you doing here?"

The royal adjutant looked at him in surprise. "Admiral Wintermourn. There you are." A slow smile spread across the lips of the younger man. "Dash it all, fellow. You're looking rather rough."

You're dead, Chesterly. You think yourself beyond my reach? Royal appointment or no, I'll see you dead and dishonored for that. Wintermourn pushed the thought aside. "What are you doing here?" he demanded again.

"Checking up on you," replied Chesterly. "The crown prince left you his Paladins but then spied them sticking out of a bunch of rubble a few streets back." He gestured towards the lagoon and the roiling battle there. "*That's* a mess. Confounded pirates are giving us a spot of trouble from above now, and we can't approach with proper reinforcements. They sank the *Titan* and the *Gargantua* when they tried to come ashore. His Highness dares not leave the *Glory* unattended, though he's having a right good time. At any rate, he sent me here to recover his clockwork troopers and to find out just what you've been up to all afternoon."

The ex-officer stared down at him, waiting in amusement for a reply that he knew wouldn't be coming quickly. Wintermourn panted. It seemed his wind just wouldn't come back.

"Are ye having a damned tea party?" shouted Euron. "Have yer stones all fallen off? Quit yer hidin' behind yer metal men! I'll have the measure of ye before I send ye off to meet the Goddess!"

"And who the daemon are you?" demanded Chesterly.

Euron drew himself up. The pirate woman in the half cloak beside him tried to shush him, unsuccessfully. "What? Ye come into my town, assail me men an' ships, and ye don't even recognize the pirate king o' these isles? I be Euron Blackheart, ye knave!"

"He's mine," growled Wintermourn. "I made the assault, and I've … taken this town. Leave … leave off, Chesterly."

"Well, well, well …" muttered the adjutant. Chesterly didn't even look at him, focusing his attention instead on the pirates and their barricade. "What a prize you've cornered."

He folded his hands beside his back and smiled down at Wintermourn. "Worry not, Admiral. I can see you've had a bit of trouble yourself. It's all over now. We'll squash this little knot of resistance for you."

Wintermourn's rage reignited. "How dare you, you up-jumped—" He tried to climb to his feet and only made it by plunging the tip of his saber into the boardwalk and using it to stand. Even still, he wobbled wearily. What was wrong with him? His side ached abominably. And his wig was hanging askew, he was sure of it.

"You can't do this!" said Sergeant Greene. "The *Colossus's* marines have cornered him, and it's we who'll take him down."

Chesterly glared at the sergeant imperiously. "Paladins!" he called out. "Present arms!"

The clockwork automatons unshouldered their heavy pepperbox muskets. Steam belched from their smokestacks in increasing puffs. Their clangor in the closed-in space was deafening.

"When you speak to me, Sergeant," replied Chesterly, "you are speaking to the crown. Remember that. Now get out of the way or be run down with that fossil at the end of the street." He turned to smile condescendingly at Wintermourn. "And as for you, Admiral, tend that wound. I'll take it from here."

He drew the saber at his side and raised it up without ever looking away. Then he lowered it sharply. The Brass Paladins all stepped forward as one, their armored feet ringing against the boardwalk planks.

"Ye cowards!" shouted Euron Blackheart. "Ye dogs! Ye milk-drinkin', lily-livered—"

"Aetherite Danica!" shouted the pirate woman in a half cloak. "Get up here! Everyone else, reinforce the barricade. Anyone with a pistol or a musket, *get up here!*"

Wintermourn opened his mouth to snarl a protest, but shooting pain stopped him. He dropped his blade to clutch at his side and then stared in shock as his hand came back red and wet, covered in blood.

When did that happen?

Wintermourn gasped in pain, his breath short, as the clockwork knights advanced. Behind their barricade, the pirates tried frantically to prepare, while the pirate king roared epithets.

CHAPTER EIGHTEEN

Captain Fengel waved his hat to clear the dust away. He stumbled
on rubble as he left the newly blasted cavern mouth, coughing. The taste of
earthy rock, sulfurous powder, and the coppery tang of his own blood was
thick on his tongue. His ears were still filled by the aftereffects of the blast,
ringing like the tuning of some rogue orchestra just out of sight.

The dust faded slowly. It cleared away just enough to reveal the firetrap
rooftops of the warehouses that made up the Waterdocks. Great shadows
came and went, the telltale sign of airships on the move. Cannon fire and
bomb blasts reached him, faintly.

So we're not entirely lost, then. Not yet.

Imogen stumbled into him. Her mask was up, and her arms were out,
seeking. She was blinded by an even thicker covering of dust than he was.

"Fengel!" she shouted, voice muffled. "Fengel, I can't … where … we?"

He grabbed her by the arm and turned her to face him. "What?" he
shouted back.

"I *said* … we … outside?"

"What?" Fengel pointed at his ears with his free hand, then remembered
she couldn't see.

The Mechanist-Aspirant tore off her mask and goggles. She blinked at
the dusty haze, then coughed. "I said, did it work? Are we outside?"

"Aye," he replied, gesturing. "Look. The battle's still going on. And it
seems Euron obeyed me, that daft old bastard; our airships are out in force."

She peered at the rapidly clearing outlines for a moment. Then she gave
a sharp nod. "I told you it would work," she said.

Fengel glanced at the devastation around them. "I still think you might have been a little excessive."

They'd rested only a few short minutes after engaging the pumps within the mine. Returning to the entrance was out of the question, so they'd sought to make a new one. The unfinished tunnel was just as Imogen had said it would be, piled full of Mechanist explosives. She'd been positively beside herself at the thought of lighting them all off. Fortunately, Mechanist Barlett was more restrained. Fengel still suspected that Imogen used more charges and powder than she should have—the blast had been titanic.

But it seemed to have done the job. They now stood again on the Waterdocks, and the fight against the Perinese was still going strong. Fengel hurt, though. The graze along his leg ached abominably, he'd bitten his tongue when the bombs went off, and his jaw was stiff where that brute Lanters had struck him repeatedly. Which had been a weirdly surreal coincidence. It felt like something from a boy's penny-story: a duel to the death with his boyhood tormentor, in the clockwork mines of a secret society. *I should write about that someday. Or get that hack in Triskelion to jot it all down.*

"I didn't get to use my bomb," complained Imogen. She sighed forlornly at the satchel slung over her shoulder.

The cloud of dust had cleared enough now that they could make out their immediate surroundings. A building lay crumpled before them, half-flattened. The roof rose like a ramp from the rubble they stood upon to the front walls that were still miraculously standing.

"Your brothers should be about finished in the Gasworks, yes?" said Fengel. He adjusted his sword belt—the extra weapons he'd taken from Lanters and his Bluecoats made it hang oddly. "They'll be firing the signal flares soon."

Imogen gave a shrug. "If we haven't missed them already, yes. We didn't spend too much time priming those explosive charges. Though it would have gone faster if we'd used more. I'm sure of it."

Fengel ignored the last. "Let's get up top, then. We should be able to see from atop this roof—" Something vile assaulted his senses. "By the Goddess above," he choked. "What is that stink?"

"It's piss," said Imogen. "Remember how I said we were trying to get Tanner Hiram to move? That's his place."

"Well, that shouldn't be too difficult now. Let's get atop—" He gagged. "Climb that roof."

Imogen shrugged and moved to clamber over the rubble. Fengel followed, trying not to touch anything with his hands. He outpaced her awkward figure quickly enough, scrabbling up the slope of the ruined roof to stand at its wobbly, sagging peak.

The air up here was better, thankfully. It still stank of sulfur and burning wood, undercut now by the smell of the tanner and the omnipresent jungle. Imogen clattered up beside him, half falling to her knees with the effort, panting.

Fengel turned his gaze again to the Waterdocks. From this vantage he could see the whole of it, all ramshackle and piecemeal. Nothing was on fire, thankfully. And only the one Perinese warship had landed. He peered at the thing where it had crashed into the northern part of the docks. *If I didn't know any better, I'd say it's been completely abandoned. Where are all the Bluecoats?* Mechanist Barlett swore they'd advanced farther into the township. But why leave their ship so completely unattended?

"Captain!"

He turned at Imogen's breathless exclamation. She was facing away, towards the cliff and the terraces dangling out from atop it, pointing. Fengel followed her outstretched arm to the Craftwright's Terrace just above them, where a well-built wooden wall hid the Mechanist's Gasworks. Great chimneys and struts rose up from the structure, supporting a wide platform, and brass piping spread out from it all like a thousand jungle vines. Fengel had never given the place much thought, let alone been inside.

Now, though, he paid attention. Stars of red-green light were shooting up from its rooftop to burst brilliantly in the sky above.

"That's it," he said in relief. "Or—you lot don't send up flares for anything else, do you?"

"No," said Imogen. "Only for a pressure breach and imminent explosion of the facility."

Fengel blinked. The girl wasn't smiling or hiding her mouth or anything else that might hint at a joke. In fact, it almost looked like she was counting under her breath.

"Twenty-nine ... thirty." Imogen nodded abruptly. "Yes, that's just the signal for the gas pumps." She turned and smiled at him, rubbing her gauntlets together. "They're pumping the light-air gas to the support cells and lift-engines. All they have to do now is blast the shackles mooring each terrace to the cliffs."

Fengel sighed in relief. "That's our bit done for now, then." He smiled. "I have to admit, I'm looking forward to this, wartime invasion and all aside. I mean, a flying city? And I get to captain it. Especially now that brain-dead old fool's been put in his place." He paused. "I mean, if all this works, of course."

"Of course it's going to work," said Imogen. Her voice was focused, obsessive. "Atherion Helmsin is the greatest engineer the world has ever known. It will work. It has to work. I won't let it fail."

Fengel snorted. "Of course you won't, little Miss Helmsin."

Imogen started in surprise. "What? How did you—"

Fengel pulled his monocle free and polished it. "Please. The truth is as plain as the days grow short."

"Actually, this close to the equator, the length of the day is consistent throughout the year, regardless of the season."

He sighed. "At any rate, we should get up top. This terrace is a loss, which is good, since we're not taking it with us. But we need to rally a real defense on the Craftwright's Terrace. If no one takes charge, it'll be a jumbled mess like the rest of the day has been so far."

Imogen brightened. "Will I get to use my bomb?"

The pop of gunfire echoed across the Waterdocks. Fengel frowned. *That wasn't in the lagoon, that was …*

He started as he saw it. There was commotion in one section of town, only a street away from the stair back up to Craftwright's Terrace. It was on Romper's Way, near that old tavern that Henry Smalls always went on about. Just past the curve of the rooftops, he spied brassy helmets shining in the daylight—they belonged to the clockwork knights, which were fighting to pull down a number of pirates standing atop a barricade.

"Thorny paws of the Goddess," he hissed. "They've come so far already? I thought we'd buried those things."

"What?" asked Imogen. "Where?"

Fengel turned to descend back down to the rubble below them. "Bring that bomb of yours. It will get used soon enough, I'm sure."

He slid down to the ground just as two figures appeared in the gloom of the recently excavated tunnel. They were Mechanist Barlett and Molly Mayhap. The former leaned heavily on a musket taken from the Bluecoats. Young Molly still clutched her doll's-head stiletto … while wearing about half a dozen other newly acquired knives.

"There you two are," said Fengel.

"Captain," gasped Barlett.

"Hello there, Barlett, Molly. Look, you two had better get a move on. The Bluecoats have been held up a bit, but they're almost to the Craftwright's stair. They've got their clockwork toys again as well."

"Captain," said Barlett. "I don't know that I can go any further."

A curse sounded behind them as Imogen tripped and slid down the rooftop. Shingles went flying, and she half fell, half stumbled down to the rubble beside Fengel. The strap of her satchel had fallen off of her shoulder, momentarily forgotten.

Fengel snatched it up off of her arm. "Nonsense," he said. "You'll have Mechanist-Aspirant Imogen here to help. And I'm sure Molly will be more than willing to skewer any malefactors you come across—right, Molly?"

The little girl nodded slowly, not blinking once.

"Hey!" said Imogen. "That's my bomb, and I'm going to fight those automatons!"

"In point of fact, you are not," replied Fengel. "You are going to escort your brother up to the Gasworks and make sure that everything goes as planned. We're leaving the Waterdocks behind, Imogen."

"So?" She scrabbled up to her feet. "Someone still needs to slow them down, and I—"

"And *I'm* going to be the one to do it," Fengel finished, putting steel into his voice. "This is an order, Mechanist-Aspirant." He met her eyes and held them.

"I don't have to obey you."

"Mechanist-Aspirant," snapped Barlett. "You may not obey him, but you *will* obey a full Brother."

A frustrated look came over Imogen. She half turned to Barlett while still glaring at Fengel. "Fine."

Fengel shouldered the satchel. "We're fighting to try and save lives," said Fengel, softening his voice. "If you move fast, we can save Barlett and the rest of this whole damned town. You've got the important job. I'm just going to try to buy you some time."

"At least give me back my bomb."

"Nope," said Fengel. "Oh, and take this with you."

An orange blur had come darting out of the cavern and across the rubble. Fengel grabbed up Cubbins and shoved him into Imogen's startled arms. Then he turned to go, only to pause and turn back.

"Right. I'm going to need this too."

He stepped forward and grabbed the musket that Barlett was leaning upon. The Mechanist swore and staggered, forcing Imogen to come to his aid. Then Fengel turned away, clambering for the way past the half-demolished tannery.

"Arsehole!" shouted Imogen.

"I'll meet you all at the Gasworks!" he called back. "Now, get going and keep to the alleys up against the cliff wall. And don't lose that cat!"

He ignored Imogen's further protests and made his way across the rubble. It smoothed out quickly, as most of the blast had been expelled into the tannery. Fengel stepped down onto the weathered boardwalk and into the shadowed alley before quickly reaching the street out front.

It was still empty. Any of the usual denizens were dead, fled, or too well hidden. He had been afraid of Bluecoat sentries roaming the streets. But it seemed they were all farther down the terrace with their mechanical monsters, besieging some brave knot of pirates trying to slow the invaders down.

Brave but foolish. They should have pulled back to the stair, at least. Fengel shook his head for the hundredth time. He could admire the bravery of his fellow pirates. They just needed to fight smarter. *At least this fellow had a sizeable force with him. If I can save his hide from the Perinese, we might be able to build a real defense together.* A massive shadow flitting past made him smile. At least his worthless father-in-law had gotten the airships moving again.

The alleys, drug dens, and warehouses of the Waterdocks flew past. Several years ago, when he'd wed Natasha, they'd almost all been burned to the ground. No great loss, in his opinion. When it had been rebuilt, though, no one had bothered with anything like civic planning, recreating the warrens that right now seemed an admirable defensive feature. The Bluecoats had made alarmingly impressive progress anyway. If Haventown were a normal city, they'd have been halfway to Nob Terrace by now.

Fengel turned a corner and quieted. Corpses littered the street, roughly piled against the walls of the warehouses. They were locals, not a Bluecoat marine among them. Fishermen, seamstresses, and simple laborers. This hadn't been a fight—they'd been hauled outside and executed. He clenched his fist around the musket and swore in every language he knew. *Damn the Kingdom. Damn it and its pride, arrogance, and cruelty. These were townsfolk, not pirates!*

A huge crash sounded on the next street over, followed by shouts and clattering swords. Fengel glared at the battle. *Well, now I'm here. And I'm going to make you pay for every moment you dared to set foot in my town, you imperialist bastards.*

Romper's Way was closed off from this street. Getting onto it in the proper fashion would have taken another ten minutes. But there were other ways, Fengel knew.

He dashed down past a warehouse to the alley between it and its neighbor. A rough wooden fence walled it off, the legacy of some long-forgotten dispute. But a dozen old crates lay about in a rough stack against the fence, making a perfect stair.

Fengel clambered up atop them, then went for the overhanging lip of a warehouse roof. He flung the musket up on the rooftop, then scrabbled up after it, the trip made awkward by the stolen pistols and blades he'd taken from Lanters. Their handles gouged into his gut as he rose to a crouch, grabbed the musket, and snuck over to the edge of the roof facing down onto the battle just below.

Romper's Way was a twisty almost-alley that ended between two warehouses and a tavern: the Cock O' the Green. Fengel hadn't much reason to come down here, but Henry Smalls swore by the pub. The whole street looked just as small and mean as he remembered it, the only difference now being the barricade choking off the end and the ranks of blue-jacketed Perinese soldiers that filled the rest of the Way.

At least seventy Bluecoats were here, almost a full ship's company. They were all rumpled, weary, and bloodied. They hung back, shaking their weapons and shouting curses down the street. Fengel spied an older officer among them who looked startlingly familiar.

Their ire was aimed at the barricade and both of the sides that warred there. Assailing it were the clockwork automatons, marching implacably forth, occasionally pausing to take a shot with their heavy pepperbox muskets. Those in the lead would clumsily attempt to climb the barrels and crates the pirates stood upon, only to slip or be thrown roughly back. Every fall, blow, or pistol ball they took failed to stop them, though. Fengel marveled again at their construction.

Atop the barricade, the pirates fought desperately. Maybe a dozen still stood. They shot at the automatons—or just hacked at them with rapidly chipping blades. The defenders were a motley lot, whom Fengel recognized from several crews. Shannon MacKinnon was here, though he wondered why she wasn't aboard the *Windhaunter*. There was the aetherite Danica too, sporting a bandage about her head. But Fengel's heart leaped into his chest as he spied the familiar shapes of Sarah Lome and Henry Smalls among the crowd.

What in the Realms Below are they doing down here? His crew knew better than to get trapped in a blind alley! Fengel felt a moment's panic. *I've got to do something! And where are Lucian and the others?* He half rose from his crouch to yell at them and shout orders. Then he stopped as he spied the bent-backed old figure screaming epithets down at the Perinese from the middle of the barricade.

It was Euron Blackheart, the pirate king.

Fengel wanted to spit. *Of course. Of course that mad old bastard disobeyed.* Now he was stuck, down here at the arse-end of the Waterdocks, about to drag Fengel's own crewmen down into the Realms Below with him.

Well. Fengel wasn't going to stand for that. Not one bit.

He set his musket down and shifted Imogen's stolen satchel about. The bomb inside was big, larger than an eighteen-pound cannonball, though not nearly so heavy. Weird spikes protruded from it, along with a fuse—a mechanism not unlike the flintlock hammer of a cannon's gun cock topped it. Fengel reached in to pull it out as he eyed the crowd below. Where would it do the most damage?

A shadow darkened the street, accompanied by a piercing whistle and the whirr of nearby propellers. The pirates quieted. Even the Perinese Bluecoats ceased shouting, and the automatons paused to look up. Fengel glanced at the dark hull of an airship coming in low, dropping a hail of fizzing black bombs as it went.

He threw himself aside, rolling back across the roof and away from the street. The detonations sounded a long second later, shivering the building that he lay upon. Fengel cracked an eyelid open when it was over, listening to the screams of men echoing up to him.

Solrun's Hammer flew overhead. The airship was battered. Dead crewmen hung limp across the gunwales. Captain Brunehilde was there, though, waving cheerfully down at the street below.

"There's a gift, Fengel!" she cried. "All I had left! Quit lying about and make use of it! I'm running back to dock!"

Fengel scrabbled to his feet and grabbed the musket. Sketching a quick bow at the already-gone airship, he ran up the roof for its other side, where it met the barricade. He'd always had a soft spot for Brunehilde—she could be counted upon in a pinch.

Fengel shouldered the musket and dropped off the eaves onto the barricade beside the still-stunned pirates. The nearest whirled at him, cutlass raised, only to stop in shock.

"Captain Fengel?" said Henry Smalls.

"Hello, Henry," replied Fengel. He clapped the man on the shoulder as he sidled past. "One side, if you please. There's a lad."

He unshouldered the musket, raised it up, and fired point-blank into the face of an automaton crawling up the side of an overturned cart. It rang like a bell and fell away. Fengel reversed the weapon, holding it like a club by the now-hot barrel. He swung the stock into the helm of another, sending it crashing below. He tried not to look at the carnage down the street where the Bluecoats screamed and died.

Turning, he glared out at the dozen remaining pirates and roared out in his best command voice, "What are you all doing? Find a way to fall back!"

"Ye damned popinjay!" shouted Euron, standing a dozen feet away atop the barricade. "What be ye doing here?"

"Saving your hides!" roared Fengel.

"Captain Fengel!" shouted Sarah Lome. The joy was plain on her face. "But there's nowhere else to go!" The rest of the pirates all called their agreement. Where before they'd been grimly determined, now both hope and relief lit their features.

"Are you blind, Gunney?" asked Fengel incredulously. "Get one of the warehouses open!

"I tried, Captain. But those doors are all rusted shut, and we don't have time to hack one open!"

Fengel paused, taken aback. "Oh. Well. Um ..."

"In here, quickly!"

Everyone turned at the voice. It came from the open door to the pub, the Cock O' the Green. An older man stood within it, dark haired and clad in a finer outfit than any of the pirates possessed, or most of Haventown, for that matter. He gestured frantically.

Fengel blinked. "Yes. Like that."

"What?" yelled Euron. "Stand and fight, ye mutinous dogs!"

Reflected light flashed in the corner of Fengel's eye. He lashed out with the musket in his hands, catching his cantankerous father-in-law by the back of his knees. The old man fell, rolling down the back of the barricade with a surprised cry, just as an automaton raised up its cannon and fired.

"Inside!" roared Fengel. "Get inside the pub!"

Then he threw the weapon aside and hopped down the barricade himself, landing on blood-stained boardwalk and the corpse of a pirate whom he felt he should know. The others didn't have to be told twice. Shannon MacKinnon fled through the doorway, followed by Danica Barker and the others. Gunney Lome and Henry Smalls hung back, falling in beside Fengel at the rear of the crowd.

"It's good to see you, Captain," said Henry.

"It's good to be seen, Mr. Smalls," Fengel replied. He adjusted his monocle and put his hands behind him. "But what are you two doing down here? Where're Lucian and the others?"

"We got split up during the retreat," said Sarah Lome. "Some of us made it aboard the airships, but the rest of us had to run back through the jungle. Henry and I barely stuck together; I don't know about Cumbers, Lucian, Maxim, or the rest. We two went looking for you, but the pirate king was rounding people up to fight down here in the Waterdocks."

Shouts rang out from down the street just as the barricade began to shift. Trailing columns of steam rose up from behind it, accompanied by the clank of the automatons. Fengel jerked his head at the pub, its doorway standing empty now but for the man within it. "Lucian knows what he's about. We'll find him after we get out of here. Oh, and Gunney, please bring that sad sack of mouldering liver spots along, if you please?"

The huge woman looked momentarily uncertain, but then she nodded sharply. Leaning down, she grabbed up Euron Blackheart from where he was rising creakily to his knees and threw him over her shoulder. He snarled and spit as she trotted into the Cock O' the Green. Fengel smiled and nudged his steward in the ribs as they trotted after. Henry returned the smile, but grudgingly and tainted by worry.

The publican slammed shut the door as soon as they were inside and threw down a bar to lock the portal. Two other men were waiting, and they pushed through the crowd with a heavy cask. Fengel stepped aside as they wedged it up against the door, then left for more things with which to reinforce their barricade.

Fengel let his eyes adjust to the gloom. The taproom they stood within was a modest one, with a cold brick fireplace along the left wall and a well-stocked bar directly across from the door. Round tables took up most of the space. Polished teak paneled the walls, which were covered in an assortment of oddities.

Trophies, caps, and tools hung in places of pride. Fengel glimpsed framed broadsheet advertisements, each proclaiming the advantages of a powder or elixir that swore to give one an advantage over one's opponents. Oil paintings portrayed men dressed in plaid standing upon verdant fields.

"Golfing equipment?" asked Fengel in surprise. Some of the things here he hadn't seen since he was a child.

"You know the Royal Sport, then, sir?"

Fengel turned to see the proprietor standing near. His dark hair was disheveled, and his brass spectacles were fogged over with sweat. "A little," replied Fengel. "It's not a game that lends itself well to my vocation."

"Are you sure? A club and a ball, and you've got a start." He reached out a hand. "Martin Pool, proprietor of the Cock O' the Green. Hello, Henry."

Henry Smalls gave the man a nod. "Good to see you, Martin."

Fengel took the offered hand and shook it. "Captain Fengel, of the *Dawnhawk*. Thank you for your timely aid, Mr. Pool."

"Well, I couldn't just stand there while you were fighting and dying outside, now, could I?"

The two other men pushed past, rolling another heavy keg. Both were older, grey-haired and with full beards. One jerked his head towards the stair just below the bar. "That goes out just below the Craftwright's Terrace stair."

"James Von Lossow is our brew master," said Martin. "And Tom O' Driscoll, our cook."

Both men set the keg up against the door, gave a wave, then pushed back through the crowd. "You brew your own ale?" asked Fengel.

"Of course!" replied Martin. "In fact, if you've a moment—"

"Let me down, ye damned freak of a woman!"

It was Euron, of course. Fengel turned to see the pirate king flailing from where Gunney Lome still had him in a fireman's carry across her back. She released him abruptly. Fengel's furious father-in-law fell with a crash upon a table beside them, then down to the taproom floor. Sarah stepped back, the contempt plain on her face. Even Henry frowned, irritated. Once, such manhandling of Euron Blackheart would have been unthinkable. Now Fengel didn't especially care, and it looked like his crew were coming around to the idea as well.

The rest of the pirates all went still. They quickly pulled away, forming an uncertain circle around Fengel, his crewmen, and the pirate king. James Von Lossow and Tom O'Driscoll pushed past carrying a table, oblivious to the fight brewing right behind them.

Euron clambered to his knees. "Ye mutinous, yellow-bellied cur! How dare ye strike me? How—"

"I dared," snapped Fengel, "because you would have died out there on that pile of garbage and brought everyone here down with you!"

"We were fightin' 'em back!" roared Euron, standing.

"You were cornered!" continued Fengel. "And besides, what are you even doing down here? I sent you up to the Skydocks, Euron!"

The crowd gasped. Euron glared up at him, hatefully. "Ye don't be sendin' me anywhere!" he snarled. "Ye don't rule Haventown—"

"Wrong!" said Fengel, taking a step forward. "I *do.*"

Another collective gasp went about the room. Everyone but Shannon MacKinnon stared at him in surprise. Even Henry Smalls and Gunney Lome seemed shocked. A rumbling murmur rose up from those assembled, even as something outside crashed. Fengel looked from face to face and realized the time was now or never. *Never let them see you stumble.*

"The *Dawnhawk* stands with me," he said, more to the crowd than to Euron, "and all her crew. So will *Solrun's Hammer* and what's left of the *Windhaunter.* I've got the Mechanists behind me, Euron. They entrusted me with the secret of saving this town while you were busy playing at war. So get out of my way! Be gone! I've still work to do, and the Waterdocks are a lost cause—"

The old man's cutlass skittered out of its scabbard, aimed for his heart. Fengel stepped aside, drawing his saber and brushing aside Euron's follow-through. The pirate king didn't let up, hacking and chopping with the brutal, artless swordplay that had served him well throughout all the long years. Even as decrepit as he was, Euron still knew how to fight.

"Me daughter can find someone else t' warm her bed!" snarled Euron. "Goddess knows she's snuck enough dockside trash past ye over the years!"

Fengel held his ground, taking the measure of his father-in-law. Fengel twisted his blade, saving his strength and letting the cutlass clang away. One opening appeared, which he declined to take. Euron rebounded, over-swinging again, leaving himself defenseless and throwing away his balance. Fengel let him recover.

The pirate king cursed him as they fought, between panting breaths. Fengel watched him slow, then stumble. *Time to make an end of this.* But how? Much as he wanted, crippling or killing the old man wouldn't sit well with Natasha, regardless of the circumstances.

A figure moved along the edge of the crowd. It was the proprietor, Martin Pool. He held a golfing club, the handle out. Fengel waited until Euron over-reached again, then took it with his free hand. He struck out with his saber in a slow, high blow aimed for his opponent's head. Euron flinched, forced back on the defensive, and raised his cutlass to parry.

Fengel lashed out with the golf club, catching Euron behind the knee. The man crumpled, his grip momentarily loosened. Fengel bound Euron's cutlass, swinging it tightly down and around until it came free and flew across the room.

Outside the pub, the boardwalk shook with the sound of many heavy metal feet.

"You're looking for an end, Euron," said Fengel. "I can see that clear as day. You want one last glorious fight with which to go out in. Well, find it on your own. *I'm* fighting to save this town and all the people left in it."

He looked up, meeting the eyes of everyone there. Then he waited. Shannon MacKinnon gave a nod, and Henry and Sarah both shifted slightly, ready to stand with him against the crowd if need be.

The remaining pirates studied him or looked among themselves. One spoke up without stepping forward. "But how are you going to do that, Captain Fengel? The Bluecoats have those blasted metal men with 'em. And a horde o' ships and men."

That's it. I've got them. There wasn't time to gloat, though. "I've already taken steps. The Mechanists have a solution. We've just got to slow the Perinese down until it's done and keep them off the Craftwright's Terrace."

James Von Lossow and Thomas O' Driscoll stepped up beside Martin Pool. "We can fire the tavern," said Thomas, looking miserable. "If everything down here is as lost as you say."

Martin winced. "All our things …" he said, glancing about the room.

Soldiers' shouts rose outside the bar. "We can't take it with us," said James quietly. "And those kegs of brandy you tried to make are more lamp-oil than anything else."

"Do it," said Fengel, sympathizing. He gestured with his saber at the door on the opposite side of the room. "The rest of you, get out the back and up to the Craftwright's Terrace. I want to see everyone up at Pillager's Square, ready to hold the line. And as for you—" Fengel dropped the tip of his blade to Euron's throat, stopping the man from rising. "Do what you want. Your reign just ended. I don't have any more need of you, old man."

Euron Blackheart glared up at him. Fengel held his eyes a moment, and then he smirked. Tossing the golfing club back to Martin Pool, he stepped past Euron towards the rest of the pirates queuing at the exit. Behind him, something slammed up against the entryway, even as James, Thomas, and Martin cracked open a keg and splashed it across the floor.

CHAPTER NINETEEN

Lina watched the Dray Engine approach.

She stood just outside the Stormhammer pyramid, on hard earth baked black. To the west, the sun hung low as it set, casting long shadows across the scorched ring at the center of the island.

The Dray Engine tromped through the southern jungle, its reptilian head bright and brassy above the canopy of snapping, rustling trees. Occasionally it would pause and look down sharply. Then it would stomp, a single metallic thump that resounded across the island entire and drowned out the death cry of some unfortunate animal. That the murderous automaton hadn't seen her yet was apparent.

This was a terrible idea. Lina swallowed and shifted her weight from one foot to the other. Sure, it had been *her* terrible idea, one she'd known Natasha would agree to. But that hadn't meant she'd wanted to be the one out here in the open acting as bait. Though in hindsight, she couldn't quite think who else would have ended up here.

"Can you see it yet?" called Natasha. The pirate captain stood inside the pyramid at the other end of the tunnel, peering out at her. Farther in, Lina knew, Rastalak was hunkering over the lever that controlled the Stormhammer itself.

Thankfully, Runt and her spawn were safely aboard the *Dawnhawk*. Her pet scryn had been exhausted after whelping and hadn't wanted to do more than curl up with a bowl of hard liquor afterward. The scrynlings had quickly followed suit, to the mutual relief of the crew. Though frankly, Lina couldn't see what all the fuss was about. Runt's babies were positively adorable, like little flying worms.

"I said, can you—"

"I heard you!" snapped Lina, who then remembered who she was talking to. "It's at the tree line to the south, coming right this way."

Silence answered her. Lina winced. Even when trying to trick an ancient Voornish death-dragon into a trap by relying on a finicky ancient superweapon, she could depend on Natasha to make her miserable.

"I thank you for your frank input," said her captain after a moment, voice tight. "Know that I am always willing to listen to anything you might have to say." There was a thump, like a book snapping shut. "Which doesn't mean I won't beat you black and green if you keep giving me lip!"

Lina winced. *That stupid book.* The threats, she could handle. But Natasha trying to be nice made her feel like the world was crawling down its own throat. "Aye, aye—"

Palm trees snapped and fell as the Dray Engine pushed out of the jungle. It stepped into the clearing and roared, a deafening, metallic sound. Lina stared at it, even as her instincts screamed for her to turn and run.

The automaton stood as tall as the mainmast of a sailing ship, a reptilian horror rendered in imperishable Voornish metal. It was squatter than a real dragon, standing on thick hind legs and powerful feet, and its tail swayed behind as it stalked. The forelimbs were shorter, its designers having traded quadruped versatility for the ability to grasp and tear. From atop the thick, armored neck, it peered about through great red glass eyes, looking for victims to devour with its coffin-long maw. Past the carapace and armored scales, its inner workings ticked along, all whirling gears and churning pistons.

The Dray Engine finished its call and paused to listen to the echo. Then it lowered its head and snorted, sending out a great gush of steam. It blinked and peered about, and if Lina hadn't known any better, she would have thought the thing looked bored.

"Captain," she said in a hoarse stage whisper. "It's here."

She could actually hear Natasha rub her hands together eagerly. "Then get *on* with it, Stone."

Glorious Goddess in the Realms Above, Lina prayed. *Guard me in this, and I'll make an* amazing *donation to your chapel in the Yellow Lantern Terrace back home. That one with the really gross priest who likes to hold your hand just a little too long. I'll even give up the old Voorn jewelry that I got back in Yrinium. I swear it.*

Lina took a deep breath, tried to ignore the lurching of her stomach, and cupped both hands around her mouth in a makeshift speaking trumpet. "*Hey!*" she yelled. "Hey, beast!"

The Dray Engine paused. It peered about, looking for her. Lina swung her arms about, and when that didn't work, pinched her fingers between her lips and let out a piercing whistle. The Dray Engine stared straight at her.

"Yes!" shouted Lina. "Right here, you great damned wind-up lizard! That's right, I'm talking to you!"

The Dray Engine snorted.

This is going to get me killed. This is going to get me killed, and I am going to die. She took a breath. Then she unlaced her trousers, turned around, and mooned the ancient Voornish machine.

The wind was surprisingly brisk.

Lina glanced back to see the Dray Engine jerk back in startlement. It blinked its great red glass eyes, its maw slightly agape. Then it roared in affront.

The ancient automaton leaped forward, its head held low for speed. Lina swore and raised her trousers, fumbling to cinch the buckle.

"What's going on?" shouted Natasha. "What's it doing?"

"It's coming!"

"What?"

"It's coming!" she yelled.

The ground shook like it was giving birth to an earthquake. Lina's ears rang as the Dray Engine roared again, far, far too close this time. And her damned belt wouldn't buckle.

To the Realms Below with it. She grabbed her belt in both hands and ran into the tunnel entrance to the pyramid. The earth bucked, twisting beneath her legs and ruining her footing. Heart in her throat, she fell, tumbling as the light from outside was occluded by the enraged machine. She hit the dusty earth as the Dray Engine slammed into the pyramid like a falling meteor.

"Now!" roared Natasha.

There was a sudden hum, which rose to a violent vibration Lina felt in her bones. Light bloomed, both inside the pyramid and somewhere outside past the Dray Engine. Then came a crackling discharge that seemed to tear through the world entire. What little Lina could see was painful and bright. The whole of the Dray Engine shuddered violently. Arcs of galvanic energy washed over it, and the grasping claws that sought for Lina just within the tunnel spasmed. She was near enough to the thing that her hair stood painfully on end, which forced her to roll away as sparks shot from the monster.

The Stormhammer's blast faded. The galvanic arcs crawling across the Dray Engine died off. Then the ancient automaton went very still. It fell away from the pyramid, and the tunnel opened again as it crashed to the ground.

Lina stared, panting. White spots danced across her eyes, like she'd stared into the sun for too long. Her ears rang too. So much so that she barely heard the crunch of Natasha's boots running down the tunnel.

"Did it work?" demanded her captain. "Did we get it?" Natasha stopped just inside the tunnel, Butterbeak flapping down to her shoulder. She peered out, wary, then glanced back at Lina. "Stone, get …" She paused. "Pull yer damned trousers up and get over here and go check that thing out."

She stared at her captain, incredulous. *I just almost died! Check it out yourself!* But Lina only sighed. "Yes, Captain," she said. Everything sounded funny, and Butterbeak was snickering at her, she was sure.

Lina scrambled to her feet, finally cinching her belt buckle. She walked over to the tunnel mouth—and her captain—to peer out at the burnished hulk outside. Out of the corner of her eye, she saw Rastalak coming out the tunnel to join them. The little Draykin rubbed his hands together as if they'd been singed.

The clearing outside the Stormhammer pyramid was a scorched, blackened mess. Clouds of stinking smoke roiled up into the bright blue sky. Little flames danced across the ground, though just as before, the jungle ringing the island exterior seemed untouched.

The Dray Engine still lived.

It lay awkwardly, a massive metal hulk toppled over onto its side. Sparks jumped from its extremities while galvanic arcs sizzled across its armored carapace. The great red glass eyes of the thing rolled about as it twitched and jerked like an old man having a seizure. From somewhere inside sounded a muted mechanical groan.

"It's still alive," said Natasha flatly.

"The creations of the Great Masters are notoriously resilient," said Rastalak.

"It's still alive."

Lina adjusted her trousers. "That was kind of the point, Captain."

"I wanted to kill it."

Rastalak made a sibilant sigh. "We know, Captain."

Natasha growled, a small weird twin to the noise the Dray Engine itself was making. She stepped outside and kicked the machine. Galvanic sparks flared at the contact, and Natasha jumped back with a yelp, flinging Butterbeak free as she cursed and shook her now-singed boot. With effort, the Dray Engine twisted its head around to glare hatefully at her.

"Enough!" she said. "Where's the damned airship?"

As if on cue, a shadow fell across them all. The *Dawnhawk* appeared from behind the peak of the pyramid.

Lina sighed in relief. She'd been reasonably sure that the airship would be safe from the Stormhammer out along the northern shore of the island, but none of them were certain. Still, the vessel was a wreck. Her ropes dangled, her hull was scuffed, and her canvas sagged in places along the gas bag to reveal the cells beneath. The shining aethersails were either torn, or hung at bent angles.

Even so, the airship maneuvered into place overhead, fifty feet above. Reaver Jane leaned out over the gunwales to peer down at them.

"Everything work out?" she hollered.

"Aye," said Natasha. "Now get down here and help me tie this contraption up!"

Reaver Jane shouted an order back down the deck, then tossed a rope ladder over the side of the airship. More ropes and cables appeared, followed by Etarin, Farouk, Paine, Michael Hockton, and Andrea Holt.

Lina moved to hold the nearest ladder for her crewmates. "How's Runt doing?" she asked as Etarin reached the ground.

The Salomcani pirate stared at her. Then he turned away in disgust. Michael was down next, though, and he smiled at her, his face covered in welts. "She's fine," he said. "The younglings too—all asleep. I think I saw a small cage in one of the storage lockers that might hold them. We can dig it out once we get moving again."

Lina jerked back. "What? We can't cage them up!"

"Stone!" snarled Natasha. "Get over here! This was your damned idea in the first place!"

She flinched. "Yes, Captain." Lina smiled at Michael, then grabbed a dangling rope from above and went to work.

Restraining the Dray Engine was awkward, haphazard work. The smoke in the air made it difficult to breathe, and residual galvanic charge shocked them wherever they touched the metal skin of the thing with bare hands. As if that wasn't enough, the monster seemed aware that they were crawling across it. Its seizures became more violent, and the muted rumble within its carapace grew stronger with every passing moment.

Impending death by mechanical dragon proved a great motivator. Lina raced across the thing, running cables under the knees, around the neck, and across the armored carapace. It was tricky, especially with the Dray Engine twisting and jerking about. The last thing she wanted was to slip and get her leg caught in the heavy gears twisting along beneath the armored plates.

The others did their parts, working quietly and efficiently. For all their trepidation and the weirdness of the situation, this was something they knew how to do and practiced regularly. Loose knots, awkward weight, weakened chains—all of these could cause a stack of freshly stolen cargo to go slipping off into the ocean on its way up to the airship holds. So Lina and her crewmates moved with care, doubling loops around brazen limbs and triple-checking the knots that would suspend the monster evenly.

Finally, they were done. Lina stepped back with the rest, regarding their handiwork. The Dray Engine lay bound in a nest of haphazard cabling and old rope, now tethered firmly to the *Dawnhawk* above them. The machine fought, its strident groans becoming stronger with every second. But their restraints would hold. Probably.

Andrea Holt stared at the giant automaton. "This is … insanely dangerous, Captain."

"Oh, don't I know it," said Natasha flatly. She turned away to climb up the ladder. "But it's time someone else suffered this miserable clockwork nuisance as much as I have. Besides, I seem to recall that it really enjoyed tearing apart Perinese warships. Good plan, Stone."

Their captain ascended back to the airship above. Lina found herself suddenly being glared at by everyone else. Even Michael looked dubious. "What?" she said, throwing up her hands. "If we can get it back to town, it'll wreak havoc!"

"Yes," said Paine. "*If* we can get it back to town."

"And what do we do when the fighting's done?" asked Reaver Jane. "Ask it nicely to leave?"

"Get yer arses up here!" snarled Natasha.

Lina's crewmates turned away from her, reluctantly, until only Michael Hockton was left. He put a hand to her shoulder, and she leaned into it wearily.

"You think it's a good idea, don't you?" said Lina. "I mean, we don't even have to do any fighting this way—just drop the thing on them and fly off."

The ex-soldier shrugged. "Well …"

Lina glared at him. Then she shrugged his hand away. "Fine, then. Just wait. This will—"

The ground shook as the Dray Engine slammed its tail into the earth. It roared, its maw closed and muted, but unmistakably enraged.

Lina swallowed. "This … this will work. It has to."

She grabbed the rope ladder and climbed up, crawling just over the gunwales as the *Dawnhawk* gained altitude again, if just barely. Natasha had taken the wheel from Ryan Gae while Allen frantically worked the gearbox controls by the helm. The propellers at the rear of the airship spun up, pushing and lifting against the massive weight anchoring it, tilting the deck at an awkward angle. Lina swore and grabbed for a handhold while the rest of the crew yelled in surprise.

"Can we even fly right now?" demanded Natasha. She held out an arm for Butterbeak to land upon.

Allen ran over to eye the propellers at the very rear of the ship. "We should be able to, if we haven't burned through all our coal stores," he said. A great scraping noise echoed up from the earth back down below, and he smiled up the deck at everyone. "See?"

"What do you mean, if?" demanded Natasha. "Shouldn't you know how much coal we have?"

"I haven't had time to check it!" said Allen, raising his voice. "I've been fighting off soldiers and pirates and every other Goddess-damned thing you people get caught up in!"

Lina blinked at Allen. Natasha too seemed surprised. "No need to be a child about it," she said, sounding uncharacteristically reasonable. "Just go check the stores as soon as we get underway."

Bit by bit, they gained speed. The scraping noise continued as they went, interspersed by the clang of a rock as they dragged the Dray Engine across the burned earth. Natasha took them around the pyramid, avoiding the jungle as they gained speed and height, and with one last dragging lurch, they leveled out and floated free.

Relief washed over Lina. The rest of the crew seemed to feel it too; big Farouk let out a whoop that the others joined in on. They were free of the Stormhammer, the Castaways, and the threat of the Dray Engine itself.

Sort of.

Oh! Runt! In all the excitement, she'd forgotten to check up on her little mother.

Lina ran down the deck, grabbing Michael Hockton by the arm as she passed him. "Michael! Quick, where's Runtie? And her adorable little babies?"

Her ex-soldier stumbled a bit as the Dray Engine shifted itself below the airship. "She's in her usual spot," he said with a strained smile. "Just over here."

Lina dragged him over to the exhaust pipe amidships, where she and Runt both preferred to spend their free time. The little mother lay there below the pipe, snug up against it in an exhausted coil about her scrynlings, who slithered back and forth, blindly writhing about.

"Aww," she sighed, looking back up to Michael Hockton. "Aren't they adorable?"

Her crewmate stared at the scrynlings, his face a frozen mask. A forced smile fought its way onto his features, fell away, and reappeared. "Sure," he replied slowly. "Why not? Here, let's get that cage."

Lina felt butterflies take flight in her stomach. She leaned into him, then rose up on her toes to give him a kiss. His attention was still riveted on the scrynlings, and it took him a surprised moment to respond. But respond he did, and she quickly forgot the taste of blood, vomit, and smoke on his lips.

The moment broke as the deck shifted again. Lina pulled away, hunting for balance, as Runt gave a weary chirp and surprised exclamations echoed from the rest of the crew on deck. Michael said nothing, only continuing to hold onto her.

"We're just at about peak ascent," called Natasha. "Swollen guts of the Goddess, that beast is *heavy.*"

Lina glanced back at her captain, only to see Allen standing a few feet away. He'd been heading up towards the bow on some errand, a coil of rope over his shoulder and a hammer in his hand. The apprentice Mechanist was staring at her and Michael Hockton. Then he threw his hammer to the deck, startling Runt, and stalked away back towards the helm.

Oh. Allen. That's right, I've been leading him on for a bit. Lina stopped to think. *Is that why he's been so out of sorts this afternoon? Or was it the fires, the fighting, and that finger he lost?* He'd always been a bit odd, even at his best. She'd have to have a talk with him later.

"Captain Blackheart!" cried Omari from up near the bow. "We need to make another pass!"

"The Dray-thing is too low," echoed Paine beside her. "It's not gonna clear the cliff!"

"Pah!" shouted Natasha. "We're fine!"

Reaver Jane bent low over the starboard gunwales. "Uh, Captain. I …"

"I don't care," snarled Natasha. "I've spent long enough on this wild goose chase, avoiding the fight back home! We're going, and all hands brace for impact if you think me wrong!"

Everyone grabbed for the nearest handholds. Lina looked to Michael, and then they both scrambled for the gunwales. She grabbed on with both hands, looking out and over to see the jungle racing by beneath them and the grey cliffs dead ahead. Her crewmates were right. They were only just clearing the canopy; they'd never clear the cliff top ring around the island.

The Dray Engine was twitching and writhing, only barely stunned now. Whatever machinery buried in that clockwork core it used to think with alerted it to the danger. The machine jerked its head forward, one great red eye half-lidded, the other open wide as it beheld the landform bearing down upon it. White steam gushed out from its maw in seeming disbelief.

Natasha was wrong, just. The Dray Engine slammed into the granite cliff face-first, its head dragged back on its long, serpentine neck as the bulk of the thing slid forward to dig a furrow in the stone. Ropes snapped, and the *Dawnhawk* jerked violently in sympathetic shock. Lina's heart shot into her throat as the deck pitched beneath them, and for a moment she thought they would all die in an impending crash.

Lina had a moment of calm, horrible clarity. *I take it back. This was a terrible idea. They've all been terrible ideas.* She held on as the deck bucked and shook. Tools flew past, and dangling rope danced crazily. Faintly, she heard Michael yell and Natasha swear a blue streak. She paid them no attention, though, focused more on every prayer to the Goddess she could make, fighting through the pain of being slammed repeatedly into the gunwales.

Amazingly, the roiling pitch of the airship quelled. The deck righted, mostly, and she wasn't flung about anymore. The airship was flying smoothly once again.

Lina opened her eyes. Her crewmates hunkered about the deck, all still aboard, if a little battered. Slowly, they stood. This time, no one cheered.

"Enough lying about!" shouted Natasha. Lina glanced back to see the captain at the wheel, confident and mad as ever, but with a darkening bruise forming across one eye and Butterbeak a frazzled ball of puffed-up feathers on her shoulder. "Stone! How's our passenger doing?"

It took Lina a moment to realize that Natasha was speaking to her. She nodded, then stood and looked over the gunwales. Below, the waters of the Atalian Sea raced by, cerulean and choppy. The Dray Engine dangled between the ship and the sea, the cabling they'd used to secure it a tangled mess. Fully a third of the ropes were torn. The automaton itself hung limp, one talon twitching on its right forepaw.

"I think it's stunned," she shouted back. Lina didn't know whether to feel relief or dread. Hauling the monster back to Haventown might give them a potent weapon to fight the invasion with. Then again, what they were doing was so much worse than holding a tiger by the tail. Lina turned back to the helm, knowing only one thing for certain. "Captain ... it's going to be *pissed* when it comes to."

"Ha!" replied Natasha. "Then my day is complete. No, I lie. All right, you laggards and reprobates, we're heading back to the Graveway—and the fight. Look sharp! It seems things have gotten thick down there."

Lina took a few steps up towards the bow. She glanced past it, to the south where the jungles of the isles met bright blue sky. A dark smudge stained the sky: smoke and fire.

Something was wrong about the position, though. Lina checked the setting sun to the west, and her stomach fell. *That's not the Graveway.*

The fighting was in Haventown itself.

"To your posts!" ordered Natasha. "Reaver Jane, check those hawsers. Rastalak, get yer scaly arse above and look to the rigging. Ryan Gae, get those bombs out from the equipment lockers and to the gunwales. Omari, go back up top and get out of the way—"

"I'm not going back up with that ape!" shouted Omari.

"Mechanist," Natasha continued, "go check the coal stores. We're making it back to Haventown in one trip, and I don't care if we have to burn—"

"I'm going!" he shrieked, already opening the aft-deck hatch.

Natasha fished out her self-help book. "And know that your efforts are valued. Probably. Hockton! Do something with those … scrynlings. I'm sure I saw a small crate in one of those lockers. Stone! Quit scowling and go aloft into the envelope. Make sure we haven't any slow leaks."

"Aye, Captain," she said, weary and indignant at the same time. Runt aside, the last thing she wanted was to climb about the light-air cells wearing a gas mask.

Natasha continued to shout orders. Lina moved to obey, first grabbing Michael Hockton's sleeve as he passed by. He looked back in surprise, and she winked at him before letting go. Then she turned about and clambered atop the gunwales, reaching for the ratlines and rigging.

Lina was halfway up when she heard the hurried tromp of boots followed by the bang of a pistol. She glanced back down to the deck, almost losing her grip in surprise.

The aft hatchway was open, and a dozen pirates stormed out onto the deck. It was the Castaways, led by Morgan One-Eye. Still battered and half-starved, they looked to have recovered from their earlier fight and flight, having bandaged their wounds. Now they stood straighter, holding gleaming weapons obviously stolen from the *Dawnhawk's* stores. One of their number had Allen as a captive, an arm locked around his throat, while the other held a smoking flintlock pistol.

It was Oscar Pleasant.

"Hello, Captain Blackheart," he said nastily.

Natasha peered out from behind the wheel. Oscar's pistol ball had slammed into it squarely, just missing her.

"You little rat's arse," she said. "I'm going to jam that gun so far up your backside you'll spit sparks when you cough. Who are you?"

Oscar tightened his grip on Allen, who choked. "You don't recognize me? I've been on your ship all this time, and you don't recognize me?"

"It's Oscar Pleasant!" snarled Lina. "He's the one that led the damned Perinese onto the Skydocks. He slipped aboard the ship afterward—no wonder we couldn't find him. Oscar! You traitorous bag of shit. I'm going to make good on that promise I made you last year."

He glanced up at her. "Lina Stone. Goddess above, I've been waiting to teach you a lesson." He dropped his spent pistol and drew another. "Now I've got your little milksop friend here, and that's not all."

"Enough of this!" snapped Morgan One-Eye. The Castaway took a step forward towards Natasha. "I'm taking command, you brat of Blackheart."

Natasha ignored him. She gave a violent shrug that flung Butterbeak into the air. Then she locked the wheel in place and pulled a series of levers on the gearbox beside it. Somewhere below the deck, the engine gave a great thump. The propellers buzzed like a nest of angry hornets and the airship lurched forward. Great gouts of steam billowed out from both exhaust pipes, damaged and not. The *Dawnhawk* strained under the pressure, pushing forward for home as hard as possible; if she could hold together, the trip wouldn't take long. Only then did her captain step out to squarely face her foes. "How did you get aboard my ship?"

Morgan laughed, the rest of his companions joining in. "We climbed the damned ladder! Running away from that big brass monster back to our village, and what did we see but yer airship and a rope ladder just dangling from it! So we climbed aboard and hid away, and then you got us away from that damned island."

Natasha glared angrily past the Castaways. "Omari!"

The aetherite was trying to find her balance as the airship sped forward. "I was busy with the ape!" she cried.

Morgan ceased chuckling. "Enough. Now we're away from the monster. So we'll be taking yer ship now."

Natasha drew her own cutlass. "Over your dead body," she snarled.

A clarion roar echoed out from below the airship. The deck of the *Dawnhawk* jerked violently; the Dray Engine had awoken.

Reaver Jane chose that moment to hurl a boarding hatchet, which hammered into the skull of a Castaway. The rest of the Lina's crewmates charged the newcomers, who raised their weapons and shouted in defiance. Then the battle was joined.

CHAPTER TWENTY

He glared down at Private Bryant, who knelt beside his makeshift chair wrapping a bandage around his bare chest. "You incompetent boob!" Wintermourn snarled. "Have a bit of care!"

Private Bryant ducked his head. "Yes, sir. Sorry, sir. It's just, the splinters left a jagged sort of wound, sir."

Splinters. Three-inch shards of wood stuck in my ribs, more like. Such wounds were common in the aftermath of a broadside. He'd watched men bleed to death from them without even realizing that they'd been wounded. But when during that mad chase after Euron Blackheart had it even happened to him? Wintermourn could not say. "Worry less about what caused the wound," he said, "and more with stanching it!"

The soldier nodded, then bent back to work. Admiral Wintermourn winced, shifting in his seat. All around them, the Haventown alley was a claustrophobic mess. He sat on an empty wooden rain barrel, watching as Sergeant Greene frantically formed a fire brigade. Those marines not too injured passed barrels of hastily scavenged rainwater down the alley in an effort to quench the blaze at its end. Adjutant Chesterly stood there too, screaming commands at the twenty Brass Paladins as they mindlessly wandered through the inferno that had been the Cock O' the Green Tavern.

Even if he hadn't been too weak to countermand the up-jumped ex-officer, the sudden overhead bombardment from *Solrun's Hammer* had been devastating, a parting blow as she fled for the safety of the upper terraces. He'd managed to avoid further injury himself, thank the Goddess, but he could only watch in frustrated rage as the Brass Paladins recovered before the men. The machines effortlessly tore apart the damned barricade, only to find the pirates had managed to flee a little farther.

The tavern had seemed a futile gesture, understandable though it might have been in the face of the clockwork monsters. But when they broke down the door, it exploded into the inferno that even now threatened to spread. The pirates had killed themselves rather than be taken alive. It was utterly mad.

And I wanted to kill you, Euron. You were mine by rights. My prize. I'd have had you, to the Realms Below with these wounds and the bombs and damned Chesterly. I'd have had you, you craven old fool. But now you're gone. Which … works to the same thing in the end, I suppose. Victory. And none of you will rise again from this pyre you've built yourself.

"About-face! No, not that way—you … you damned wind-up machines! Just … just listen to me! Argh!"

Adjutant Chesterly stood as close to the burning tavern as he could get, sweating profusely and getting in the way of the Bluecoats. Wintermourn listened to his frustrated screams in amusement. With any luck, the fire-blinded automatons would melt into slag.

"High Admiral Wintermourn?"

Wintermourn looked up to see a fresh-faced young naval field officer, a lieutenant commander he did not know. The man was smudged and dirty from battle, but he still wore his embroidered jacket neatly. A squad of similarly uninjured Bluecoats stood at his back, black-capped, holding their muskets at the ready.

Where in the Realms Below have you come from? "Yes?"

The officer gave a salute. "Lieutenant Hollyway, off the *Leviathan*. His Highness Crown Prince Gwydion requires and requests your presence along the docks."

Wintermourn's irritation rose anew. "And how am I to reach him through that war zone? Besides, I'm overseeing this operation here. If we don't get it under control, this whole damned part of the city could burn."

"The *Glory of Perinault* has landed, sir. We've taken the lagoon and quashed the pirates there. Their airships have fallen back, crippled. Deployment of the marine companies is taking place all along the Waterdocks." Hollyway nodded up the street. "As for this …" He gestured at the screaming adjutant and the blinded, tottering forms of the automatons in the skeleton of the burning building, "I'm instructed to let the royal adjutant see to it."

A great crash sounded at the end of the street as the roof of the tavern fell in. Fire and ash flew out, choking Chesterly and those Bluecoats nearest him.

Wintermourn shrugged. Chesterly wanted to be responsible for this mess? Let him, then. Good, even. "Very well," he said. "And it's about time the rest of you showed up."

He rose to his feet, shrugging off Bryant. Gingerly, he dressed himself again; first his shirt and then his jacket, and then he yanked his sheathed saber from Bryant's outstretched hands. He took his time straightening his wig, even though Hollyway fidgeted impatiently. The man might be here on an errand of the prince, but he seemed to have forgotten that he was fetching the Lord High Admiral of the Sea, one of the king's own Order Gallant. Wintermourn hurried for no one.

Especially that infuriating fop of a crown prince.

His breath came easier now than before. "Greene!" he shouted, buckling his sword back in place. "Put someone else in charge and get over here."

The sergeant obeyed, limping over to attend him. Wintermourn sighed. He actually missed Sergeant Lanters, he realized. Where in the Realms Below was the fellow? Cleaning out that pirate bolt-hole should have been simple. He would have to think on an appropriate chastisement when the sergeant finally returned.

At least Greene had found his hat. Donning it, Wintermourn looked to Lieutenant Hollyway. "Well? What are we waiting for?"

Hollyway made his salute. Then, obviously wanting to be off, he marched them all back down the street, following the winding path that led out of this mazelike warren of a town.

Something had indeed changed, Wintermourn realized. Away from the clangor of the alley, he realized what it was: the omnipresent sounds of battle had faded. The occasional musket pop still sounded, but the blasts of cannons and bombs had disappeared. Overhead, the pirate airships clustered in tight knots around the Skydocks, lit by early evening twilight, looking battered and worn. Hollyway was right—they'd won the lagoon.

And I've won the city. With Euron dead and the rest of the Waterdocks scourged by their invasion, there shouldn't be anything stopping his reinforcements from climbing up through Haventown. It would be hard, messy work, digging out every last pirate, whore, and urchin still hiding in their hovels. But now it was only a matter of time until the sunburst sigil of Perinault flew from the highest terrace. The Copper Isles truly belonged to the Kingdom now.

The close-knit boardwalk streets widened as they made their way out to the lagoon. Echoes reached Wintermourn, of many polished black boots marching in unison. Hollyway led them around a corner, and he sighed in relief at the sight.

Navy warships filled the piers lying directly ahead. The *Leviathan* and the *Cyclope* sat in port, their gangplanks down to disgorge mostly fresh marines onto the docks, the sunburst sigil flying proudly from atop their rigging. Other ships filled the lagoon behind them, their splintered and broken masts poking up through clouds of roiling smoke as they jockeyed for position. They thumped and collided, their captains screaming epithets at each other. Wintermourn wanted to snap at them—he wanted to take direct control and bring order to the mess. But, no. The faster the better. He was tired of these pirates. It was time to bring this action to an end.

Hollyway gestured to a nearby building with all the hallmarks of a dockside tavern. It was squat and low, with a rickety stair leading up the back to a shanty atop the roof. Stray cannon fire had cleared most of that away, leaving an almost perfect landing pad for the bulbous form of the *Glory of Perinault.*

Wintermourn didn't wait for the lieutenant commander. He crossed the boardwalk and ascended the stair with Sergeant Greene limping along after him. The steps shook and wobbled alarmingly as he climbed.

Gwydion was waiting for him. The crown prince sat at the base of the gangplank in a fine chair that had obviously been brought down from the airship, wineglass in hand. An attendant stood beside him, quietly waiting with a bottle of wine. The airship captain, Broadlow, leaned against a remnant of a wall with a glass of his own, staring up at the pirate city. Spaced out along the rooftop stood the royal guards, eyes cold and halberds at the ready.

"Ah!" cried Gwydion as Wintermourn climbed up past the staircase. "My good admiral, how wonderful of you to join me." The prince rested his wine on the arm of his chair and snapped his fingers at his attendants. "Another glass—and be quick about it."

Wintermourn wanted to refuse on principle, but after the smoke and fire and all the action, a bit of wine sounded rather fetching. He took the offered glass and raised it in salute, then drank deep.

"Your Royal Highness," he said, putting a bit of edge to his voice, "should you really have landed the *Glory* here? Pirates could fall on this location at any moment." He glanced pointedly back up the terraces of Haventown, past the edifice of the Gasworks, to where the airships floated, around the Skydocks so high above.

Gwydion made a dismissive gesture. "Oh, you worry too much, Admiral. I'd say it's one of your charms, but you haven't any, really. No, after the drubbing we gave them, the pirates are in full retreat, at least for now. Didn't get any of the captains, but there's been a hideous cost of lives, both theirs and ours—they've barely enough men left to fly their ships, from what

I can tell. Any bombing passes they make now would wreck their own city—not that I think they've munitions enough left for it. So drink your damned wine and tell me what you've been up to here." He held out his glass for a refill. "You are to be commended, my good admiral. Not a one of the other useless captains made landfall save yourself."

A part of Wintermourn just wanted to needle the prince. To prod and poke at him like one would a chained bear. Anything to twist that smirk off his face. The man—the youth—really, was insufferable. The wine was good, though, and the day had been effectively won.

"Landfall *was* the objective," repeated Wintermourn. "I swear, some days there isn't a sailor in the fleet worth a damn. Everyone was getting fouled up by these reprobates, so I went ahead and created a beachhead. *Myself.* When it was apparent that no one would be joining me, I conquered this terrace." He took a sip and smiled. "Single-handedly, I might add."

Gwydion snorted. "Until the Mechanists deployed that screamer of theirs." He laughed. "I'm going to want what's left of it later. And you have been trying to capture those madmen in gas masks, yes? I gave an explicit order, I recall. But! It was a good thing I gave you my Paladins. They've certainly proved their worth by now." He paused to shake a finger. "Though you could have taken better care of them."

"They did prove their worth," agreed Wintermourn frostily, "and then old Euron Blackheart dropped a wall on them. Your wind-up toys proved nearly useless after that, so we pressed on." He paused to sip his wine, enjoying the crown prince's frown. "Good men of flesh and bone served out where clockwork failed. Not that the pirates gave us any real resistance."

Gwydion raised an eyebrow. "No?"

Wintermourn thought back to dead men who wouldn't fall. He saw their rotting claws scrabbling for his eyes, empty maws hungry for his flesh. The scents of wine and ash faded against the memory of rot and desperate sweat. Wintermourn drained the rest of his wine, forcing away the image.

"No *real* resistance," he affirmed heatedly. "And even when the so-called pirate king found the stones to make another appearance, I managed to corner him. He's surely dead now, but I'd have his head here if your bumbling adjutant hadn't driven him to his demise in a fiery deathtrap."

The crown prince drained his own glass. "Was that who that was? Worry not, my good admiral. I saw a bit of the action from above and signaled to Adjutant Chesterly. Turned into a mess, well enough, but we'll have another chance."

Wintermourn froze. "What do you mean?"

"That pub that burned down? All those pirates escaped out the back. Deftly done too. I barely noticed before *Solrun's Hammer* flanked us."

Euron escaped! That damned pirate played me for a fool and escaped! Wintermourn shoved his empty wineglass at the attendant. "We've got to go after him!"

Gwydion rolled his eyes. He held out his glass for the attendant to refill. "Well, of course we're going after him," he said. "That was kind of the point, to kill the pirate king and all the captains, though we've pretty much already won, now. Once the *Oliphaunt* lands and we've enough men, it'll be back into the fray. Oh. I'll need to recover my adjutant as well, I suppose."

"No! We've got to go after Euron!" Wintermourn turned back to Sergeant Greene. "Go back below and grab three squads of men. I don't care who's in charge!"

The sergeant made his salute, then froze at a cutting gesture from the prince. "Belay that, sergeant. Is that how you say it?"

Rage blossomed in Wintermourn's stomach. He rounded on the man. "What? What is the meaning—"

Gwydion leaned back in his chair and threw up his hands. Wine from his just-filled glass flew through the air, splashing the attendant. "Admiral, they've already fallen back to the second terrace by now. Even with just a few defenders, that means a long, hard climb and a lot of dead marines. And while I have no doubt that's something you'd favor, I'm not willing to risk the *Glory* ferrying small squads of troops up to another part of the terrace, such as that Gasworks or wherever. The pirate airships have been driven back, but if we move from here, they could easily decide to damn the consequences and fall on us from above with whatever few surprises they've got left."

"You yourself wanted Euron dead," said Wintermourn. "And he's just slipped through our fingers!" He thought of the pirate king, mocking him from atop his barricade, distracting Wintermourn and keeping them from cover just long enough for his treacherous airship to bomb them from above.

"Admiral!" replied Gwydion. "What's our hurry? Where are they going to *go?* The pirate airships are battered, and they're not nearly large enough to carry the populace of a town this size. It's not like they're going to just fly away!"

An explosion cut across Wintermourn's retort. It erupted from above, too loud to be a cannon—and coming from the wrong direction as well. He glanced up to see smoke rising from the highest terrace, along the Skydocks. A second blast followed it, from the south this time, where intelligence suggested the Brotherhood Yards were located. Then came a third explosion and a fourth—from the Yellow Lantern and Flophouse terraces, respectively—ejecting smoke high into the sky.

Crown Prince Gwydion rose to his feet, and Wintermourn rounded upon him. "Did you bomb the city?"

"No," said Gwydion. "Just a bit of opportunistic sharpshooting on our final pass. What in the name of the Goddess ..."

Wintermourn clenched a fist. "If some fool is shelling Haventown *now*, of all times, I'll have his command *and* his head. I'll—"

He fell silent as a great rumbling noise roared into life. It started small up above and grew in intensity until it seemed the highest terrace was shaking. Wintermourn watched as those pirate airships not docked suddenly changed course away from their port. Then he felt his jaw fall open—as the highest part of Haventown lifted into the air.

Small white gas bags were inflating beneath the boardwalk, lifting taverns, houses, the Skydocks, and the Brotherhood Yards entire. He could see propellers, just like those aboard the *Glory* and the pirate airships, spinning away, helping to lift. Great hawsers rose up with the terrace, attached securely to the boardwalk and connecting it to the rest of the city below.

The second terrace, Yellow Lantern, gave a mighty shiver. Then it too rose into the air on swelling canvas gas bags and arcane machinery lit by the light of the sinking sun. Dust and debris rained down, and the great immovable brass pipes twisted apart with the shriek of tearing metal. The terrace itself, though, ascended in one piece.

Next came Flophouse Terrace. The poorly built shanties and firetrap lean-tos collapsed in droves. The whole edifice shuddered and sagged. Screams echoed down to Wintermourn, even from so far away. Yet it rose as well to join the rest of the now-aerial city.

Then the whole sequence ... stopped. The three terraces of the city floated aloft ... just hanging there, a trio of floating steps into the sky connected to each other by thick hawsers and chains. The pirate airships circled around, half-protective, half-uncertain.

Wintermourn blinked. He closed his mouth, opened it to say something, then closed it again.

Beside him, Gwydion dropped his wineglass from between limp fingers. It shattered on the rooftop. Then he laughed. Great big belly-shaking whoops erupted from the crown prince. He doubled over, slapping his hands on his thighs as he fought for air.

Wintermourn shook himself as urgency, anger, and irritation at his liege lord all warred for primacy. "Stop your howling!" he snarled, forcibly straightening his wig as if it was about to crawl away.

Gwydion half stood. His cheeks were flushed, and there were tears in his eyes. "I … I just—oh come now, Admiral. This is just impossible! And the timing. I *literally* just asked—"

"I know what you said! And if we don't hurry, they're going to actually do it!" Wintermourn clenched his teeth and thought furiously.

"Ha!" continued Gwydion. "I never would have imagined *this*. I mean, really. The airships were impossible enough. And we still have Helmsin back at the capital—they shouldn't have been able to come up with anything else! Oh, every day brings new wonders, certainly."

Wintermourn rounded on the crown prince. He grabbed the man with both hands by the lapels of his jacket. "Will you cease your irreverent prattle?"

Gwydion's face froze. He gestured to check his guards, who were already moving to action. His grey wolf's eyes were focused, intent, and dangerous. "Take your hands off of me, Admiral. And have a care—"

"No, you have a care!" Wintermourn gestured at the terraces of the city, still rising above them. "The pirates of Haventown aren't just fleeing, they're taking the city with them! The only reason we're still here is to crush them and conquer this ridiculous shantytown. If they get away, then everything we've done is wasted. And I will *not* have my efforts wasted!"

He held the eyes of the crown prince a moment, then let him go and turned to face the Craftwright's Terrace. "Something's wrong, though," he said, largely to himself. "Why hasn't the second terrace taken off? They're tethered to it, just like the others, so it's supposed to go as well."

"A malfunction—" Gwydion sulked, brushing his jacket where Wintermourn had grabbed him.

"There," said Wintermourn. He pointed at the bundle of pipes, smokestacks, and gas reservoirs all squatting together at the opposite end of the terrace: the Gasworks. "That's where the next charge should have gone off."

"How can you be certain?" asked Gwydion, still irritated.

Wintermourn wheeled about. "Because Euron and all the others are *pirates*. Craven-hearted reavers. We know they didn't build the airships—the Brotherhood of the Cog, the Mechanists that live here, did. This is their work. They're the ones really behind this escape. Greene!"

The sergeant made another salute. "Sir!"

"Go below and grab three squads of men. Bring them back up here aboard the *Glory*. Have a message sent to Chest—the royal adjutant that he is to assault that stairway with everything he has, clockwork men included." He jabbed a finger at Captain Broadlow. "You. Go prepare to … lift off—or whatever it is you do to make that swollen cow of a vessel fly."

The *Glory's* master opened his mouth to object, but Gwydion cut him off. "Admiral," he hissed. "That is enough. Your old-fashioned pomposity has been amusing to me, and you're *so* very easily pushed. But I give the orders here. And I am not going to risk the Kingdom's sole airship on your uninformed hunch!"

"Then get out of my way while I do!" snarled Wintermourn. He took a step towards the prince, his saber banging against his hip, and stabbed a finger in his direction. "*I* am the Lord High Admiral of the Seas. *I* am in command of this fleet, and it is *my* responsibility to crush our foes and send them fleeing, for glory of the Kingdom and the king. I do not care if your father has given you command of this battle, and I do not care if he gave you Danlann itself! You are not king yet. Your ridiculous, irreverent plans have gained us victories, it's true, though they've broken with all tradition and honor to do so. But now the foe is about to fly away! I will not stand idly by while that happens. So for once, prove yourself worthy of a modicum of my respect, *my prince,* and obey!"

He quieted, holding Gwydion's gaze. The youth stared at him in return, resolute and unyielding. Then slowly, ever so imperceptibly, he nodded.

"Very well," said Gwydion in a slithering hiss. "Have your way, Admiral. But you will never speak to me so again. And when this is over, we will have further words."

"Oh, indeed we will," snapped Wintermourn in reply. "Greene! Get moving."

The sergeant completed his salute and hurried off. Taking their cue, the attendants, Captain Broadlow, and the royal guards moved to board the *Glory* again. Wintermourn pushed past Gwydion to join them.

He wasn't worried about Gwydion, though the prince was truly dangerous. The king still reigned, and victory absolved everything. In short order it would be his, and the Haventowners' plans would be crushed for the ridiculous gambit that they were.

CHAPTER TWENTY-ONE

He stood in Pillager's Square on the base of Euron's ridiculous statue. All around it swarmed pirates and townsfolk alike, both those who'd escaped from the Waterdocks as well as reinforcements from the upper terraces. They tossed their hats into the air and fired pistols in excitement. Fengel wanted to rebuke such a waste—*but no let it pass.*

Because they had won. Nob, Yellow Lantern, and the Flophouse terraces floated above them on gas bags and propellers, connected in a daisy chain by long hawsers, free from the cliff face they'd rested upon for so long. Haventown was rising aloft.

It wasn't a *real* victory. At least, not a military one, not against the invaders. That wasn't ever going to happen, though. The Perinese were too advanced, too organized, and there were simply too many of them.

But Haventown had survived. Fengel had saved the whole damned city. With the Mechanists' help, of course. Now all that was left was to fly somewhere the Perinese could never trouble them again.

And he would be the one in charge.

Fengel hopped down from the base of Euron's statue. "Well, Mr. Smalls. I bet you never thought to see the day, hmm?"

His officers, Henry and Sarah Lome, both stared slack-jawed at the terrace districts floating above them. Rejoicing pirates jostled his steward, who didn't even seem to notice.

The *Windhaunter's* mate, Shannon, went dancing past with Martin, the publican who'd sacrificed his tavern in their escape. Fengel smiled and adjusted his monocle. He turned back to his officers, who hadn't moved a muscle.

"Oh, come now," he said. "A little decorum, you two."

Henry shook his head. "Yes, sir. Sorry, sir. It's just … how did they even build that?"

"And under Euron's nose!" exclaimed Sarah.

Fengel rolled his eyes. "Please, Gunney. The Mechanists built this town. And Euron never cared one whit what happened here so long as everyone paid him respect. Now. I'm going to want order and a central command restored as soon as possible. Henry, you're going up to the Brotherhood Yards. I want a straight answer from the Mechanist Cabal on how we go about piloting a city." He paused to tap his chin thoughtfully. "Wait—they probably all split up to crack those terrace shackles. Never mind then— continue on to the Skydocks. Our airships look half-crippled, but tell Brunehilde and that bastard Weatherby to keep a perimeter about the town, if they can fly. Remember that the navy still has an airship of its own, though it has to have taken quite the beating itself by now."

"Aye. But, sir—" interjected Henry Smalls.

"Gunney Lome, I've a different task for you."

Sarah straightened. "Yes?"

"Captain, shouldn't—" continued Henry.

"Sarah, grab a knot of bruisers here from the crowd. Townies and pirates both. Everyone here knows I've taken charge, but there's a whole town of people hiding away behind barricades. Spread the word—and knock heads if you have to. Take a few of the older fellows, as that might give a bit more credence to—*what*, Henry?"

His steward licked his lips. "It's just … sir? Shouldn't Craftwright's Terrace have lifted free by now?"

Fengel blinked. He looked to the cliff face past the nearest buildings to the east. Then he followed the great hawsers rising there up to the daisy chain of buildings floating above. Finally, he glanced to the west, past the stair and down to the Waterdocks.

Henry was right. He could feel it. *Something has gone wrong.*

Fengel swore under his breath. He pushed past Gunney Lome ran for the stair, slammed into its railing, and peered down at the terrace below.

The great clouds of battle smoke were clearing from the lagoon, revealing a graveyard of broken ships foundering in the water. Despite that, Perinese vessels had docked against the piers and were disgorging hundreds of marines into the streets, an entire ship's company's worth. The *Glory of Perinault* had even landed, far back enough along the waterfront that it was protected by the rest of the invasion force. Only a block away from the bottom of the stair stood the shining brass forms of the clockwork knights, at attention in the smoking ruins of Martin Pool's pub.

They're coming straight for us.

Fengel turned around, grabbing the rail with both hands behind him. Everyone still rejoiced, save Henry and Sarah, who looked at him in alarm.

All right. All right. We're not dead quite yet. But what to do? What to do? Fengel thought furiously. What he really needed right now was a status update from the Mechanist Cabal. He glanced to where the arcane machinery of Atherion's Siren lay in a broken heap at the corner of the square. No one remained here to service it, as all the Mechanists had apparently run off to tend to the Cabal's master plan.

Past the siren, past the other buildings of the terrace, rose the pipe-bundle edifice of the Gasworks. Fengel snapped a finger. *There. That's where I sent Imogen and the others. That's where the shackle for this terrace is? Or was it somewhere else? Why didn't I bother to ask?* He rubbed his beard for a moment, then shook his head. It didn't matter. They had to act, and fast. He'd figure this out as he went along. If nothing else, he'd find Mechanists at the Gasworks. *Never let them see you stumble.*

Fengel pushed away from the railing stair and back across the square. He hopped up onto the base of Euron's statue and adjusted his hat, then gestured to Sarah Lome while jerking his head towards the pirates about them.

Sarah nodded, then put two fingers to her lips. Her piercing whistle cut across the square, silencing the revelry. Fengel clapped his hands together in the aftermath and held them out, gathering everyone's attention.

"Hold, lads," he said. "Hold just a moment now. We're not out of the woods quite yet."

"I thought we only had jungles hereabouts," called a hook-handed young pirate in the crowd.

Fengel rolled his eyes. "It's a figure of speech. And what I mean is that we're not quite ready to take off entirely. There're … things that still need doing. The Mechanists have work to do yet. And those blue-backed bastards down there are coming right this way." He gestured down past the stair to the lowest terrace of the town.

The assembled fighters pressed up against the terrace railing. Whispers of alarm spread among the crowd as they beheld the forces encroaching upon them.

"They've taken the piers! What happened to our ships?"

"Look at all th' Bluecoats!"

"Ha! I ain't paying that bar tab back now."

"So!" shouted Fengel. He waited until the others turned reluctantly back before continuing on, and he stabbed the air for emphasis. "What we're going to do is protect this stair! Shannon MacKinnon—take some people and grab some of those Mechanist barricades I see poking out that alley. Set them up right where you're standing. Martin Pool, you and your friends break into that cooper's place across the square and grab his tools. Realms Below, grab him if he's still in there and cut the damned stair apart—we don't need it anymore, and our enemies do. The rest of you lot, gather up all the powder and shot you've got and keep the Perinese off this terrace!"

"What are you going to do, Captain Fengel?" asked a grizzled old woman with a pike.

Fengel plucked free his monocle, wiped it on his sleeve, and replaced it. "I'm glad you asked that. I'm just going to step over to the Gasworks and make sure that everything's going smoothly."

"Everything's gone wrong!"

A squat figure wearing a scorched greatcoat and a gas mask ran into the square from the northeast entrance. It was Imogen, judging by the muffled tone. And she was deeply, deeply upset.

"What's that?" asked someone from the crowd.

Fengel made a curt gesture at his gunnery mistress. Fortunately, Sarah was paying attention. As the frantic Mechanist ran past, she reached out and grabbed her up in a bearhug, wrapping her powerful hands around the ventilator of Imogen's mask.

"Just what I've been waiting for," said Fengel to the crowd, his tone overloud and cheerful. "Now get a move on, you lot, while I tend to things."

He didn't wait to see the results. Instead, he hopped down from the base of the heavy statue and hurried over to where Sarah held the writhing apprentice Mechanist. Henry Smalls joined them as Fengel gestured across Pillager's Square to the street she'd emerged from.

Once away from the crowd, they found a stretch of shadowed wall on the path leading up to the Gasworks. Sarah released the flailing Mechanist, who dropped to her knees.

"Hello again, Imogen," said Fengel.

The Mechanist-Aspirant ripped off her gas mask and took a great, gasping breath. "What did you do that for?" she demanded, staring accusingly up at him. Her eyes were bleary and red from weeping.

"Because you were about to panic the only people left who can buy us enough time to save this town," snapped Fengel. "Now, what's happened? Why hasn't this terrace taken off? And where's my cat?"

"It's the Gasworks," said Imogen. "That Perinese airship flew past and just started shooting at us while we were setting the shackle charges outside. They hit Gas Reservoir Number Four and ruptured it. The safety valves kicked on, but they created a back-pressure build—"

"Imogen!" snapped Fengel. "Get to the point. Also, cat?"

The Mechanist-Aspirant flung her hands out. "I don't know what happened to that flea-bitten furball! There was an explosion! Graye and Barlett kept it from setting off the whole system, but then one of the walls collapsed. I … I think everyone of the Gasworks crew is dead but me, even Mechanist Second Class Harland, who came down to oversee! And there's worse: the Craftwright's Terrace shackle is buried now!"

Fengel felt cold. He glanced to Henry and Sarah, whose worried expressions made clear their thoughts. Without any Mechanists around and the terrace shackle buried, there wouldn't be any kind of escape for Haventown.

Never let them see you stumble.

"Very well," said Fengel. He removed his monocle and buffed it, replacing it slowly. "Then we'll just have to do the work ourselves. Pity we haven't Lucian and the others on hand. And I'm sure Cubbins is fine."

Imogen, Henry, and Sarah all looked to him. "But we can't," said Imogen. "There's collapsed machinery everywhere and light-air leaks and—"

"Come now, Miss Helmsin. Failure provides us the stepping-stone to success, after all."

"That's ridiculous," said Imogen, still distraught. "Failure by definition implies an attempt that can no longer succeed due to unreachable objectives."

Beside him, Gunney Lome gave an approving nod.

Fengel frowned, nonplussed. "It's a figure of speech," he snapped. "Anyway, *I* am the captain of this pseudoaerial city, and I'm far from ready to abandon ship—er, town." He gestured up the street towards the towering smokestacks of the Gasworks. "Whatever. Lead on, young apprentice Mechanist."

"It's Mechanist-Aspirant. And what—"

A piercing whistle from down below in the Waterdocks echoed up to Pillager's Square. Fengel glanced back to see the pirates there all freeze. One looked over the rails and turned back in alarm. "They're coming!" she cried. "Those clockwork monsters are coming for the stair!"

Past him, out beyond the rooftops of the Waterdocks, the great pale gas bag of the *Glory* shifted, beginning to rise. Fengel cursed under his breath and turned back to Imogen. "To the Gasworks. Now!"

The young Mechanist-Aspirant swallowed and gave a nod. Then she turned and jogged down the street. Fengel gave one last look at Pillager's Square, then followed, his officers in tow.

Empty boardwalk streets rumbled beneath their feet as they ran, their boot steps echoing from the structures around them and the rubble they strode across. The shops and shanties there, pressed shoulder to shoulder, cast the early-evening shadows of Haventown that Fengel knew so well. The shacks had been made into jagged, sinister things, marked by happenstance bombardments that had torn rooftops and toppled walls. Townsfolk hid within those buildings even now, clearly, as their casements were cracked just enough to reveal an ancient blunderbuss or outdated crossbow poking out in front of worried eyes.

For the hundredth time today, Fengel wanted to despair. *We needed you. We still need you now. You should all be out here fighting.* If only Euron had ever given a damn. If only they'd had more time. If only ... if only Haventown wasn't full of *pirates*.

The Mechanist's Gasworks appeared ahead. A mad tangle of brass pipe and arcane machinery, its exhaust stacks and struts towered above the nearest rooftops, rising up to support the airship platform sitting almost level with the now-empty cliff the Flophouse Terrace had been built upon. Something was obviously wrong with the place. Smoke and steam billowed up from it, and a great broken pipe belched jets of flame into the air.

"We're almost there!" shouted Imogen. "Careful—the air isn't clean."

Fengel grimaced as the young Mechanist-Aspirant donned her gas mask again. Hopefully, there would be spares inside the structure.

She dove into an alley as the street twisted away, leading them between a pair of well-built workshops. For all the haphazard civic planning of Haventown, the Mechanists didn't brook shoddy construction near their own enclaves. Fengel sucked in his gut to pass a rain barrel, then stepped out into the street beyond.

He ran into Imogen, who had abruptly stopped on the boardwalk beyond. Just across the street rose the Gasworks. It was a strange structure, even for Haventown. Ten-foot-high walls hid most of the place, just like the Brotherhood Yards up above on Nob Terrace. A towering mass of brass pipes and gantry walkways climbed up from behind the wall, winding around a central stack of chimneys. At the peak of the structure spread a platform landing pad, moored to the rising columns and a frail-looking network of stairways that looked for all the world like cobwebs attached to an upthrust branch. In the middle of the wall, a massive double gate provided entrance. One of the doors sagged in place, now only barely connected by a hinge.

Unlike the Brotherhood Yards, Fengel had never been inside the Gasworks before. "All right, then," he said. "Where are we going, Imogen?"

Henry Smalls appeared beside him, panting. Behind them in the alley, Sarah Lome gave a curse as she collided with the rain barrel. Water rushed out into the street as the young Mechanist-Aspirant turned back to him.

"There is a small hall just past the gate," she said. "That's where most of the … damage … is. If we follow it through to the other side, there will be an open courtyard with the shackle and the stairway up to the airship pad. It's usually hidden from sight by the wall that fell in. But even if we get back there, what can we *do?* The shackle is probably buried!"

Henry Smalls sniffed beside him. "I smell light-air gas too, sir."

"Wait," said Fengel. "Probably buried?"

"I … I didn't go back there. But the wall collapsed, and the explosion—"

Fengel felt a glimmer of hope. "*Probably* isn't *certainly*. And I've a plan," he lied. "Henry? There should be gas masks inside. So lead on, Imogen. Every second—"

The pop of gunfire echoed over from the southern part of the terrace. Fengel glanced back down the alley behind them, but Haventown's confines prevented any sight of its contents.

"Every second brings our enemies closer to victory," he finished. "Now move."

Imogen gave a nod and led the four of them across the street to the gate. There was an opening where it hung askew, not tall, but just high enough for a grown man to crawl through. Imogen did so easily, followed by a frowning Henry Smalls. Fengel ducked down onto his hands and knees to crawl behind his steward.

The gates opened onto a small yard layered with brass pipe and ovoid gas canisters, so thick that Fengel couldn't see where it all ended or began. Valves, levers, and gauges sprung from it all, their functions opaque. Steam shot out from cracked pipes, lending the whole edifice a misty, mysterious air. Faintly, Fengel smelled the old-milk stink of light-air gas.

Imogen ran down the only opening in the mess, a simple path between two huge pipes, shrouded by a jet of hissing steam. Fengel made to follow, one arm up to hide his nose, when the gate rattled behind him. Glancing back, he saw Sarah Lome half-crammed through the opening. The boards had her tight, though the whole gate rattled and shook as she bucked it.

"Gunney Lome?" he asked, his voice muffled from behind his sleeve.

Sarah paused to look up at him. "Sir?"

"This *really* isn't the time for games."

"I'm stuck, sir."

"Go on, sir," said Henry. His steward knelt down to help the huge woman. "I'll get her free; you go on ahead. And, sir! Careful—I smell a gas leak here."

Fengel rolled his eyes. "I've a working sense of smell as well," he replied. Then he turned to follow the now-missing Mechanist-Aspirant.

The interior of the Gasworks wasn't much clearer on the inside. It was quite a bit darker, in fact. A single path wound itself beneath the omnipresent forest of hoses and ducting clear enough, though myriad secondary trails branched off only Goddess knew where. What ceiling there was shifted in accordance with a logic Fengel knew he wouldn't understand. Just enough early-evening sun reflected down through the brilliant brass piping to impart the fog of steam all around him with a pale, sourceless glow.

This is just perfect. The Mechanists can build a flying city, but they can't keep adequate illumination or any damned maps up on where to go. Which wasn't charitable, he realized. There had been an explosion or some sort of mishap here, after all. Then he ran into a bit of low-hanging pipe.

Fengel decided the architecture was wholly their fault. As he turned a corner and the curdled stink of light-air gas washed over him, panic shot through him—he crushed his sleeve to his nose and tried not to breath. Then he took a step back and surveyed the devastated room he'd stepped into.

The Gasworks here opened into a wide chamber, which must have been the heart of the facility. Shafts of faded twilight illuminated the space, tumbling in through a collapsed section of the left-most wall to reveal instrumentation dancing madly among the twisted wreckage. Crumpled figures in leather greatcoats lay about the space, some half-buried by burned and misshapen metal—the Mechanists. One of them knelt just ahead over one of her colleagues. Imogen, by her size.

This is going to be the death of me. Fengel held his breath and dove forward, trying not to think about what light-air poisoning would feel like.

A fallen section of pipework lay atop two of Imogen's fellow Mechanists. The first was trapped from the waist down. Imogen had him propped up in her lap, both of her hands pressed over a jagged tear in his greatcoat. Blood pooled beneath the fellow, and his breath rasped beneath his mask. The second was just an arm and a head sticking out from beneath the wreckage.

"How is he?" asked Fengel through his sleeve as he knelt down beside them. His throat burned, and everything stank of spoiled milk.

Imogen turned to look at him in surprise. Tears choked her voice, muffled by her mask though it was. "I was wrong! He's still alive, but badly inj—"

"I'm dying," rasped the Mechanist wearily.

Fengel paused. His voice sounded familiar. "Hold on. Do I know you?"

The dying man rolled his head in exasperation. "Of course … you know me, Fengel. You tit. I'm the reason … you're back in Haventown at all. It's me, Mechanist Second Class … Harland."

Blank spots kept appearing in front of Fengel's eyes. He tried blinking them away. "I'm sorry, who? You just all look so similar in those masks."

"I'm Mechanist Second Class—"

"Clangfoot," sobbed Imogen. "You called him Clangfoot."

Now his lips were numb. "Oh." Fengel blinked again, then pointed with his free hand at the other Mechanist lying still beside them. "I'm sorry, is this other fellow dead?"

"Mechanist Third Class Terence," rasped Harland. "Yes."

"One moment, then."

Fengel tore off his hat and monocle even as he bent over the dead man at their feet. The gas mask came off only grudgingly, but desperation led to success quickly enough. Fengel slid his head into the mask and pulled it tight, even as he started to choke.

His lungs burned. His face felt numb. Slowly, though, through his gasping and retching, the mask went to work. Breathable air replaced the toxic gas. Fengel realized he wasn't going to die. Probably.

"There," he croaked after a moment. "That's done it."

"You didn't properly tie the straps," said Imogen, her voice a flat monotone. "Proper mask-donning procedure requires you to completely untie—"

"Well, I'm sorry that I was too busy choking to death on this stinking gas!" snapped Fengel. The mask made his voice sounded tinny and muffled.

Mechanist Harland gestured sharply between them. "Enough. None of us … have much time."

Fengel nodded, then put up a hand to hold his mask in place as it shifted. "The terrace shackled here in the Gasworks—you didn't blow it free."

"Pressure back-build cascade," gasped Mechanist Harland. "Graye … was out setting the charges … when it happened. Everything should be in place but the primer. I saw … the wall fall. The shackle is still … reachable. "

He coughed wetly. Imogen bent over him, pressing tighter on the wound in his side. Then she looked back to Fengel. "We have the primer in here still," she said, jerking her head towards the wreckage. "It's buried now. We'll never get to it."

"What's the primer?" asked Fengel. "Just an explosive?"

"Yes," gasped Harland. "But there's nothing left in the facility with enough power to set them off."

"My bomb!" shouted Imogen.

"What?" asked Harland. "Those ridiculous munitions ... I expressly forbade you from experimenting with?"

"No—I mean, yes. Fengel, you've still got my bomb!"

Captain Fengel blinked, then he peered through the glass lenses of the mask at the satchel he still wore. "Oh. Right. What about it?"

"We can use it to blast the shackle free! Now give it here!"

Fengel put a protective hand to the satchel. "No. Harland, where is the shackle?"

The Mechanist Second Class pointed feebly at the opening blown through the wall above them as Imogen complained. "Courtyard ... just outside. Hidden before, until the incident. Should be free of gas."

"Right, then." Fengel stood and made to climb atop the wreckage. "Harland, I apologize for calling you *Clangfoot*, though not overmuch. Imogen, leave him and get some of these masks here. Bring them back out to the front of the facility for Henry and Sarah Lome and anyone else who shows up."

"What? No! Give me back my bomb. You don't even know how to set it! And I'm not leaving Mechanist Second Class Harland here. We could still go get help!"

"Mechanist ... Sixth Class ... Imogen Helmsin," said the dying man. "Do as Captain Fengel says."

Imogen jerked her head down to stare at him. "What? Why? And why did you call me Mechanist Sixth Class?"

Harland lay back with a sigh. "Because I've just promoted you."

"But what about the tests?"

"You've the skill ... and we all know it. The tests would be a ... formality."

"But I've been preparing for them for months now."

"Then you can take them ... for fun ... later!" snapped Harland. "Right now, do what you're told ... Mechanist."

"But why?" asked Imogen, her voice thick.

"Because Captain Fengel is in charge of the city," he replied. "And he's putting you where he needs you to be. Obey my orders, Mechanist. And Fengel!"

Fengel paused in his climb, exasperated. "Yes?"

"Once you've escaped ... with Haventown ... find Atherion Helmsin. Find ... the First Mechanist...and bring him home safely!"

Mechanist Harland spasmed, gasped, then fell still. Fengel gave the corpse a hurried nod. "Of course. Imogen? He's dead now. *Please* obey his last wishes and get moving."

He didn't wait to see what she'd do. They'd already wasted enough time. It was harsh to act so callously, but there were more important things to worry about at the moment. And his mask still didn't quite fit right.

Fengel clambered up the wrecked pipeworks and through the breach back outside. He pushed through a cloud of jetting steam to see the Gasworks exterior and a small courtyard built onto the boardwalk, just as Harland had said. It lay snug up against the face of the cliff and the external wall of the facility. The accident had exposed it, however, revealing the rooftops of the Waterdocks through a hole blown through the wall. Thin, rickety-looking metal stairways ran up along the cliff, still intact, leading up to the airship platform and other parts near the top of the facility.

In the center of the courtyard, among piles of rubble, sat the shackle. It looked like nothing more than the top of a thick iron spike surrounded by a ring of toothed gears biting down upon it. Ominous black explosive charges covered the gears, and the boardwalk they stood upon was warped, the boards slanting towards the shackle as if under great pressure.

There. That's it. Fengel opened the satchel at his side and lifted out Imogen's bomb. He eyed the fuse at the top, then he swore.

He didn't have any way to light it.

Henry. Henry smokes—he'll have one of those new lighters. Or Gunney Lome, she'll know a way to jury-rig this thing. If Imogen can get them up here.

He stopped as an armored ovoid emblazoned with a sunburst appeared above the Waterdocks. It was that Perinese airship, the *Glory*. The vessel was swinging around into view, a whole complement of Bluecoat marines crowding her gunwales.

Coming right for him.

CHAPTER TWENTY-TWO

LINA SLIPPED DOWN THE AFT HATCHWAY STAIR. The cutlass in her hands was a heavy thing, far more unwieldy than her lost daggers.

She was angry about that, more so at the Castaway who'd fallen overboard with them buried in his spine. As for the smoke rising dead ahead from Haventown, she tried not to think on that—or how half of her home port seemed to be … flying. Those were problems for later. Instead, she shifted her grip on the stolen sword and carefully descended down below the decks of the *Dawnhawk*.

Oscar Pleasant, I'm going to cut your Goddess-damned head off.

The fight had been furious from the start. Caught off guard and outnumbered by just a few, her crewmates rallied. It wasn't like they hadn't beaten these curs off once already. The Castaways had the twin advantages of numbers and surprise, though. Worse, they'd rearmed themselves. Properly equipped from the *Dawnhawk's* own stores, Euron's abandoned crewmen seemed like a different group altogether.

As if that weren't enough, the Dray Engine was almost fully awake again. It roared and flailed within its bonds, shaking the whole airship with its gyrations. The deck pitched and yawed while they fought as if in a storm. The ancient Voorn monster was going to free itself, of that Lina was certain. It was only a question of when.

So there had been battle aboard the *Dawnhawk* for the second time today. Natasha met Morgan One-Eye head on, with Reaver Jane coming to her aid. Etarin and Farouk fought back to back against their geriatric assailants while the aetherite Omari protested her neutrality vociferously. At least, until a Castaway devoted himself to taking her head off, forcing her to flee.

Rastalak and Michael Hockton worked together until the crate containing Runt's scrynlings went sliding madly for the breach in the gunwales. Then her lovely soldier pitched himself across the deck, catching it before it could fall overboard. Lina loved him for that.

For her own part, Lina tried repeatedly to get to Oscar Pleasant. The traitor needed to die for his numerous betrayals—screaming, if possible. For all his tough talk, though, he'd backed firmly out of the melee, maneuvering away, keeping a flailing Allen as hostage the entire time.

Then the Dray Engine gave a particularly violent jerk, pitching the *Dawnhawk's* decks so that not even Rastalak could keep his footing. Lina recovered just in time to see the rat-faced bastard slip belowdecks via the aft hatchway.

So now she hunted.

Lina crept down the hatchway stair, moving as quickly and quietly as she could down the creaking boards. She reached the landing of the captain's cabin, then down to the crew deck where the stair opened onto a hall. Off to her left, the hall opened onto the quarterdeck, where a single open porthole provided illumination. To the right, the hall continued down to the engine rooms and the Mechanist's domain, as well as to the stores and the stair that led to the cargo.

Which way did you go, you bastard?

The deck pitched wildly beneath her feet. Lina fell hard, dropping her cutlass, which clattered against the stair behind her. She cursed as the Dray Engine gave a thunderous roar outside, loud enough that she felt it through the planks more than heard it. The mechanical monster thrashed again, tilting the airship madly about.

A more human cry of pain reached her, along with a snarl for quiet. Lina narrowed her eyes. It had come from off to the right, up from the stairwell that led down to the hold.

There.

But why would Oscar go that far down? If he'd been hiding onboard since Haventown, he had to know about all the Revenants they'd put in the hold after the fight with the *Glory.*

Lina swallowed her discomfort. *He's trapped. There's only one way out of that hold. And the Revenants are harmless enough, if you don't attack them. At least, that's what Omari always says.*

Which seemed true enough. The things had never run amuck or done any of the things that the penny-papers always seemed to go on about.

Still, the soldiers *had* been trying to kill her when they died. *And Goddess in the Realms Above, do they stink.*

Allen gave a startled yell. This time Oscar said nothing, though she heard the thump of a blow. A low groan echoed up the stairwell.

Enough. Lina grabbed up her cutlass again. She slipped down the hall to the hold stairwell and made her way down. What little ambient light there'd been disappeared completely. The stair was dark and close. It seemed to swallow her up, like she was descending into a wooden grave.

The cargo hold of the *Dawnhawk* opened up at the bottom of the stair, a wide, airy space meant for packing away all the illicit booty that Fengel and Natasha could steal. Both captains had emptied it earlier that morning, leaving only a single oil lantern dangling from a chain overhead. That lantern was freshly lit, and it swung back and forth now, casting long, mad shadows from the dozen corpses rising to stand. Their stink filled the air, a perfume of dead flesh and congealed blood.

Allen knelt in the middle of the room beneath the lantern. He clutched one arm to his chest and sobbed openly.

Lina forced herself to ignore the undead. She stepped into the room, cutlass hefted. "Allen!" she hissed. "Allen, are you all right? Where's Oscar?"

The apprentice Mechanist glanced up at her, eyes wide. "Lina, don't!" he croaked. "It's a trap!"

Someone moved in the gloom to her left, faster and with more purpose than a Revenant. Lina threw herself to the right, hitting the deck and rolling as the pistol went off. The crack and flash was brilliant. But the ball went wide, splintering the bulkhead behind her.

"Of course it's a trap!" she snapped, rising back to her feet.

Oscar Pleasant stepped out from the corner. In the faint lighting, his features appeared even more ratlike, exaggerated. He tossed the emptied pistol aside to clatter on the boards, then drew a cutlass.

"I don't even know why anyone bothers with those things," he growled. "Has anyone ever hit anything with them? Even once?"

Lina backed away as the Revenants rose up between them. They groaned and rasped. A dead Bluecoat from the *Glory's* crew reached out to her, bringing up her gorge as she ducked away.

"Captain Blackheart shot an ape once," she said.

Oscar snorted. "She couldn't miss!" A Revenant lurched his way, and he dodged it, sticking out a leg. The corpse tripped with a loud thump, and its groans turned strident and angry. "Natasha Blackheart is the worst shot on the Atalian Sea," continued Oscar. "Decent with a blade but downright hazardous to everything around her with a firearm."

Lina thought back to all the near misses that she'd had around the captain. Intentional or not, it seemed Captain Blackheart was always trying to kill someone. "That's neither here nor there," she said as she wove around behind an undead Nate Wiley. The Revenant looked past her, hunting for his brother, probably. Lina tried not to focus on how that made her feel. "Why are you doing this, Oscar? You've always been an absolute shit, but mutiny? Helping out the Perinese against the whole town?"

Oscar Pleasant snarled. He leaped past dead Nate Wiley, lashing out at her with his cutlass. She parried, feeling the shock of the blow run down her blade and up her arms. It forced her back and off-balance. Lina snarled, threw her weight back against the sword, and shoved it forward again. Her opponent bent to the side and let her go past as their blades slid against each other, sending sparks up to flash and die in the air between them.

"Why *I* did this?" asked Oscar. "I had no damned choice! You all left me behind! Months ago, when we threw Fengel and his bitch out on that deserted island. I got knocked cold when we attacked the *Kingfisher*, and you left me behind! It was the Perinese who picked me up, and they were going to hang me!"

Lina rounded on him. "You should have let them," she panted, swinging for his knees. The cutlass was *heavy*.

Oscar danced back, then came forward with an overhand chop. Lina parried and leaned, letting his blow slide aside. A dead Bluecoat reached out for her—it seemed to remember her as an enemy. Lina ducked its outstretched arms and darted around behind it, appearing on the opposite side and lifting her blade up at Oscar.

The traitorous pirate parried her blow and shoved her back. Then he cursed as the Bluecoat reached for him. They separated, circling around, avoiding the Revenants excited by their fight.

"That's a stupid weapon for you, girlie. If you keep swinging it around, you're going to get tired."

Lina tried to respond through her panting. The cutlass was heavy and big and not at all what she usually used. But it would serve. It would have to.

They came together again. She hacked out at him twice, which he parried aside before slugging her in the gut with his off hand. Her breath rushed out, and pain filled her belly. She barely pulled away as his own blade splintered into the wood of the hold at their feet.

Lina readied herself again, struggling for air. Something was wrong. *Why am I so tired?* The sword was big for her—but not that big.

"Getting tired yet?" mocked Oscar. A Bluecoat clambered to its feet in front of him and he shoved it contemptuously aside.

There was something in his voice. Lina narrowed her eyes. "What did you do?" she demanded.

Oscar laughed. He turned to face her, cutlass held lazily at his side. With his other hand he reached into his shirt. "Remember this?" he asked, pulling something up to dangle in the lantern light.

Lina stared. It was a long braid of golden hair, tied together at each end. Beads and charms dangled along its length. Even a year later, Lina still recognized the tresses that she'd cut away.

"You've still got my hair?" she said.

"Oh yes," laughed Oscar. "Thought you'd recognize it. I kept it this whole time, waiting to teach you a lesson. Saved up my shares and took it to an aetherite down on Flophouse Terrace. You really shouldn't have just *given* it away. That Salomcani sorcerer said that made it extra potent."

"Salomcani …" Lina blinked. She stepped aside as a dead Jahmal lurched her way, one hand to a lethal chest wound, the other out for succor. "You mean Xavier Ravalan? You gave my hair to Xavier Ravalan to make a Worked charm? That fool isn't even a real aetherite!"

Oscar rocked back. "Yes, he is!"

"No," said Lina. "He's not. He just wears a turban and talks in that ridiculous accent!" She panted, fighting for breath.

The deck of the cargo hold shifted abruptly. Lina jammed her cutlass into the planks beneath her feet and held on. All about her, the Revenants toppled. Even Allen went tumbling, clutching his arm and crying out in pain. A high-pitched ringing sounded somewhere outside past the bulkheads— the chains and cables restraining the Dray Engine were tearing apart.

The cargo deck rocked back the other way. Lina held on to the cutlass, trying not to fall. Something slammed into the hull beneath them—a dreadful, resounding impact that echoed about the space. Wood crunched and snapped; it was one of the most sinister things Lina had ever heard.

Amazingly, Oscar Pleasant still stood. He crouched around his sword, just as she did, and held the Worked braid of hair in his other hand. When the airship stilled again, he looked about, ratlike in the swaying light. His gaze fell again on her, and he stood with a wordless snarl.

"Liar," he hissed. "I can see it. You're tiring, and fast. The charm works. In just a minute, you're not going to even be able to move."

It … it can't be true, can it? She was tired. She felt exhausted. But that had to have been the long night and the longer day. Lina pulled the heavy blade from where it stuck, then lifted it up in guard. It felt like a bar of solid iron.

Oscar made to pull his cutlass from the planks of the cargo floor. It was stuck tight, though, lodged deeper than he'd meant to send it. He scowled and tried again. The sword barely budged.

The traitorous pirate wrapped his hand again around the hilt, glared at Lina, and then pulled up as he kicked down at the boards holding his blade. He kicked a second time and then a third, each blow a resounding knock that echoed throughout the cargo hold.

Finally, he yanked the blade free. Oscar snarled and raised it high, preparing to charge. Lina fought a wave of weariness, trying to anticipate Oscar's blow.

Wooden splinters exploded into the air as the boards of the *Dawnhawk's* hull erupted beneath Oscar Pleasant. They peppered Lina, as massive brass talons scythed up all about her startled foe. He screamed as they closed tight, catching him in a crushing grip that clipped his left arm neatly off. Oscar flailed and fought, swinging away ineffectively at the Dray Engine's claws with his cutlass, spraying blood all about him from his horrible wound. Reflected daylight shone up through the holes past the talons, illuminating him in full for a brief, awful moment.

Then the Dray Engine pulled away. It ripped open a breach in the hull, and Oscar Pleasant disappeared like a cork popped free from a wine bottle. His screams dopplered up from outside the airship's hull for a few moments, then went ominously silent. There was silence, and then a victorious mechanical roar sounded from just outside.

Allen shuffled again to his knees. "It's on the hull!" he shouted, his voice raw. "That monster has got ahold of the—"

He collapsed with a cry of pain, one arm holding the other, which hung at an unnatural angle; obviously, it had been broken by Oscar. Lina snapped her jaw shut. She dropped the cutlass and raced over to him.

"Allen!" she said. "Hey, Allen, don't worry, I'm here."

"My arm," he whimpered. "It's broken. And my ankle's sprained. He yanked me around for *ages* during the fight."

"I know. Hey? It's fine now."

"Oh, what do you know about it?" snarled the young apprentice Mechanist. "You're flailing around just like you pirates always do. You never think of consequences." Lina jerked back in surprise, but he shook his head. "Never mind. We've got to cut that monster free before it brings the whole ship down. Using it was a *terrible* idea!"

Lina felt a twinge of irritation. She *had* come down here to help him, hadn't she? And to kill Oscar, of course. Lina shook her head. They had bigger things to worry about. She bent to help Allen stand. He did so with a cry of pain, then took her shoulder in support.

As they hobbled back to the stair above, her eyes alighted on her old braid. She stared at it for a long moment, then shook her head. It was nothing.

Just hair. Oscar never could have afforded the services of an aetherite. She put it out of her mind, helping Allen to skirt the hole in the floor, and the groaning, flailing Revenants.

Back up top, the fight with the Castaways was over. Bodies littered the deck, which was awash in blood that ran madly back and forth as the Dray Engine fought down below. Lina's crewmates had won, it seemed. No one cheered, though. Everyone stood about in varying stages of shocked exhaustion. Natasha stood scowling amidships above the corpse of Morgan One-Eye, wrapping a rag around one bared, bloodied arm while a blood-spattered Butterbeak hunkered on her shoulder. Nearby, big Farouk knelt numbly over the corpse of his friend, Etarin. Young Paine hid behind the airship's wheel, sobbing while Michael Hockton talked to him quietly. And up near the bow, her friend Andrea sat cradled in Ryan Gae's lap.

Lina felt her heart catch in her chest. She wanted to go to them. *Oh no. Please. I've lost so many friends already.*

"Where in the Realms Below did you run off to?" snapped Natasha. "I needed your blades up here!"

Lina blinked back at her, but Allen spoke first. "Oscar Pleasant is dead," he shouted, half-panicked, his voice raw with pain. "And that's not important! We've got to cut the monster loose, or it'll tear us apart!"

"I know!" said Natasha. "The deck is pitching and yawing like mad. You'd think it would have fallen free by now."

Lina shook her head. "It's on the hull," she said. "It's got at least one claw gripping the hull."

Natasha stared at them. Then she spat. "Of course it does. Cut it free, then. Anyone who can still move! I'm going to try to shake it loose. The rest of you, cut it free!"

The captain ran back down the deck for the helm while Allen pointed with his good arm at a thick clump of hawsers tied around the starboard gunwales. Lina helped him over as Farouk, Michael, Reaver Jane, and Rastalak all sprang wearily back to action.

She led Allen up near the cleat anchoring the thick bundle of rope that went over the side. Then she tried to draw a dagger that wasn't there. *Damn it all.* A sword. She needed a sword, a dagger, or a boarding hatchet.

A Castaway's corpse lay wedged up against the exhaust pipe a little farther up, the handles of two cutlasses poking out from beneath it. Lina ran there, rolled the corpse aside, and fetched them.

The Dray Engine roared out as she did so, heaving the *Dawnhawk* to one side. Lina threw herself across the exhaust pipe as the deck fell away and grabbed at the gunwales with her forearms, trying not to drop the blades clutched in her hands. The hollow pipe rang beneath her. Runt and her scrynlings went sliding past in their small crate while the little mother shrieked and spit and tried to stop it. Half straddling the boundary of her vessel, Lina looked out beyond the airship.

They'd come home. But things had changed in the short time they'd been gone. Haventown Lagoon lay dead ahead, a column of smoke rising thickly all about it. She spied warships in the water down past the curve of the cliff top, filling it almost completely. The Waterdocks writhed with the march of bluecoated soldiers filling its alleys. Popping muskets echoed throughout the lower township where pockets of fighting still occurred. The stair at Pillager's Square between the Waterdocks and the Craftwright's Terrace was besieged, and pirates and townsfolk were fighting from behind a makeshift barricade at its top against columns of soldiers trying to make the ascent. At their head marched the same brightly armored automatons they'd fought earlier today.

That wasn't the strangest thing. Fully half of Haventown had ... taken off. Nob, Flophouse, and the Yellow Lantern terraces all floated, like a string of vast, oversized airships—but rather than being hung from large gas bags, as airships were, the terraces were borne up from below on clusters of miniature gas bags and whirling propellers. Two massive hawsers at the edge of each platform connected them together, the last in the line attaching to the Craftwright's Terrace, which still sat in its usual place against the cliff. At the pinnacle of the floating town clustered the battered and burned pirate airships, which had all pulled away from the fighting to flit around the Skydocks, at last now aptly named.

The twanging snap of overstressed cable rang out behind her. Lina glanced back to see one of the cables attaching the *Dawnhawk's* gondola to its gas bag go flying free, sending a shudder throughout the whole airship.

"Cut the monster free!" snarled Natasha back from the helm. "Hockton, port side! Jane, the bow! Ryan Gae, quit yer sobbing and join her! Paine, if you don't move we're all dead, but I swear I'll throw you overboard myself before we go!" She threw the wheel hard to the right, then hard to the left, sending a violent shudder through the *Dawnhawk.*

It was true. The ship jerked again as the ancient Voornish war machine writhed from its hull. Lina swore to herself, shimmied back to the deck, and ran to the bundle of cables anchoring the Dray Engine to the airship. She dropped a blade near Allen, who snatched it up with his good hand and began to saw awkwardly away.

They worked quietly together for a moment. She pushed out the sounds of battle, the clanking mechanical struggles of the Dray Engine below, and the cries of her crewmates. Only then did she realize Allen was speaking.

"Stupid," he muttered as he sawed. "Stupid."

Lina quit sawing. She flung out her hands, nearly hacking off his ear accidentally. "I know! It was a terrible idea! My ideas are always terrible!"

The young Mechanist didn't even flinch. He paused to glance up at her with eyes like ice. "Not you," he snapped. "Me."

Lina blinked. "What?"

Allen shook his head. He went back to sawing, and one cable in the bundle gave away with a twanging snap. "This whole time. Ever since Breachtown, I thought I had a chance with you, that we could be … more than friends. When really, it was never going to happen."

Lina stared. "That's what you've been worked up about?" she almost shouted. "All day long you've been in *such* a snit."

"No!" he yelled at her, his voice choked with unshed tears. "I'm cranky because my ankle is sprained, my arm is broken, I lost a finger which aches abominably, there's a monster trying to kill us all, and because my home is being invaded by the Perinese! And yes. Because I just realized today what an *idiot* I've been."

Another cable gave a snap and fell away. Several more joined it across the deck of the airship, and the crew shouted their progress to each other. Runt and her crate went sliding past, this time in the other direction.

"I've been an idiot!" continued Allen, not even looking her way. "I should have just asked you, clearly, and been done with it. But I'm a coward! So I've been carrying a torch this whole damned time, hoping to win you over. Which was stupid! But you didn't have to play me off like some sort of tool. You've been using me. Just so that *he* would jump through a few more Goddess-damned hoops for you!"

Allen jerked his head back towards the bow of the deck, where Michael Hockton hacked away with a boarding hatchet at an almost-severed bundle of cables. Just the sight of him made Lina feel warm. Then she felt ashamed.

"Allen. I … I was probably wrong in doing that."

Allen stared up at her, incredulous. He still kept sawing, though. The bundle was almost severed. "How in the Realms Below can you even say that? Probably? Probably wrong?"

Runt and her scrynlings went sliding past. Lina gave a shrug.

"I'm sorry, all right? I mean, I know you've always had a crush on me, but that's just it, right? A crush. I thought it would pass! And come on. When we first met, you were sobbing your eyes out on Euron's old derelict airship. That's not exactly a great first impression. I've never really been able to take you seriously after that."

Allen stopped sawing. He stared up at her. "Lina Stone," he said. "You are an utter bitch."

Ropes snapped audibly all across the *Dawnhawk*. The cries of her crewmates reporting severed cables echoed down the deck. The airship lurched then, listing to starboard—the weight of the Dray Engine was now supported by nothing more than the strand of cordage in front of Lina and its own grip upon the hull. Even that gave way suddenly as they felt a shudder through the deck of the ship. The ancient Voornish war machine swung into view, roaring, and the deck pitched even further. Panicked yells rung out as the others aboard slammed into the starboard gunwales, along with all the corpses sliding unceremoniously about. Lina barely held her footing. She looked down and out at the Dray Engine, covered in cables and flailing furiously. She looked past it, where the shantytown buildings of the Waterdocks swarmed with Perinese soldiers. The bundle of ropes in front of her snapped and popped with a twang.

"Stone!" shouted Natasha from where she clung to the wheel. "Cut that damned rope!" Butterbeak punctuated her cry with a fearful shriek of his own.

Lina yelled, her fear, frustration, shame, and anger all finding outlet in her voice even as her balance gave way. She swung desperately, furiously, and felt the cutlass in her hands bite home.

The bundle of cable seemed to explode in a hail of snapping fibers. They shot out over the gunwales with skin-shredding force, leaving the scent of burned wood in the air. Lina toppled with the force of her swing, slamming into the gunwales alongside Allen. She barely hung on as the airship violently righted itself.

A blur of brilliant brass fell through the air like a comet: the Dray Engine, free from any bonds save those of gravity. It roared out, less in defiance and more in something like panic, its dinner-plate eyes wide. The ancient machine toppled end over end on an almost parallel path along the rear cliffs between the Waterdocks and the Craftwright's Terrace.

Almost.

It slammed into the cliff face, the force of its impact echoing across the entirety of the lagoon. Granite dust rose in a plume as it skidded down, impacting with a tannery and sending filthy timbers flying in a blocks-wide explosion. The monster wasn't done yet. It rolled like a lost cannonball, smashing shacks, warehouses, and homes in a devastating path. Soldiers' screams were only barely heard over the clamor. The stairway up to Pillager's Square collapsed as the monster took it out and the twenty brass automatons there fell. Finally, the monster came to a stop, buried beneath rubble just before the southern edge of the Waterdocks.

Lina stared. She panted, her emotions a tangled mess. *What have I done?*

"What's going on?" demanded her captain from back near the helm. "What happened?"

Beside her, Allen pulled himself slowly away from the ledge, cradling his arm. "I … I think we killed it, Captain." he said, voice quavering with pain.

Lina had to agree. The world just wasn't fair if the monster could survive a fall like that.

"Hey!" called Michael Hockton from farther up the deck. "Isn't that Captain Fengel?"

Lina followed his outstretched arm to the Mechanists' Gasworks on the northern tip of the Craftwright's Terrace behind them. The structure was a mess of pipes and exhaust stacks topped by an airship landing pad that would have almost reached the Flophouse Terrace above, were it still in place. Part of the place had collapsed, though, revealing a small courtyard past a tangle of broken wall and wreckage. In the middle of it moved a man in a blue officer's coat and a tricorn hat. Something he wore flashed in the reflected light of the setting sun.

Someone shoved Lina roughly aside. It was Natasha. The *Dawnhawk's* captain peered down before nodding sharply. "That's him. And he's about to be in a mess of trouble too."

Lina glanced at her quizzically, then caught it. Past them, coming in low and slow, was the Perinese airship. It had twisted aside as the *Dawnhawk* appeared, but now it circled back, heading straight for the Gasworks.

Natasha turned and ran back to the helm, her parrot flying beside her. "Prepare to come about!" she ordered. "Grab up whatever you can—muskets, bombs—Realms Below, get something heavy from the galley." The pirate captain spun the wheel hard as they reached the southern end of the lagoon. "We're bearing back around and then straight at that overinflated balloon. And this time, *we're* the ones on the attack. Oh, vengeance is—Omari! What are you *doing?*"

The Yulani aetherite was crouched against the starboard gunwales like the rest of them, but rather than gawking, she was furiously attempting to lift the corpse of Morgan One-Eye overboard. She stopped, panting, and stared at them.

"You've got to help me!" she cried.

"Help you what?" asked Reaver Jane.

"We've got to throw them overboard. They're going to come back!"

Natasha pulled at the wheel before her, throwing levers on the gearbox beside her to adjust the airship's ballast. "We know. We'll just have to work around those things, for the time being. Grab a gun!"

Omari shook her head. "No, you don't understand! The Bluecoats, they were just soldiers, and your crewmates were friends. But these men … they really, really hated you!"

Farouk let out a yell as something grabbed his leg and he tripped heavily to the deck. Runt hissed from her scrynlings' crate, now wrapped around it with wings spread wide, trying to flap away from the bodies stretched up and down the gunwales. Omari yelped and jumped back away from the corpse of Morgan as it angrily swiped at her.

Lina felt the hairs on the back of her neck stand up as the bodies of the dead Castaways began moving with awful purpose.

CHAPTER TWENTY-THREE

Admiral Wintermourn climbed down from the *Glory of Perinault*.

The rope ladder he descended whipped and jerked like a thing alive. It seemed to catch every errant gust blowing across the lagoon, threatening to fling him atop the heads of the dozen or so marines standing in the breach of the Gasworks wall.

"Hold it steady!" he shouted.

"Sorry, sir!" cried Sergeant Greene. He and Private Bryant set their footing, as if they could moor the great airship above them through force of will alone.

Wintermourn snorted. He climbed down the last six feet to stand on dusty boards and broken piping.

Their intelligence called this facility the Gasworks. Purportedly, it was where the Mechanists developed the light-air that lifted their airships aloft. To Wintermourn's eyes it looked like nothing so much as a child's tangle of brass piping and arcane machinery, all wrapped around a central smokestack spire surrounded by a protective wall. A wide platform landing pad stretched itself across the top of the structure, supported by struts and the spire itself. Originally, the *Glory*'s captain had thought it an ideal point from which to dismount and attack. That was before the other airship, though.

The *Dawnhawk* had come out of nowhere, bedraggled and battered. Unlike its sister ships, who hung up high near the Skydocks nursing their wounds, she came in low, cutting straight across the town to drop something awful on the Bluecoat columns spreading throughout the Waterdocks. Wintermourn hadn't quite seen what it was, but the clamor had been enormous.

He ignored the men still waiting to descend and paused at the bottom of the rope ladder, one hand resting on the hilt of his saber while he looked out from the breach to survey the damage along the Waterdocks below. A great furrow had been torn through it, the buildings shattered and the boardwalk itself crushed through in places. It almost seemed like the pirates had dropped some great cannonball from on high, letting it roll across the lowest part of Haventown with abandon. The stairway leading up to this second terrace had been completely knocked to flinders, leaving cheering pirates to mock Adjutant Chesterly and his clockwork soldiers where they were stuck down below.

Which made his current objective all the more imperative. Fortunately, the *Dawnhawk* appeared to be having trouble coming back around, battered as she was.

"Where to, sir?" asked Sergeant Greene. The officer eyed the structure about them with deep suspicion, which was only appropriate, really.

Wintermourn snorted. "Don't be an idiot. We go inside."

Greene ducked his head. "Aye, sir. But ... then what?"

"We kill all the damned pirates." Wintermourn let go the ladder. The remaining marines descended as he stepped farther into the breach. A makeshift passage led inward, though it was twisty and haphazard. "I spied a courtyard just past all this while still above," he continued. "We make our way there, and then we see."

Crown Prince Gwydion shouted something from over the gunwales of the airship up above. Wintermourn couldn't make it out, and he didn't quite care to, either. Instead, he peered into the gloom, shadowed by the curve of the lagoon and the setting sun. Something stank here, like burned metal and old milk.

"There could be anything in here," he said to Greene darkly. "Another screaming cannon, more treacherous explosives. Any sort of perfidious Mechanist trap. Tell the men that anyone who lingers—"

He paused at another shout from Gwydion back aboard the *Glory*, this one amplified by a speaking trumpet. Wintermourn let loose a sigh. "What does he want now?"

Greene shook his head. "I don't know, sir, but I think he's worked up about something back down on the lower terrace."

"It was a rhetorical question," snapped Wintermourn. He turned away from the ragged passage and back to the airship up above. "Speak up, curse you!"

"Clear all that grey hair out of your ears, Admiral!" boomed Gwydion. The crown prince was leaning out over the side of the airship gondola, even as more Bluecoats climbed down the ladder. "There is something happening down on the Waterdocks! Along the south—"

A mechanical roar cut him off. It boomed, enormous and malevolent. The sound of it echoed about Haventown Lagoon, moving like a thing alive itself. Wintermourn thought it sounded vaguely familiar, and the hairs on the back of his neck stood straight at the clear promise of vengeful wrath it contained.

"Hairy knuckles of the Goddess!" shouted Gwydion from on high. For once, the youth sounded utterly surprised. His exclamation was joined by those of the men still on the ladder, all staring southward.

Wintermourn pressed into the now-tight crowd of Bluecoats. He shoved, swore, and elbowed until the men moved aside, coming abruptly to the end of the breach where the Gasworks wall gave way to a slope of rubble spilling down over the cliff top. Admiral Wintermourn looked out over the Waterdocks, then felt his jaw go slack as he stared.

A massive pile of rubble was heaped on the southern edge of the Waterdocks. Wintermourn watched as it shifted, twisted, and rose up. The debris slid away to reveal the brazen hide of a reptilian mechanical monster.

It appeared like nothing so much as a land-bound dragon standing on its two hind legs. Thirty feet high and covered in scales of Voornish brass, it had a heavy torso, a long, segmented tail, and a serpentine neck. It raised up its head and opened its maw, unleashing another mechanical roar.

Wintermourn stared. *It can't be.* He'd last seen that monster three months ago, after barely dislodging it from his own battered *Colossus*. They'd destroyed it, though, certainly, knocking it into the ocean deeps. There was no way something like that could have been recovered from the depths of the Atalian Sea.

And yet, the pirates appeared to have done it. Somehow.

A trio of Brass Paladins had reassembled after their fall from Pillager's Square. They formed up to face this new threat, moving as one to open fire with their clockwork muskets. Sparks flew from the hide of the mechanical beast as they unleashed volley after volley, ricocheting away into the city. The monster paused in its tirade and swung its head down low to glare at the metal men. The thing cocked its head back and forth, peering out from great malevolent red eyes before exhaling a cloud of steam that washed over them all.

Then it charged.

Bluecoats all around Wintermourn called out to the Goddess as the thing attacked. It moved with startling speed, plowing through a half-collapsed shanty and kicking through the rubble at its feet. It reached out and caught up one of Gwydion's Brass Paladins, flinging it a hundred paces to slam into a warehouse. Another of the Paladins tried to move aside, but it grabbed the mechanical soldier up in a titanic paw, pausing only to step down with mortal finality upon a screaming Bluecoat who'd had the bad luck of getting too close to the thing.

Adjutant Chesterly screamed for order, and the marines moved to action. Soldiers fell into firing formation and unleashed a rippling report of shots at the thing. The machine-dragon whirled suddenly, its tail lashing out like a cannonball to hammer through their ranks, separating several poor souls entirely from their lower portions. Reinforcements from the waterfront paused as they entered the scene, as bewildered and horrified as the officers at their head.

The Brass Paladins proved more stubborn. They rose from where they'd fallen and joined straight to the fray, firing with their heavy pepperbox muskets—or using them like clubs if they were close enough. Before long, the southern side of the Waterdocks rang with the sound of metal hammering on metal.

"That thing is going to wreck our entire advance!" yelled Crown Prince Gwydion from on high.

Reflexive anger at the princeling snapped him back to himself. Wintermourn glanced back up at the *Glory* where it floated above. "So take that fancy airship of yours up and go do something about it!"

"Exactly my thought, Admiral! Now quit dawdling and go do *your* job!"

The crown prince disappeared, even as his orders rang out from over the edge of the gondola. Those marines still on the ladder descended quickly. Before long the airship was moving away. Wintermourn watched it go peevishly. *Always something new. Damned pirates!*

Sergeant Greene coughed beside him. "Orders, sir?"

Admiral Wintermourn took a calming breath. "We do our job, Sergeant." A quick count revealed three dozen marines clustered together, half of those he'd gathered from the docks before lifting off. Numbers enough for what lay ahead. "It's our task to stop these damned pirates from getting away."

The Bluecoat sergeant jerked his round, black cap towards the lagoon. "That other airship, sir. It's coming around again. Looks like they're back in control."

Wintermourn followed his gaze. The *Dawnhawk* was indeed circling back over the lagoon, straight for the *Glory*. It shuddered and shook as the navy forces below fired a rain of musket balls into its ragged hull, but still, it came on.

"So it is," agreed Wintermourn. "So it is, Sergeant. Well. Let the crown prince deal with it. Come."

He turned and pressed back through the soldiers for the Gasworks interior. At Greene's orders, a pair of Bluecoats flanked him, peering about at the weird structure as if a piece of it might come alive to do them harm at any minute.

It wasn't an unfounded concern. Mechanical dragons, screaming cannons, and airship bombardment from above—even a flying city! The damnable Mechanists meddled with all manner of perfidious mechanical wizardry. Well. Their time had come, at long last.

Admiral Wintermourn ducked under a length of pipe, then clambered up a pile of broken wood. The wreckage sloped away, revealing the small courtyard he'd seen from aboard the *Glory*. It was built atop the boardwalk, butting up against the cliff wall at its rear. The rest of the Gasworks held it close, the outer wall and the slumping interior both. A single stair of wrought steel climbed the cliff before bridging across to the Gasworks proper and the great airship landing pad moored to the smokestack spire. The air was heavy with the stink of spoiled milk.

In the center of the courtyard was a thick, waist-high metal spike surrounded by a ring of toothed gears the size of carriage wheels. The boards beneath the gears were warped, and they squealed and groaned as if under great pressure. Beside this array knelt two figures: one in the greatcoat of a Mechanist, the other a pirate wearing a mockery of Wintermourn's own naval finery.

The man wrestled something from his companion, small and black like one of their aerial bombs. "Imogen! How in the Realms Below do you light this damned thing off? And where's Henry and the others?"

Imogen, the Mechanist, snatched the bomb back from him. "That ogress of yours is still stuck, and I don't care! I got them masks and came straight back because I knew you'd screw this up! What have you done to my bomb?"

The pirate waved a small box her way. "I've been trying to light it off! Why do you Mechanists make everything so complicated?"

Imogen stared at him. "What is that, a tinderbox?" She glanced down at the bomb. "What were you thinking? You have to *prime* this first! It's a clockwork fuse, it lights itself!"

Her companion sat back and crossed his arms. "Well, that is a serious design flaw!" he huffed.

Wintermourn drew his saber. The rest of the Bluecoats pushed out past him, forming two ranks on the slope at either side, with more ready behind. "No one will be lighting any fuses, clockwork or otherwise," he said.

Imogen and the other pirate turned simultaneously to stare at him. A monocle fell free from the pirate's face to dangle on its chain at his breast.

He stood quicker than Wintermourn would have thought possible. The saber at his side slid out and into guard more easily than most men lifted their forks at mealtime. In spite of himself, Wintermourn was taken aback. Still, the fellow was pompous, something more than the overblown individualism the pirates thought to call panache. *I've heard of this man before. But where?*

"I'd ask how you got up here," said the pirate, "but I don't particularly care. Men of Perinault! Be glad. You've driven us from the Copper Isles—I concede you your victory. However, attempt to prevent us from leaving, and you'll be accounted as suicides when I send you to meet the Goddess."

"Fengel!" shouted the Mechanist from behind him. "You broke it! I don't know if I can fix this thing."

The pirate half turned to call back at her, trying, and failing, not to ruin his pose. "Now is *really* not the time for pessimism, Mechanist Sixth Class."

Now Wintermourn knew where he'd heard the name. Fengel was one of the pirate captains, master of the missing airship *Flittergrasp*, according to the dossiers. That idiot Chesterly had been going on about him just yesterday. Wintermourn smiled.

"Pirate Captain Fengel," said Wintermourn. "I've heard of you. You're a mutineer and traitor as well as a pirate." Sergeant Greene appeared beside him, at the tail of the Bluecoat column pushing its way into the courtyard. "By rights you should hang," Wintermourn continued, "though I'll be just as comfortable pitching your headless corpse over the side of this cliff."

"Many have said the exact same thing," replied Fengel. "And I'm sure they will continue to. But who are you? An admiral, by your braid." He jerked his head forward, indicating the lagoon behind them. "You've a bit more gumption than most, if that's the case. I dare say your command is floundering down here."

"The Lord High Admiral of the Sea does what he pleases. And unfortunately for you, I prefer to take a more personal hand in things."

"I ... I think this might be doable," shouted Imogen.

"Not *quite* so loud, if you please," said Fengel. He stared at Wintermourn, nodding slowly. "Yes. You're Wintermourn. High Admiral of the Sea. I know of you." Fengel narrowed his eyes. "You're everything wrong with the Kingdom. The epitome of the whole rotten system and every cruel, nepotistic, imperialistic action it takes. You've the ear of the king himself, who isn't any better. It's a small handful of men like you that makes everything so much worse."

Wintermourn allowed himself a slow smile. Finally. "It is men like me who will make this world something glorious. It's a pity that you're a turncoat. Deckhand or drudge, at least you'd have lived long enough to see the rise of an empire." Wintermourn paused. "Well. Possibly."

Fengel shook his head. "You are a burden upon the world," he said. "And I will fight you as long as my body draws breath."

"Unfortunately for you," replied Wintermourn, "that will not be long." This banter was amusing, but it was time to put an end to it. Once he stopped this idiot in whatever mad plan he had, there was still the matter of the mechanical dragon to tend to.

"I've got it!" cried Imogen.

"Enough," said Wintermourn. "Greene? Fire."

Captain Fengel swore and turned back to cover Imogen, who looked up as if she'd only just then noticed the kneeling ranks of Bluecoats taking aim. Muskets steadied as Greene called out, slashing down with his sword.

A wash of caustic brilliance splashed over the men to his right. They fell back, screaming, their cerulean jackets and round black caps—as well as their weapons and very flesh—eaten away by arcane malevolence.

Wintermourn stepped back behind the sergeant at his side reflexively. The aetherite who'd thrown the blast stood just across the courtyard where a passage led to the Gasworks interior. He wore a half cloak and a gas mask, and his hands gripped a seething Working, something that dripped down to spatter at the boards beneath his feet. Wintermourn swore that the vile necromancer eyed the fallen eagerly, as if just waiting for them to die so that he could raise them up again.

Other pirates appeared beside him, bearing gas masks and an assortment of differing weapons and ragged clothing. One stepped forward and pulled off his own mask, revealing a cocksure smile beneath.

"Lucian!" shouted Captain Fengel from where he stood covering Imogen. "About damned time!"

"Sorry, sir!" replied Lucian. "We all got split up from Henry and Sarah back at the Graveway—Goddess knows where the rest of us are. Took near forever for Konrad to track you down, even with a Working."

A big, hirsute fellow to his left gave a grunt.

Lucian jerked a thumb back through the Graveway. "Then we found Sarah's huge arse jammed into the door."

"It fell on me!" snapped a large, red-haired woman.

"Well," said Fengel, seemingly practiced at stalling arguments. "Now that you're here, help me hold off this lot so that we can blast this shackle free and leave these Bluecoat-infested isles."

"Aye, sir," drawled Lucian. "Also, something's making a terrible ruckus down on the Waterdocks. If I didn't know better, I'd say it was that Draything you found on Almhazlik."

Captain Fengel stared, his monocle popping free again. "What?"

Admiral Wintermourn glanced about his side of the courtyard. The soldiers stared, somewhat stunned by the surprise reinforcements. At least, those soldiers who weren't screaming at his feet. "What are you buffoons standing around for?" he snarled. "Charge!"

Sergeant Greene jerked as if he'd been slapped. He raised his saber and roared out the order. The Bluecoats all threw themselves forward, crying out as they raised muskets or drew their smallswords. Captain Fengel whirled to meet them while Lucian and the others came to his aid. In seconds, the ruined Gasworks courtyard rang with the sounds of clattering steel and ringing musket shot.

Wintermourn let the men run past him, throwing themselves into the fray. He hung back, letting them expend themselves, as was only right and proper. From the slope of rubble he watched the field of battle, calling out commands in an effort to direct it.

Which unfortunately was somewhat needed. Unlike Euron and his lot down on the Waterdocks earlier, who had constantly retreated, these pirates could *fight*. The Bluecoat charge slammed into them, knocking them back … only to be blunted and fought back. Lucian and his pirates found their footing and stood as firm as any trained regiment. They parried smallswords or cut the marines down, even as fresh soldiers replaced those who stumbled or fell. Then, incredibly, the pirates moved forward. They fought foot by foot, not to throw the Bluecoats back but to force them aside as they made their way to the captain, giving him the time and cover he had asked for.

The huge, red-haired woman hacked away with her cutlass as she met the brunt of the Bluecoat charge, bowling men aside and cleaving their skulls with abandon. Beside her worked Lucian, mixing dirty tricks and a bandolier of pistols with his more-than-competent swordplay. A small man, heavyset and scowling, darted in and out between the two to cover them. The aetherite came next, wielding his awful liquid light. As if that wasn't enough, Fengel apparently had two of the heretical necromancers at his call. A thick, heavyset man with a wild beard and wilder eyes blew gouts of living fire that crisped skin and burned flesh. Wintermourn tried not to think of what these two would do with the corpses after the fight, though an image of rotting claws and hungry jaws came unbidden.

There were a few victories for his side. Blood ran freely from dozens of wounds: gashes, nicks, and musket-ball wounds. A vicious-looking pirate with a mouthful of filed-down teeth was skewered by two marines at once, grasping feebly at the smallswords transfixing him. The hirsute aetherite cried aloud and lost his fiery Working as a Bluecoat stepped up and shot him in the shoulder. Others fell as well, cursing, gasping, and pleading for help. Still, though, the pirates tried to reach their captain.

Who stood alone. Impossibly so. A full squad of marines had rushed Fengel when the fighting started, but rather than be immediately overcome, he stood firm. His saber whirled faster than Wintermourn could see, a blinding blur of steel that parried, cut, parried, and rebounded. Bluecoats fell back clutching severed wrist-stumps, mangled feet, and torn-open throats. Behind him the Mechanist Imogen knelt, working feverishly.

Outnumbered at least three to one, the pirates were holding out.

"Can't *anything* go right today?" Wintermourn muttered incredulously.

Sergeant Greene glanced his way. "Sir?"

"Grab a squad of men!"

Admiral Wintermourn slid down the slope of rubble for the boardwalk of the Gasworks courtyard. The saber in his hand was heavy, with a comfortable, well-worn heft. Surely he'd held it more in the last twelve hours than in the last twelve years.

He certainly wasn't as spry as when he was a mere ship's captain. The aching tear across his ribs and his shortened breath attested to that. Any other high-ranking officer in the fleet would have held back. Realms Below, they wouldn't even have left their ships! Wintermourn knew they all thought him reckless—or simply bloodthirsty. Well. There was some truth to the latter, he had to admit.

But in this world of buffoons, incompetents, and moral degenerates, the only one he could count on was himself. And he would be damned to the Realms Below before he bore responsibility for any failure today.

A Bluecoat fell back ahead of him, screaming and clutching his nose, bleeding a torrent that soaked his chin and the bright white shirt beneath his jacket. Captain Fengel appeared in the opening, and Wintermourn struck out. It was an overhand swing aimed for his opponent's crown. Fengel whipped his blade up to block it, just barely. He turned aside as a Bluecoat lunged for his heart with a bayonet-tipped musket, lashing out with the bell guard and breaking the man's cheekbone. Wintermourn pulled back into a traditional fencing stance, honed from years of dueling and warfare.

"How kind of you to join us, Admiral," said Fengel. He parried a blow from a Bluecoat beside him, bound the man's smallsword, twisted it down, and stabbed the man in the thigh.

Wintermourn aimed a cut at the pirate's head, which Fengel dodged. "If I have to intervene personally to stop you pirates and necromancers from escape, then I will do so gladly."

Fengel suddenly lashed out at him, skewering his hat and forcing him back. "Ah. You found the Revenants. I never did ask Gunney Lome where she hid those things."

He hacked a kneecap off a marine, shoved the man away with the bell of his saber, then parried a blade to his left. Another Bluecoat took the opportunity to circle right, only to find Fengel's blade there, sawing across his face. Wintermourn found himself momentarily alone, and then the pirate captain went on the attack.

Fengel's saber was everywhere—to the left and aimed at his head, then down in a cut at his thigh as Wintermourn blocked it. He pulled his leg back just enough and raised his saber against the cross-cut now coming for his shoulder before beating back the blade. The pirate captain drew back and raised an eyebrow, though not so much as to dislodge his monocle again.

"You can actually fight," said Fengel, pausing for breath.

Sergeant Greene arrived at his side with fresh troops. Wintermourn sneered at the pirate. "Of course I can. I'm Lord High Admiral of the Sea, you criminal dog. A member of the Order Gallant. The king doesn't reward wilting lilies with such an honor."

"I've got it!" cried Imogen from the shackle ahead. She stood and backed away from the fight, from whatever she'd been working on. "It's ready and armed—get away!"

Captain Fengel either ignored her, or didn't hear. He knocked away the Bluecoat's attacks, almost contemptuously, before flicking the tip of his blade at Wintermourn's eyes. "What you are, Admiral, is *old*. Old-fashioned, worn out—you remind me of my father-in-law, curse his bones."

Wintermourn tried not to focus on the growing ache in his side from the wound earlier or the burning of his lungs. "And you are tiring, Fengel. I can see it in the sweat on your brow. Let me teach you a trick or two that I've picked up over the years."

A thunderous crash sounded from above them, the thump of a wooden hull on armored plating. Captain Fengel drew back in surprise, glancing up above and behind them, back towards the lagoon and the air above the Waterdocks. Abruptly, he barked out a laugh.

"Ha! It seems that my wife is the one teaching your lot a thing or two."

Greene and a Bluecoat tried to take advantage of Fengel's distraction. Wintermourn pulled back to leave them to it, half turning to see what the pirate captain thought so amusing.

It was the *Glory*, floating just near the Craftwright's Terrace, out above the Waterdocks. Gwydion hadn't managed to lift off fully before the *Dawnhawk* had taken her from above. The pirate airship was in sad shape and appeared to have just barely managed the attack; her canvas gas bag was torn in several places, and her hull hung weirdly off-center, dinged, scraped, and broken. The delicate skysails were torn and twisted. Gwydion must have had Bluecoats or his royal guard stationed up top, however. Already, Wintermourn spied desperate fighting on the pirate airship, along the gunwales and even up in the rigging connecting the envelope.

Admiral Wintermourn turned back with a vicious smile. "Foolish pirate. The crown prince is already aboard your derelict, see?"

The Mechanist, Imogen, danced and waved her arms at the back of the courtyard near the stair rising up the cliff. "The bomb is armed! We need to flee!"

Wintermourn ignored her. "Give up, Fengel. We'll have your whore of a wife—"

Something burst through the Gasworks at his back, raining rubble from the wall out among the courtyard as it went. A huge, brazen object sailed through the air to slam into the granite wall of the terrace cliff with a sound like a ringing gong. Imogen darted aside with a yelp as it landed, and all the fighting paused for an involuntary moment.

Wintermourn stared. It was one of Gwydion's Brass Paladins, smoldering and barely recognizable. The thing still twitched and steamed, flywheels spinning beneath its heavy armor.

A great roar echoed out across Haventown and the lagoon. It rebounded from the cliff walls, triumphant. Wintermourn glanced back at the Gasworks boundary, which had been blasted open to clearly reveal the rooftops of the Waterdocks and the forest of masts made by the warships in the lagoon beyond. The mechanical Voornish dragon stood there, distant, half-atop a collapsed warehouse out in the middle of the lowest terrace, raising its great maw up to the sky. The thing roared out again, bestial and bloodthirsty, for all of its mechanical nature.

The rippling report of a musket volley sounded above. It was the *Glory*, her crew taking shots at the pirates aboard the *Dawnhawk*. The mechanical dragon paused, glancing up at the warring airships. It snorted, and a great fume of steam gushed out. For a moment it stared, as if reminded of something. Then it narrowed the great glass eyes and stomped angrily, crushing a portion of the warehouse it stood upon.

The monster turned away, hunkering low. It seemed to shake and shudder, its interior machinery working furiously. Then it straightened abruptly out, maw open, to breath a lambent bolt of lightning at the *Dawnhawk* above.

Wintermourn stared. The bolt barely missed the armored envelope of the *Glory*. Bluecoats still fell from the rigging, spasming to their doom just from proximity. It hammered up into the hull of the *Dawnhawk*, passing through it and shattering out the deck on top, then up into the gas-bag envelope of the airship before exiting on the opposite side.

Fire exploded out from the *Dawnhawk's* envelope. It burst out into the sky and washed across its deck in a wave of red-orange flame. Amazingly, the rest of the airship still hung in the sky, though burned and badly crippled. Below, the Voornish dragon gave a satisfied snort.

"No!" cried Fengel.

"Why are you all standing around!" sobbed Imogen.

Then her bomb went off.

Admiral Wintermourn felt pressure, then saw light, and everything became a confused jumble. The world seemed to wink out, then come back in a completely different orientation. Long moments passed as he struggled to set things to order.

He was lying on his side upon the courtyard boardwalk, his back bent at an awkward angle. Bodies lay all about him. *How did I get down here? What happened?*

Something was ringing in his ears. He ignored it. *Wait. The fight. Captain Fengel and the airship.*

His saber. He had to find his saber and get to his feet before the enemy could finish him off. Something was strange, though. The world—it wouldn't stop wobbling.

Admiral Wintermourn rolled onto one arm, then gasped as a riotous, shooting pain lanced through his side and his wound from earlier. He forced himself through it with the experience of many long years, looking up past the dead or unconscious Bluecoats just in front of him. Then he stopped, trying to make sense of the scene.

Bodies lay all about, Bluecoats and pirates both. A hole gaped in the middle of the courtyard boards. On the opposite side, the cliff wall was moving.

No, passing. It was falling away. Wintermourn realized that the structure he lay upon was *rising*.

No. No, they won't succeed. He tried to force himself to sit up and coughed violently. The taste of blood was thick on his tongue.

Movement caught his eye. It was the Mechanist, Imogen. She pulled at a stunned, bloodied, half-standing Captain Fengel, still holding his blade. The short, bulldog-looking fellow, now covered in blood, helped her. He gestured at the airship landing pad above them, then back out at the lagoon.

No. You won't get away.

Wintermourn licked raw lips and adjusted his wig. "Greene," he gasped. "Greene! Attend me!" The man was useless. What had ever happened to his adjutant, Sergeant Lanters?

A shadow covered him. He glanced up to see the *Dawnhawk* on the approach, a madly burning wreck falling straight for the Gasworks. The *Glory of Perinault* was out of his field of vision, escaping catastrophe for the moment, it seemed.

"Sir?" croaked the body before him. It was Sergeant Greene.

"Get on your feet, soldier," rasped Wintermourn. He grabbed a saber, not his own, and used the blade like a crutch, forcing himself to one knee. Wintermourn glowered down at the Bluecoat. The man said something, but he didn't catch it this time. The ringing in his ears would just not stop.

Sergeant Greene was an oozy wreck. His eyes were gone; it was obvious he wouldn't long survive.

Damnation! Wintermourn glanced at Fengel and his minions, who were slowly climbing the stair away from them, to the landing pad above.

"Everything myself," he muttered. "Have to do everything myself."

More movement appeared across the courtyard. A shock of fear shot through him, but no, it wasn't Revenants. It was a group of still-living Bluecoats, thank the hairy knuckles of the Goddess. Though whether they'd be of any more use than Green was questionable.

"To arms!" he croaked, grabbing up his fallen saber. "Attend me, you whoreson laggards! They're getting away!"

Slowly, with his lungs burning and black spots dancing in his vision, Admiral Wintermourn straightened his wig. Then he crept after Fengel in pursuit.

CHAPTER TWENTY-FOUR

Captain Fengel forced himself up the Gasworks stairway. It rang with every step he took, the metal clangor a counterpoint to his own labored breathing.

He *ached*. Each breath was like fire. His ankle was stiff. Blood ran freely from his tattered clothing and the dozen wounds beneath them. That omnipresent ringing in his ears was fading, though the pounding in his skull couldn't have been worse if his head were placed in a vise.

Henry Smalls was at his side, propping him up and helping him in his climb. His faithful steward was saying something, but Fengel couldn't make it out. Ahead of them, giddy with excitement and possibly a concussion, Imogen Helmsin raced for the airship platform at the top of the stair. She stopped to point at the rapidly disappearing cliff wall and then up at the Flophouse Terrace floating above before running forward again.

We've done it. We're aloft. They'll never catch us now. But how steep the cost? In the courtyard below were dozens of the dead, men and women he'd known for years. Crewmates he'd led to freedom, then victory, and then finally to the skies. Some lived still, he was sure, and he was leaving them even now to the Bluecoats!

Because there wasn't any time. The *Dawnhawk*, with Natasha, was coming in hard, crippled by the damnable Dray Engine. Where in the Realms Below had it even come from? And breathing lightning? Never on Almhazlik had he seen it do *that*.

Not important. It just wasn't important right now. He felt shame over his abandonment of those still injured below, Lucian and Sarah and anyone else that was left. But his wife …

Fengel grabbed for the handrail, failing because of the saber still clutched tight in his hand. That was surprising; he hadn't even realized he still had it. Fengel sheathed the blade roughly, stopping Henry with a mumbled command and looking back out over Haventown's lagoon. Then he stared, monocle falling away. The *Dawnhawk* loomed hugely just ahead, a falling star awash in flame heading straight for them.

"Brace!" screamed Imogen, all her giddiness gone now.

His airship passed just overhead, so close that Fengel felt the heat from the flames up on her deck. He could have reached out and touched it, had he wanted to lose a finger. She tore railing away as she slammed into the Gasworks platform, skidding across it to ram the central smokestack spire rising up from the structure.

Fengel experienced a horrible moment as the entire world seemed to shake. Steel gave way with the screeching snap of metal pushed just too far. The Gasworks—or was it the unmoored Craftwright's Terrace itself?—shook with the force of the impact. Orange light washed over them all, cutting through the early evening gloom and illuminating the shattered pieces of steel that fell like clattering rain into the Gasworks interior. The *Dawnhawk* burned up above, a torch for the whole of Haventown.

The shaking ceased as his airship settled on the platform above with a mighty groan. Fengel grabbed a wincing Henry with one hand and gestured up to it, past where Imogen clung to the stair they stood on. "She's stopped! Henry, if ever you've borne me any love, get me to the ship! We can still save them—we can still save Natasha!"

His steward stared at him, appalled and uncertain. Then he nodded, spat blood out over the courtyard, and helped Fengel forward. They stepped past Imogen where she was clambering unsteadily to her feet, and climbed the last few steps up onto the airship landing pad.

It wasn't large, certainly not like the piers up at the Skydocks. An oval-shaped platform of wood and steel, the Mechanists had built it for their own purposes, and it stuck out from the central smokestack spire of the Gasworks. The Dawnhawk lay perpendicular to it, having touched down in its middle and slid to a violent arrest up against the now-bent smokestacks.

Fengel felt his throat catch. Past the broken boards and burning debris that littered the platform, his lovely airship was dead. Her hull was snapped in two, her uppermost deck presented to him as if to show what would never be again. The great gasbag envelop burned, half-floating, half-dangling from the smokestacks like the awning of some great pavilion.

My ship. My crew. Natasha!

He let go of Henry and stagger-stepped across the platform, oblivious to anything beyond or below it. Images flashed through his mind's eye of the last time this had happened, of the last time he'd lost an airship. But the *Flittergrasp* hadn't been carrying the woman he loved.

A piece of debris reached up and grabbed his leg. Fengel toppled, falling to the creaking platform and slamming hard into it. *That had to have been a hand …*

Fengel rolled onto his back. He looked down the length of his body at a bedraggled, crumpled figure lying at his feet. It stared back up at him with eyes like hard glass set above a hawklike nose and greying beard.

"Euron?" choked Fengel, incredulous.

Euron Blackheart relaxed his grip. He coughed, then hawked and spat. "Popinjay. Realms Below, but I wish ye were anyone else."

Fengel couldn't help himself. "What are you even doing up here?"

The old pirate sighed. He sat painfully upright, debris from the *Dawnhawk* sliding off of his ruined yesteryear outfit. "What do it even matter anymore?"

Fengel didn't even feel his temper rise. "I asked you, what—"

"I came up here to watch th' end," Euron snapped back at him. "Ye damned mutinous cur! Ye took everything, rose up against me, an' those cowardly dogs followed! Ye think yer so clever, that ye'd find a way out. So I came up here to watch ye cock it all up." He shrugged. "Then I smelled light-air gas, and something exploded down below. Then ye arrived along with yer Bluecoatie friends, ye traitor."

"They're not my friends," growled Fengel. He knew the answer, but still felt he had to ask. "And if you saw us fighting down there, why didn't you come help?"

Euron made a flippant gesture, ignoring the approach of Imogen and Henry Smalls. "What would be th' point? Ye'd already gotten what ye wanted, ye coward. It weren't enough to cut and run yerself, ye had to take the whole town! Better death than that. Better to fall before a worthy enemy." He looked up at the rapidly darkening sky. "It should have been Reddon, back then. Only one ever worth a damn. An' now I got nothin'."

A small explosion roared behind them from the envelope of the *Dawnhawk*. Fengel glanced back to it, feeling all his earlier panic and fear again. He turned back and lashed out at Euron with his right fist, catching the old pirate by surprise and connecting squarely with his jaw. Wooden teeth sailed through the air to bounce off the shirt of a surprised Henry Smalls. Fengel followed through, scrabbling to his knees and grabbing the old man by his ragged shirt before he could fall.

"You incompetent, glory-hungry old fool!" he screamed. "Nothing? Have nothing?" Fengel gestured at the wrecked airship only a couple dozen paces away. "Your daughter is on that ship! She could be burning alive while you wallow here in pity!" He made to climb to his feet, then stumbled. Henry Smalls ran to help him up.

Euron glanced up at him hatefully. He rubbed his jaw, then stopped as if he'd just made sense of Fengel's words. "Natasha?" He looked back at the *Dawnhawk*, eyes widening. "But I sent her away! What is she doing back here?"

"It doesn't matter!" screamed Fengel. He found his balance, then let go of Henry to hobble towards the *Dawnhawk*. Out of the corner of his eye, he saw his father-in-law clamber up after him.

The wreck of the *Dawnhawk* was complete. She lay not quite sideways, her starboard side facing out, ruined deck shown in full. The hull was cracked in half, and he could see down past her decks almost all the way into the cargo deck. Debris covered her: tangles of rope, mounds of canvas, and torn metal struts from the skeleton of the gasbag above. To say nothing of all the bodies. Jets of flame shot out from the gas bag as light-air cells cooked off, like the breath of angry dragons.

A staggering figure was illuminated by the flames. She was short and clutched a boarding hatchet in two trembling hands.

Fengel put both hands to his mouth and yelled. "Stone!"

Lina Stone whirled, raising up the hatchet defensively. She bled from a myriad of cuts, scratches, and gashes. Upon seeing Fengel she froze but did not lower her weapon.

"Captain Fengel?"

Fengel clambered up the wreckage and through a broken section of the gunwales until he stood on the deck. "Stone, where are the others? Where's Natasha?"

"They just kept coming," said Lina. "Not tame like all the others—or like Omari had ever said. They … they just kept coming, and they wanted us dead, and they were clutching at us with dead fingers, and it was just like Breachtown all over again, and I saw Andrea, only she's not herself any—"

Fengel grabbed the small woman by the shoulders. "Focus!" he snarled, only inches away from her face. "Where's Natasha?"

Lina stared at him. "Stern, near the hatchway stair," she said in a rapid-fire monotone. "She's trapped. Omari and Allen are helping, but I can't find Rastalak or Runt or even Michael to help."

Something seemed to give way in her. "Oh Captain, it's all gone tits up. The ship. She's dead. There was the Stormhammer, but it was broken, and Euron left a bunch of angry pirates marooned there … look out!"

She shrugged free of his grip and reared back with the hatchet. Fengel followed her eyes, the twist of her arms. He stepped to one side, drew his saber, then whirled. The blackened, wizened head of a dead pirate went rolling down the deck as he cut it neatly from its shoulders. What was left of the corpse fell limply back down to the deck, still reaching for him. Then Fengel's injured leg voiced a complaint, forcing a gasp from him.

"Come on!" he yelled to Euron and the others as they picked their way aboard the airship. "Aft hatch stairway. Watch out for Revenants!" Then he pushed past Lina and staggered his way down across the deck.

It was easy to see where to go. The Yulani witch and his ship's apprentice Mechanist worked feverishly to free Natasha, who had both her legs pinned beneath a heavy metal strut. Her awful parrot, Butterbeak, hopped back and forth between the wreckage. The parrot was too fat to fly with its feathers so singed.

"Put yer damned backs into it!" snarled Natasha.

"I am not some draft horse!" said Omari.

"We need a pulley," said Allen, his voice tight with exhaustion and pain, who had one arm bound tightly to his chest with a length of rope and looked as badly off as Fengel felt. "If … if we can attach it to the envelope with some rope, we can—"

A section of that very gas bag fell away, crashing to the deck and sending soot spraying across them both.

"Or … not," he continued. Allen's eyes lit up as he spied Fengel. "Captain!"

Fengel swept his arm back and forth to clear the air as he staggered forward. "Natasha!" He sheathed his saber and fell down to his knees beside her.

His wife was gorgeous, as always, even though she was covered in soot, grime, and dried blood. She smelled like an abattoir, though. And part of her hair had caught fire, which also wasn't doing her scent any favors.

"About time you showed up," she snarled. Her face froze in a rictus, then she sat up and slapped Omari across her shoulder. "Argh! Be careful! That's my legs under this thing, not some loose change you're digging for!" She glanced back at Fengel, face softening. "You look half dead."

"I know," agreed Fengel. "I know." He waved the others over. "Move your feet!"

Fengel staggered over beside Omari and put his hands to the strut. It was made of steel and thick as his torso, buried at one end by a massive heap of canvas. "Here, Omari. You and I both lift. Allen! See if you can jam a lever underneath."

The young Mechanist grabbed up a much-battered boarding pike with his good arm. But rather than help, he looked around worriedly.

"We have to hurry," he said. "The … the Castaways are all dead, but they're not like the other Revenants. They're almost unstoppable, and they're recovering from the crash."

"I told you!" snapped Omari. "They hate you! They really wanted to kill us in life, so they'll keep on trying in death."

"We can deal with them afterward," yelled Fengel. "Now shut up and lift this strut!"

Allen and Omari both shared a look, then bent to work. A shadow fell across them all, and Fengel felt a moment's relief. *Finally.*

"Henry, help Omari. Lina, put your weight on that lever with Allen. Euron, try not to get in—"

He froze at the look of alarm on Natasha's face. She opened her mouth to shout denial, reaching for a broken plank at her side. Then a cutlass speared down past Fengel's shoulder and buried itself in her chest.

Natasha's eyes popped wide as she slammed back down to the deck. Her breath left in a gasp, and she grabbed at the blade.

"No!" Fengel turned and rose, raising both fists in a two-handed blow at the swordsman behind him. He connected, staggering the man back.

It was a Revenant. He wore a tattered outfit several decades out of date, with a greying beard and wrinkled, well-tanned skin. An eye patch covered a missing eye, a lesser injury than the gaping wound in his chest that had killed him. Fengel didn't know him, and he didn't know how he'd gotten here.

The dead man seemed to notice him for the first time. Fengel drew his saber as it swung its cutlass, slow and awkward, though still fast enough to be lethal. Their blades clashed, sending sparks between them both.

The head. Take off the head! Omari's accursed undead were usually slow and easily handled. She'd said again and again that they weren't dangerous unless first threatened.

A cutlass blade chopped neatly through the neck of the one-eyed Revenant. Its head tumbled away off down the deck, and it seemed to freeze. Then the corpse toppled, revealing Euron Blackheart with blade in hand. Henry, Lina, and Imogen stood behind him.

"Morgan One-Eye!" he snarled. "Ye traitor! I warned ye I'd kill ye if ye ever left that island unguarded."

Henry caught Fengel's eye. "There are others on the deck, and they're just as angry."

A chorus of undead groans echoed about the *Dawnhawk*, underlining his point. Fengel didn't reply. He turned again and dropped to his knees, letting go his saber and fumbling for a handkerchief, a rag, anything at all to stanch the bleeding. Omari and Allen were there, trying to help but just getting in the way. Natasha was gasping, clutching at her shirt where the cutlass had impaled her. He shoved the two crewmen out of the way and came in close to help her, but she only growled and swatted him away with her free hand.

Natasha reached into the tatters of her puffy pirate's shirt and fished something out. She flung it to the deck and then fell back with a groan.

It was a small book, the one he'd given her. *How to Pillage Friends and Intimidate People*. The little folio had been almost severed through by the Revenant's cutlass. Almost.

"Looks like … it came in handy … after all," she gasped at him.

Fengel wanted to laugh and cry at the same time. "I told you," he said.

"That you did." Natasha rubbed her chest. "Argh. Still fells like someone took a hammer to my tit. Now quite staring, and will you three get this damned strut off of my legs?"

"Oh," said Fengel. "Right. Allen, grab your lever. Omari—"

"What are ye doing down here!"

Euron staggered over to stand above them all. "Dad?" said Natasha, surprised.

"Aye! And I asked ye a question, girl. I sent ye off to secure the Stormhammer. So what are ye doing back here?"

Natasha looked as if she'd spit black tar. "You sent me off to keep me away from the fighting," she snarled back. "To the Realms Below with that! I leave for a day, and you let the whole town get overrun by Perinese! It's a *damned* good thing we found our own, working Voornish weapon. Unlike that junk pile up north."

"Well, of course it didn't work! Ye would have had to fix it. Should have taken ye days!"

Natasha's eyes widened. "You knew. You knew that it wasn't working!"

"Of course he did," said Fengel. "He never intended to save Haventown. All he wanted was a glorious death."

As the old pirate rounded on him, a volley of musket fire rang out. Hot lead whipped all around them, splintering wood and ricocheting off metal. Euron jerked violently, almost falling over. Then he looked down at his ragged shirt with a grunt. He touched his chest gingerly, pulling back fingertips tinged by blood. Looking up at Fengel, he narrowed his eyes.

"Me only regret," he said clearly, "was that I never killed ye myself, popinjay." Then, turning to Natasha, he reached out to her and collapsed.

"Dad!" yelled Natasha.

Fengel whirled, grabbing up his saber as he did and ignoring the pain in his ankle.

A dozen Bluecoats with smoking muskets knelt on the platform just below the *Dawnhawk*. They looked ragged, bloody, and angry. Admiral Wintermourn stood in their midst. He clutched his side with his spare hand, and his wig hung askew, but his grip was sure on his saber, and he glared at Fengel hatefully.

Captain Fengel ran down the deck, heedless of all the little protests his agonized body responded with. Using his momentum, he climbed up the starboard exhaust pipe, then leaped down into the Bluecoats. He landed hard in their midst, and something in his injured ankle crunched.

Agony shot up through his leg. Fengel let out a yell and tried not to fall. Wintermourn and the Bluecoats, momentarily taken aback, moved to swarm him. They dropped their muskets and drew their smallswords.

Fengel cursed wordlessly. *Never let them see you stumble.*

He parried the first, awkward, desperate blow aimed for his head. Returning the riposte, he skewered the soldier through his shoulder, then brought the bell guard of his saber around just fast enough to deflect the next blade that came for him.

"You've failed, Fengel," said Wintermourn. The admiral stood behind the soldiers and let them do his fighting. "Now you're injured and outnumbered. Lie down and get this over with, so that I can execute the rest of you degenerate pirates."

Fengel's leg flared with pain as he moved. He shifted his weight, bit his tongue, and used every bit of sheer, bloody-minded willpower he had to keep his footing and keep on fighting.

A ragged battle cry echoed out from behind Fengel. Henry joined him at his side, along with Lina Stone. Others seemed to appear from nowhere: Farouk and Rastalak and Reaver Jane, all converging from wherever they'd been thrown in the crash, bloodied but able to fight.

The pop of pistol shots sounded behind him as well. Fengel cut at a Bluecoat's eyes and used the time to risk a look back. It was Natasha, standing on the gunwales of his wrecked airship, free now and supported by Omari, with Allen limping painfully behind her. His wife glared coldly at the Perinese and fired shot after shot at them, taking pistols from a hastily donned bandolier.

Fengel choked up. Then an errant shot took his hat clean off. He ducked with a curse, the movement forcing agony up his leg. Natasha wasn't a great shot, even at the best of times.

He rounded back to the fight, bringing his saber back up into guard. No one was trying to take his head off, at least for the moment. The Bluecoat marines fought his crewmen, who'd earned him a moment's respite.

"I'm hardly alone, Wintermourn!" he yelled to the man.

Admiral Wintermourn glared back at him. "A more ragged band I've never seen. Lambs coming to slaughter. They won't … save … you …"

The admiral trailed off, his look of disdain twisting into one of horror. He stared, not at Fengel, but past him. Natasha shouted a warning back aboard the *Dawnhawk,* but it was Wintermourn who took a step backward.

Fengel turned to see Allen and Omari both flee from a lurching figure rising up out of the wreckage. It grabbed for them with undead claws, and Natasha fired a pistol straight into its chest. The Revenant staggered, then reached for her again. Imogen tripped the thing with a broken length of wood, then all three of them scrabbled off of the airship's deck.

Revenants appeared all over the *Dawnhawk,* like maggots from a burning corpse. There were a mere dozen still on deck, though all moved with malevolent purpose. Others were crawling out from belowdecks, from out the crack in the hull leading to the cargo hold. They were Perinese, pirate, and even a few of his own crew.

What in the Realms Below happened on my ship? Fengel didn't have time to wonder—the Revenants were at his back, but they were slow. The Perinese were right in front of him.

He looked back to see the fight spreading out across the platform, turning into a general melee. Admiral Wintermourn stood frozen in sheer horror. Then he turned and tried to flee, shoving to get through the Bluecoats at his back.

Revenants later. Time to push the advantage! Fengel threw himself into a limping charge after Wintermourn, trying not to cry out at every breath. *You won't get away. You're mine now.*

He hacked and cut, forcing the men before him to dive aside into the waiting blades of his crewmen. The admiral cast a glance back at him and swore, grabbing a Bluecoat and pushing him out in front of Fengel as a shield. Fengel bashed the fellow in the face with the guard of his saber, then pushed on with an overhand chop at the back of Wintermourn's head. Someone—the soldier he'd just hit or one of the ones at his side—fell against Fengel, pushing him back at the last second. The tip of his saber caught his quarry just barely, nicking through the white wig of curls and down his back rather than burying itself in his skull.

Admiral Wintermourn yelled and turned to face him, bringing up his own blade while he tore away the wig with his free hand and sought out the wound. His fingertips came back crimson, and he stared at them in surprise before fixing his gaze hatefully upon Fengel.

"Your abominations won't save you," he snarled.

"Worry less about me," said Fengel, assuming a guard. "And more about yourself." He gestured with his head at the melee around them.

Wintermourn opened his mouth to retort and was stopped short by a battle cry. Past them both, at the edge of the platform, new figures appeared. Ragged and bloodied, they looked like Revenants themselves, but were infinitely more welcome to Fengel's eyes. Lucian led the charge with a cutlass in each hand, followed by the towering form of Sarah Lome and then his aetherites, Maxim and Konrad, empty of Workings but clutching blades of their own as they shouted Omari's name as a battle cry.

His reinforcements charged the Perinese, adding their weight to the fight and evening the odds even further. Behind them all, the Revenants continued to advance from the burning airship.

Fengel smiled maliciously. "Well, now. Not so easy, is it? When numbers aren't on your side?"

The Lord High Admiral of the Sea glanced about in a panic, his eyes wide, seeking for escape. "No," he said. "I am a Wintermourn. I do not fail. I do not fall here, at the claws of these abominations."

Enough talk. The admiral dropped his blade half an inch, and Fengel saw an opportunity. He beat forward, knocking his adversary's saber aside, then twisting to stab down through Wintermourn's thigh. The man fell to one knee with a scream as Fengel pulled back his saber, red and wet with gore.

Captain Fengel reared back for the killing blow. Then the staccato pop of musket fire rang out somewhere ahead. Deadly lead flew past close enough for Fengel to feel, and one bullet even slammed into his upraised saber. It jerked and snapped, and the ball continued on, taking half of the blade with it.

A huge shape appeared through the gloom and the smoke. It was the enemy airship, the *Glory of Perinault*, coming in low on the opposite end of the platform from the wreck of the *Dawnhawk*. Great galvanic lanterns flared into life, casting stark, brilliant illumination across the fight. Then a ramp slid out from the gondola to slam onto the Gasworks platform.

Perinese reinforcements strode out from the *Glory*. A single figure led them, a handsome young man in rich, dark clothing. He wielded not a saber but an old-style longsword, obviously Worked and glowing with a golden light. At his back came four Perinese royal guards, hefting long-bladed halberds etched with the sunburst of Perinault.

"You seem to be in a spot of trouble!" said the youth. "Worry not, my good admiral."

"Gwydion?" cried Admiral Wintermourn.

"Of course! Now just sit tight while I save the day."

Wintermourn stared behind him, then snarled wordlessly in rage and frustration. He flung himself up at Fengel, tackling him and throwing them both to the ground. Fengel tried to hold on to the hilt of his broken blade, but Wintermourn had one hand around his wrist and slammed it into the platform until he was forced to let go. Fengel grabbed with his other hand for the admiral's throat, finding a grip on his jacket instead.

They rolled on the ground, flailing. Boots stomped all about them. Fengel fought his hand free, then formed a fist and slammed it repeatedly into the admiral's gut. There wasn't any art now, no swordplay. Just two men trying to kill each other. A distant, detached part of Fengel wondered why it always seemed to come to this.

Wintermourn wrapped his hands around Fengel's throat and rolled atop him, trying to choke the life out of him. Fengel heaved, throwing the man aside, though he still had ahold of his neck. Someone yelped and fell past: Lina Stone, with a bloodied hatchet.

Fengel kicked with his good leg, trying to knee the wound he'd made earlier. He connected, but Wintermourn butted his head forward and left Fengel seeing stars.

The admiral rolled atop him again, his hoary old hands still locked tight upon Fengel's throat. Fengel's lungs were ragged now, crying out for air. He battered against his opponent's grip, but nothing seemed to work.

Someone moved into view just above them both. Hands burned into black claws reached down for Wintermourn, who did a double-take, then threw himself aside with a hoarse scream of pure horror. Fengel gasped, then looked up into the undead face of Euron Blackheart.

"Euron?" gasped Fengel.

The Revenant gave a satisfied groan as it grabbed him by the face with both hands. *Oh,* Fengel realized, as he flailed and fought anew. Euron's corpse hadn't come to help him at all.

A blade flashed out, lopping the head off of Fengel's undead father-in-law. The Revenant spasmed, and Fengel threw his claws away. Euron Blackheart toppled, revealing Lucian standing behind him with a cocksure grin.

"I know you wanted to do for him yourself," he said. "But I think we're a bit pressed at the moment."

Fengel laughed, his throat sore. "So long as I was able to watch," he replied.

Lucian reached out a hand to help him up. "Well," he said, pulling Fengel to a half-standing position. "I do apologize for being late. Both here and below. It's been—"

Two feet of glowing, golden steel burst through his chest.

"Tsk," said Gwydion from just behind the dying first mate. "Mind your surroundings, now." He pulled the gleaming blade free, and Fengel's first mate crumpled to the ground.

"Lucian!" cried Fengel.

Gwydion smiled and brought his longsword back into a two-handed guard. "Captain Fengel, I presume? Your bitch of a wife gave me a thrashing, earlier. I intend to repay the debt now. Know that when you meet the Goddess, it was Crown Prince Gwydion of the Kingdom of Perinault who—"

He folded around a massive fist and was flung suddenly away. Sarah Lome appeared, yelling in rage. Royal guards charged out of the gloom, moving to protect their charge as she turned to face them. The first she knocked down with her cutlass, but then two more were there, one spearing her in the side with the tip of his halberd.

"Gunney," croaked Fengel. He cast about for a sword, a dagger, anything to help her with. *No, wait. Lucian. Stanch the bleeding. I can still try to save Lucian.*

It dawned horribly upon Fengel that he couldn't do both.

A fist slammed into his jaw, knocking him back and preventing him from doing either. It was Wintermourn. He threw another punch, catching Fengel still off-balance while grabbing his jacket with his off hand. Fengel grabbed him in turn, rolling with the blow. They fell, tumbling together across the Gasworks platform, fighting for advantage.

Fengel lashed out, took blows of his own, bit, spat, and swore. The old man was tough, like teak hardened by time. He clouted Fengel across the sides of his head with both fists, and for a moment the world swam. When he blinked it away, the admiral was atop him again, squeezing his throat with an iron-hard grip. Fengel flailed. The old sailor would not budge.

"Your time ... is ... over," snarled Wintermourn. "I can see you ... flagging. Failing. You've got nothing left!"

Fengel let go the admiral's grip. He grabbed about him for a weapon, some debris, anything. His fingers scrabbled across nothing. It was true. He had nothing at hand, nothing left to change the odds with.

Almost.

He grabbed with his left hand for the chain on his chest. It brushed against his fingers, still there after all this time and trouble. He made a fist around it, yanking at his monocle. It came free, small and round and weirdly-shaped ever since Almhazlik.

Captain Fengel slammed it onto the platform. The cracked lens broke free of its housing and fell into his palm. He gripped it between his fingers and rammed the sharpest edge up into Wintermourn's throat.

The admiral let out a croak of surprise. He let go of Fengel and reached up to stop him. Fengel followed, reaching up and grabbing Wintermourn by the back of the neck with his free hand. Then he *sawed*.

Admiral Wintermourn fought. He flailed at Fengel and tried to twist away. Fengel held on as blows and blood both rained down on him, blinding him as he worked. The admiral gave a keening cry of agonized denial. Fengel ignored it. He thought of Lucian, Phred, Geoffrey Lords, Mechanist Clangfoot, and all those who'd been killed in this pointless, brutal invasion.

The blows lessened. They turned to slaps. Fengel couldn't see anymore through all the blood. Gradually, Wintermourn weakened. There was a burbling noise, as of someone choking on their own ichor. Then Wintermourn went limp. Fengel didn't stop cutting until the man fell off of him.

He lay a moment, panting, ears ringing and a thick coppery tang filling his mouth. *Lucian. Sarah. I've got to help them. And where's Natasha?*

He wiped his face with a shirtsleeve. Admiral Wintermourn lay right beside him, still, staring off into the Realms Beyond. Fengel forced himself up with a groan.

Lucian lay a few feet away, still clutching the wound that had killed him. A look of shock suffused his rogue's features, dashing no longer. Past him, Gunney Lome kneeled upon the platform. Three separate royal guards had her transfixed with their polearms, spearing her through the thigh and the shoulders.

The other Bluecoats fought the few still-standing Revenants—there weren't much left of either. His own crew, however ...

They lay or knelt in a semicircle around Crown Prince Gwydion. Farouk clutched a bleeding arm tightly to his chest. Henry lay on the platform, dead or unconscious, along with Reaver Jane. Maxim rolled across the platform, wreathed in the pale flames of some arcane mishap. Konrad chased after him, trying to put him out. Omari crouched over a hysterical young Paine, though she was weeping herself at the horror of the battle, while a bleeding, gasping, Ryan Gae struggled to draw a pistol from his bandolier. Lina Stone crawled forward along the ground for a dropped cutlass. He did not see Rastalak.

Gwydion himself stood fine. His clothes were still only slightly scuffed. His Worked blade gleamed bright, slicked with blood as it was. He stalked over to Lina Stone and put his boot upon the small of her back, causing her to yell out.

"Hold the big redhead steady," he called to his guards. "I'll deal with her after I cut this one's head off."

Fengel put out a hand, trying to focus through fading vision and the roaring in his ears.

Gwydion raised his blade up high, then swung down.

Something darted through the gloom. It glowed red and spat viciously, flitting down into Gwydion's face. He swore and dodged aside, swinging wildly. The Worked blade in his hands connected, splitting the enraged, flying scryn in two.

Runt fell as Lina screamed and Gwydion continued to curse. The crown prince raised his blade again, just as another figure went sprinting past the royal guard.

It was the ex-soldier, Michael Hockton. He held a small crate in both hands, whose contents he emptied in full at the crown prince.

Small, wormy things flew through the air. They hissed and spit and writhed and landed upon the arm Gwydion raised to block them. He screamed as they slithered and bit, flinging his longsword out reflexively. The tip of it caught Hockton across the face, sending him back with a yell of his own.

Gwydion dropped his blade and staggered away. The scrynlings writhed all over him now, though still mostly on his outstretched arm. His well-tailored jacket was ragged and tattered, bulging with the little monsters as they burrowed beneath into his flesh.

The roaring in Fengel's ears grew louder. He saw the royal guards shouting, but he did not hear them. They dropped their halberds and went for their liege. Fengel blinked, and suddenly they were all together, swatting at the scrynlings. Then he blinked again, and Natasha was there, lying beside him. She fired pistol after pistol at the retreating crown prince, the whole of it weirdly silent. Gwydion screamed and flailed with the remnants of his arm, and Fengel thought he saw glistening bone. Then they hauled him back aboard the *Glory*.

Fengel blinked again, and Natasha was looking at him now. She was filthy, gore-slicked, and shouting. He had never loved her more.

Then the roaring in his ears reached a crescendo, sweeping Captain Fengel away into the dark.

EPILOGUE

CROWN PRINCE GWYDION STARED AT THE LETTER BEFORE HIM.

It was a report to his royal father, one of the rare pieces of bureaucracy he dared not shirk. The letter was blank, and the pen beside it untouched. Two balls of crumpled paper lay nearby, next to a mostly drained glass of whiskey, evidence of earlier drafts. Anything he found to say just seemed so utterly insufficient.

Gwydion's private cabin aboard the *Glory of Perinault* was luxurious. Warm teak paneled the walls, punctuated here and there by wide windows with armored shutters, a change he had insisted upon from the original design. Exotic rugs from far-off Zhong-hei covered the floor, and the desk atop it was richly inlaid. Gwydion fingered a splintered gouge in that inlay, the legacy of some stray shot that had breached the hull. He stared outside, where the Atalian Sea stretched endless beneath the sky.

Gwydion picked up the mechanical ink pen and tried to start again. After only a few sentences, he paused, distracted by the implement itself.

Machinery fascinated him. The wonders he'd seen crafted back home were going to change … everything. Steam engines, volleyguns, advanced automation—to say nothing of aerial flight. The *Glory of Perinault* was just a test, a prototype; soon there would be a fleet.

And these were just the things under development by the Kingdom! The artificers of Triskelion regularly experimented with mundane wonders, and the Mechanists of the Copper Isles worked with such ingenious skill that it rivaled aetherite magic.

That was what had finally attracted his attention to the navy—why he had insisted to his royal father he join in the action. His own people were decades behind the Mechanists in terms of what they were accomplishing. The chance to capture working examples of their technology, or even some of their number, was simply too good to pass up.

Not that it had worked out even remotely well. Oh, the *Glory* had been a blazing success, as had the Brass Paladins. But his crowing over them could only fill a small part of the report to his royal father. The rest would be filled with miserable failure: three dozen ships, thousands of soldiers, hundreds of officers, and the Brass Paladin themselves ... all lost. Even the legendary sword of the Kingdom, the priceless relic Danlann, was gone. Gwydion felt downright queasy at that last bit. How was he going to explain that he had lost an eight-hundred-year-old royal treasure?

And what did they have to show for it all? Future maps would certainly claim the Copper Isles for the Kingdom of Perinault—not that they could hold them. But the enemy they'd sought to crush had just taken their town and ... flown away.

He could try to blame everything on the Lord High Admiral of the Sea. Wintermourn had been a wasteful, bloodthirsty tyrant, an old stuffed shirt who Gwydion had enjoyed prodding, and there was much that could be laid at the dead man's feet. But no one would believe that Wintermourn had been the one to so recklessly order the fleet into the island interior—there were far too many witnesses to the contrary.

Gwydion set the pen back down with a sigh. The *Glory* flew back to the Kingdom, while what was left of the fleet remained behind to cordon off the Copper Isles and receive any survivors of the retreat. There had been a few, last he'd heard. The rest were dead—or stuck on the isles with that brazen Voornish monster the pirates had unleashed.

How was he to make any of that look good before his father?

A dull ache began again in his other arm. He looked to the freshly bandaged stump terminating at his elbow. Then the Crown Prince of the Kingdom of Perinault reached for the whiskey, once again, with a groan.

The Dray Engine hunted.

It pushed through thick green jungles, cracking palms and flattening undergrowth as it stalked. The native wildlife hooted as it passed, a mild irritation. Of far more import were the slave-humans in blue pelts who ran ahead. There were just so very many of them, screaming and hiding, gloriously panicked at its approach.

Things hadn't gone terribly well of late. First the Dray Engine had been stuck on the bottom of the ocean. Then, following the oh-so-weak aether-bands, it had found itself trapped on an island to the north. And as if *that* wasn't enough, the slave-human female reappeared, the irritating one with the golden eyes and shrill voice who had woken it back within the Foundry of Garaam.

At first, that development had excited the Dray Engine. The female had bested it, mocked and escaped it. The Dray Engine positively dreamed of squashing her beneath its armored feet. Killing the humans on the isle where it had been trapped was positively boring compared to the joyous thought of crushing her.

Well, only a little. It *did* love squashing slave-humans.

But she'd come back! The Dray Engine ignored the why and how and unlikely odds of such a thing. It focused instead on how it would step on her, slowly, like a mob of vermin Draykin—or maybe a cow that couldn't move fast enough.

Surprise, then, when not only did she manage to stun it but bind it to the bottom of her sky-boat! Injury and insult followed, and then it was dropped like a rock atop a primitive collection of hovels in the middle of some lagoon, which was just *crawling* with even more repulsive slave-humans.

It was that fall which changed things.

Something had been jarred within the Dray Engine. Whether knocked back into place or simply unlocked, it didn't matter. Systems long forgotten came online, ready to be used. Testing them on the golden-eyed female's sky-boat had proven immensely satisfying.

Then the human hovels … flew away. Which was perplexing. And infuriating. The Dray Engine had wanted to climb up atop them. It wanted to find the wreck of the sky-boat and the golden-eyed woman's corpse, just to grind it flat.

Oh well. There were plenty of slave-humans left for it to crush. The ones with the blue pelts were just *everywhere.*

There still hadn't been any commandments across the aether-bands. Though, with its newly unlocked capabilities, the Dray Engine *did* sense a few, faint, coded signals. It pondered this development before ultimately deciding they were just more dead noise from abandoned installations like the one to the north, not worthy of investigation.

So it hunted.

The Dray Engine wasn't happy, really. Such a state may not have been possible for it. Yet as the pitiful, blue-pelted slave-humans ran before it, the Dray Engine felt a sort of contentment. The time and people that had created it were long gone. It could not truly fulfill the purpose for which it had been made. Still, it decided to focus on the little pleasures. And maybe that would be enough.

The sun shone down as Fengel left the Skydocks. Slowly, he made his way across Nob Skywalk—it was the same terrace he'd always known, apart for the flying. It didn't quite seem right to call it by the same old name anymore. So he'd changed it. The other captains didn't seem to care; they were all too preoccupied with their own losses, crippled as they were now. As for the townsfolk, they were just happy to have someone in charge again.

Pirate King *has such a nice ring to it.*

He staggered down the boardwalk, done arguing with Brunehilde and the others for the moment, leaning heavily on his cane. Cubbins, the fat orange tabby cat, wove figure eights between his legs. The little fur ball had lost an ear sometime after they'd parted but had seemed to be in otherwise good health when Fengel found him after the battle. His steward, Henry Smalls, walked behind them both.

"All right back there?" asked Fengel.

"Aye, sir," said Henry. His steward had two splinted arms, in contrast with Fengel's much-fractured leg. Still, he insisted on attending Fengel, even though Fengel was forced to trim his own mustache for the time being like some kind of barbarian.

Fengel paused to let a stream of Mechanists pass, along with a column of drafted townsfolk. The Brothers of the Cog had been busy in the days since the escape shoring things up, repairing structures, evaluating resources, and starting new construction. Fengel hadn't taken the time to talk with them, and so far they hadn't sought him out.

It could wait. Now didn't seem a good time for discussion anyway. The groaning and swearing townsfolk labored under the weight of a brazen humanoid machine while the Mechanists chastened them along towards the Brotherhood Yards. They carried one of the Perinese clockwork automatons, thankfully inert at the moment. Fengel dimly remembered it crashing down into the Gasworks during that last frantic, frenetic fight. He could only imagine how eager the Mechanists were to study the thing.

After the column tromped on past, two stragglers came limping after the rest of the Mechanists. He recognized them. Allen ambled along with a crutch under his arm, one leg in a brace, his hand bandaged, and his other arm splinted. Beside him walked Imogen, eagerly shoving a stack of papers in his face.

"Look," she said to him. "The math all works out. You'll have to carry a small steam boiler, but the functionality should be close to 50 percent more than what you have right now."

"Imogen," panted Allen, "can't this wait? I don't know why I'm even out here right now. I should be resting."

"Oh, I told the Cabal that you were fine. *I'm* a full Brother now, and you're a Mechanist-Aspirant still. Now, with my design for a mechanical hand, we can even add *extra* fingers …"

Fengel noted how closely Imogen walked beside the maimed young man, something of which Allen seemed completely oblivious. They disappeared around a corner, following the others. Fengel just shook his head and smiled.

Music drifted to him from up ahead. Henry paused, a small frown of surprise on his bulldog features. "Oh," he said. "Is that a patter song?"

"Well," replied Fengel. "Why don't we go see?"

Common sailors always expected Copper Isles pirates to love sea shanties, when in truth it was the patter songs that rang throughout Haventown. That was how Fengel knew things had finally changed; everyone was singing lately. There was so much cheer in the air, now that they'd escaped invasion and certain death.

The song came from the Bleeding Teeth, Euron's old tavern and the center of what passed for government in the pirate city. The place was more festive now than it had been during his reign, with a crowd sitting and hanging off of the porch, all caught up in the song; even the White Ape was there, its fur half-burned away, crouching atop the roof and trying to catch gulls as they flew past. Fengel stopped to appreciate it all, thumping his cane in time with the cadence. As the song ended, a familiar young woman emerged from the tavern, staggering beneath a platter full of mugs. She passed them out, lingering over a pirate wearing an eye patch. Someone catcalled at her, and she replied with the empty platter flung like a discus. It caught a drunk pirate across the forehead and knocked him out cold.

"Miss Stone!" called Fengel.

Lina turned to look at him in surprise, and then she waved. Grabbing the hand of the eyepatch-wearing pirate, she hauled him out onto the boardwalk where Fengel stood.

"Captain Fengel," she said. Beside her, Michael Hockton fidgeted with his eyepatch.

Fengel shook his head. "No. No, Miss Stone. Captain no longer."

Lina rolled her eyes. "Pirate King Fengel, then."

Fengel nodded. "That's better. How have you been?"

The waif looked away and sighed. "I'm … I've been all right."

Fengel made an effort. "I'm sorry for your loss. Runt was … a novelty, aboard the ship."

She looked at him cynically. "You don't have to pretend, sir."

"Oh," said Fengel, relaxing. "Good."

"Besides," continued Lina, "she whelped, just before the final fight. And some of her scrynlings survived!"

Her shirt writhed, and Fengel watched in abject horror as three shiny black heads poked up from behind Lina's collar. He took a staggering step back, then turned in place on his cane, ready to hurriedly limp away. "Well, that's all good, then! Don't let me keep you!"

"Sir? Wait."

Something in her tone made him stop. He turned back to see her looking up at him, her face serious. "Yes?"

"I've had enough."

Fengel blinked. "Oh?"

"I … I want to say thank you. For taking me aboard, back in Triskelion. But … I've had enough." She reached out and took Michael's hand. He returned her smile, then fidgeted with his eyepiece. "I'm moving into the town. We're going to marry, Michael and I, and settle down. If you could perform the ceremony, I'd appreciate it."

Fengel studied the pair. "You're sticking around then, Hockton?"

Michael flushed. "A-aye, sir," he stammered in reply.

Fengel snorted. *She could do better.* "Very well, then. The eye patch suits you. Come see me and Natasha aboard the *Dawnhawk* later. We'll talk further. And Stone?"

"Yes, sir?"

"It was a pleasure to have you aboard."

Lina flushed and looked away. Michael Hockton beamed at him.

Fengel rolled his eyes and turned on his cane. Slowly, he stalked off down the boardwalk. Henry followed along, saying nothing.

Shortly thereafter, their destination came into view. Just alongside the Brotherhood Yards stretched another pier, much like those along the Skydocks. The remnants of a ship sat there, supported by scaffolding and small, temporary gas bags on loan from the Brotherhood Yards.

The *Dawnhawk* would never fly again. In fact, he couldn't even call her an airship proper anymore. Just … a remnant. Still, he had insisted on recovering her bisected hull to add to the Haventown infrastructure. Holding court in a tavern may have been traditional, but it struck Fengel as unseemly. And he got to make the rules now, didn't he? For her part, Natasha had decided where to stick the thing, choosing the empty pier where her father's airship, the *Copper Queen*, had sat for so long. Fengel agreed that it felt appropriate.

Pirates swarmed over the construction, hammering, sawing, and ferrying where necessary. Fengel saw most of his surviving crew: Sarah Lome, Reaver Jane, and Rastalak, among others. They replaced charred sections of the ship and washed the deck clean of blood. Maxim and Konrad worked with especial fervor, racing to finish, no doubt so they could visit Omari in the empty part of the town she'd been exiled to. All her Revenants were gone, thank the Goddess, pitched over the side to contend with the sharks. Later, Fengel would talk with the crew. He'd talk with all of them. There would be celebration, reminiscence, and toasts to the fallen.

The fallen. So many lost, either dead now or just … missing: Ryan Gae, Andrea Holt. He'd never heard what happened to Simon and Cumbers after the Graveway. And Lucian … *ah, Lucian.* A black mood threatened to wash over him. He fought it back the same way he had ever since waking two days ago, by ignoring it. *Never let them see you stumble.*

Orders buried within a string of snarled profanity carried across the deck of the *Dawnhawk*. Fengel looked to the figure who was overseeing all this construction, then crossed the pier and up the gangplank to be with her.

Natasha looked weary. She limped, but she wasn't splinted like he was. A bandana was wrapped around her head, hiding the bare spots where her hair had burned away in the fires. At her side hung the Worked longsword she'd recovered from that last battle. According to her, the wielder had been the Crown Prince of Perinault himself. That seemed unlikely. Though if it was the blade Fengel thought it was … no. Time enough for that later. On her shoulder squatted Butterbeak, cranky and malevolent. The fat little parrot had been badly singed during the fight and wasn't doing much flying these days. Of all the injuries suffered, this one had been a source of joy to every crewmember still alive.

His wife saw his limping approach and turned away from the work, walking down to the stern of the vessel. Fengel followed, coming to a stop beside her to lean wearily upon the railing. Natasha shook off her parrot, which fell to the deck with an unceremonious thump. It let loose an irritated shriek before glaring at her and waddling away.

Beyond, past the railing, what was left of Haventown fell away. The Atalian Sea glittered far below them, unbroken but for the waves stretching as far as Fengel could see.

"So," said Natasha eventually. "How'd your meeting with the captains go?"

Fengel made a face. "They're licking their wounds and doing little else. I'm not surprised they all fled there at the end—each airship is barely aloft as is. Khalid and Weatherby will be trouble, when they've time for it. Brunehilde will stand with us. Better than that, *Solrun's Hammer* is well enough off to ferry supplies. No one's going raiding anytime soon. Though Shannon MacKinnon's *Windhaunter* will be the first to do so, once she gets a new rudder assembly."

"Mmm."

"Something wrong?"

Natasha leaned on the railing. "So many of our crew, gone. Our ship, wrecked. The Copper Isles, gone. Even ..." She looked away. "Even my father."

"I'm still sorry about that."

"Don't lie."

Fengel had nothing to say to that.

"We've lost so much," he said eventually. "But we survived. And we'll thrive."

He reached an arm out behind her back. She leaned into it. "Is that all? Just survive?"

"Well. We've got a flying city now," he said. "Our enemies will learn to fear us."

"You always say the sweetest things."

They watched the clouds skid by, an impermanent ceiling hanging just above them. The sun beat down, warm and bright though the air was cold.

"It's all different now," said Natasha. "Isn't it?"

Fengel nodded. "All of it. I don't think we can even be pirates anymore. Not with the Perinese making airships. Time to find something else to do."

His wife didn't have a response to that. She leaned into him, and they held each other, suspended between the sun and the sea. They watched as whitecaps broke far below—always changing, always in motion, yet ever the same. Fengel mused on what tomorrow would bring. Beside him, he knew Natasha would be wondering the same thing.

END BOOK THREE

ACKNOWLEDGEMENTS

Well. That certainly took awhile. Four long years of writing, revising, critiquing, and such a crazy adventure that I would have to write another novel to do it all justice. Now we've come to the end. There were high points and low points, travel across thousands of miles, and involvement from people all over the world. I couldn't have come even remotely close to getting this far all on my lonesome.

First thanks go to Shawna, my wife, for putting up with me. I'd also like to thank my first readers: Tyler Netzel, Aaron Simons, Rori Bumgarner, and Erik Hansen. Jennifer Lerud and the rest of the Screaming Sandcrabs did a great job with critiques over the years. Thanks go to Jeremiah Reinmiller for convention support. Susan DeFreitas did a stellar job editing the entire trilogy—a truly herculean task. Ksenia Mamaeva did an amazing job with the art, which Vladimir Verano then turned into covers. Susan Morman, Anthony Thurber, Jim Holzkamm, Willy Traub, Nicholas Petrous, Leilani Corell, and Martin Pool: thank you all for helping with characters.

A shout out to all those who helped in the Kickstarter project for this novel! Paul Lamb put up with filming my ridiculous self for the video, while the amazing Erica Mulkey permitted the use of her wonderful music (check out her work at www.unwoman.com). Thanks to Rob Balder for suggestions. To all my Kickstarter backers around the globe: thank you. You're the best. I hope you enjoy the novel, and that it proves worthy of your support.

ABOUT THE AUTHOR

I haunt the Pacific Northwest.

Find out more at WWW.JONATHONBURGESS.COM.